ALPHA ALPINE

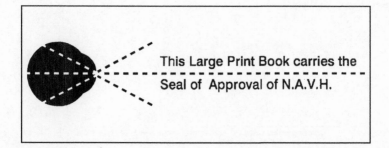

This Large Print Book carries the
Seal of Approval of N.A.V.H.

AN EMMA LORD MYSTERY

ALPHA ALPINE

MARY DAHEIM

THORNDIKE PRESS
A part of Gale, a Cengage Company

GALE
A Cengage Company

Farmington Hills, Mich • San Francisco • New York • Waterville, Maine
Meriden, Conn • Mason, Ohio • Chicago

GALE
A Cengage Company

Copyright © 2017 by Mary R. Daheim.
Thorndike Press, a part of Gale, a Cengage Company.

ALL RIGHTS RESERVED
Alpha Alpine is a work of fiction. Names, characters, places, and incidents either are products of the author's imagination or are used fictitiously. Any resemblance to actual events, locales, or persons, living or dead, is entirely coincidental.
Thorndike Press® Large Print Mystery.
The text of this Large Print edition is unabridged.
Other aspects of the book may vary from the original edition.
Set in 16 pt. Plantin.

LIBRARY OF CONGRESS CIP DATA ON FILE.
CATALOGUING IN PUBLICATION FOR THIS BOOK
IS AVAILABLE FROM THE LIBRARY OF CONGRESS

ISBN-13: 978-1-4328-6599-3 (hardcover alk. paper)

Published in 2019 by arrangement with Ballantine Books, an imprint of Random House, a division of Penguin Random House LLC

Printed in Mexico
1 2 3 4 5 6 7 23 22 21 20 19

ALPHA ALPINE

CHAPTER 1

I couldn't believe my ears. Maybe I was going deaf. As editor and publisher of *The Alpine Advocate,* I've heard some startling revelations, but this one almost zapped me through the roof of the cubbyhole I call my office. I gaped at Vida Runkel, my House & Home editor. "Are you serious?"

"Yes, Emma, I'm going to retire," she repeated, her imposing figure moving closer to my cluttered desk. "I'd like to enjoy some leisure time in my remaining years. I've earned it, I think."

"You surely have," I assured her, glancing into the empty newsroom. "I just can't imagine the *Advocate* without you. You've been here much longer than I have. You're an Alpine icon."

"Perhaps," she allowed, sitting down in one of my two visitor chairs. "Close to thirty years. I prefer not telling anyone just yet. But it's time."

I was still flummoxed. "You'll stay on until I find someone else, won't you?"

"Of course." She adjusted a floppy magenta rose on the pillbox hat that looked as if it was made out of twine. "I'm in no great rush. You know I'm not the sort of person who has any desire to start gallivanting around the country in a motor home."

Despite fighting back tears, I smiled. "No, Vida, that's not your style. I'm having trouble thinking what the paper will be like without you. You broke me in. The previous owner of the *Advocate* left town as soon as my check cleared the bank."

"Yes," Vida murmured. "I suppose he had a reason, though I often wondered why."

Vida always wondered why anyone would ever leave her beloved Alpine, short of hot pursuit by rabid mountain goats. Not that I'd ever seen such a thing, but normal mountain goats are no strangers at our three-thousand-foot level in the Cascades. "It may take time to find a replacement," I said, noting that our receptionist, Alison Lindahl, was approaching with her gaze fixed on Vida.

"Your daughter Amy has been trying to reach you, Mrs. Runkel," Alison said. "She's on hold."

Vida stood up. "Goodness, what now?"

She tromped off in her splay-footed manner.

I managed a smile for Alison. "You seem more like yourself these days. I'm so glad you decided to stay on with us."

Alison had been a temporary hire after our regular receptionist, Amanda Hanson, quit to have her baby in early July. "I'm glad I was needed here," she replied. "I was totally wiped after the college canceled my cosmetology program. But I realize the state system is short on funds. Skykomish Community College may cut a couple of other courses come winter quarter."

"So the rumor mill says," I said. "I'll remind Mitch to check on that. I don't know if the administrators are on campus right now. They usually take a break after summer classes end in mid-August. Where *is* Mitch, by the way? I haven't seen our reporter since he went on his rounds earlier this morning."

"He mentioned going to the library to do some research for a Labor Day weekend follow-up," Alison said. "I think he wanted to write the story and put it online before it runs in the paper."

"Right." I glanced at my Blue Sky Dairy calendar. It was Thursday, the first day of September. "The office will be closed Monday, so that's why Mitch wants it online by tomorrow. Are you going over to Everett to visit your parents for the holiday?"

Alison grew glum. "I might as well, since Justin and I broke up."

The failed romance had dealt her a double blow, as it had happened right after she'd learned the bad news from the college. Justin Graham also taught there, but his job was safe. No administrator ever canceled a math program.

"You've had a rough summer," I said. "I'm sorry we can't meet your college salary."

"That's okay," Alison responded. "I'm going to offer makeup lessons in the evenings at my apartment. Lori says she'll help. My roommate wants me to show her how she can look more glamorous."

"She couldn't look any less," I said, and immediately felt like biting my tongue. Lori Cobb was the sheriff's receptionist. She had a decent if lean figure, but otherwise was as plain as a street lamp. "Hey," I went on, to make amends, "I could use some improving."

Before she could comment, Mitch Laskey came into the newsroom, heading our way. Alison excused herself as my reporter entered the cubbyhole I called the editorial office.

"I'm glad I did my homework about labor unrest in Skykomish County," Mitch said, parking his lanky frame in the other visitor chair and tugging at the collar of his dress shirt. It had been a year since he and his wife, Brenda, had left the Detroit area and his longtime job at the *Free Press* and he'd started working at the *Advocate,* but it was taking him time to shed his big-city ways. "Until the Great Depression, there weren't many unhappy workers around here," he said. "The manpower shortage during World War Two increased opportunities. Then things really heated up in the next couple of decades."

I nodded. "Vida recently filled me in on some of the town's earlier history. Are you thinking about revealing unsavory deeds from the past?"

Mitch ran a hand through his thick gray hair. "That's a series. You told me that Alpine itself was never incorporated. The ballot issue to eliminate the three county commissioners and the mayor seems long overdue for eight thousand people, even if SkyCo has grown in recent years. Replacing all four positions with a county manager will save a lot of money."

I'd considered delving into some of the shady doings in the past to show how bad things happen under corrupt leadership. But Vida had warned me that I'd be risking lawsuits from descendants of previous generations. Worse yet, it might discourage voters from risking a change. In small towns, tradition can trump progress.

"Have you talked to the sheriff about how he feels on the issue?" I asked. "As you know, he reports to the three county commissioners."

Mitch shot me as quirky look. "You don't know?"

"I mean an official statement, not hearsay."

He gazed at the low ceiling. "When does Sheriff Dodge get back?"

"Milo will be in the office tomorrow. It was a one-day meeting."

Mitch stood up. "I'll see him first thing in the morning when I check the sheriff's blotter." Looking a bit glum — not an uncommon expression for our reporter — he returned to the newsroom.

Ten minutes later, Vida stood in the doorway. "I'm off to the retirement home to take photos of the Lundstroms' seventieth wedding anniversary. It's a shame he's in a coma," she said. "Of course, he never was very social."

"I can't remember ever meeting them," I admitted.

"You wouldn't," Vida asserted. "They're quite unremarkable people." Huffing a bit, my House & Home editor stomped back into the newsroom. I watched with a misty eye, trying to imagine the *Advocate* without her.

My ad manager, Leo Walsh, returned just as Vida headed out on her rounds. After setting his briefcase on his desk, he came into my office and sat in the visitor chair Mitch had vacated. "Jack Blackwell's got his mill employees handing out broadsheets on Front Street urging a no vote on the government issue," Leo said in a grim tone. "Should I put that online or let Mitch do it?"

"He's touchy about turf," I responded. "Half the town must already know what Blackwell's doing, since he's one of the three commissioners. I'll check with Mitch. The mill employees must've shown up after he came back from his early rounds. But we'll have to go public."

"Jack's fighting for power," Leo declared. "Hell, if he could run the government as well as he runs his logging operation, maybe he should play a bigger role around here."

13

I was shocked. "Are you out of your mind? Jack and Milo might end up killing each other. Blackwell's first move would be to fire the sheriff. Have you forgotten Jack recently spent the night in jail after beating up one of his ex-wives?"

Leo sighed. "We should've seen this coming. As a commissioner, Jack's against government change. He may demand equal time when Mayor Baugh gives his Labor Day speech."

"I wouldn't doubt it," I muttered. "Have you any *good* news?"

"Let me think. . . ." His gaze traveled to the low ceiling, rested on my SkyCo map, and finally fixed on me. "We should have an eighty-twenty split for this week." Leo grinned, making more creases in his weathered face. "The special fall section for the week after that ought to up the ante in the *Advocate*'s kitty."

"You're a wizard!" I exclaimed. "That's the best we've done all year."

Leo shrugged again. "It's a combination of Labor Day and back-to-school ads. With the community college not starting until October first, we can draw out ads aimed at students. We got another bump because the merchants had to let patrons know about the four o'clock closing in deference to the

14

Labor Day picnic. I figure we can go twenty-four pages."

I couldn't stop smiling. "Having Liza living here seems to have juiced up your enthusiasm for the job."

"In a way, it has," Leo agreed, growing serious. "Up until our son was transferred to Raytheon, south of Seattle, I knew if I wanted a second chance at my marriage I'd have to go back to Santa Maria. But Brian's move meant our little grandson was heading north, too. It was an easy decision for Liza."

"And a lucky one for me," I said.

Leo smiled again, though with a bittersweet edge. "The luck cut both ways, babe. If you hadn't taken a chance on me, I'd have drunk my way into oblivion ten years ago. Liza owes you, too." He stood up, rapping his knuckles on my desk. "Back to man the oars on the good ship *Advocate*. Your ad manager never rests."

I smiled as he ambled back to his desk. Then I took a deep breath and set to work on my editorial. Labor Day. Work. American enterprise. Innovation. Technology. What could I say that I hadn't said every year since I'd bought the newspaper and moved to Alpine? In fact, three weeks ago had marked the sixteenth year since I'd arrived with a college-bound son, a used Jaguar, and ownership of the *Advocate*. Back then, I'd had no plans to spend more than a few years in the small mountain town a mile off the Stevens Pass Highway. Alpine was in economic upheaval. Logging had been sharply curtailed by the environmentalists, and Skykomish County was in the wood chipper.

But if my editorials are often predictable, life isn't. I deleted all the overused words and stared at the blank computer monitor. Then I got up and went out to the front office. To my surprise, our receptionist was sitting at her desk and looking dazed. "What's wrong?" I asked.

Alison blushed. "A really hot guy just came in. How rare is that?"

"Well . . . I'm prejudiced, being a married woman. Who was it?"

"His name is L.J. — just initials," Alison replied. She handed me a pale green sheet of paper. "It's against the new government plan."

I scanned the four paragraphs. "The hot guy must work for Blackwell. Leo says Jack has his employees handing these out."

Alison's blue eyes grew wide. "You mean L.J. might live here? How come I've never seen him before? He wasn't wearing a wedding ring."

I laughed. "Aren't you getting a little ahead of yourself?"

"Emma." Alison grew serious. "Face it — the local gene pool's majorly shallow when it comes to seriously hot guys."

"Feel free to check him out. He might win you over to the no-change side and I'll have to fire you."

Alison didn't seem to realize I was teasing. She sighed. "Maybe I should move back in with my parents in Everett. The naval base there has lots of eligible men."

"Oh, stop!" I exclaimed. "You're doing such a good job, and if I can squeeze any money out of the budget, I'll —"

She uttered a weak little laugh. "Hey, don't worry. I'm just in a bad place right now."

I glanced at my watch. It was almost noon. "I'm in a hungry place. Let me treat you to lunch at the ski lodge. We're unofficially closed in the noon hour. If anybody's desperate, Kip MacDuff can handle it. He rarely leaves his production duties in the back shop."

"Oh . . ." Alison looked sheepish. "I feel silly. You sure?"

"Yes. We haven't had a real chance to visit since you started here in early July."

She gazed into the empty newsroom. "I won't be much fun."

I kept a straight face. "Should we go to the Heartbreak Hotel Diner instead?"

In spite of herself, Alison laughed. "No! You're a good boss. I bet you had a bad breakup back in the day, right?"

"I suppose I did." She didn't know the half of it.

"L.J.?" Vida echoed, standing in the door to my office while I grabbed my purse and applied a fresh coat of lip gloss. "What kind of a name is that?"

"His initials. What else?"

"I've never heard of such a person," Vida declared in the familiar tone that indicated whoever it was must be an impostor. "Why would a stranger oppose the ballot measure? If he's new, he can't understand our issues. Perhaps my nephew Billy knows who he is. I'll call him after lunch."

Billy was Deputy Bill Blatt, and like all of Vida's kin, he was obliged under pain of God only knows what to pass on any gossip-worthy items. After she'd tromped out the door, I told Alison we should head for the ski lodge. The coffee shop is always a busy lunch venue, since Alpine has only four eating places that serve something other than fast food.

I drove us in my aging Honda, heading out of the downtown area and up through the stand of third-growth timber flanking Tonga Road. There had been no sign of anyone handing out anti-change broadsides. Maybe L.J. and his ilk had already gone to lunch.

"Weird," Alison said under her breath as I pulled into the parking lot. "I haven't been to the lodge since last winter. Skiing was awful. There wasn't enough powder. Justin was being a real jerk that day."

"Was he often a jerk?" I asked as I parked between a red Ford pickup and a dark blue Nissan Pathfinder with California plates.

"He could be moody," Alison murmured. "Nobody's perfect." She sighed as she opened the car door.

It was still a few minutes shy of noon, but the coffee shop was filling up. We were shown to a table by one of the rough-hewn cedar pillars. Despite its basic design to resemble a Scandinavian hostelry that would fit into a Norwegian fjord, the lodge also featured Native American touches. On our way to the coffee shop, we'd passed a trio of pen-and-ink drawings of Salish symbols.

"I'm not very hungry," Alison said, looking almost as if she were hiding behind the menu. "I think I'll have a salad."

I tried to look severe. "If you do, make it the crab Louie. I don't want you passing out on the job from malnutrition."

A faint smile touched her mouth. "Okay. I'll try not to be a twit."

"You're not a twit," I assured her. "You're merely heartbroken. That isn't fatal."

A fair-haired waitress named Bridget came to take our orders. We both ordered crab Louies. "So," I said after Bridget departed, "did the breakup come as a surprise?"

Alison looked beyond me and didn't answer right away. "I guess it did," she finally said, "but looking back, it shouldn't. Even before he finished teaching summer quarter, he seemed to be distancing himself from me. I figured it was because he was cramming everything into the last couple of weeks for the students. But it got worse after classes were over. He went hiking on the Olympic Peninsula with an old friend. In fact, I was getting worried when I didn't hear from him after a week." She lowered her eyes. "It turned out he'd been back for three days and hadn't called me. Everything started to fade to black after that."

"Do you think he met someone else?"

"I don't know." Alison sighed. "We'd dated for almost a year. I really thought we might have a future." Again she looked away, so crestfallen that I wondered if she'd practiced the spurned-woman role in front of a mirror.

"Don't give up," I said, hoping to sound sympathetic. "You're all of twenty-two."

Alison scowled. "I'll be twenty-three at the end of this month."

"So? I waited until I was fifty-two to get married."

"That's not very encouraging," she declared. "Besides, you had a son before you were my age."

"Yes, and I had to raise him on my own," I said. "Enjoy your freedom. I never got do that when I was young. I was too busy getting my college degree and then working full-time to support Adam."

"I really am a twit," she said and again averted her gaze.

I smiled. "Don't be so hard on yourself. I never met Justin, but I suspect you were too good for him. You'll find someone better."

Alison looked at me, though she seemed dubious. "You think?"

"I do. I did." I thought back to all the years I'd waited for Tom Cavanaugh to be free of his rich, loony wife. Over a year after

21

she ODed, we became engaged — and then Tom was killed. "I know you've got courage, Alison. I found that out when you were twelve and your mother was murdered. You were a real trouper."

She smiled wanly. "I guess. But my stepmother has always been the real deal."

I smiled back. "So are you."

"That's really nice of . . ." Her blue eyes widened as she looked beyond me. "Omigod," she said under her breath, "it's L.J.! With a woman! Don't look!"

I didn't have to. Bridget was leading Mr. Love God right past us to the other side of the pillar. He wasn't alone. His companion was a young and very attractive raven-haired girl who looked as though she'd just stepped off the runway at a Nordstrom fashion show.

Alison closed her eyes, "Oh, shoot! I'm doomed," she whispered.

"Maybe it's his sister," I suggested.

"Dubious." She pushed her chair back a few inches. "I can't see anything but the back of his chair. She must be sitting across from him."

I felt like saying that was better than if she were sitting on his lap. But Alison lowered her voice again before I could say anything. "Do you think she came to Alpine with him? She's got killer looks. Have you ever seen her before?"

"Never," I said. "Admittedly, we're a little short around here when it comes to gorgeous. But you're a beautiful blonde, Alison."

"I'm savvy with cosmetics. She looks like she doesn't need any."

"Maybe she has the same knack."

"You can't tell unless you get up close," Alison shot back.

Our salads arrived. We dropped the subject of L.J. and his knockout companion. Alison asked about my son, Adam. I told her he seemed to be getting along fine at St. Mary's Igloo in Alaska and had just returned from a meeting in Fairbanks with other priests.

"He's probably coming to Alpine for Thanksgiving," I said. "Maybe you'll get a chance to meet him."

Alison regarded me with a sardonic expression. "You showed me a picture of Adam once. He's good-looking. I'm not Catholic, but it's a real waste that a guy like him can't get married just because he's a priest."

I didn't argue, since it meant I'd never have grandchildren of my own. I'd been upset when my son told me he had a religious vocation, but a decade later he seemed

23

content.

However, Alison had a one-track mind and seemed determined to derail herself. As much as I hated to do it, I decided we should change the subject and talk about work. With any luck we could get out of the coffee shop without our receptionist hurtling around the other side of the pillar and throwing herself into L.J.'s arms.

"Say," I said, at my most ingenuous, "Leo gave me some good news about our ad revenue. Ever since Ginny Erlandson left last October to have her baby, none of our temporary help has been assigned to her office manager's job. It's been kind of catch-as-catch-can. If you wouldn't mind taking on that task, I can offer you a raise." And maybe have to chisel on the annual holiday bonuses . . .

Alison brightened. "I'll try. What does it involve?"

"The budget, mostly. Paying bills, making out paychecks, handling ad revenue."

"I can do that," she assured me.

"If you need help getting started, call Ginny. She knows more about the job than I do."

Alison nodded. "I've met her a couple of times." She frowned. "How many kids do she and her husband have now?"

"Three boys," I replied.

"Three." She stared at the pillar. "How old is Ginny?"

I wasn't sure, math not being my strong suit. "Early thirties?"

Alison nodded again. "Good. That makes me feel a little better."

I didn't ask why. The answer might make me feel like a fossil.

Around four-thirty, Vida announced that she needed items for her front-page "Scene Around Town" column. The homely snippets of everyday Alpiners were the best-read part of the paper.

"Since we only have Tuesday before deadline, I want a head start, but not entirely focused on Labor Day," she explained. "The only one I have that isn't, is Janie Engelman shooing a rabbit out of her yard. Well?" The gray eyes behind the big glasses seemed to pinion us all in place.

Leo went first. "Seventies VW hippie bus parked by Old Mill Park. California plates, no hippies sighted. Sorry."

Vida nodded. "Mitch?"

"The architect in the remodel by the golf course is getting new lighting. The Mel-something-or-others?" He looked at me for help.

"Scott and Beverly Melville," I said. "Scott

25

worked on our remodel."

Kip stroked his goatee and smiled. "Last night I saw a beaver family crossing the truss bridge over the Sky. I was wondering why they didn't go under the bridge and swim the river. They're *beavers.*"

"Maybe," Leo suggested, "the little beavers can't swim yet."

We all chuckled before Alison spoke up. "Handsome young man handing out flyers on Front Street?" She winced as she saw Vida's glare.

"That's a news item," she asserted, usurping my editor's role. It was a common occurrence during the sixteen years I'd owned the *Advocate.* "Try again, Alison," she urged.

Our receptionist frowned, then brightened. "Dr. Ferris changing a flat tire on his minivan a block from RestHaven's medical rehab building."

"That's Farrell," Vida corrected her. "Dr. Iain Farrell. He heads their psychiatric division in the main building, where they also have the drug and alcohol rehabilitation patients." She turned her gimlet eye on me.

I resorted to Crazy Eights Neffel sitting in his long underwear on a block of melting ice and feeding tacos to pigeons in John Engstrom Park.

Vida frowned. "You know I dislike using Crazy Eights's antics, but if we come up short Tuesday, I'll allow it. Really, Emma, you should be more aware of your surroundings."

Under her withering glance, inspiration struck. "Oh! Mickey O'Neill getting out of his Blackwell Timber rig to check his load after crossing the truss bridge."

Vida was still frowning. "You're sure you want to mention Blackwell?"

I shrugged. "He *is* the town's largest employer. And he advertises."

"Very well," she said. "But I'll change the tire reference to 'inspecting his vehicle.' "

Vindicated, I retreated to my office. By quitting time, I was the last to leave except for my back shop guru, Kip, who was always grateful for downtime to deal with high-tech problems. He seldom offered details, knowing my eyes would glaze over. To me, a computer is just a fancy typewriter with pictures. During my tenure at the *Oregonian* in Portland, I was flummoxed when they went high-tech. I begged my editor to let me keep my IBM electric typewriter. He refused. The first time I tried to log on to the thing with its sickly green screen, I'd blown out the entire system. I was mortified. But they'd been warned.

27

With a clear conscience, I left Kip lost in cyberspace. He could lock up. I shut the door behind me — and almost collided with Jack Blackwell.

"Where's Dodge?" he barked, forcing me up against the building next to our entrance.

"Out of town," I said. "Are you reporting a crime?"

Jack sneered, an expression well suited to his dark, saturnine features. "Hell, no. Unless it'd be how that bastard runs this county's law enforcement. When's he due back?"

"I don't know," I replied honestly. Blackwell was six feet tall and in decent shape for being in his late fifties, and his eight-inch height advantage was more vexing than intimidating. "Move it, Jack. I'm going home."

To my surprise, he backed off. "I want to see him the minute he gets here. Got that?"

At least five pedestrians and a couple of drivers were staring at us. "Where do you want to see the sheriff? With guns drawn in the middle of Front Street?"

Blackwell's eyes narrowed. "You've got a big bark for a little bitch. One day somebody may shut it for you." He stalked off to a new silver Lexus parked near the corner.

It took me a few seconds to gather my

composure. Maybe we should dump the Mickey O'Neill sighting in "Scene." Black Jack may not have intimidated me, but the confrontation was disturbing. Milo reported to the three county commissioners. The other two, Leonard Hollenberg and George Engebretsen, were way past their prime when it came to butting heads over county issues.

I got into my aging Honda and tried to forget about Blackwell.

But I couldn't.

CHAPTER 2

Driving away from the office, I noticed that Blackwell's employees were gone from the streets. The mill whistle had sounded its usual quitting time at five, so his workers were off the clock. With a sense of relief, I headed up Tonga Ridge to my now not so little log cabin. *Our* log cabin, since Milo had paid for the entire remodel, insisting that was the only way it could be home to both of us after our February marriage.

His Yukon SUV wasn't in the new double garage. I went inside through the kitchen but left the door open. The summer heat wave was ebbing, though the house still felt too warm. After changing into cotton slacks and a well-worn Jamie Moyer T-shirt, I was peeling potatoes when I heard Milo pull into the garage. He looked grumpy when he entered the kitchen. I set the peeler down and kissed him, in case he'd forgotten that I was his wife.

"What's wrong?" I asked. "Was the Olympia meeting a pain?"

He tossed his regulation hat onto the dishwasher. "Yeah. Let me change. Traffic was a freaking mess."

I didn't comment. After sixteen years of being together — more or less — I knew when to keep my mouth shut. I didn't bother to tell the sheriff that he shouldn't have left his hat in the kitchen. Instead, I took it into the living room and put it on a peg by the front door.

By the time Milo returned, I'd made us each a drink — Scotch for him, Canadian for me. I set the potatoes on the stove and waited for him to speak. To my surprise, he picked up his drink and headed for the living room. I turned on the burner under the potatoes, grabbed my drink, and left the kitchen to join him.

"Well?" I said, flopping down on the sofa.

Milo shifted in the easy chair across from me. "It was a waste of time. Most meetings are. Just a lot of bullshit about seasonal weather changes and upcoming highway projects and why it's a bad idea to take a shot at your neighbor just because he looks like a deer. Especially if you've just polished off a half rack."

I stared at him. "This lecture was aimed

31

at law enforcement?"

Milo ran a big hand through his graying sandy hair. "It was about reminding us lowly county sheriffs that the big shots in Olympia know we exist."

"Did they feed you?"

He nodded. "Decent doughnuts, but the coffee was weak. Lunch was okay. It's a hell of a long drive. Worse for the guys on the other side of the state. Four of them flew in. Anything going on around here?"

I took a deep breath. "I had a run-in with Blackwell. He's retaliating about the ballot issue." I described his anti-change campaign.

"Jesus," he muttered. "The sonuvabitch won't go quietly. Did he touch you?"

"No. I told you — we were in public. Jack's evil, but he's not stupid."

"Damn. I need a refill," Milo said. "Anything else I don't want to know?"

"Sort of." I grimaced. "Vida's quitting."

Milo swirled the dregs of his drink in his glass. "Is she serious?"

I nodded. "You know she's gotten harder to deal with ever since her grandson, Roger, got into trouble last year. She's been touchy, moody — whatever. Vida's been my rock from the moment I took over the paper. At least she won't quit until I find a replacement."

Milo downed the last of his drink and hoisted his six-foot-five frame out of the chair. "That could take some time."

"True. Are you still hoping to find money for another deputy?"

He shook his head. "Not right now. But it has to happen. The county's growing. You want a refill?"

"I'm good."

"You are," Milo said, pausing to muss my hair. "Good for me, anyway. I feel better already."

The dinner hour passed without annoyance. Just as we finished eating, I remembered that *Vida's Cupboard* was on KSKY. Her weekly program was must listening in Skykomish County. Tonight's guest was Kenneth McClelland, the new pastor at her Presbyterian church. Milo nodded off a couple of times during the fifteen-minute segment, but I paid attention in case Vida was preparing a quiz.

My husband yawned and stretched. "Did I miss anything?"

"Not really," I replied as I perched on the easy chair's arm. "The usual newcomer reaction to life in the majestic mountains, with a touch of Christian fellowship for his flock. It's a wonder Blackwell hasn't insisted that Vida put him on her show."

Milo shook his head. "She'd never go for that."

"She might. He's an advertiser. Face it, Jack owns the only timber company in town. Even you can't criticize how he runs his business."

"I never have. It's his private life that's sketchy. Speaking of that sort of thing," he went on, putting an arm around my waist, "I think I've recovered from the drive. That kiss when I came home was half-assed."

"*I* had to kiss *you*," I snapped.

"Want me to make up for that?"

I smiled. "Yes."

Half an hour later, I was drifting off to sleep when the phone rang in the living room. I started to get out of bed, but Milo grabbed my arm. "Stay put. If it's important, whoever it is will leave a message."

"You know I hate doing that. It could be Adam or Ben. I haven't talked to my son or my brother in over a week." But the ringing stopped.

"Where's Ben now?" Milo asked. "The last I heard, he was somewhere in Texas."

"He's back on the Mississippi Delta. He

34

spent so many years there after he was ordained that he's still drawn to that part of the church's Home Missions. It seems to have a stronger hold on him than Tuba City and the desert." I heard a phone ring again, but this time it was nearby. "That's your cell," I said to my husband. "Where is it?"

He looked irked. "Under my shirt. Grab it, will you?"

I leaned down, fumbled a bit, but finally got a grip, and chucked it at Milo. He palmed the cell and answered with his usual "Dodge here." At first his expression didn't change, but when it did, the sheriff looked irked. "Tell the SOB to stay the hell out of the office or you'll arrest him for harassing a law officer. You got that?" He paused. "Good. You earned your keep this week, Mullins. For once." He disconnected.

"What?" I asked.

Milo set the cell on the nightstand. "Blackwell came roaring into headquarters this evening. I was tired of fighting traffic, so I didn't check in at the office. Mullins doesn't know I'm back, and I'm keeping it that way. He'd tried calling here first, so that was probably the ringing you heard."

"How do you plan to avoid Blackwell tomorrow?" I asked, getting out of bed and reaching for my robe.

35

"Damned if I know," Milo replied. "I'll deal with him when it happens. The jerk's avoided me ever since I busted him earlier this summer for beating up his ex-wife, Kay Burns. I guess he didn't like the food when he spent a night in one of our jail cells."

"Promise you won't try coaxing him to take a swing at you?"

"No. I don't want to have to lock him up again. I hate just looking at that bastard."

I didn't comment. But again, I worried.

On Friday we were busy making up for the short work week to come. Leo had managed to get enough ads for a little more than the desired eighty-twenty split.

"Some is co-op advertising between us and Fleetwood," he said, leaning against the doorframe. "You can't say your archrival isn't willing to share."

My original animosity toward Spencer Fleetwood had all but disappeared during the seven years since he'd set up his KSKY-AM station. "Like us, Spence struggles to survive," I said. "But his chances are better than ours. The print media's disappearing faster than radio."

Leo nodded, then glanced at Vida's vacant chair. "What's up with the Duchess? She seems subdued."

"She's fine," I said. "Like most natives, Vida's not fond of heat."

My ad manager chuckled. "Even after living here for ten years, you people still amaze me. Frankly, I'm dreading what happens in October when the gray clouds and endless rain start. Liza may head south."

"Hey, she might enjoy the change of seasons," I said. "Has she ever seen snow?"

"Only the fake kind," he replied, stepping aside for Alison, who was bringing me the mail. "By the way, I hear Blackwell hired a pollster to see how the voters are leaning. Ronnie Something-or-other. Hope the guy shows up here. He'll get an earful. Later, babe." He strolled back to his desk.

Our newly created officer manager set down a six-inch pile of what looked mostly like junk. To my surprise, I realized the spring was back in her step. "You recovered?" I blurted.

She laughed. "I talked to my mother last night. She told me I was an idiot. Mom's always been cool in a crisis."

I nodded. "I remember that from over ten years ago, when your dad was a suspect in your birth mother's murder. She was a tower of strength for you and your father."

"She's been a good role model," Alison said.

My phone rang. When I heard Milo's voice blast my ear, I wondered why he needed to call instead of just shouting from his headquarters a block and a half away.

"Blackwell's goons are handing out more crap," Milo bellowed as I held the receiver an inch away from my ear. "He claims a search for a city manager costs —"

"Stop!" I yelled. "Calm down before you have a stroke. I don't want to be a widow before we've celebrated our first anniversary."

I heard Milo let out a heavy sigh. "Okay, fine. Black Jack says he did a study on city manager salaries. They don't come cheap."

"That may be true," I allowed, "but it depends on the city's size. Or, in our case, the county. With only eight thousand people, a county manager shouldn't command a huge salary."

"That's another thing," he said, still irked. "Blackwell figures no one qualified will take the job."

"Dubious," I responded. "Lots of people would like to move to a quiet, scenic area like this. Cities can be very wearing."

"Shit," Milo muttered. "You used to be a city girl. What happened?"

"You happened. Are you through bitching?"

"Yeah. For now. But I'm still pissed off."
He hung up.

Mitch had returned to the newsroom just as the sheriff rang off. My reporter lingered by my door. "Are you busy?"

I smiled. "Your boss is always busy. Have you any weekend plans?" I hated to ask, sensing I already knew the answer.

"Brenda and I are visiting our son at the Monroe Correctional Complex," he replied. "Troy's only got a year left to finish serving his sentence. We'll stay over in Monroe to see the Evergreen State Fair. We moved here too late to take it in last September."

I didn't want to admit I'd never been to the fair at Monroe. When Ben and I were growing up in Seattle, my parents had taken us to the Puyallup Fair a couple of times. It had been fun, but there are only so many pot-bellied pig races, giant gourds, and steroid-induced dahlias that I can admire without getting bored.

"Did you have a state fair in Detroit?" I inquired.

Mitch looked at me as if he thought I were kidding. "With exhibits featuring rusted-out GM cars, a wax figure of Jimmy Hoffa, and a bunch of panhandlers outside of the gates? In a word, no. The state fair is at Novi, about twenty miles from where we lived in

Royal Oak, and it's huge. We never went there."

That sounded typical of the often gloomy Mitch and his troubled wife, Brenda. "The one at Monroe should be more . . . homey," I said for want of a better word.

"Anyway," Mitch went on, "we may stay at a motel to give us more time with Troy. It's not a long drive, but I don't want to tire Brenda."

Since he'd brought up a touchy subject, I asked how she was getting along.

"She really is improving," Mitch replied. "Brenda's gotten back full bore into her weaving, and Christmas orders are already coming in."

"That's good news," I declared and meant it. Mitch's wife had suffered a breakdown when Troy escaped from the correctional complex in December. "The weather should hold," I went on. "I'm sure Brenda will enjoy the craft displays."

"I hope so." Mitch tugged at one of his long earlobes. "Before the weather gets bad we'd like to go up to Vancouver or maybe Victoria. When we lived in Royal Oak we only went to Ontario once."

"You should check out British Columbia," I said. "Especially since the tourist season is over. You can take the *Victoria Clipper* out of

Seattle for a day trip."

"I'll think about that," Mitch said without much enthusiasm.

I changed the subject. "Anything of interest in the sheriff's log?"

"The usual." He started to turn away, but stopped. "Oh — we don't run names, but the guy who beat up his girlfriend was that Mickey O'Neill you mentioned for Vida's 'Scene.' I wondered if you'd still want to run it even if nobody knows he's a bad guy."

"I considered it because of the Blackwell connection," I said. "Yes, I'd better delete it. Vida never checks the paper after it comes out. Who was the girl?"

Mitch grimaced. "Mullins didn't know. Mickey refused to say and apparently she wouldn't talk."

"Maybe she couldn't," I said. "Or she was too embarrassed. Mickey comes from a rough background. His father and two uncles were wiped out in an infamous feud with another equally bellicose family."

"Sounds like Detroit," Mitch remarked. "I'm almost sorry I missed that one."

I wish I'd missed it, too. But that was another story.

An hour later Vida returned from her rounds. "I've been lacking in hospitality,"

41

she declared, sitting down at her desk. "I've never hosted the Laskeys to dinner since their arrival a year ago, so I'll invite them for tomorrow. I received a new casserole recipe in today's mail. It sounds very tasty, with chicken gizzards and turnips. Would you and Milo care to join us?"

I glanced into the newsroom to make sure Mitch was gone. "The Laskeys are leaving for the weekend."

"Oh." She frowned. "A visit to Troy, I presume?"

I nodded. "In fact, more than once over the holiday."

"Yes, of course," she murmured, shoulders slumping. "So difficult." She quickly brightened. "Would you and Milo like to come anyway?"

"Milo hasn't told me his work schedule for the three-day weekend." *And he'd rather shoot himself in the foot than eat one of your gruesome casseroles.* "Will Buck Bardeen be in town for the weekend?" I asked, referring to the retired Air Force colonel who was her longtime companion.

"Yes, I planned to ask him, too." Vida repinned what resembled a flying saucer on her unruly gray curls. "Maybe we'll go out to dinner — perhaps the French place on the highway. He enjoys restaurant meals."

I didn't doubt it. The colonel might prefer eating scientific specimens to Vida's cooking. Her phone rang, so I headed to my office.

My own phone started ringing. "Why don't you wander down here to see me?" the sheriff asked.

"I just saw you this morning before you left for work," I replied.

"You're never awake when you get up. We need to talk." He hung up on me.

Wondering why it couldn't wait until lunch, I dutifully trudged off to the sheriff's headquarters. Deputy Sam Heppner was in charge of the front desk and receptionist Lori Cobb was looking wistful. Sam, not a talkative type, nodded at me. Lori uttered a big sigh.

"Have you seen the hunk who seems to be working for Blackwell?" she asked in a breathless voice.

"No," I replied, assuming Lori was referring to the same guy who'd dazzled Alison. "Is that why you're hyperventilating?"

She nodded. "He's real eye candy. Are you here to see the sheriff?"

"Yes, but maybe I should ogle the hot dude, even if he'd think I was his mother."

"He was on the corner of Third a while ago," Lori said.

"I'll take a look when I leave." I opened the half-door in the counter and headed for my husband's office. "The door's closed. Should I go in?"

"What?" Lori was still dazed. "Oh, sure, go ahead. But he's not in a very good mood."

"Oh?" I said in mock surprise. "He's always such a sweetie at home." I heard Sam grunt as I entered Milo's office. "Well?"

My husband was holding his head. "Blackwell's having the county commissioners investigate how I run my operation."

I was so rattled that I almost missed the chair when I sat down. "No! Why? I mean, why now?"

"Because he can," Milo replied. "Those two old duffers who serve with him as county commissioners can't say no to Blackwell. Hell, Engebretsen and Hollenberg are too senile to remember that they *are* county commissioners."

"What does Blackwell think will come of an investigation?"

Milo shrugged. "Unless they plant stuff, nothing. But announcing an investigation sends a message that something's wrong. By the way, he's dropping off a news release for you. I suppose Fleetwood will get one, too. Avoid Black Jack when he shows up."

44

"No biggie. The last time he pitched a fit in the office, I found out Mitch knows martial arts. Unfortunately, he didn't have to use his skills."

Milo leaned forward in his leather chair. "Did Jack threaten you back then? You told me at the time he only shot his mouth off."

"Well . . ." I felt sort of silly. "I didn't want to upset you. . . ."

Milo's hazel eyes narrowed. "Did or did he not threaten you?"

"Not really," I replied.

"Did you feel threatened?"

The sheriff's intense gaze made me feel like a perp in a lineup. "Kind of. But I didn't think he'd —"

"Stop." Milo sat back in his chair. "If there's any fear a situation might get physical, it's enough to file charges. You know that from the domestic abuse stuff you run in the paper."

"Damn," I said under my breath. "I wish I'd kept my mouth shut."

"You should've told me at the time." He took a cigarette out of an almost empty pack and offered me one. I declined, not having smoked for almost two weeks. "But you might be right about holding off on busting Blackwell right now," Milo went on. "It'd look like retaliation for his dumb-ass investigation. I'm not forgetting about it, though. And for God's sake, give him a wide berth from now on."

"You think I like dealing with him?"

"Hell, no." Milo waved his free hand. "Here's one more pain in the ass. My brother, Clint, called from Dallas. He and his wife, Pootsie, are coming this way. He claims he feels bad about missing his nephew's wedding. Hell, Bran hardly remembers Clint. They've only been back up here four times in almost thirty years since he got his biology Ph.D. from Wazzu and took the Texas job. They'll hit the road tonight in their fancy RV."

"I've never met him," I said. "Did you tell him we got married?"

Milo looked a bit sheepish. "Yeah. I had to. I couldn't explain you away as some stray I picked up at the Icicle Creek Tavern."

The comment annoyed me. "Why didn't you tell him in the first place, jackass?"

Mile let out an impatient sigh. "Because Clint wouldn't give a damn. He's always been full of himself. It took three years before I told him Mulehide and I were divorced. He only saw her twice after he was the best man at our wedding."

"Did he like Mule . . . I mean, Tricia?"

"Clint only likes himself — and Pootsie.

46

Oh, maybe their twins, Muffy and Duffy."

"You made up those names."

"No. They did. I saw those kids only once on their second trip up here. They were about eight."

I stood up. "I'd better get back to work. Any chance you can meet me for lunch?"

"I can't," Milo replied, coming around the side of his desk. "It's Dustin Fong's birthday. I told him I'd buy lunch at the ski lodge."

"Give your deputy my best —" I never finished. Milo had wrapped his arms around me and kissed me. It was a very intense kiss.

"I think," I gasped, "you were lonesome."

"Hey," he said, "we're still newlyweds."

I laughed. "After more or less sixteen years together?"

"Should've been more." He swatted my rear. "Beat it. You're still a distraction."

I left, still smiling.

Leo stopped me halfway through the newsroom. "I saw one of those broadsides Blackwell's guys are handing out."

I perched on the edge of my ad man's desk. "It's worse than you think." I told him about Black Jack's investigation of the sheriff.

Leo looked grim. "That's not good. Are

47

you putting it online?"

"There's nothing official," I replied. "I'll wait until Blackwell or one of his stooges gives out the announcement."

"You won't wait long," Leo said, lowering his voice. "Black Jack just came in. He's talking to Alison."

I glanced into the front office. Jack wheeled around and left. "That's weird," I murmured before hurrying to quiz our receptionist.

Alison looked chagrined. "No, I didn't ask about L.J., because Blackwell was in a rush. He told me to give you this." She handed me a typed sheet of paper. "I think it's a news release."

"It is," I said. "The county commissioners are going to investigate the sheriff's department."

Alison looked aghast. "Why?"

"Jack's a world-class jerk. He and Milo never got along, back to when they were both in their twenties. They clashed from the start."

"He's not originally from here, is he?" Alison asked.

I shook my head. "Jack's from California — the northern part, I think. But I heard he had mills in Idaho and maybe Oregon before he came to Alpine thirty years ago."

Alison frowned. "If he was only in his twenties, where did he get the money to buy up timber mills?"

"I haven't a clue," I admitted. "Maybe Vida does, since she knows all things Alpine." But glancing into the newsroom, I saw no sign of her. "I'll ask when she gets back."

I took the news release into my office to give it my undivided attention. When it came to his business, Blackwell was beyond reproach, disliked only by those of us who had to deal with him away from his timber company offices. He'd been married and divorced before coming to Alpine. There had been two failed marriages here early on, but they were before my time. Jack had stayed single ever since, living off and on with Patti Marsh, who didn't mind being his regular punching bag. At least she'd never filed charges against him. I got the impression she actually loved the guy. In my opinion, even that wasn't any excuse for beating on her.

I steeled myself for what I figured was Blackwell's announcement of investigating the sheriff. But I was mistaken. In fact, I had to read the first sentence twice to make sure I wasn't hallucinating.

49

As a longtime resident and an experienced county commissioner, if Tuesday's vote favors a change in government, I feel not only well qualified for the task, but also a personal and professional obligation to become manager of Alpine and Skykomish County.

Maybe I should have expected this. Taking a deep breath, I continued reading.

After completing a thorough study of the process to hire a city manager, I discovered that this is a costly and time-consuming task. I've discussed it with my fellow commissioners, George Engebretsen and Leonard Hollenberg, two conscientious men who have served this county so long and so well. They have given me their full support to take on the responsibilities of governing our honest, courageous, and compassionate citizens who have built our community from its very beginnings ninety years ago. I look forward to leading Skykomish County when Alpine celebrates its centennial in five years.

I was quivering with aggravation by the time I finished. Jack made his case for the manager's job sound like a fait accompli. Milo would really explode. My next thought

50

was how Mayor Fuzzy Baugh would take Blackwell's power play. Fuzzy might be old and sometimes addled — or maybe it was the result of taking too much Southern Comfort right out of the bottle. But he was from New Orleans and well steeped in what I might kindly describe as bayou backstabbing. I called the courthouse to see if the mayor was in. And sober.

The mayor's secretary, Bobbi Olsen, informed me her boss was "under the weather." I asked if that meant he was still on the job.

"No," Bobbi replied. "He felt some heart palpitations earlier, so Mrs. Baugh insisted he go to the clinic. They're still there, as far as I know."

"Would the palpitations have been set off by Commissioner Blackwell?" I inquired.

"They usually are," Bobbi said. "Jack called on him earlier today. It was a closed-door meeting, so I don't know what went on between them. I doubt it was pleasant, though."

I opted for discretion. "Just talking to Blackwell could bring on a spell for Fuzzy. Keep me posted, please."

"Will do. I worry about our mayor. He's no spring chicken." Bobbi rang off on that worrisome note.

I looked into the newsroom to see if Mitch was around, but he was nowhere in sight. Vida, however, was heading for her desk. I hurried out to meet her. "It's almost noon," she said. "The Venison Inn?"

"Sure," I agreed.

The VI, as it's known, is two doors down from the office. To my relief, I saw no sign of Blackwell's stooges. With the long weekend under way, traffic on Front Street was heavy by Alpine standards. I saw at least three out-of-state license plates. The morning clouds had lifted, revealing Alpine Baldy to the north and Mount Sawyer to the south. A BNSF freight train crawled through town a block away by Railroad Avenue. Warning bells clanged to alert drivers that the train was approaching the truss bridge over the Skykomish River. When I first arrived, it had taken some time to adjust to a small town after sixteen years in Portland. By now the warp and woof of my adopted home were second nature. If I had changed, so had Seattle, the city of my birth. It was no longer a woodsy Northwest outpost, but an influential, progressive metropolis. Maybe my hometown and I had become strangers.

All this flashed through my mind as Vida made her usual royal progress through the

52

VI. The restaurant was busy, so we headed for the rear as she paused to greet several locals. I trailed along like an afterthought.

"Well now," she said, surveying her surroundings. "No window booths." She held on to her saucer-like hat as she slid into the last available booth. "I do hate it when I can't see what's going on outside."

Vida always had to see what was going on. I remarked that I had noticed some pedestrians who looked like tourists.

"Yes," Vida said. "There were six people I didn't recognize." She opened the menu and made a face. "The special is creamed shrimp on a bed of rice. Rather peculiar for lunch, don't you think? Of course, seafood is rarely fat-making. My diet, you know."

I shrugged, accustomed to Vida's alleged war with her weight. "I'm having the hamburger dip."

She set the menu aside. "Oh, I'll try the special. It comes with one of their nice, plump rolls." She leaned out into the aisle. "Did you notice if my niece, Nicole, is waiting on tables?"

Seeing a waitress coming our way, I realized it wasn't Nicole. In fact, I didn't recognize the frizzy-haired blonde, whose name tag identified her as Sarah.

She smiled as she stopped at our table.

"Are you ready to order?" she inquired in a small, breathy voice.

Vida nodded. "How generous is the creamed shrimp?"

Sarah's smile disappeared from her overly made-up face. "You mean . . . the portion?"

"The amount of shrimp," Vida replied. "I'm quite fond of shrimp, so I don't want a skimpy serving."

"I'll make sure there's plenty," Sarah said, making a note.

Vida was still looking at the menu. "I see it comes with potato salad. The last time the mayonnaise dressing was weak — on mayonnaise. Could you bring extra butter pats for the roll? They're often a bit dry."

Sarah nodded. "Is there anything else? A beverage?"

"Hot tea." Vida put the menu down and glanced at the sugar and sugar substitutes. "I see only two real sugar packets. I prefer three or four for my tea, if it's no trouble. Oh — and cream. Real cream."

I kept my order simple. "Hamburger dip, medium rare, honey mustard dressing on the salad. And a regular Pepsi, please."

"Where," Vida asked after Sarah scurried off, "did she come from?"

"College student?" I suggested.

"Perhaps. Now, whom does she resemble?

54

Think, Emma. She could be related to someone we know."

"She probably had parents," I said.

Vida gave me her gimlet eye. "You lack curiosity about people. That's not good for a journalist. Besides, I'd like to put Sarah in my 'Scene Around' column. Perhaps I'll interview her before we leave."

"Go for it. By the way," I went on, not really interested in whether Sarah had recently moved here or had escaped from RestHaven's psych ward, "I hear the mayor's ailing."

"According to my niece, his wife, Irene, took him to see Doc Dewey," Vida said, referring to Marje Blatt, who worked as the clinic's receptionist. Like all of Vida's relatives, including Marje's brother, Deputy Bill, she was expected to deliver the latest news to her aunt. "Which reminds me," she continued, again lowering her voice, "Marje's mother, Lila, might be qualified to take over my job. She's only in her early sixties and was editor of the high school newspaper. When Marius Vandeventer owned the *Advocate*, Lila did a series on well-known Alpine High alums."

"I didn't know there were any," I said without thinking.

Vida took umbrage. "What about Bobby

Lambrecht? He's the new president of the Bank of Alpine after being the chief financial officer at the Bank of Washington in Seattle."

I confessed to being guilty of omitting Bob. "Sorry. He doesn't start the job until after Labor Day. I understand they're moving into their new home over the weekend."

Vida beamed. "Yes, they bought the house in The Pines that was on the market for going on a year."

I remained quiet as Sarah brought my salad and our beverages. The pause allowed me to change the subject. I told Vida about Blackwell's self-professed lock on the city manager's job.

She sniffed. "We may not have a manager. The issue hasn't been decided. Jack wants to have it both ways."

"Hedging his bets?" I suggested.

Vida frowned. "Well now . . . yes. Jack can't predict which way the wind is blowing. Don't worry about something that hasn't happened."

But of course I did.

CHAPTER 3

Sarah had declined even a brief interview. The VI was still very busy and she couldn't spare the time. Vida was miffed. "Really," she fumed as we returned to the office, "how can a newcomer expect to fit in if she isn't willing to make herself known?"

"She *is* on the job," I pointed out.

Vida ignored my remark. The poor girl had no idea it was virtually against the law to deny information to my House & Home editor. It didn't occur to me that Sarah might have a reason for being discreet.

After I returned to my office, Leo leaned in the doorway. "Guess what?" he said, looking pleased. "Liza and I are moving over the weekend. An unexpected vacancy came up at Pines Villa."

"Unexpected?" I was curious. "Did somebody croak?"

Leo shook his head. "One of the high school teachers got a better offer from

Wenatchee. She gave notice last week."

"I imagine Liza's pleased."

"She is." The lines on his face deepened. "Sure, she's anxious to sell the house in Santa Maria, but real estate sales slow in August before school starts. On the other hand, she's glad to move out of my apartment. I'm used to Dolph Terrill, but Liza isn't. Seeing the owner usually smashed reminds her of me in my bad old days. Last night Dolph fell down the front steps and asked her who the hell had moved the damned things." He started to leave, but halted for a moment. "Did I hear that Dodge took his own house off the market?"

I winced. "For now. Bill Blatt's mother made him move back home, which left Milo's daughter, Tanya, living alone. Things are sort of up in the air right now."

Leo frowned. "You mean the romance is kaput?"

"No, but Lila Blatt's making it awkward," I replied. "She's a widow who needs a man around, if only to do the heavy lifting. It's no wonder Bill and his sister have never married. Marje Blatt may not live at home, but Lila makes sure her daughter's at her beck and call."

"Those Blatt women . . ." Leo paused to make sure our House & Home editor wasn't within hearing range. "They're a tough-minded bunch, even if they only married into Vida's family. I'd hate to . . ." He stopped again. "Was that a siren close by?"

I listened, but couldn't hear anything except what sounded like a truck rumbling out on Front Street. Leo went through the newsroom, calling to Alison. I didn't hear a response, so he kept going, apparently to look outside. A moment later he hurried back into my line of sight. "It's Sam Hepp-ner. He pulled his cruiser up by the VI. Shall I check it out?"

"I'll come with you," I said, moving quickly to join him.

By the time we got outside, Sam had gone into the restaurant. A half dozen people had come together on the sidewalk, including the Presbyterian church's Pastor McClel-land and the Bank of Alpine's Rick Erland-son.

"What's going on?" I asked Rick, the husband of our former receptionist, Ginny.

"Darned if I know," he replied. "A rob-bery, maybe?"

Leo tried the door, but it was locked. "Weird," he murmured.

I moved to the curb, listening for more emergency vehicles, but there were no other sirens. I motioned to Leo that I was going back to the office. He nodded but stayed put.

Alison was at her post when I returned. "I saw you and Leo take off as I was coming from the rest room," she said. "What happened out front? I heard a siren."

I explained about Deputy Heppner's arrival at the VI. "For all I know, somebody flew into a rage over the daily special," I said. "It didn't appeal to me, but Vida lapped it up."

Alison smiled. "She's in a better mood today. Maybe she's come to terms with her grandson being in jail. Has she visited him?"

"No," I replied, glancing out through the plate-glass door, but seeing no sign of Leo. "Her daughter Amy told me Vida can't bear to see Roger caged up like an animal and surrounded by real criminals."

"As opposed to fake ones?" Alison said with a droll expression.

"Right." I shook my head. "Vida still can't accept that he's a genuine perp. Dealing drugs was bad enough, but luring young girls into prostitution was reprehensible." I shut up as Leo came in the door.

"Weird," he said, shaking his head. "Heppner finally came out and took off in his cruiser, but didn't say anything. Typical of Sam. I went inside to ask Sunny Rhodes,

60

who wasn't sure. Her hostess duties had tapered off, so she'd been getting something to eat. She thought some guy was hassling their new waitress. I asked if he was a drunk in the bar, but Sunny said no." Leo shrugged and pulled a pack of cigarettes from his shirt pocket. "Sounds weird to me, but Sunny can be kind of vague."

"Sarah's the new waitress," I said to Alison, waving off Leo's offer of a cigarette. "She waited on Vida and me today."

Leo grinned as he lighted his cigarette and inhaled. "Say, Alison, I caught a glimpse of that hunk you were swooning over. He came out of the bar while I was talking to Sunny."

"Oh, shoot!" Alison looked as if she might vault over the desk and fly straight through the front door. "Was he alone?"

"He was." Leo paused to take another puff on his cigarette. "But there were three or four pretty girls chasing after him. Maybe that's why Heppner was called in." He sauntered off to his desk.

"Leo!" Alison shrieked — and then stared at me. "Is that true?"

I laughed. "Relax. You know Leo likes to tease."

"What if he's serious this time? Or is he ever?"

"Only when he's selling ad space," I said.

"Oh — that waitress, Sarah, could use your cosmetic talents. She's just shy of looking like a clown taught her to do her face. It's a shame, because her features are good."

"I'll have to see for myself," Alison responded. "Maybe the majorly hot guy will show up there again."

"Hey — Mr. Hottie works for Blackwell, so he's the enemy. Avoid him." I started to turn away, but stopped. "Unless, of course, you'd like to become a spy."

"Do you mean that?" she asked, her blue eyes enormous.

I considered the question. "Yes, maybe I do."

Sometimes I have really bad ideas. I hoped this wasn't one of them.

With the long weekend under way, there wasn't much sleuthing I could offer Alison. In fact, I asked if she still planned to spend the time off with her parents in Everett. But the senior Lindahls were taking advantage of the good weather to go camping by the ocean.

"I suppose," she said, looking thoughtful, "I could do a makeover for Lori. But if her boyfriend's still hanging out, she doesn't need one. Cole Petersen works for Microsoft and travels all over the world, so how come he spends so much time with Lori in Alpine?" She sighed and then, apparently not expecting an answer, shrugged. "Oh, well."

Her regress to gloom goaded me into suggesting she get chummy with Sarah the waitress. I explained how she'd turned down Vida's offer to write her up as a newcomer feature. "Sarah might respond to someone in her peer group. She could be a college student, so maybe you'll recognize her."

A small spark of interest flashed in Alison's eyes. "The VI does takeout. I'll ask Lori if she'd like to have me pick up something for us. And for Cole, if he's still hanging out." She paused. "Maybe Cole's anti-marriage. Lori's twenty-nine and still single."

"So?"

"Well . . ." She frowned. "I suppose it makes me feel not so old."

There are times when I don't know what to say. Maybe that's because I'm so old.

I spent the rest of the afternoon making sure everything was close to camera-ready since there was only one workday before the paper went to press Tuesday night. Barring breaking news, the big story would be the Labor Day picnic — and the droning speeches. Then there would be the usual vehicular mayhem of a three-day weekend, especially on dangerous Highway 2 and the Stevens Pass corridor. At least the weather was good. That might cut down on the carnage.

For once, I was the last to leave. Front Street was backed up from Eighth to Alpine Way. That was unusual even at our so-called rush hour. Apparently there were quite a few tourists in town, though I didn't notice any out-of-state vehicles. Since I usually arrive home first, it's my task to open the door and a couple of windows. The thermometer by the kitchen door showed a tolerable seventy-five degrees, but it was misleading. The third-growth forest behind our log cabin shields us from the late afternoon sun.

The phone rang as I came back into the kitchen. I had to hurry into the living room to grab the receiver off the end table before the call trunked over to voice mail.

"Emma?" said my stepdaughter, Tanya Dodge. "Where's Dad?"

"He's not home yet," I replied. "Did you try him at work?"

"Yes, but Dwight Gould told me he'd just left. That was ten minutes ago. I didn't try his cell." She paused. "I hate to bother him, but they let us off work early at the Forest

64

Service. After I came in the house I heard a noise downstairs. Maybe something fell off a shelf, but I didn't want to go down to check it out."

"Did you talk to anyone at headquarters?" I asked, going to the big picture window to see if my husband was in sight. He wasn't.

"Lori Cobb, but she was in a rush," Tanya replied. "I feel dumb. It could be a mouse."

"Go ahead and call back —" I stopped, seeing the Yukon turn into the driveway. "Here comes your father. Do you want to hold on?"

Tanya didn't answer right away. "What?" she finally said, a bit breathless. "Bill just pulled up. I think he must've come on duty at five. I'll tell him what happened. Thanks, Emma." She rang off.

I went into the kitchen to greet my better half. Or louder half, at any rate. Milo was cussing as he came in the door. I leaned against the counter and waited for him to defuse.

"What?" he barked. "Have you got a problem, too?"

"No," I responded calmly. "But I gather you do."

"Damned Fred Iverson," Milo grumbled, taking off his regulation hat, but stopping before he threw it at the dishwasher. "He

65

called right at five to say his new waitress had run off. What the hell am I supposed to do about that? It's a personnel problem, not a crime."

"Did Fred want her reported missing?" I asked in my mildest voice.

"You got it," Milo retorted, heading to the living room. "I told him nobody's officially reported missing until after forty-eight hours have . . ." He stopped and turned around. "Why are you still in the kitchen?"

"I can hear you from here," I declared. "Keep bitching. Consider me another appliance. A cheap one. I don't use up electricity."

"Shit." Milo tossed his hat aside. "Why do you put up with me?" He loped into the kitchen and took me in his arms.

I leaned against him. "You need to vent and I'm used to it."

"Yeah." He leaned down to rest his cheek on my head. "Damn, you must be the only woman on the planet who'd put up with me."

I moved just enough to look up into his intense hazel eyes. "I hope so. No other woman's getting you. Now let go, change, get a drink, and then tell me about Fred's new waitress. Her name's Sarah, by the way. She served Vida and me today at lunch.

Didn't Heppner tell you about the call he got from the Venison Inn?"

Milo had released me. "He logged it, but no details. You know Sam never runs at the mouth. You don't have any weird news, I hope?"

I shook my head. I wouldn't bother him about Tanya's report of a noise downstairs. Deputy Bill was her knight in regulation dun brown. Unlike her mother, the daughter was sympathetic toward law enforcement. Tricia had never appreciated the demands of her ex-husband's job.

Milo reappeared five minutes later. "Why don't we eat out? Even with visitors in town, we shouldn't have to wait long at the ski lodge."

I looked questioningly at my husband, but before I could speak, his cell rang. He yanked it out of his shirt pocket with one hand while the other opened the liquor cupboard. I saw him tense.

"Okay, Bill," Milo said in a beleaguered voice, "you know the drill. Call in the emergency crews and stay put. How's Tanya?"

I moved closer, but couldn't hear Bill's reply. "Right, I'm leaving now." Milo put the cell back in his pocket. "Hell of a way to start a weekend. Blatt found a stiff in the lower level of my old house. What next? He finds Santa Claus's corpse in the chimney? I have to go over there." He started for the kitchen door.

"Milo!" I yelled. "What about Tanya?"

"She's fine," he replied over his shoulder. "Shocked, but okay."

I grabbed him by the back of his cotton shirt. "I'm going, too. Tanya's my step-daughter, remember?"

Briefly, my husband looked conflicted, but finally he shrugged. "Fine. Hold her hand while Bill and I do whatever. You know the drill, you ornery little twerp."

I ignored the comment. "What kind of stiff?"

"The dead kind — female. That's all I know. Get into the vehicle."

I was still fastening my seatbelt as Milo reversed out of the garage, down the drive, and onto Fir Street. "Tanya called to say she heard a noise downstairs," I said.

"When?" He hadn't put the flasher on the Yukon, but he was exceeding the speed limit by at least twenty miles an hour. Luckily, traffic was sparse in our residential part of town.

"Just before you got home," I informed him. "But Bill showed up. Tanya talked to Lori. You must've already left."

68

"I was probably outside talking to Iverson," Milo said, turning by the high school to get on County Highway 187, more commonly known as the Icicle Creek Road. "Fred stopped me just as I was coming out of headquarters." He slowed for the arterial by the cemetery. "The EMTs must be on their way."

"It could be a burglar," I said.

Milo darted me a sharp look. "A female burglar? Hell, why not? Equal rights and all that. Keep quiet now. I'm on the job."

The fire engine and the EMTs had pulled in just ahead of us. I couldn't see Bill's cruiser, only the split-level roof of what had once been the Dodge family home. Tricia's affair with a high school teacher had trashed that American dream twenty years ago.

There was no room in the driveway for the Yukon, so the sheriff parked at the curb by the next-door neighbors' house. I glimpsed an elderly man at the front window and recalled that an older couple named Swenson lived there. By the time I hit the ground, Milo was already out of sight. The first person I saw was one of the EMTs, Del Amundson. Despite whatever disaster he encountered, Del was always upbeat. He waved and disappeared on the other side of the fire engine.

Suddenly it dawned on me that this was news. I dug out my cell and started to call Mitch, but remembered he'd left early to pick up Brenda for the trip to visit Troy in Monroe. I was about to dial Kip's number when Tanya rushed out from behind the EMT van.

"Emma!" she cried, sounding breathless. "Am I hexed?"

I put an arm around her. "No, but you do attract drama. Did you minor in theater at the UDub?"

She managed a rueful smile. "How could anyone get inside the house and . . . die? It's too weird."

"You're sure she's dead?" I asked as we took our time heading toward the house.

"Bill says so. I never saw her. He wouldn't let me come downstairs. Frankly, I didn't want to see another corpse." She broke away from me and shook herself. "Not after getting shot by my crazy ex-fiancé before he killed himself. Mom will insist I go back to Bellevue!"

"That nightmare happened in Bellevue," I said, as if she needed reminding. "You're in your thirties, Tanya," I went on, trying to ignore the handful of neighbors who were edging ever closer to the Dodge house. "Your mother can't make you do anything.

70

Your father won't let her."

"She could always find ways to get around him," Tanya declared. "I'm not criticizing her. She had to run everything at home. His job came first. I get that — now. But still . . ." Her voice trailed off.

I was familiar with the first Mrs. Dodge's rationale for running off with Jake Sellers. I wasn't without sympathy for her as a wife and mother of three. It wouldn't have been easy being married to someone in law enforcement. Even now, instead of dining at the ski lodge, I was standing by a fire engine while my stomach growled. But I wouldn't trade places with Tricia for all the high school teachers on the planet. Ironically, Sellers hadn't changed his stripes. He'd cheated on her, too. Their divorce had been final at the end of July.

I was tempted to say as much, though I tried to avoid criticizing my predecessor in front of her daughter. "Are you sure you locked up after you left for work this morning?"

Tanya grimaced. "I did. But I got a call around eleven at work from a Monroe real estate agent about someone who wanted to see the house. I told the agent it was temporarily off the market, but he said his client wouldn't move here until after the new year

71

and wanted to see any homes that might be available then. I stopped by on my lunch hour to put my key under the mat. It was there when I came home."

"What real estate company was it?" I asked.

Tanya rolled her eyes. "He gave me the name so fast that I didn't catch it. We were busy today because of the holiday and trying to finish up so we could leave early. I feel like an idiot."

"You're not," I assured her as I saw Bill Blatt coming in our direction. He greeted me with a brief nod before putting an arm around Tanya. "You want to come back inside?" he asked her. "When they're done, they'll be taking the body out the back way."

Tanya leaned against Bill. "I guess so. I'm kind of numb."

I stayed put while they went inside. Then I called Kip at home to ask him to take a picture. He asked where and why. I quickly summed up Bill's discovery in Milo's house.

"Wild," Kip said under his breath. "A corpse in Dodge's basement? Isn't that kind of freaky?"

"Yes," I replied. "It's as if whoever did it planned to save the sheriff some bother."

Or, it suddenly occurred to me, wanted to cause him some trouble.

72

■ ■ ■ ■

I started for the door as the firefighters came back outside. Obviously, they weren't needed. The split-level's front door was open and I heard voices coming from downstairs. Being squeamish, I steeled myself before facing any gruesome sights. I'd only been in the lower part of Milo's house twice. In all the years we'd known each other, I'd rarely spent much time on the premises. Right from the start, he'd felt more at home in my log cabin.

"Emma!"

I gave a start, hearing my husband's voice before I saw him coming out of what looked like a bedroom. "Is it grisly?" I asked.

Milo shook his head. "Not really. She may've been strangled. No apparent struggle. But Del and his partner are taking her out through the back. The front stairs are too awkward."

"Do you know who it is?"

"No ID on her," Milo said, indicating I should lead the way upstairs. "But it shouldn't be hard to find out." He paused until we reached the main floor. "She's wearing a uniform, like the ones at the Venison Inn." While I gaped at him, he took

73

out his cell. "I'm calling Heppner. I wonder if he missed something earlier. Go home, Emma. There's nothing you can do, so . . . Sam?" The sheriff turned his back on me.

I wanted to ask the big jerk how he expected me to get home. Walk? Or maybe ride in the EMT van with the body? I assumed it was Sarah. Who else could it be? I stomped upstairs, in search of Tanya.

She was in the kitchen with Bill, who asked what was going on downstairs. I told him what little I knew.

"A waitress?" Tanya looked puzzled. "I don't recall anyone named Sarah at the VI."

"She's new," I responded. "Was new." Now dead. I grimaced, then remembered to offer a quick prayer for the poor girl. Leaning on the back of an empty kitchen chair, I asked Tanya how she was feeling.

Tanya pointed to a shot glass. "Dad still had some Scotch here. Bill thought it might help." She offered the deputy a grateful smile. "Go, get back to work. I'll be fine." He hesitated, but she made a shooing motion. "He's a good guy," she said softly after he was out of the room.

I sat down. "He should tell his ornery mother to stick it. You won't want to be alone tonight, so if Bill can't stay with you, come to our house. You haven't been there since we finished the remodel. We put my old double bed in the spare room."

"I suppose," she murmured, "Bill could say he has to work because of . . . this." She gestured in the direction of downstairs.

"He may have to," I said, hearing someone call my name. It was Kip — with Alison right behind him.

"I got a shot of the EMTs loading the body into their van," Kip said after greeting Tanya. "Should I take a couple of pictures downstairs? Del told me that's where the poor girl was found."

I considered briefly. "No. I won't invade the house's privacy." Nor did I want the owner threatening to strangle me when we got home.

Kip nodded, "Good. I'd better get back to my barbecue duties. Can I ID the victim when I go online?"

"Hold off," I said. "I'll have to talk to the sheriff first."

He nodded again before hurrying away. I looked at Alison. "How come you're here?"

"Well . . ." She glanced quickly at Tanya. "I'd gone to the VI to pick up dinner. Sunny Rhodes was still fussing about their missing waitress. When I left, I saw Kip coming out of our office. He told me a young woman had been found dead here, so I thought . . ."

Her blue eyes not only widened but seemed to sparkle. "I know it's not espionage, but it sure beats eyebrow plucking."

I shot Tanya a quick glance, but she was looking past me. "Dad?"

Dad, however, was staring at me. "I thought I told you to beat it. Take Tanya with you. This place is a crime scene." He glanced at Alison and then frowned at me. "I just saw Kip leave. What's going on? Are you holding a staff meeting?"

"No! And how did you expect me to get home?" I shot back. "I have no car. Did you forget we were married?"

Milo looked sheepish. "Maybe I did. Sometimes I live in the past. Tanya has a car."

His daughter stood up. "Can I get my stuff out of your old room, Dad?" she asked.

"Go ahead, but make it quick. You, too," he said to me, "and your camp followers." Milo turned around to head back downstairs. "This is going to be a long night."

No kidding, I thought. But for once I kept my big mouth shut.

"The sheriff didn't throw me out," Alison whispered as Tanya left the kitchen. "How come?"

"He's preoccupied," I said. "Let's vacate the scene before Milo remembers we're here

76

and forcibly ejects us. Did you drive or walk from the *Advocate*?"

"I never went back inside the office," Alison responded. "I've got my Audi parked by the development entrance."

We trudged through the dining room and kitchen but stopped short of the front door. Sam Heppner was stepping over the threshold. He gave us a baleful look before asking where he could find his boss. I told him to go downstairs. He knew the way, having worked for Milo back when the sheriff's wife was still Tricia.

"Let's wait for Tanya," I said to Alison. "I don't want her to think she's been abandoned. Tanya can ride with us and collect her car later when the driveway's freed up."

I'd hardly gotten the words out when Tanya came into the living room. She'd already met Alison on a couple of other occasions. We trooped outside. The fire engine was gone, but the EMT van remained in place. As we started to go around it, Del Amundson appeared from the back. For once, he seemed to have lost his usual jovial manner.

I let my two companions go on ahead of me as I waited for him. "Is something wrong?" I asked.

Unlike some of my pricklier sources, Del

has always been cooperative. He stopped, shifting his weight from one foot to the other. "I don't know." He looked around, apparently making sure Alison and Tanya were out of earshot. "One of the gurney wheels got stuck in a rut coming out of the basement. There's not much room to maneuver because the lot abuts the golf course fence. The body got jostled, and . . . her hair fell off."

I stared at Del. "Fell off? Or fell out?"

"No, no, I mean . . ." Del grimaced. "That blond hair wasn't hers. She was wearing a wig. Kind of creepy for a young gal like that, huh, Emma?"

I wasn't sure if "creepy" was the right word for it.

CHAPTER 4

"We thought we'd lost you," Alison said after I hurried to join her and Tanya in the Audi. "Is the backseat okay?"

"Sure." I clambered inside in my usual graceless fashion. Tanya obviously had been recounting Bill Blatt's discovery of the body.

"Wow!" Alison exclaimed, heading up the Icicle Creek Road. "So if you heard a noise downstairs, whoever killed the poor girl must've still been in the basement!"

Somehow, that thought hadn't occurred to me. Or to Tanya, judging from her reaction. "I hope not! Bill was armed, of course. I wouldn't have gone down there alone."

"Bill?" Alison said, giving Tanya a quick, innocent look.

"One of Dad's deputies," Tanya replied primly. "He'd just come on patrol at five."

"Lucky you," Alison remarked. "I mean, lucky timing."

Tanya didn't comment. Fred Iverson would be summoned to make an official ID as soon as the EMTs delivered the corpse to the morgue in the hospital basement. I decided to speak up. "She's the new waitress who served Vida and me at the VI," I said. "Her first name is Sarah. She wore a wig."

"Really?" Alison gaped at me in the rearview mirror. "How do you know? Did the sheriff tell you?"

"No, Del Amundson did," I replied. "He and Tony Lynch were the EMTs. They're probably telling the sheriff right now."

Alison braked at the corner by the football field as a trio of teenage boys crossed the street. "Was the girl bald?" she asked, darting another glance at me in the mirror.

"I don't think so," I said. "Del told me her own hair was covered with some kind of mesh. A hairnet, maybe. Hey, Alison, how do you know where I live? You've never been to my house."

"I know it's that killer cabin tucked in the forest," she replied. "It's the only log house in town."

"So it is," I murmured, wishing she'd used a different word than "killer" to describe the place. We were now only a block away. "Do you want to come inside? I can show you how it was remodeled."

"Thanks, but no," she replied, slowing for the turn into the driveway. "I've got to deliver dinner. Lori's probably starving. Maybe over the weekend, okay?"

I told her that sounded fine. With a homicide on Milo's plate, any plans we might have had were put on hold. Tanya and I thanked Alison and went inside via the front door.

"She seems sharp," Tanya said after we were in the living room. "Too bad her cosmetology course was axed. I was thinking of taking it if she offered classes at night. Wasn't her mother murdered years ago?"

I nodded as I checked my phone messages. There weren't any. "Linda Petersen Lindahl was the bank president's daughter. She also worked for the bank. Linda and Howard had been divorced for many years when she was killed. Would you like a glass of wine?"

"Yes, thanks. I can get it for myself after I stash my stuff in the spare room." She smiled just enough that her angular face looked almost pretty. "It still seems amazing that you and Dad finally got married. I'm thirty-four years old and was on the verge of marrying at least two other men before I started dating Bill. How do you know when you've finally found the right person?"

I looked into the hazel eyes that were so like her father's, though not nearly as intense. "I didn't know. Why do you think it took us fifteen years to get married?"

Tanya laughed. She did look pretty then.

I had no idea when Milo would be home, so I didn't start dinner. If he worked for another hour, he might grab takeout from the Burger Barn. Tanya had lost her appetite. Not that I blamed her, even if she hadn't seen the body. But my stomach still growled. I decided to make scrambled eggs and toast to tide me over.

I'd just closed the dishwasher a little before seven when the phone rang. "Well now!" Vida exclaimed. "What's this I hear about a dead woman in Milo's house? How can that be? Was she a Realtor?"

"No," I replied, sitting down on the sofa. "Why would she be?"

Vida made a disparaging noise. "You know how people confuse things. Buck and I had dinner at the ski lodge. The early bird special, though there was nothing special about it — beef brisket, very dry, like chewing twine. And the service was soooo slow! Which is why I asked Henry Bardeen if his staff was shorthanded. He said no, but they were busier than usual — and not just because of the long weekend. The VI had been shut down, perhaps by a health inspector. Doesn't that beat all?"

"Where did the ski lodge manager get that news?" I asked.

"From one of his guests who had gone there for dinner," Vida replied. "Henry went on to say a dead woman had been found in Milo's house in the Icicle Creek Development. He assumed it must have been a real estate agent showing someone around. Well?"

I gave Vida the brief version. "Tanya's staying here tonight," I added. "She's in the spare room doing email on her laptop."

"My, my," Vida said in a distracted voice. "Sarah. How peculiar. Do you think she wouldn't let me interview her because she was frightened?"

"You mean . . . what? She was frightened of publicity?"

"Perhaps," Vida allowed. "Or frightened because she knew someone was after her. Have you talked to Fred Iverson since she was found?"

"No, but I'm sure Milo has."

"Men! They don't know how to talk to people. Oh, Milo will ask the standard questions that elicit standard answers. Conversation, the ordinary exchange between people, that's how to learn what you need to know. Shall I call Sunny Rhodes? I gave her an Avon order last week. I could ask how soon my Skin So Soft lotion will be delivered. It was on sale, two for one."

"Go ahead. But except for the bare facts, I'm not posting anything online until I've talked to the sheriff."

"I wonder . . . ," Vida began, but paused. "If Mitch is gone for the weekend, should I help with the hard copy? You may need sidebars."

"Let's see how it plays out," I suggested. Vida's folksy style was fine for her House & Home page but not suited to hard news.

"If you say so," she said a bit stiffly. "My wretched sister-in-law, Mary Lou Blatt, lives two doors from Milo's house, you know. I heard she was going out of town for the weekend. Won't she be livid when she finds out what she missed practically in her back-yard!"

"No doubt," I agreed. Hearing what sounded like the Yukon pulling into the driveway, I told Vida I had to see how Tanya was getting along. If I'd mentioned Milo had arrived, she might insist I put him on the line. That would not be a good idea.

Judging from my husband's grim expression, nothing was good in his world. The only non-inflammatory thing I could think of to say was asking if he was hungry.

"Yeah," he replied, stalking off to the living room. "Got a spare steak, or should I have stopped at the Grocery Basket deli?"

I assured him I had the situation under control, though I didn't mention the steak was still in the freezer. Milo apparently remembered he hadn't made himself a drink before being called to duty. He came back into the kitchen to get his Scotch, but didn't talk. I pretended he didn't exist as I dug out the T-bone, thawed it in the microwave, cut up some new potatoes, and husked an ear of corn. After everything was cooking, I made myself a short CC on the rocks and came into the living room, where Milo was in the easy chair, staring into space.

I sat on the sofa and waited. Chipmunks chattered in the evergreens and the Empire Builder whistled as it passed through town on its way to Seattle. After a couple of minutes, Milo looked at me and said, "It's a setup. I'd bet good money on it."

"How do you mean? Because the girl was killed at your house?"

He shook his head. "We don't know that for certain. Maybe that's what it's meant to look like." His expression was grim as he

85

lighted a cigarette. "Where's Tanya?"

"In the bedroom," I replied.

"She's okay?"

I nodded. Milo started to speak, but stopped. "I'll tell you more while I eat. Or is Tanya eating, too?"

"She told me she's not hungry. I already ate something."

He grinned. "You surprise the hell out of me. You're not asking a lot of dumb questions. Are you sick?"

"I'm learning how to be a sympathetic wife instead of a prying journalist, okay? However," I went on, given that there are limits to my patience, "I'd like a brief statement that Kip can post on our website."

"You've got a website?" Milo said in mild surprise.

I never knew when he was teasing about his ignorance of my job. "We've had one for ages," I told him, my eyes narrowed. That wasn't true, but I wished it were. It had been only about a year, and even then, it hadn't been my idea, but Kip's. "Give, Sheriff, or I'll dump your dinner out in the yard."

"No, you won't. It'd attract bears and they scare you." He uttered a weary sigh. "Okay, the basics are Sarah Williams, twenty-four, resident of Redding, according to her

86

California driver's license, staying at the Lumberjack Motel, started at the VI Monday. She'd worked evenings until today, when she had to take over for Vida's niece, Nicole, who had an emergency dental appointment. Sarah was polite but not friendly with her co-workers. That last part's from Fred Iverson."

"Weird," I murmured. "She moves to Alpine a week ago and almost immediately gets murdered? Someone must've followed her. Or did she come up here with a friend?"

"Fred didn't think so," Milo replied. "I had Heppner check with the owners of the Lumberjack. Mel and Minnie Harris were sure she was alone."

"Has her family been contacted?"

"Not yet. The Redding address is an apartment house. I've got Blatt working on that."

Hearing the timer on the stove, I got up. "Your dinner's ready."

"Good," Milo called after me. "Give me a minute. I want to see how Tanya's doing."

I smiled to myself. After so many years of being friend and lover to the sheriff, now that I was his wife, I was adjusting to him being a father. He'd taken on that role long before I met him. But until Tanya had moved to Alpine after a horrendous experience with her now dead fiancé, Milo's main obligations had been occasional visits to his family in Bellevue. As selfish as it sounded even to me, I wasn't used to sharing him.

I turned off everything on the stove before calling Kip to tell him what to post on our website.

"Not a great start to the Labor Day weekend," he remarked. "How come Fleetwood wasn't there?"

"Maybe he left town for the weekend," I said. "Now that I think about it, he hasn't taken a real vacation this year. Spence may have trouble rustling up a reliable college student to fill in for him at KSKY."

"He never does live stuff on weekends," Kip pointed out. "It's mostly music and canned programming. On Sunday mornings he has some crazy reverends. They sound like they're preaching in a tent."

"Be thankful they aren't preaching in Old Mill Park. Are you sticking around over the weekend?"

"I think so," Kip replied. "We're having dinner tomorrow with my brothers and their families. You want me to take pictures at the picnic?"

I told him Mitch was supposed to be back late Monday afternoon, but to be prepared for details on the murder investigation. I was disconnecting when Milo entered the kitchen.

"Tanya seems good," he said. "Where's the food?"

"I'm getting it out now," I informed him, not so sweetly. "I, too, have job responsibilities, you big jerk."

"How come you're so crabby?" he shot back, sitting down at the table. "You're not the one who's stuck working over a holiday weekend."

"Oh, yes, I am," I asserted, unceremoniously shoveling his food onto a plate. "I have to keep up on what you're doing."

"Are you going to stand there glaring at me or sit down and enjoy my company?" Milo asked in an annoyingly complaisant voice.

I started to snap back, reconsidered, and plopped down in my usual chair. "Someday I'll stay mad at you for . . . how long is my record?"

"Eleven minutes. Not bad after sixteen years."

"You stayed mad at me for months after we broke up the first time," I reminded him.

"I didn't like being dumped," he declared after downing more steak. "Back then, despite what you insisted when we first got together, you hadn't finished chasing the

89

impossible dream that was Tom Cavanaugh. Hell, unless my memory's gone south, he was still married to his nutty wife."

"He was." I smiled wanly. "But Tom was Adam's father, and after Sandra died, I thought marrying him was the right thing to do."

Milo shook his head. "It wasn't. If you'd done that, you wouldn't have this plush remodeled log cabin." He gestured at the expanded kitchen with its all new appliances.

"Tom was rich," I asserted. "He could've built me a castle."

"You wouldn't have liked it. You like being cozy. Castles are drafty."

I was quiet for a moment or two. "True. Most of all, I wouldn't have had you. That's what I always wanted. I just didn't know it."

He shrugged. "That's okay. I did."

I growled low in my throat. Milo ignored me and kept eating.

After we'd adjourned to the living room, I asked Milo why he thought the murder had been a setup.

"You know I hate to speculate," he began, putting his feet up on the ottoman, "but have you ever heard of anyone who found a murder vic they didn't know in their house?"

I thought for a moment. "Yes, when I worked for the *Oregonian*. Four people, two couples. One pair was in Portland, the other in the suburbs. Tigard, to be exact."

"That's cheating," Milo declared. "I thought you didn't cover crime in Portland."

"I didn't, but you asked if I'd ever *heard* of anybody like that."

He stared at me. "God, but you can be a pain in the ass."

"You're right," I conceded. "The last few days have been kind of nerve-racking. You think Blackwell set you up?"

"He seems like the obvious suspect," my husband said, settling back into the easy chair. "But it doesn't make sense. Would Jack — or one of his stooges — murder a waitress just to cause me trouble? Even he wouldn't pull a stunt like that. His goal is to run the county. Getting rid of me comes in second."

"Except for knocking Patti around, Jack keeps his public image clean," I allowed. "Will you learn much from the crime scene evidence?"

"What evidence?" Milo made a face. "That's Bran's old room. It was pretty well cleaned out ten years ago after he went off

91

to WSU. All that was left were some bookcases, a few books, and a beat-up desk. But I'm borrowing one of Snohomish County's crime scene magicians to give it a once-over. If they send somebody tomorrow, they'll have to charge SkyCo triple time because of the holiday."

"What about the wig?" I asked.

"What about it? You women are always doing weird stuff with your hair. Maybe Sarah had a different wig for every day of the week."

"I never do anything weird to my hair," I asserted. "It looks weird because I have a styling disability."

Milo stood up. "I like your hair the way it is. You never get mad if I mess with it. Why don't I do that now?" He eased his big frame onto the sofa. "Well? Why are you looking like a prune?"

"Because," I said quietly, "your daughter is in the next room. Do you want to shock the poor girl?"

"Shit. I forgot. Why didn't I have Blatt ask Tanya to help him hold down the fort at headquarters?"

I gave him my widest doe-eyed look. "It's not too late."

Milo reached for his cell phone.

CHAPTER 5

The first phone call of the morning was from Alison at nine-twenty. Milo had already left and I was still in my usual foggy state.

"Do you want my report over the phone?" Alison began, sounding irritatingly cheerful. "Maybe I should stop by in person to see the inside of your amazing log cabin."

I told her to come over. Only after I hung up did it occur to me that I had no idea what kind of report she was talking about. While I was pleased that she sounded in better spirits, I didn't want her taking my spying suggestion too seriously with a murderer on the loose. I was pouring a third mug of coffee when Tanya stepped into the kitchen.

"Bill and I are going to breakfast at the Cascadia in Skykomish," she informed me, looking pleased. "He got off work a little after midnight. I went on patrol with him after he finished up at headquarters. It was really kind of interesting."

Her remark jolted me out of my fogged-in state. "What happened?"

"Nothing dramatic," Tanya replied, darting a glance at the living room window. "He only made three stops. Two loud party complaints and teenagers looking as if they were about to break into a house that was dark. Oh, he pulled over some other kids for speeding and a guy who ran the arterial on Spark Plug Road. Gus something. He apologized to Bill and said he was looking for some lost bears. He was kind of weird."

"I know Gus Lindquist," I said. "He had to shoot a mama bear a while ago and it sort of unhinged him." I spotted the deputy's Ford Focus pull into the drive. "Bill's here," I said as he honked the horn.

As Tanya went out the front door, I waved from the window. The lost bears story could be put on hold. Intermingling with wildlife wasn't uncommon for those of us who lived so close to nature on the rocky face of Tonga Ridge. Tanya's childhood may have been spent in Alpine, but she had come of age on Seattle's Eastside. Twenty years ago her mother had carted the three Dodge children off to suburbia in Bellevue. Ironically, back in the fifties, when I was born, the town had just begun to emerge from what had been little more than forest, orchards, farms and, during World War Two, military housing. Half a century later, over a hundred thousand people called Bellevue home. Ironically, the downtown skyscrapers reminded me of the Seattle I had known in my own youth. I, meanwhile, stared out at a handful of homely midcentury modern houses flanked by towering evergreens and Alpine Baldy.

Alison's Audi appeared just as the Ford drove out of sight. Its owner practically bolted out of the car, hurrying to the front door.

"Well?" I said in greeting. "Have you solved the case?"

"No," she replied, swiveling around to take in the living room. "But I talked to some people. Wow! This is one very cool cabin! You say you remodeled it? How long have you lived here?"

I explained that I'd bought the cabin when I moved to Alpine. It had belonged to a couple who'd used it as a family ski retreat. Eventually the children moved away and the parents' knees gave out. I'd spent less for the cabin than I'd paid for my Portland bungalow.

"Milo took on the remodel when we got

married," I continued. "It started with a den out back for him and went on from there. We doubled the kitchen's size to include a laundry area, enlarged both bedrooms, and added a second bathroom."

Alison seemed duly impressed, especially with the appliances. "Stainless steel," she said wistfully. "Someday when I get married — if I ever get married — that's what I want. Maybe by that time, robots will do all the work."

I shot her a hard stare. "If you don't stop saying things like that, I'll be tempted to shake you. Why are you so anxious to get married?"

Alison sank down onto a kitchen chair. "Good question." She studied her navy crocheted flats. "Maybe because my parents flunked marriage. They always told me they were too young and didn't know what they were doing."

I nodded. "But you lucked out. Susan's been a great stepmother."

"Sure, but that's not the point." Alison paused again. "It turned out she couldn't have kids. After my parents split, my real mother didn't want me. She died before I was old enough to talk to her about it. I was born when she was twenty-four, but I'm sure she resented being tied down with me. Then she and Dad split when I was six and she let him have custody. I want to get married and have kids to prove that I'm not like her."

I thought back in time to when I met Alison ten years ago. "Your mother was making more of an effort to spend time with you before she died," I pointed out. "She was in her midthirties by then. Maybe she realized what she'd missed by giving custody to your father."

Alison's expression was wry. "You mean she matured?"

"Yes, I suppose I do," I allowed. "She'd succeeded in the banking business, so you know she was smart. But it took her longer to become a full-fledged adult."

"That's what I mean," Alison said with a lift of her chin. "I want to prove I'm an adult now. I don't want to be like my mother."

"Getting married won't make you an adult," I declared.

"It will if I find the right man. Isn't marriage about helping each other grow?"

I shrugged. "Don't ask me. I stayed single until last February."

"But . . . you have Adam, right?" She saw me nod. "Look at poor Sarah. She was only a little older than I am and she'll never get married or have kids. Life's too short to take chances by putting off important things."

"I did."

"Not really," Alison said. "You had a son. How old were you when you had him?"

"Twenty-one," I replied, not wanting to dredge up my personal history. "Maybe we should talk about the people you interviewed."

Alison sighed. "You think I'm weird."

I laughed. "Would I turn a weirdo into a spy?"

"You might. Mrs. Runkel is the biggest spy — okay, snoop — in town and she's a little weird. Those hats! Where does she find them?"

"That's a mystery we'll never solve," I said, laughing. "Let's stick to something easier — like murder. Who did you talk to?"

Alison reached into her straw handbag and pulled out a Nokia tablet. "I started with that old couple next door. I figured they might have seen something because elderly people like to check out the neighborhood. It turned out the only person they noticed until the sheriff's deputy pulled up was the mailman, Marlowe Whipp. According to Mr. Swenson, he didn't stop at the Dodge house. Is that unusual?"

"No. Milo had his mail changed some

time ago. I'm not sure if Tanya ever officially switched her place of residence from Bellevue."

"Got it." Alison glanced at her tablet. "Next is Cookie Eriks, who lives with her daughter and granddaughter a couple of doors down. Mrs. Eriks was walking the baby in her stroller around four and saw a U-Haul van go by, but she didn't see where it went."

"Cookie's not the noticing kind," I murmured. "How big a U-Haul?"

"Fairly small, not moving van size," Alison said.

"That'd be easy to check through the company. Besides," I went on, "there are only a dozen houses in the whole development. What else?"

"Do you know who lives in the ultramodern house? It looks out of place."

"The Melvilles. Scott's an architect who redesigned that house when they moved here from California ten years ago. He also worked on the remodel for all of this." I gestured at the living room. "Beverly's an interior designer. Did you talk to them?"

Alison shook her head. "I saw . . ." She glanced at her tablet. "Anagreta Amundson, lives this side of the sheriff's house and next to the Melvilles. She was leaving for a meeting, but had been in and out during the afternoon. The only things she noticed were a carpet company van and a FedEx truck. But she hadn't seen either of them stop."

Anagreta was the wife of Wes Amundson, Del's cousin, and one of our forest rangers. "Did she notice the carpet company's name?"

"Not really," Alison replied. "She thought it had letters, not words, in it."

That rang no bells, but Alpine didn't have a store that specialized in flooring, unless I counted Harvey's Hardware, which I didn't, since it'd require a DIY job. "No suspicious strangers?"

She looked apologetic. "Only the pollster dweeb."

"You mean . . . Ronnie whatever? Leo mentioned him to me. What did he look like?"

She nodded. "Young, midtwenties, maybe five-eight, average build, short brown hair, brown eyes. Nothing special."

"Find out who ordered a new rug," I said. "The carpet truck's of interest."

Alison stood up. "Will you pass this on to the sheriff?"

"Yes," I asserted, walking her to the front door. "He may want to talk to you later on today. Be careful, Alison. There may be a random killer on the loose, an outsider who preys on young women."

Alison looked startled. "Like Ted Bundy or the Green River Killer?"

"Like that," I said — and impulsively squeezed her arm. "Be careful!"

"I will," she said, flashing me a smile. "I promise!"

I smiled back. But promises are flimsy things and easily broken.

Alison had been gone for less than half an hour before the doorbell chimed again. Remembering Milo's caution about checking through the peephole, I peered out to see Kay Burns, RestHaven's PR person.

"To what do I owe this visit?" I asked after Kay sat down in the chair Alison had vacated.

Kay, a well-preserved and oft-married woman in her midfifties, adjusted the pleats of her mauve slacks. Her blue eyes darted around the living room and up to the beamed ceiling. "I'm on a mission. What I have to say would be better suited to the dark corner of an out-of-town bar."

I glanced at my watch. It was eleven-twenty, too early to haul out the booze. "How about coffee?"

"Fine." She rose from the chair. "I'll join

101

you in the kitchen. You must think I've gone over the edge." The sharp little laugh she uttered suggested that maybe she had.

There was only enough left in the coffee-maker for one cup. I poured it into a Seahawks mug and joined Kay at the kitchen table. "I can make more if you like," I offered.

"No, thank you." Kay took a sip, frowned, and briefly closed her eyes. When she opened them, her expression hardened. "Thirty years ago Jack Blackwell ruined my life. It turns out I'm not the only person he's trashed along the way. And no, I'm not talking about his first wife, Jennifer Hood, whom he married in California. She and I have bonded since we both work for Rest-Haven."

Jennifer was the RN in charge of the medical rehab unit and had only been in Alpine since the facility opened in February. But Kay was a native. Her first husband had been Milo's future deputy, Dwight Gould. The union lasted only a year before Blackwell swept her off her feet. But after suffering his physical abuse, Kay left Jack and fled Alpine. Thirty years and two more husbands later, she'd finally returned to her hometown.

"Then who is this other victim?" I asked.

Kay grimaced. "That's the problem. I don't know. Both Jennifer and I got anonymous postcards yesterday from Koblenz, Germany, with the same message — 'You will be avenged on Jack Blackwell.' "

I think my jaw dropped. "Weird." It was the only thing I could say.

"Very." Kay looked faintly amused. "I came to see you because of the longtime animosity between Milo and Jack, not to mention your own run-ins with him. Did you get postcards, too?"

"No. Not here or at Milo's house. You have no idea who sent the postcards?"

Kay shook her head. "I also came here because not long ago, rumor also had it that you threatened to expose Jack as a world-class abuser of women. You were right, of course. Not only did he put me in the ER after a confrontation at RestHaven a while ago, but he's been knocking Patti Marsh around for over twenty years. She's a fool to take it, but I assume she actually loves the beast. But Jennifer and I are willing to come forward." Kay paused to sip more coffee.

"I suppose," I said, "you're wondering why I haven't followed through on Jack's abusive ways."

Kay hesitated. "Well . . . a little. I heard you threatened Jack in front of at least one witness, but I thought you might be gathering evidence. It's possible that Patti and I aren't the only women he's knocked around lately. Jennifer swears he's never hurt her since she moved here."

I nodded in a vague sort of way. "Back in July, I intended to do a series on abuse and include Jack as a local example. He could sue, but there's documentation. I've already done background research, both regional and national. But I put the series on hold because summer isn't the right time for a newspaper crusade. So many people are on vacation and the focus is on relaxation, not problem-solving. I plan to start the series in October and end it before the holiday season." In my mind's eye, I envisioned a Norman Rockwell–esque Thanksgiving dinner setting with the family wearing bandages and casts.

Kay's expression was bemused. "I've always felt that summer unofficially ends with Labor Day."

"You're forcing my hand," I said.

She leaned closer in the chair. "I can help with research. We get all kinds of statistics at RestHaven because they pertain to the mentally and emotionally disturbed. The vote for government change is only two days away. I know Fuzzy hatched his plan months

104

ago and it's a good one, but it'll backfire if Jack has his way. I'm surprised he hasn't gone public about wanting the county manager's job."

"He has," I informed her. "Jack dropped off his announcement Friday. I didn't put it online. His self-proclaimed qualifications aren't news, but self-promotion."

Kay looked at me with apparent pity. "You might as well post it. Jack's had several hundred copies printed to hand out at the picnic."

"I should've guessed," I declared bitterly. "And the bastard didn't even give us the printing job."

"It could be worse," Kay said grimly. "He's giving everybody else the shaft."

Milo arrived home shortly after one o'clock. "The body's gone to Everett. Doc Dewey still doesn't have the equipment for a full autopsy. With the long weekend, we may not get the results until midweek."

"Maybe," I suggested, "if the voters favor change, SkyCo can stop relying on SnoCo for help."

"Maybe Blackwell will turn into a baboon," Milo muttered, taking a Budweiser out of the fridge. "He's already a horse's ass. The vic's real hair is dark, by the way.

What did you put on your website?"

"Just her alleged name, age, and where she worked. We don't know the California driver's license is real, right?"

My husband scowled. "You didn't say where she was found?"

"Only that it was a house in the Icicle Creek Development. I omitted that she was staying at the Lumberjack. The Harrises don't need curiosity seekers bothering them."

Milo snorted. "Motel owners have to have a thick hide. Occupational hazard. I'm going outside to commune with the bugs." He loped to the back door.

"Hey! Why aren't you changing?" I called after him. "Are you still on duty?"

He turned back toward me. "Yeah. With Blackwell trying to run me out of town, I can't look as if I'm sloughing off on the job. Hell, I may sleep in my uniform." He kept going and banged the screen door behind him.

I started to follow Milo outside, but after six months of marriage and sixteen years of semi-togetherness, I knew when to give him time to unwind. Taking the SkyCo directory out of the end-table drawer, I dialed the Lumberjack's number. Mel Harris answered on the third ring. He sounded relieved when

I identified myself.

"That big-mouthed Fred Iverson should never have shot his face off about the poor kid who got killed staying here," Mel complained. "All sorts of ghouls have come by to gape at her unit. Phone calls, too. It's enough to almost make me wish I were back doing the divestiture dance with U S West."

I laughed. "I thought you were glad they offered you early retirement. Nobody forced you to buy the Tall Timber and Lumberjack Motels. But I'm glad you did. They needed new ownership."

"Heck," Mel said, "having escaped the rat race in Seattle, we wanted to slow down, but not atrophy. Sam Heppner came by half an hour ago to finish doing whatever Dodge wanted done in the girl's unit and our office. That leaves us with a vacancy tonight." He uttered what sounded like a grunt. "I sound crass. But man, Sarah was too young . . . what a waste! Anything new on who did it?"

"Not so far," I responded. "When did she check into the motel?"

"A week ago Friday. Claimed she'd driven straight through from Redding. Maybe she had. The young have endurance. Hold on — got another call coming in."

I sat staring out the front window, where

a Forest Service van was passing by, followed by a couple of boys on unicycles. A pair of cedar waxwings hopped among the dogwood tree's branches, apparently looking for lunch. Over two minutes passed before Mel spoke again.

"I just filled Sarah's room," he said. "Where were we?"

"Youthful endurance," I informed him. "How did Sarah get a job here so fast?"

"One of the VI's waitresses quit a couple of weeks ago to head for WSU," Mel replied. "They're on the semester system, you know. The Iversons were on vacation and didn't get back until last Sunday. They put up a Help Wanted sign and Sarah saw it. It was a lucky break for her. About the job, I mean," he added hastily.

"Right," I murmured, thinking it had been lucky for Fred Iverson, too, since the cheapskate hadn't bothered to take out a Help Wanted ad in the *Advocate*. "How long did she plan to stay at the motel?"

"She never told me. What Minnie and I couldn't figure out was why she came to Alpine in the first place. She didn't seem to know anybody around here. No visitors, either, though except for yesterday, she worked the late shift. What I'm saying is, we're not on the main route from California.

Sarah had to go out of her way to get to Alpine."

"What kind of a car did she have?"

"A Mitsubishi Eclipse, eight, ten years old, kind of beat-up." Mel chuckled wryly. "She never drove it after she got here. I guess she walked to the VI. Your better half impounded the car. Ask him about it."

"I'll do that," I said, seeing Milo enter the living room. "Thanks, Mel. If you think of anything else, let me know."

He assured me he would. I put the phone down and looked up at my husband, who was looming over me. "I thought you would've nodded off outside," I said. "Did the bugs chase you in here?"

"No," he replied. "I have to go back to work. Gould called to say they ran Sarah's car through the system and it belongs to some woman who lives in Seattle. She's not answering her phone, but we'll keep trying." Milo frowned. "It sounds as if you're on the case, little Emma. Keep your distance, okay?"

I bristled. "Dammit, I have to cover the story. Mitch is out of town and won't be back until Monday."

"So?" Milo said. "What's the rush? The paper doesn't come out until next week. Wednesday, right?"

I felt a kink in my neck from looking up at Milo. Awkwardly getting to my feet, I whacked my elbow on the end table. It hurt, making me fractious. "Stop acting as if you don't know when the paper's published, you big jackass! That drives me nuts!"

Milo shrugged, his expression bland. "I'm pretty sure you publish on Wednesday. By the way, you're standing on my feet." He lifted me up and set me down on the carpet. "Can you stay put until I get back?"

"Yes!" I glared at my aggravating mate as I rubbed my sore elbow. "But why should I? Do you think there's a crazed random killer loose?"

He started to say something, thought better of it, and shrugged. "Probably not. This murder appears to have been planned."

"What do you mean?"

"Sarah's killer may've been waiting for her to come off work when her regular shift ended. But," he went on, his big hand brushing my overlong bangs out of my eyes, "one of Vida's thirty or forty nieces, Nicole Gustavson, begged off after a rough root canal session with Dr. Starr. Sarah worked a short shift Thursday, so Fred asked her to fill in for Nicole. Are you still pissed off?"

I was momentarily puzzled. "About . . . ? Oh. No. You know I can't stay mad at you.

110

Will you be home at the usual time for dinner?"

Milo hooked one arm around my neck and drew me close to kiss the top of my head. "Yeah, maybe sooner. There's not a lot more we can do before we get the autopsy report or find some witnesses. Hey, let's eat out. It's getting warmer. I don't want my wife to wilt."

"Bad idea," I said, looking up at Milo. The usual thirteen-inch height difference seemed greater because I was shoeless and he had on his regulation boots. "You'd be accosted by other diners asking about the murder. Don't worry, I'll have Kip put online only that you're waiting for the full autopsy report."

"Good." Milo kissed my nose before letting go of me. "With any luck, I won't be gone long." He grabbed his regulation hat and left.

I decided to work in the backyard, where there was sufficient shade from the evergreens. But after an hour, I started to sweat. Then I remembered that the University of Washington was playing Air Force and the game was on TV. Having spent my first three years of college at the UW, I set guilt aside and went indoors to root for the Huskies. The phone rang just as Air Force kicked a field goal to take the lead.

"R. L. Burnside died day before yester-day," my brother announced in words that would have suited the death of a world leader. "His great heart finally gave out."

"The Mississippi blues man!" I blurted out. "I remember when you and I went to hear him at . . . Centreville?"

"Not quite in the town," Ben said, his voice taking on its usual crackling tone. "The juke joint was out on the highway. Burnside wasn't Catholic, but I'm saying a couple of Masses for him anyway. God's got to love the blues. By the way, I think I can make it to Alpine for your birthday in November. Is Adam still on board for that?"

"As far as I know," I said. "He's at the mercy of Alaska's weather. It may not be officially winter in St. Mary's Igloo, but he could still get snowed or iced in if the float-plane can't land."

"Right," Ben agreed. "Are you sure you don't want a Mass when you and Dodge get your marriage blessed?"

"I know Milo would rather not," I admitted. "But he'd do it for me if I insisted. You know he's a believer, but not a churchgoer. Besides, having lived most of his adult life in the public eye and being a very private person, he loathes calling attention to himself."

"He could wear a disguise," Ben said solemnly. "How about fixing him up as a Douglas fir?"

"That sounds about right," I muttered, hearing sirens heading for Highway 2 and wondering if a major vehicular accident would make Milo late coming home. "May I point out that for a priest, you sometimes lack spiritual sensitivity?"

"How much spiritual sensitivity do you need when you'll have three priests blessing the marriage? Or are you giving Dennis Kelly a pass?"

"That depends on Father Den," I said. "I like my pastor. He's a lot nicer to me than you are, you jerk."

"He didn't grow up with you as a weird, whining sister," Ben retorted. "Give him thirty more years and see how he acts. Hey, got to go shoot a gator for dinner. Prayers and peace, little brat."

I set the phone down, but I was still smiling when it rang again. Wondering if the gator had gone after Ben before he went after it, I grabbed the receiver and shouted hello.

"Emma?" Alison said in a startled voice.

"Oh!" I laughed. "Sorry, I thought you

were my brother. We just rang off. Have you cracked the case?"

"No," she replied, sounding disgusted. "I went door-to-door in the Icicle Creek Development. There was nobody home at four of the houses and Mrs. Melville told me three of the families had left town for the long weekend. She and Mr. Melville and their kids weren't around at the time of the murder. They'd gone to Deception Falls for a picnic supper. The four other families live far enough back that they hadn't seen or heard anything. In fact, the Lundquists didn't know there'd been a murder. I ended up wasting ten minutes explaining what happened. I feel like a major flop as a detective."

"Hey, it's what we veteran amateur sleuths call early days in solving murders," I asserted. "Do you want to stop by or are you worn out from pounding the pavement?"

Alison sighed heavily. "I'm home now and Lori's going out to dinner at Le Gourmand with Cole. She wants me to do her makeover. I'm stuck."

"Good for her. Cole must make good money at Microsoft. Le Gourmand is pricey."

"Maybe he can write her off as a business expense," Alison grumbled. "Justin and I

114

had dinner there once. It really was amazing. Too bad he wasn't."

"Don't dwell on him," I advised. "There really are other men, even in Alpine."

"Oh?" She sounded dubious. "How many locals did you date before you got married?"

"The only man I dated here was Milo. We went together for a long time before we got married."

"For fifteen years?" Alison sounded incredulous.

I didn't blame her. "Well . . . not exactly all in a row. Skip the history. You don't have a kid to raise. You are, as you once told me, 'a fancy-free single girl.' That's not a bad thing, so stop beating yourself up. And never mind that you came up empty interviewing potential murder witnesses. Did you take notes?"

"Yes," she said in a leaden voice. "I mean, just their names and that they didn't see anything weird. I thought maybe after I do Lori's makeup, I'd go to the VI and have dinner. By then the rush should be over, so the staff may have time to talk to me."

"Good idea. Hey," I said, trying to boost Alison's spirits, "it's been less than twenty-four hours since the murder. Investigations take time."

"I guess," she murmured, still dejected.

"Has the sheriff made any progress?"

"Not yet. It's too soon. Even if he gets a lead, he might not tell me. To quote him at his most aggravating, 'I can't reveal anything at this stage of an ongoing investigation.' "

"That's mean," Alison declared. "You're his wife."

"I'm also the press," I said, hearing more sirens. "I can deal with it. Go make Lori look gorgeous and then get back on the case. But be careful. Please."

"Okay. Hey — here comes the ambulance, turning off Alpine Way. I think it's going to the hospital. Should I see what that's all about?"

"Hold off," I suggested. "I heard sirens heading for the highway a little while ago. It's probably the usual Stevens Pass pileup with drivers who don't know how to navigate Highway 2."

"I could take a picture of the wreckage," Alison offered, sounding less gloomy. "Wouldn't Mitch do that if he were here?"

"He would. Well . . . go for it. But don't take chances."

I rang off, wishing Alison wasn't so eager. I sensed something reckless in her attitude. Breakups can play havoc with even a sensible person's emotions. I recalled Vida's old saying about sending a boy to the mill.

116

Maybe I'd sent a girl into danger.

Milo returned just before five. He kissed the top of my head and kept going. I got off the sofa to follow him. "Was Alison taking pictures?"

"Of what? Me sitting on my ass talking to one of SnoCo's senior deputies? Get real."

Justifiably confused, I yanked at the short sleeve of his summer-weight regulation shirt. "The accident out on Highway 2. What else?"

"Oh — that." He removed my hand. "Don't paw me, woman. I'm beat. The wreck was no big deal, just a rear-ender with out-of-towners when the first car slowed to make the turn into town and the other driver didn't hit the brakes."

I was puzzled. "So a minor collision exhausted you? That's not your style, big guy."

Milo let out a heavy sigh. "That's not the problem. The waitress isn't Sarah Williams. In fact, she might not be the murderer's first victim. We may have a serial killer on the loose."

CHAPTER 6

"So who got killed here?" I asked in a puzzled voice. Maybe my brain was going south.

Milo tossed his boots into the open closet. "The vic's brother came in this afternoon. She's Gemma Anne Jennings from Coeur d'Alene, Idaho."

I leaned against the bureau. "I don't get it. Why the wig and the phony name?"

"Apparently Gemma — weird name, isn't it? — liked to do that kind of thing," Milo replied, standing up. "It's damned odd. The brother's handing out Blackwell's broadsides. He calls himself L.J."

I told my husband about seeing L.J. and the dark-haired girl at the ski lodge. "None of this makes sense. Why did they come here? Why was the brother helping Blackwell?"

"He insists he volunteered to pass the time," Milo replied. "Gemma was a writer, researching small towns for a travel book. L.J. came with her."

I had more questions for Milo, but he held up a big hand. "Let me unwind, okay?"

"Jackass," I muttered. "I'm going to post the victim's name on our website. Then I'll make drinks and go sit outside."

Ten minutes later, Milo joined me on the patio. He took a quick gulp of Scotch before he sat down and lighted a cigarette. "You want one?" he asked, proffering the pack of Marlboro Lights.

I shook my head. "I *am* trying to quit, even if it's for the tenth time. You're good about not smoking in the house. Now unload before I hide the rest of your cigarettes."

He tugged at his right ear and sighed. "I knew Snohomish County had another young woman vic over in Maltby last month. She was found in a vacant house off the Paradise Lake Road. Chelsea Warren, nineteen, no permanent address since she ran away from home three years ago." He paused to sip his drink.

I asked if she'd had ID.

"Not on her," he replied, "but she'd been reported missing by her grandmother. Chelsea had been staying with her recently.

I'm guessing the girl had a rocky upbringing."

"Sad," I murmured.

"But," my husband continued, "I hadn't heard about the one a fisherman discovered yesterday evening in a vacant cabin by the Snohomish River. Her name was Erin Buchholtz, twenty. She'd been dead for at least a week, strangled in the same way as Chelsea, according to the SnoCo ME." He paused to sip from his drink.

"Had Erin been reported missing?"

"Yeah, by her boyfriend. Erin worked at a Snohomish antiques store. She planned to enroll fall quarter at the UW's Bothell campus."

Despite the late afternoon heat, I shivered. I asked the only question that came to mind: "Have you checked Gemma's motel room?"

Milo put out his cigarette. "Doe Jamison did that this afternoon. Bare bones, but you'd expect that since she was actually staying at the ski lodge. I talked to Minnie Harris at the Lumberjack and she admitted they hadn't seen the girl since she checked in over the weekend."

I nodded faintly. "Have you searched Gemma's room at the ski lodge?"

Milo rolled his eyes. "Yeah, Dustin Fong's

120

up there now. The Jennings duo wanted the Valhalla Suite. I sent Fong because he's the most tactful of my deputies. You know how touchy Henry Bardeen is when it comes to his managerial reputation."

"Should I go public about the previous murders?" The question was for me as well as for Milo.

He shook his head, the hazel eyes fixed on my face. "I'm speculating. That's the price I pay for my wife running a newspaper. Maybe I should keep my mouth shut. But damn, I've gotten used to talking about the job. I couldn't do that with the first Mrs. Dodge."

I touched Milo's face. The fine lines weren't only from his hard-earned experience in the trenches of law enforcement. After Tricia left him and took their three children with her, he'd lived alone for almost twenty years. I'd spent fifteen of those years skittering around on the periphery, not willing to sacrifice the independence I'd fought for after Adam's father had forsaken me. But Milo was a patient man.

"Why are you smiling?" he asked, putting his big hand over my smaller one.

I smiled at him. "You. Us."

He smiled back.

■ ■ ■ ■

Tanya had returned to Milo's house, where Bill would later join her. My husband was unclear how his deputy had dealt with his ornery mother and he didn't want to know. I guessed Bill had told Lila Blatt that between the homicide and the Labor Day weekend, he was pulling extra duty. Now that he was in his midthirties, it was time he asserted himself.

It was too late to start the barbecue and not hot enough in the kitchen to make me pass out from turning on the stove. I thawed a couple of lamb steaks before putting them under the broiler, made a green salad, and put egg noodles on to boil. Milo would want to know what happened to the potatoes, but I'd ignore him. I was slowly trying to wean him away from the dietary rut we'd gotten into over the years. At least now that we were living under the same roof he'd stopped eating frozen dinners out of boxes.

To our relief, the evening passed quietly. The only phone call was from Alison, who hadn't gone to the VI after all. Cole Petersen had come down with a late summer cold, so the date with Lori was off. Apparently she needed her roommate to console her.

That was just as well. I didn't let on about the possibility of a serial killer in our midst, but if Alison was staying home, I didn't have to fret about her becoming the next victim.

Sunday brought more sun. I went to Mass, leaving Milo drinking coffee and reading the *Seattle Times.* St. Mildred's was crowded, as it had been off and on during the summer. I'd admit to drifting occasionally during Father Kelly's homilies. Before becoming our pastor, he'd taught in a California seminary. Thus his take on the gospel was more scholarly than devout. But that was my sole criticism of our pastor. However, I sensed there was a small minority who wished Den could change his skin color from black to white. *I* wished they could shake their prejudices. But after his thirteen years in Alpine, that wasn't going to happen.

What did happen after Mass was my former ad manager, Ed Bronsky, barring the way to my Honda. "Emma," he said in an unusually solemn voice, "is Fuzzy Baugh dying?"

"I doubt it," I said, seeing Ed's wife, Shirley, and their five offspring getting into the secondhand Kia SUV they'd recently bought. "I only heard he wasn't feeling very good."

Ed nodded somberly, his third chin almost touching his chest. "If the mayor's out of commission, he won't be able to give his annual speech at the Labor Day picnic. Fuzz and I got real tight over the years after my aunt in Iowa left me that big inheritance. He always kidded me about being his secret weapon with voters because of my advertising experience. He knew I could swing the undecided ones around to his side." He paused as someone in the Kia honked the horn — or maybe sat on it.

I nodded, knowing the mayor usually ran unopposed because nobody else wanted the figurehead position. "And . . . ?" I said.

"So I figured I should take his place as a featured speaker," he went on, still serious. "It's a God-given opportunity to present my new plan for Alpine and Skykomish County."

I felt like saying that God had an odd sense of humor. In fact, I was having trouble keeping a straight face. "Plan?" It was the only word I could get out of my mouth.

Ed nodded again, this time with more vigor. "You got it. See, now that we're settled in our new place on the river, I've had time to think. Reflect, you might say." Furtively, he glanced around as the rest of the vehicles began leaving the parking lot.

124

"You notice how many of the people at Mass were visitors?"

"That's been true off and on all summer," I said.

Beaming, Ed wagged a chunky finger. "Exactly! Now think about those deserted shacks in the east end of town by the garbage dump."

"Weren't they old outhouses for the railroad workers?"

"They were more than that," Ed declared, ignoring another blast on the Kia's horn. "Why not use that old stuff to bring more tourists, visitors, and vacationers to town? Turn them into miniature versions of the original mill, the social hall, and town founder Carl Clemans's house, and you've got a gold mine!"

Over the years I've heard many weird, outrageous, and just plain stupid ideas from Ed. Before and especially after he frittered away his inheritance on expensive cars, lavish vacations, and the villa that was now RestHaven, he couldn't stop the craziness.

"See?" Ed continued. "This is the ticket to move out of the economic blip this country's going through. If I take Baugh's spot on the podium, my plan's perfect for the Labor Day theme." He took a deep breath, slamming his fist into the palm of

125

his other hand. "I call my speech 'Let's Put the Sky Back to Work!' What do you say about that, Emma?"

I felt like saying it sure beat putting Ed back to work. Instead, I forced a smile. "Why not? Go for it."

And I went — to my Honda, with another loud toot of the Kia's horn ringing in my ears.

"Well?" Milo said in greeting when I came into the living room. "You look pissed. Did Kelly tell all of you you're going to hell?"

"Priests don't do that," I replied, sinking onto the sofa. "It cuts down on the collection. If I look grim, blame the usual suspect."

My husband looked askance. "Bronsky? What now?"

I related Ed's latest madcap idea. "When he worked for me on the *Advocate,* his ad copy was one cliché after another. Tomatoes were 'right off the vine,' apples were 'hand-picked for you,' steak was 'so tender you could cut it with a knife.' Of course he meant a fork, so I had to change it. But I honestly can't say Ed doesn't have imagination, because he does. It's just that he finds such dumb, self-serving ways to use it."

"Hey," Milo said, stretching his long legs out on the ottoman, "even if Baugh can't

126

give his own boring speech, we don't have to listen to Ed. Didn't you say Laskey's coming back in time to cover the picnic?"

"That's what he told me. But," I added, "if Blackwell's going to hand out his self-promoting propaganda, he'll probably speak, too."

"Maybe Kay will show up with a bunch of hecklers," Milo suggested with a hopeful expression. "After what you told me last night about her going on the warpath, that wouldn't surprise me. It could be fun."

"Speeches are never fun," I said. "At the *Oregonian,* I got stuck with the dullest speakers south of the Columbia River. They were part of my so-called Lifestyle beat."

Milo's cell rang. After his usual "Dodge here" I saw him roll his eyes. "Hey, don't kill yourselves getting here for the picnic, Clint. You're covering two thousand miles. Besides, I have to work the event."

If the sheriff really had to be on duty doing the Labor Day bash, he hadn't informed me. I decided to change out of my church-going clothes. When I emerged from the bedroom in beat-up slacks and a red tank top, my husband was saying goodbye to his brother.

"Where are they?" I asked.

"Somewhere near Ogden in Utah. They

think they can get here by late afternoon tomorrow. That damned motor home they've got must have wings." He held his head.

I perched on the easy chair's arm. "Does Pootsie help drive?"

Milo nodded. "She's kind of a squirt, but a gamer. She was a cheerleader at Wazzu."

"Have they always driven up here?"

Milo caressed my lower back. "No, they flew the other times. Clint's close to sixty and thinking of retirement in a couple of years. I suppose they plan to see the country in their motor home. But how much can you see when you're driving five hundred miles a day?"

"True. Do you really have to work the picnic?"

Milo shook his head. "I gave that job to Gould. But I should show up, if only to let the local working stiffs know I support them. Hell, I probably put in more hours a week than most of them do."

The phone rang on the end table. I hopped off the easy chair's arm to pick up the receiver. "I'm on the case," Alison said. "Do you know Todd and Wendy Wilson in the Icicle Creek Development?"

"Yes, Todd manages the Public Utility District," I replied. "Why do you ask?"

"They were the couple who were gone yesterday, but stayed in town and got back late," Alison explained. "Their daughter, Julie, was home, but she had on headphones, so she didn't hear me knock. In fact, none of the Wilsons knew what had happened until this morning when Mr. Melville told them. That was when Julie remembered seeing the girl."

"What girl?" I asked, aware that Milo had paused to glance my way before heading to the kitchen for a coffee refill.

"Julie had to let out their dog, Jabba," Alison responded. "Jabba's old, so it takes him a while. Julie's thirteen and she was listening to music, sort of getting down with it. But she saw a woman she didn't recognize who was wearing what looked like a waitress uniform walking into the development. Julie wondered who she was because strangers don't usually show up without a reason."

"Did she see where the girl went?" I asked.

"No. Jabba was ready to come back in the house by then — unfortunately," Alison added. "I'm not sure she could see Dodge's split-level from her front yard. The Wilsons are behind Mrs. Eriks's house."

"Julie didn't see anybody else?"

"I asked her, but she said otherwise everything was quiet there. I suppose it would be, with a lot of them gone for the weekend."

"Okay. Good work. I'll let Milo know. Say," I continued, "take it easy for the rest of the weekend. There's not much that can be done until the autopsy report is released."

"I can still talk to the Venison Inn staff," Alison said. "I'd rather not stick around the apartment. Lori's caught Cole's bug and I don't want to get sick. My resistance could be low because . . . well, because emotional stress can trash your system."

"You're tougher than that," I declared as Milo returned from the kitchen. "Take it easy, okay?" I didn't want to repeat my warning to be careful. My husband might ask why, and I was reluctant to confess that Alison was playing sleuth at my urging.

"Who was that?" he asked after I hung up.

"Alison," I said. "She's trying to avoid Lori because she's sick."

Milo frowned. "I hope Lori recovers by Tuesday. She runs the front part of our operation better than anybody else ever has."

"It's only a cold." I paused, wondering how to explain why my own office manager had talked to Julie Wilson. I didn't look directly at Milo. "Alison happened to run into Todd and Wendy Wilson's daughter today."

"Oh?" My husband sounded skeptical.

I summarized what I'd been told, hoping it sounded like a casual encounter. Apparently it didn't.

"Dammit," Milo bellowed, "did you put Alison up to that or is she just another pain-in-the-ass would-be detective like you and Vida?"

"Research is part of a journalist's job," I shot back. "May I point out that sometimes we've figured it out before you and your deputies did?"

"Luck," Milo said. "Skip the background. What's up with Alison?"

"She broke up with her boyfriend," I replied. "I thought doing a little background digging on the news side might distract her."

"So now she's a reporter *and* a receptionist?" Milo shot back.

"I also made her the office manager," I confessed in a meek voice.

"Good God," Milo muttered. "Hell, maybe she should be the county manager. That might really make her forget the boyfriend. Who was he?"

"A math instructor at SCC, Justin . . . something. I forget. I wish she'd forget *him*."

131

Milo heaved a beleaguered sigh. "Make sure she forgets about playing Nancy Drew, okay? After her mother got herself murdered, I'd figure Alison would avoid being involved in anything sketchy. There seems to be a bounty around here on girls her age."

The sheriff didn't have to remind me.

After lunch, I asked Milo if he wanted to get out of town for a few hours. He didn't. Too much traffic, too many people who didn't know how to drive Highway 2, too far to go to see the sights he'd seen too often while patrolling the area. He also felt compelled to check in at his office in case there was any new information pertaining to Gemma's murder.

"But," he said, hooking his arm around my neck, "we'll eat tonight at the Cascadia in Skykomish. It's a short drive and I won't have the locals ruining my digestion with a bunch of dumb questions."

That was fine with me.

Half an hour later I looked up from weeding the garden out front to see Vida's Buick pulling into the driveway. "Well now!" she exclaimed, erupting onto the lawn with one hand holding her beribboned straw hat in place. "Why haven't you kept me informed about poor Gemma? The more I think about it, the more I believe she was afraid of publicity. Wouldn't you agree?"

"Honestly, I don't know what to think," I admitted.

"I should never leave town," Vida declared, "but Buck wanted to spend yesterday with the Klinkenburgs, his old friends who live between Startup and Gold Bar. We didn't get back until quite late. Excellent fried chicken and quite a good molded salad. I must ask Leona Klinkenburg for the recipe to put on my page."

That was a good place for it, I thought. Much safer than Vida trying to actually make it. There should be a county ordinance preventing my House & Home editor from getting within ten feet of a cooking implement. "Sounds . . . pleasant," I remarked.

"It was," she agreed, "but to learn this morning that Sarah — that is, Gemma — was murdered . . . Why didn't my nephew Billy tell me as soon as he found out? He discovered the body, for heaven's sake!"

"He had his hands full at the scene," I pointed out. "And Tanya was unnerved by —"

"Oh, these young women!" Vida cried. "Where's their gumption?"

"Tanya recovered fairly fast, but she was alone when —"

"Yes, yes," Vida interrupted again. "That's

not the point. Billy is well aware that I hate not knowing what goes on in Alpine."

That was always the point with Vida. Heaven help us if even a smidgen of news slipped under her radar. Still, I couldn't resist a gibe. "If you hadn't taken off for the day, you'd have found out sooner."

"Had I known before I left, I wouldn't have gone out of town," she retorted. "I suppose Billy spent the night with Tanya. Lila must be wild."

"Lila can stick it," I shot back. "If a homicide victim was found in your house, Bill — or one of the other deputies — might have stayed overnight with you. Killers sometimes strike more than once." I stopped short of telling Vida about Milo's serial killer theory. I might be the next murder victim if I mentioned that out loud.

But it takes more than logic to defuse my House & Home editor when she's on the warpath. "I should talk to Minnie Harris. She's quite good at learning things from their motel guests. Discreetly, of course."

"Of course," I echoed, thinking it was generous of Vida to compliment another person's talent for prying into private lives. "Do you want to come in for a cup of tea?"

"No, but thank you." She resettled the straw hat that a sudden breeze had threatened to blow askew. "We met after church to discuss the telephone tree. Some members aren't diligent about passing news down the line. It simply won't do to have a breakdown in communications. If that happens, there's no point in having the tree."

"I assume you're still at the top of the tree?"

"Well, certainly. I *am* the only journalist in the congregation." Vida paused, her eyes studying my front yard. "Is Milo hiring Mountain View Gardens to do your landscaping?"

"No. That was contingent on work in his own yard, but with Tanya living there, he's taken the house off the market."

Vida was surprised. "Does she plan to live there permanently?"

"She has to live somewhere," I said.

"True," Vida allowed. "Perhaps Tanya expects Billy to move in with her. Lila would have six cat-fits if that happened."

"They're both in their thirties," I reminded her. "By the way, did you know that Blackwell's conducting a poll on the government issue?"

"What kind of poll? Door-to-door or by phone?"

"The former. Alison spoke to a young man who said he was a pollster. He called himself

Ronnie Davis, but I've never heard of him."

Vida tapped an index finger against her cheek. "It's a common name, though I can't remember any Davises ever living here."

I had to take Vida at her word. I'm convinced she has every resident registered in her head. "Maybe he's a recent hire," I suggested.

"Perhaps. You recall that two of Jack's workers retired in January. He should have let us know, but you and Blackwell aren't on good terms." A hint of reproach was in her tone.

"How," I demanded, "can I be on good terms with that jerk when he not only threatens me but declared war on Milo thirty years ago?"

"Yes, yes," Vida said airily, "I understand all that, but I hate to lose a news source. It's a pity none of my relatives work for Blackwell."

It was more than a pity, it was a marvel, given the many branches on her family tree. "Call their office Tuesday. You'll want to mention Ronnie Davis as a newcomer."

"I'll ask at the picnic. I'm on the dessert list. I considered baking a cake, but it's too warm to turn on the oven. I'll bring cookies instead."

"Good idea," I said, wondering if she'd

baked a cake in the last decade. I hoped not. Noticing that Vida's eyes had darted beyond me in the direction of my troublesome neighbors, Doyle and Laverne Nelson, I asked what had piqued her interest.

"I heard a child over there," she said, lowering her voice. "The Nelson granddaughter, Chloe, correct? She must be going on two."

"That sounds right. As you know, I avoid them at all costs."

"Yes." She tapped a finger against her cheek. "You had an incident with them last spring, as I recall."

"It was one of their unsavory hangers-on," I said. "Doyle's doing time along with his older son for poaching maple trees, and the two younger boys are in juvenile detention."

"You never elaborated on that unpleasantness." Vida's gray eyes were reproachful.

I shrugged. "I called 911, Evan Singer sent help. End of story."

"The hanger-on may still be around," Vida said in an ominous tone. "Do be careful, Emma." Still holding on to her hat, she stalked off to the Buick.

Half an hour later when I'd begun to wilt again, I gathered up my garden tools and trudged back toward the house. Before I reached the front door, I heard a horn honk.

Turning to look over my shoulder, I saw a silver Lexus creeping along Fir Street. The horn honked again. The tinted windows prevented me from seeing who was inside, but I knew only one person in town who owned a new silver Lexus — Jack Blackwell. The car slowed almost to a stop just short of the Marsdens' property next door. I tried to keep walking at an unhurried pace, resisting the temptation to look back at the street.

After what seemed like forever instead of mere seconds, I went inside and locked the door behind me. I felt foolish, but barricaded myself by securing the rest of the doors and closing the bedroom window. To pass the time, I wrote a letter to my old friend and former *Oregonian* co-worker, Mavis Marley Fulkerston. She'd hoped to visit Alpine during the summer, but her husband, Ray, was still recovering from quadruple bypass surgery and, according to Mavis, extreme grumpiness.

I signed off, feeling sleepy. It was overly warm in the closed-up house, but I was too lazy to get off the sofa. A sudden noise startled me. My eyes flew open as I tried to focus.

"Are you nuts?" Milo demanded, coming from the kitchen and opening the front door. "It must be ninety degrees in here. If you want a steam bath, go to the gym."

"I'm an idiot," I mumbled, falling back on the sofa. "Anything new with the case?"

"*You're* a case." He loomed over me. "Are you sick?"

"No. I worked in the yard for a while. I got quite a bit done out front. Vida came by. Then I wrote a letter to Mavis. I nodded off after that. Tell me what you did. Is it really that hot outside? Aren't you going to make a drink?"

Milo sighed and sank down beside me. "Okay. What happened?"

I didn't want to mention Blackwell for fear that Milo would explode. "I got too warm outside."

"So you came in here and closed up the house? Dammit, Emma, you know you can't lie to me. You never could, even back when I didn't let on. In fact," he went on, capturing my chin between his thumb and forefinger, "you're the worst liar I ever met. Now give or I won't tell you what went down at headquarters."

"Let go of my chin," I said through clenched teeth.

My husband complied. "Well?"

I heaved a sigh before unloading. "Blackwell — I think it was him — drove by slowly and honked his horn." I winced. Even to me, it sounded stupid.

"Shit." Milo leaned back against the sofa. "You sure it was Jack? You can't tell one car from another."

"I know a Lexus when I see one. I owned one for a short time."

"So you did." Milo's hazel eyes sparked. "Cavanaugh's gift. Why did you get rid of it?"

"You know damned well why. I couldn't bear to keep it after Tom died. It was too flashy for me."

"Bull." He put his arm around me and kissed the top of my head. "You drove a Jag when you moved here. I'll open up the house and then you can ask your usual wacky questions. But let's do it outside, okay?"

Ten minutes later, we were on the patio, drinks in hand. "Well?" I said, giving Milo an expectant look.

"Not much to tell," he replied, batting at a mosquito. "I spent most of my time getting details from SnoCo about the other two murders."

"I still want to know why Gemma was wearing a wig," I said.

"Her brother told us it was a whim, like playing waitress and getting experience in

140

small-town life. My SnoCo contacts can't connect the dots between their two vics, either. That's why a serial killer is a possibility. But don't go public with that, okay?"

I told him I wouldn't. We sat quietly for a few minutes, hearing an occasional car passing by, a couple of crows cawing in a nearby Douglas fir, and a dog barking in the distance. I stared at a squirrel on our new cedar shingles. The squirrel stared back with big black eyes. He looked saucy, clever, even shrewd. Maybe he knew who killed Gemma.

I certainly didn't.

CHAPTER 7

The Cascadia's staff knew Milo from way back when he'd been a young deputy patrolling Highway 2. They also knew to not pester him with questions. We both ordered the fried chicken. It was a pleasant interlude, ending with brandy in oversized snifters. My husband suggested we work off our dinner with a leisurely walk along the river. We'd been married for almost six months before I found out that every morning after he left the house at seven-thirty, he usually spent the next half-hour at the gym before it opened to the public. He'd assumed I knew that. I'd pointed out that although we'd met sixteen years ago, there were obviously some things he'd kept to himself. Then, just to get even, he asked if I dyed my hair. I told him I had never done that and never would. Not turning gray was hereditary, since he must've noticed that my brother still had brown hair, despite being two years older.

Around nine, Alison called to say she'd seen L.J. at the Venison Inn. He wasn't dining there, but had emerged from Fred Iverson's office at the rear of the building.

"He looked super upset," Alison told me, sounding aghast. "I'd seen your posting and I felt so sorry for him that I wanted to say something, but I couldn't. He brushed past me and kept going."

"Did he leave the VI?" I asked, seeing Milo look up from his *National Geographic.*

"By the time I came out of the rest room, I didn't see him anywhere, including the bar," Alison replied. "I asked one of the waitresses — Emily whatever — but she was clueless. He must not have eaten there because nobody remembered waiting on him."

"Did you talk to Fred?"

"No. It turned out Mr. Iverson wasn't there. Kind of strange, huh?"

"Fred can't spend all his time on the premises. Are you settled in for the night?"

"I guess." Alison sounded woebegone. "I'm keeping my distance from Lori. I don't want to get sick."

"Then get plenty of rest," I advised, and rang off.

I pretended Milo wasn't staring at me. Or

maybe he was glaring. I kept my eyes focused on the Alan Furst spy novel I'd been reading.

"Dammit," he exploded, "call off Alison. I mean it. She's a kid. Do you want her to be the next victim? And who the hell is 'he'?"

"She was stalking L.J. before the murder," I said. "She thinks he's a real stud."

"Great. Now Alison's some kind of double agent. What next? *She* gets a wig and goes around in disguise? I think I liked it better when Vida played detective. The only weird thing she wore was her crazy hats." He fingered his chin. "I wonder who this guy is. Have you run anything about newcomers in SkyCo lately?"

"If," I said archly, "you ever read the *Advocate,* you wouldn't have to ask. Since you don't, we haven't, except for Bob and Miriam Lambrecht. Of course you know about him taking over as the bank president because he's your old high school chum and fishing partner. Thus, I assume he hasn't forgotten to tell you about his new duties or anything else he's been doing since he got here, which mustn't be newsworthy."

Milo rubbed at his forehead. "That almost makes sense. If you wrote the way you talked, it's a wonder anybody reads the paper. They'd need a translator."

"I hate you."

He ignored the remark. "Okay, if Alison's so hot for this guy, let her interview him for the paper. Do you think she could handle writing a news story?"

"She might," I conceded. "She's smart and I could help her."

"Then give it a shot. Want to sit on my lap?"

"No. I'm not quite done hating you."

"Okay." Milo resumed reading his *Geographic*.

I went back to Furst's spies. The dangers of pre–World War Two Paris didn't seem as frightening as what was happening in present-day Alpine. Maybe that's because when reading fiction, I live in reality.

To my surprise, I awoke Monday to see Milo putting on his uniform. I fought off my usual morning fog to ask if he was on duty.

"Not officially," he replied, "but I want to check some things at the office. Go back to sleep."

I forced myself to focus on the clock next to the bed. It read eight-fifty. "I'll get up, too," I murmured.

"Don't," my husband said, sitting on his side of the bed to put on his boots. "You like to sleep in."

I told him I already had. But when I opened my eyes again it was almost ten and the house was empty. I was in no rush to get up, so I allowed myself the luxury of waiting until I felt reasonably alert. At ten-thirty, I was eating a bowl of Grape-Nuts when someone came to the front door. I dutifully looked through the peephole to see who was on the porch. It was Alison, who seemed to be dancing a jig on the mat.

"You're home!" she exclaimed as I let her in. "I thought you and Dodge might take off for the day."

I shook my head. "He's working. Do you want coffee?"

Alison declined. "I'm already hyper. I know where L.J. works."

"Where?" I inquired, indicating she should sit at the kitchen table.

"I stopped by the VI and he'd left a business card for Mr. Iverson. Mandy Gustavson had seen it and she told me the card read Lawrence Jonathan Jennings from Boise and he's a salesman for Micron Technology."

I asked Alison why he'd be handing out Blackwell's propaganda. She insisted Mandy was clueless.

"So," I responded, "you intend to track

him down and seduce him?"

Alison's cheeks turned slightly pink. "No. I mean, I was curious."

"Of course." I offered what I hoped was an encouraging smile before refilling my coffee mug. "Blackwell's from northern California, but early on he had mills in Oregon and Idaho. I doubt he still does since I haven't heard about them in years. I figure that back when logging was curtailed, he hedged his bets and focused on the one here."

Alison was looking thoughtful. "Does he really beat up women?"

"I'm afraid so," I said, sitting down again. I kept mum about Kay's plan of attack on her ex.

"Jack must've been fairly young," Alison said. "Where did he get the money to start his mills?"

"I don't know," I admitted. "Maybe he inherited it. Jack was still in his twenties when he arrived here." A thought popped into my head. "Marius Vandeventer — the *Advocate*'s previous owner — must've done an article about Blackwell back in the early seventies. I know that because Milo was already a deputy. They butted heads from the get-go."

"Real macho stuff," Alison commented,

blue eyes dancing. "I suppose that was a big deal back then."

I avoided saying it still was, as far as Milo and Jack were concerned. Alison volunteered to find the original story on Blackwell's arrival. I gave her my spare office key and wished her luck. I also told her to make a copy of the article for me. Milo had never revealed specifics about what had set off the two men's mutual antagonism. The first time I'd witnessed hostility between them had been fifteen years ago, during the homicide investigation of Patti Marsh's former son-in-law. When Blackwell hadn't liked how the case was being handled, he'd criticized Milo to his face. I'd been a witness to the encounter and had admired the sheriff's restraint.

Alison returned just before noon. "May sixteenth, 1973, issue. Who's Nolan Ryan?"

I thought I'd misheard. "What?"

"The big headline was about a baseball game the previous day, but it wasn't in Alpine. A guy named —"

"Never mind," I interrupted, not wanting to explain a historic baseball no-hitter. "I only met Marius Vandeventer twice. I didn't realize he was a baseball fan. I might've liked him better if I'd known that."

Alison looked bemused. "Ryan got more

148

space on the front page than Blackwell, who was down in the left-hand corner. Here's the article."

There's a new Bull of the Woods in Alpine now that Jacques (Jack) Blackwell has arrived to add his youthful enthusiasm and cerebral prowess to our thriving timber industry. The dashing twenty-six-year-old native Californian has run successful logging operations in Albany, Oregon, and Lewiston, Idaho. Skykomish County residents should welcome him with outstretched arms.

I winced at my predecessor's florid style, and gave myself a little shake before reading further. If Vida's folksy style was hard to swallow, Marius could give her a run for her verbiage. Of course I'd read some of his articles before I bought the paper, but I'd forgotten just how fulsome he'd been in print.

"There's a picture on page three," Alison said.

I skimmed the next graf about Blackwell's earlier ventures and followed the jump. The reproduction of the original page was a bit fuzzy, but Jack's studio portrait made him look like a movie star. Flattering as it was, he still came off as more villain than hero. A suave villain, of course. Then again, maybe my imagination was running away with me. The rest of the article was about Jack's plans for the two small mills he'd bought out. One had been owned by a couple of brothers whose names I didn't recognize, and the other had belonged to Clarence Munn, who was living out his final years in the Lutheran retirement home's medical wing. Marius allowed the new mill czar only one quote: "I'm very excited about my move to Alpine. It feels like a place where I can leave my mark on the local economy and its citizens." Blackwell had a way with words when he wasn't vilifying me.

After I told Alison there was nothing in there to offend Milo or anyone else in SkyCo, she looked pensive. "Maybe," she said after a pause, "they fought over a woman?"

"No," I replied. "Milo would've told me. In fact, I think he and Tricia got married that year."

"How old were they?"

I had to think, since it involved math. "His birthday's in March, so he would've been twenty-three. Tricia was a year or so younger."

Alison leaned forward in the chair. "You

see? They were my age; she was even younger. These days people either get married in their early twenties or wait forever."

"Like I did?" I asked in a droll voice.

"I told you, that was different."

"May I point out that the youthful Dodge marriage didn't last?"

Alison sighed. "That's a whole different kind of scary. Half the marriages in this country don't last."

I changed the subject. "Are you going to the picnic this afternoon?"

"I guess." Alison didn't sound enthusiastic. "Lori may feel better by then. Cole has to leave later today because he's flying to Brussels on business for Microsoft tomorrow. If he and Lori get married, do you suppose she'll move to Bellevue or wherever he's based?"

"For all I know, Cole may be based in Brussels," I said. "I didn't know they were that serious."

"They seem to be." Alison bit her lip. "Looks don't really matter, do they? I mean . . . Lori wanted a makeover, but why? She's got a man."

I was losing patience. "Would you please stop harping on the subject? You're driving me nuts."

Alison sighed. "Sorry. Really. Okay, I'll

151

see you at the picnic." She forced a feeble smile and left.

Half an hour later Milo returned, looking testy. "Tanya and Bill stopped by the office. They saw the Yukon and knew I was on the job. She unloaded about the phony Realtor. Why didn't you tell me about that?"

"I figured she had — or that she'd told Bill and he told you."

Milo shook his head. "Witnesses are a pain in the ass, but when my own daughter doesn't open up, that pisses me off." He slammed his regulation hat against the wall. Luckily, it wasn't brim-first. "I had the call traced. It was from the Bank of Alpine's courtesy phone."

I kept calm, knowing my husband needed to blow off steam. "Have you talked to anyone at the bank?"

"On Labor Day?" he shot back, starting for the hall. "I tried Rick Erlandson — no answer. Bob Lambrecht's in town, but he would've been in his office, not out front where the call was made. I'll check with the rest of them, but I don't expect much. The Friday before a long weekend is always busy." He disappeared, apparently to change clothes.

But I was wrong. When he reappeared five minutes later, he was still wearing his uniform. I asked why.

"I told you," he said, still grumpy. "I want to stay official. I changed my shirt because I worked up a sweat. I heard that Baugh's supposed to be on hand, but he won't give his usual 'work is swell' speech. How soon do you want to head for the picnic?"

I checked my watch. "It's only a little after four. Let's wait until closer to five. They don't start hauling out the serious food until then. Make us drinks while I change into something more presentable. We can sit outside while you tell me how you solved Sarah's murder."

"Funny Emma," Milo muttered, swatting my rear as I started for the hall. "I'll grab a beer. That's standard for picnics. I don't want that asshole Blackwell saying I hit the hard stuff when I'm in uniform."

"Beer has alcohol. Are you letting Jack dictate your lifestyle?"

He frowned. "You're right. Gould's on picnic duty. Screw Blackwell. Let's change our clothes together. That'll make things more interesting."

"*Too* interesting," I declared. "We might not get to the picnic in time for the speeches."

"So? You want your ears to wilt from listening to bullshit?"

"You know you have to make an appearance to show support for SkyCo," I said. "So do I. We're public figures. And the people in this county pay your salary."

Milo shrugged. "It was just a thought."

We arrived shortly after five as the high school band was playing "Tequila." Frankly, it sounded as if they'd been drinking it first. Judging from some of the adult attendees, they'd made too many trips to the big ice-filled wooden tub that held the beer. High school coach Rip Ridley and insurance agent Brendan Shaw were engaged in a heated argument that caught my husband's eye.

"Damn," he breathed, hauling me in the opposite direction. "Let's hope I don't have to break up a fight. When that happens, I miss out on the Grocery Basket's good fried chicken."

"Gould's on duty," I said. "Jack and Nina Mullins are here. He can help if there's trouble."

We wound our way to the food, greeting various Alpiners. Spotting RestHaven's security chief, Sid Almquist, and his wife, Mary Jean, I made a mental note to call them. Their recent return to Alpine after an absence of ten years was worthy of a feature story.

The bandstand and podium seemed smaller, or maybe the high school band was bigger. The surrounding Douglas firs, Western cedars, and other evergreens dwarfed the man-made structure. Despite another official year of drought, the forest seemed to have thrived. Since living in Alpine, I've learned that nature has a way of evening out the score when dealing with humans.

I didn't see Mitch Laskey, but as we reached the picnic fare, I spotted Ed Bronsky talking to Fuzzy Baugh. Sensing the subject of their conversation, I almost lost my appetite.

"Damn!" I exclaimed. "I'll bet Ed is going to speak."

"So? We can take our plates down the bank to the river."

"But we have to cross the railroad tracks. What if a freight stops and we get cut off?"

"From what? The speeches? Why do you care?"

"I haven't spotted Mitch," I replied. "He and Brenda may not be back from visiting Troy. I'll have to listen to the speakers so I can write them up for the paper."

"Just make up a bunch of stuff," Milo said as the music stopped playing and the band members shuffled around, apparently taking a break. "Nobody listens to speeches at

155

the picnics. Besides, half the people here are gassed. Maybe I'll bust some of them for being gassed in a public park. I could use the fines to pay for painting my office."

I saw Ed getting up on the podium. "Ed's sober. And he's definitely going to speak. Is there something you can bust him for?"

"Shit." Milo put his arm around me. "Let's grab our food and disappear."

"We can't! I have to hear what he has to say. I pride myself on journalistic integrity." I literally dug in my heels. "Let go. You can get our food, but I have to listen to Ed."

Milo groaned. But he stayed put.

"At least," I said, keeping my voice down, "he doesn't have a script or notes. Who else is up front? I can't see over all these people."

"Blackwell, for starters. A couple of his managers, including Bob Sigurdson and the new guy, McVey or McKey. Baugh's off to one side in a wheelchair, so he probably won't speak. Oh — the vic's brother is there, too. The guy's a gamer — or a suck-up to Blackwell."

The crowd quieted, but not enough for Ed to be heard, at least not as far away as we were. Someone I couldn't see handed him a microphone. As Ed opened his mouth, the mic let out an ear-shattering squawk that made me and probably everybody else wince.

"Sorry, folks," Ed began. "Technical difficulties. Ha ha."

"Oh, bother!" a voice behind me said. "Must he make a spectacle of himself?"

I turned to see Vida, holding on to a big orange sun hat. A breeze had come down from Tonga Ridge. Or maybe it was Ed's hot air. "Be thankful," I said, whispering to Vida, "Ed's not wearing shorts."

"My, yes!" she declared in her normal speaking voice. "The less seen of Ed, the better. Whatever is his latest self-serving idea?" She paused long enough to catch the gist of his plan for the old outhouses. "Oh, really now! Has he gone quite mad?" She poked Milo in the back. "You must have your deputies burn down those eyesores. That should have been done years ago."

"Right, Vida," Milo said without turning around.

"Soon!" she practically shouted as Ed droned on. "Oh, here comes Buck. You two must try the casserole I brought. It contains tasty fresh geoducks Amy and Ted dug up on Whidbey Island last weekend."

Luckily, Vida couldn't see my expression. I love seafood and I love clams — but not geoducks, which have the texture of thick rubber bands. Ed had finished speaking and been replaced by our freshman state representative, Jason Plebuck, who had lived in a yurt on the Tye River until he decided to run for office. He claimed to earn a living as a property manager, but neither Mitch nor I had been able to figure out where his properties were located. For all I knew, they were made up of the land that included the old outhouses.

But I had to credit Jason with good sense. He kept his remarks to three minutes, urging us to cherish the wonders of our natural environment and honor the work ethic that had made this country great. Fortunately for him, no one asked what kind of work *he* did. But Jason earned more applause than Ed had gotten, which wasn't saying much.

"Crap," Milo said under his breath. "Blackwell's going up to the podium."

I stood on tiptoe trying in vain to see around a couple of burly young men in tank tops. "You mean at the mic?"

"Right. Here comes the bullshit." Milo sighed. "I knew we should've gone into hiding. Just listening to that asshole ruins my digestion."

"Friends and fellow citizens of Skykomish County," he began, "I know you'd all like to enjoy the wonderful repast that so many of you have brought for our annual Labor Day celebration. Thus, I'll be brief."

"Like hell he will," Milo muttered, and grabbed my arm to steer me away. "Let's go. If we can't get at the food, we should —"

A loud, sharp sound cut through the air, followed by screams. It seemed that the people near the podium had gone berserk, thrashing and shouting. Milo had frozen in place, causing me to stumble. I would have fallen if he hadn't had a firm grip on me.

"What the hell . . . a gunshot?" he said out loud as we both tried to take in what looked like panic overcoming the crowd closest to the bandstand.

Blackwell's voice came over the sound system. "Please stand back from the podium," he urged in a voice that lacked its usual aplomb. "Please! Move back!"

"Stay put," Milo said, letting go of me. "That sounded like a rifle. I've got to check this out."

I nodded, but had no intention of standing around like the nearby statue of town founder Carl Clemans. Maybe I imagined it, but the original mill owner's bronze image looked as curious as I was. Milo had disappeared into the crowd near the podium. Several parents were rounding up children for safekeeping. I noticed at least two women who were crying, and one man was pumping his fist while cussing a blue streak.

Taking out my cell, I called Kip to ask him to post the gunfire online. He didn't pick up, so I left a message. For all I knew, he and his wife, Chili, might be somewhere in the park. Hesitating, I saw Jack and Nina Mullins breaking away from the others up front. He had his arm around her and looked unusually somber.

"Emma!" he called. "Can you take care of Nina? She feels faint."

"I — sure," I replied, wishing he hadn't asked. "What happened?"

Jack gently propelled his pale wife toward me. "Somebody apparently shot at Black-well," he said as I heard sirens nearby. "Here come the medics. Got to go help the boss. Gould's already there."

I turned to Nina, whose eyes were enormous. In fact, I wondered if she was in shock. "I think you should sit," I said, taking her hand. "Let's go to one of the picnic tables."

Nina nodded dumbly and walked like a zombie. I held on to her to make sure she was safely seated. I'd just started to join her on the cedar bench when I saw Tanya and Bill hurrying through the park entrance.

"What's going on?" Bill asked. "The emergency crews just arrived."

"There's been a —" I was interrupted by a squawk behind me.

"Billy!" Vida cried. "Where have you been?"

"Tanya and I decided to drive to —"

"Never mind," his aunt interrupted. "You must pitch in to help. You too, Tanya. A young man has been shot and several people are panicking. Buck is trying to get things organized. His military background, you know. Now come along and . . ."

I was left with Nina. To my relief, she seemed to be refocusing. I asked if she wanted something to drink, but she shook her head. "It's such a shock," she murmured. "The poor young man . . ." She shook her head again. "I've never understood how my poor Jack can put up with so much violence. The man's a saint!"

I was glad Milo wasn't on hand to hear Nina's declaration. According to my husband, Jack was not only the most laid-back of his deputies but also the smartest. "What exactly did you see?" I asked.

Nina put a hand over her eyes. I hoped she hadn't erased the incident from her memory. "It happened so fast," she finally said, her sweet face pale. "Mr. Blackwell was speaking, and then there was such a noise! A young man jumped in front of him and fell down. The young man, I mean. Jack — my Jack — thought he was shot in the shoulder. That means he'll live, I hope. Oh! Here's the ambulance. Have you seen Doc Dewey or Dr. Sung?" Nina didn't wait for an answer. "Oh, my! How can they drive an ambulance to the podium?"

"They'll use a gurney," I said, seeing Tony Lynch and Del Amundson getting out of the vehicle. "It's not that far."

Nina nodded, then folded her hands. "I'll say a prayer for the poor young man. And everyone else here."

"Good idea," I mumbled, wishing I'd thought of that sooner. And also wishing I wasn't stuck away from the action. Where was Mitch? We needed pictures for the paper. Maybe he and Brenda had gotten stalled in cross-state holiday traffic. My only hope was that Vida had brought a camera. She was a decent photographer, certainly better than I am. Despite some minor successes earlier on the *Advocate*, I'd regressed with age.

Nina was still praying. Maybe she was saying a rosary without holding the beads. The medics were coming our way with the victim on the gurney. Being squeamish, I didn't

162

take a close look, but a quick glance told me he was the young man I assumed to be L.J.

I jumped when Nina spoke. "Isn't that poor fellow a newcomer? Does he have family here?"

Before I could answer, I realized that Del Amundson's broad form had blocked out a smaller figure next to the gurney. It was Alison, and she was holding L.J.'s hand.

CHAPTER 8

I wanted to ambush Alison, but the little group was almost to the ambulance. I could wait until the medics pulled out. But to my amazement, she got into the back with L.J. and the gurney. Del and Tony didn't notice me as they hurried to get inside the cab.

"Rats!" I said softly as the siren sounded again.

Nina jumped. "What's wrong? Do you think the poor man is dead?"

I shook my head. "He was breathing. They wouldn't turn on the siren if he was a . . . ah . . . deceased." I caught myself just before saying "a goner." I didn't think Nina would approve of my crass journalist's language.

"Why," she asked, her pretty face pale, "would anyone shoot him? Or Mr. Blackwell, for that matter?"

"Good question. Maybe our husbands can find out. It's their job." I stood up to see if I could spot the sheriff or his deputy. The crowd around the bandstand had begun to disperse, though no one seemed to be leaving the park. There was still food to be devoured and beer to be guzzled.

Nina also got to her feet. "Then Jack will have to work. My son Jackie's here with his girlfriend. We gave him a used car for his birthday. I'll ask if he can take me home. I'm afraid I've lost my appetite. Nice to see you, Emma." She moved away, if a bit unsteadily.

I intended to find Milo, but Mitch was coming my way. To my relief, he held a camera. "Emma!" he called, his lanky frame hurrying in my direction. "What's going on? I just got here. I dropped Brenda off at the house first. Those visits with Troy are really hard on her."

I explained what had happened as we continued to the bandstand. "For all I know, they may've apprehended the shooter," I said as I spotted Milo surrounded by at least two dozen people.

"I don't see anybody in cuffs," Mitch said. "Blackwell's holding court by the podium. Are you sure the bullet was meant for him? He seems pretty calm."

"His sangfroid is admirable," I grudgingly allowed. "Maybe Jack feels he's immortal. He didn't seem to notice when one of his exes literally stabbed him in the back last winter."

Mitch chuckled. "True. He's really quite a character."

That wasn't the word I'd have used, but I didn't say so. My reporter started taking pictures. I moved closer to Milo just as he broke through the anxious gathering of people who had been besieging him with questions he couldn't possibly answer.

"Don't," he said to me. "I'm not going public."

"Did I ask?"

"No, but you will." He ran a hand through his graying sandy hair. "The only thing I can say is what I've been telling the nervous Nellies around here. The shot was fired from a distance, probably a rooftop at the shopping mall on the other side of the park. But that's a guess, so don't go public with it. I'm stuck here for a while. Why don't you head for home?"

"Are you crazy?" I snapped. "This is news!"

Milo was looking beyond me. "Shit. I suppose it is. Here comes Fleetwood. Keep him from pestering me. I've got work to do." He turned around and loped away.

Mr. Radio had spotted me. His usual suave mien seemed ruffled. "I knew I shouldn't have left town for the weekend. What happened?" he asked, cutting to the chase.

I couldn't resist taunting him. "What's it worth to you?"

Spence didn't answer right away. He was pinning a mic on the front of his pale blue Ralph Lauren sport shirt. "You can tell me all, or when I break into our current programming I'll announce that you've been uncooperative with a fellow member of the media. That won't go down well with the voters when they go to the polls tomorrow to say yea or nay to the government change."

Not wanting to push my rival too far, I told him what had happened.

Spence frowned. "I heard a siren after I left Rosalie at Parc Pines. Which Blackwell employee caught the bullet?"

I grimaced. "He's a newcomer, a young guy. I only found out his name this morning. In fact, I'm not sure he works for Blackwell Timber."

"Negligent of you," Spence said, giving me one of his lupine smiles. "I often wonder if you're spending too much time being mauled by your favorite bear instead of practicing your journalistic skills."

"My bear has been working most of the weekend," I asserted. "You missed not only

167

a shooting today but a murder victim late Friday afternoon."

"Good God, woman, I am bereft! I owe you." His tanned hawk-like features showed genuine dismay. "Don't abandon me. What's the shooting vic's name?" After I told him, he glanced at his Movado watch. "It's almost six, so I can actually make the hour turn. Is there a chance I can interview you for our KSKY listeners?"

"There is not," I stated firmly. "But after you're done, I'll fill you in on the details."

"You're a sport," he declared. "I'll move away to a quieter corner."

The next half hour was a bit of a blur. Ominous gray clouds were forming over Alpine Baldy and the air felt oppressive. As the crowd began dispersing after six-thirty, those who remained were subdued. From what I could tell, Milo and his deputies were questioning as many people as possible. Maybe someone could pinpoint where the shot had come from or might even have an inkling of who had fired it.

Deciding to do my own share of interrogating witnesses, I was coming up empty. Grocery Basket owners Jake and Betsy O'Toole hadn't seen the incident. They'd been busy arranging their deli's fried chicken at the food table. Coach Ridley's wife, Dixie, had had her back turned and thought someone had set off leftover fireworks. Reverend Poole of the First Baptist Church was clueless, but he felt that the shot had broken at least three of the Ten Commandments. I didn't ask which ones.

Just before seven, my weary husband finally joined me by the cook-stove area. "Waste of time," he muttered. "Nobody knows jack squat. Dustin Fong's working the desk, so I called in Doe and Sam to check out the buildings at the mall. So far they've got zip. Nobody's around because they're closed."

"Have you heard anything about Jennings?" I asked as I heard the rumble of distant thunder.

"Jennings? Oh — the shooting vic. No, I'll check later after he's been evaluated. That'll take —"

He was interrupted by a sharp voice calling out, "Dodge!"

Milo blocked my view, but I was sure it was Blackwell. My husband turned away from me. "In my office," he barked, seeing his nemesis immediately turn balky. "You have to answer some questions. Now!"

"*You're* giving *me* orders?" Blackwell shot back, his face darkening. "You work for the county and that means me!"

169

The sheriff shrugged. "So you want to stall the investigation of who tried to kill you? Your call, Jack."

Blackwell stopped some six feet away. "I don't want you running the investigation," he declared in a loud voice. "As a county commissioner, I'm suspending you as of now and asking for the state patrol to step in."

I could tell that every muscle and sinew in Milo's body tensed. But when he spoke, his voice was calm. "Go ahead. I have a right to appeal your decision and to appoint someone to take my place." He waved a hand toward the podium. "Gould! Come here!"

Dwight, who was a couple of years older than his boss and built like a small bull, took his time ambling over to join us. He shot Blackwell a sharp glance that would have withered anyone with a normal heart rate.

"Sure, boss," he said to Milo. Whipping out a pair of handcuffs, he snapped a cuff on Blackwell's wrist. "I'm arresting you on the grounds that you threatened Kay Burns with bodily harm and the intent to kill her. Come along quietly. You're going to jail."

In all the years I'd known the glum and often belligerent deputy, I'd never seen Dwight look so happy.

170

"Well?" I said to Milo after Mullins showed up with a cruiser to take Blackwell away. "Did Kay get to Dwight?"

"Damned if I know," he said, scanning the crowd. "I don't see Kay, but I'll bet you're right. She set this up with Gould."

I nodded. "Kay may've left him for Blackwell, but she always liked Dwight better. Are you really suspended?"

"Hell, no. Does that jackass think I don't know the county bylaws? He can't do a damned thing without a unanimous vote of all three commissioners. I haven't seen Engebretsen or Hollenberg this afternoon. The last I heard, Hollenberg was confined to his house. They're both older than dirt. Let's go. Blatt can stick around to interview witnesses still sober enough to have noticed anything important."

"Okay," I said as he propelled me toward the park entrance. "Do you want to grab something to eat?"

Milo shook his head. "No time for that. I have paperwork to do. Most of the good stuff is probably gone by . . . What the . . . ?" He slowed his pace as I saw what looked like a tour bus pulled up on Alpine Way. "Oh, crap!" my husband cried. "It's Clint!"

"Are you sure?" I asked, startled by the sheer size of what was actually a sleek mo-

171

tor home.

"Yeah," Milo said, stopping abruptly. "See that outline of Texas on the side of that monster? Who else would it be but my show-off brother?"

"Do you want me to detain them?"

My husband grimaced. "Well . . . no. You've never met them. I'll deal with Clint and Pootsie. Damn!"

We started moving again. By the time we reached the sidewalk, a tall, burly man with a full head of gray hair was stepping out of the behemoth conveyance. Lightning flashed, turning the amber color of the motor home to gold.

"Bro!" Clint shouted. "We've landed! How do you like our Newmar Dutch Star? It's the only way to travel, almost as good as being at home in Dallas. And here comes the little woman!"

Pootsie appeared from the other side of the front end. She wasn't so much "little" as almost emaciated. I wondered if she was ailing or if she was some kind of diet freak. Even though she was a couple of inches taller than my five-four, I figured she must weigh at least fifteen pounds less than my hundred and twenty. I hurried to meet her while Clint wrapped his kid brother in a bear hug.

"Amazing!" Pootsie exclaimed, taking my hands in hers and kissing me on both cheeks. "We've heard so much about you, Honoria!"

"Actually," I said, trying to sound friendly, "it's Emma."

Pootsie dropped my hands and stared in confusion. Her thin, bare arms were very tan, as was her curiously unlined elfin face. "Oh! Really?"

I forced a smile. "Yes. Emma Dodge."

Her blue eyes grew enormous. "Really!" she screeched. "You're married? Why didn't Milo tell us?"

"He told Clint," I said.

Pootsie laughed, not quite piercingly enough to rupture my eardrums. "Oh, men! They don't pay a hoot of attention, do they?"

We both gazed at the Dodge brothers. Clint had let go of Milo, who was explaining that he was on the job. "So," my husband said, moving to where Pootsie and I were standing, "*Emma's* following the story for her newspaper. If you haven't had dinner, the ski lodge won't be busy, with half the town at the picnic. We can get together later. In fact, we'll meet you at the ski lodge bar in about an hour, okay? Hey, *Emma,* meet Clint."

I caught Milo's emphasis on my name as the elder Dodge wrung my hand in a manner that must be a family trait. When I first met the sheriff, I was sure his vise-like grip might crush my bones.

"You work for the newspaper?" Clint said, glancing at Pootsie and then back at me. "I thought you taught school."

"I don't," I replied, noticing that the motor home was drawing several Alpiners' attention. In fact, a couple of teenage boys were about to get in the cab. "Say, Clint, maybe you'd better check —"

"Actually," Milo said in his laconic manner, "you should move that thing. It's in a no-parking zone."

Clint threw his arm around his brother's shoulders and guffawed. I noticed he had a bit of a paunch that the big Lone Star belt buckle couldn't conceal. "You'd give your own flesh and blood a ticket, bro?" He stared at Milo. "Damn, I do believe you would. You always were a straight arrow. Okey-dokey, we'll move on out. Come on, Poots, let's find a spot to park."

I edged closer to Milo as his relatives headed to the motor home. Clint shooed the curious teens away, but he was good-natured about it.

"Holy crap," Milo muttered. "He's gotten

worse with age."

"How could you two be so different?" I asked, clinging to his arm.

"We always were," Milo murmured. "He was the family star. Good grades, popular in school, girls were nuts about him." My husband paused to salute as Clint pulled the Dutch Star out into the middle of Alpine Way.

"Pootsie thought I was Honoria," I said. "Clint took me for Linda Grant." I gave Milo a steely look. He'd never mentioned his relationship with the high school PE teacher. I'd gathered they'd been a duo before we met, but I'd never pressed him for details.

"Hey," Milo said, "didn't I say Clint's all about Clint? What did you expect? Let's head for the office."

"You're going to let me sit in on your latest attempted homicide investigation?" I asked in surprise.

"Let's not call it that yet," Milo said steering me to where he'd left the Yukon on Park Street. "You might as well stick with me as long as we have to meet up with Clint and Pootsie. What did you tell Kip?"

"Just that a shot was fired and a non-local was wounded."

"Good. Keep it that way for now." He

175

paused by the SUV, giving me a puzzled look. "Linda Grant?"

"Right." My expression was noncommittal.

Milo sighed. "Long time ago. Move, woman. I've got work to do."

I moved. But I was still curious about Linda.

It took only two minutes to reach headquarters. Dustin Fong was at the front desk, exhibiting his usual calm manner. "Mullins brought me up to speed, sir," he said. "I just talked to the hospital. The shooting vic's still in surgery, but he's expected to recover."

Milo nodded. "The guy's young and seemed in good shape. That helps. But make sure I get that bullet." He poked me in the arm. "Okay, Dustman, you can entertain Mrs. Dodge while I do the paperwork."

Dustin looked mildly surprised. "She's not Ms. Lord?"

"That's up to her," Milo said, already inside the open area behind the counter. "She knows more than you do, so she won't have to pump you for information about the shooting. Hell, she was an eyewitness. You can interrogate *her.*" He went into his office and closed the door.

I opened the counter's half-door and came

inside to sit by Dustin's desk. "How's the prisoner?" I asked, keeping my voice down.

Dustin shook his head. "At least Blackwell's stopped yelling. He wants his attorney, of course. I suppose he'll post bail tomorrow. Did he beat up Kay Burns again?"

"Not that I know of," I said, thinking back to July, when Kay had filed assault charges against her long-ago husband after he'd slugged her during an altercation at Rest-Haven. Jack had been arrested, but Patti Marsh posted bail for him. Kay later confided that when she left Jack, she'd been carrying his child and had given her up for adoption. "I'm guessing there's more to it than Blackwell slugging Kay," I hedged. "I wouldn't put it past him to have threatened to kill her. The jerk's got a terrible temper. Busting Jack made Dwight a happy man. I almost expected him to break out in song."

Dustin grinned. "I'd like to have seen that."

The phone rang. The deputy answered with the standard "Skykomish County Sheriff's Office." I stood up and wandered around while Dustin dealt with a mountain lion sighting on Second Hill. At the three-thousand-foot level in the Cascade Mountains, it wasn't unusual for wildlife to wander into town.

"People shouldn't panic like that," Dustin said after hanging up. "Most animals won't bother humans if humans don't bother them first."

"True," I agreed, having been visited by deer, bears, beavers, and generations of gophers who dug their homes in my backyard. "Who called? I could use the sighting for our 'Scene Around Town' column."

Dustin smiled. "She wouldn't give her name. Too embarrassed, I guess. I think it was one of the Gustavsons, though. She's always seeing wild animals. Once she claimed a mountain goat got into her mailbox and ate her PUD bill. Maybe it did. I guess goats will eat anything."

"Billy goats will," I said. "I'm not sure about mountain —" I stopped as Milo emerged from his office.

"Done," he announced, looking at me. "How come you aren't interviewing Blackwell?"

"Are you kidding?" I shot back. "And have him insult me and rant about what a nasty bastard you are? No thanks."

Milo nodded before turning to Dustin. "Make sure we get the bullet that hit Jennings. And find out when he'll be lucid so I can talk to him."

"Yes, sir," Dustin replied. "Are you sending somebody to stand guard at the hospital?"

"I don't think so," Milo replied, glancing in the direction of the cells. "Unless I'm nuts, the bullet was meant for Blackwell. Maybe I should talk to the SOB now. He'll probably post bail first thing tomorrow. He can't vote in the election from jail unless he gets an absentee ballot."

"I'll be in the Yukon," I called after him.

The rain started to fall just after I settled into the passenger seat. I called Kip to bring him up to speed. He asked if I wanted to post Blackwell's arrest online, but I told him no. We'd handle it the way we always did, by taking it off the sheriff's blotter in the morning.

Five minutes later Milo got back behind the wheel. His expression was grim. "Well?" I began. "What did Blackwell have to say?"

My husband didn't answer right away. There was more traffic than usual on Front Street, probably from picnickers who were heading home to avoid the rain. It wasn't until we'd turned off onto Tonga Road that he finally responded. "The prick says one of my deputies shot at him. He's going to press charges — and file a lawsuit. How are you going to handle that story, my little objective reporter?"

I felt it was prudent not to say I'd like to turn it into a humor feature. The sheriff seemed to be taking Blackwell seriously. "That's bluster on his part. But the shooter's timing was perfect. Jack never got a chance to harangue the locals about voting against the government change tomorrow. Does the jerk have any idea who'd want to shoot him?"

"According to him, he doesn't have an enemy in the world — except me," Milo replied as more thunder rolled, scaring a bunch of crows off a phone pole by The Pines, the upscale housing development. "Do you know of anybody he's fired lately?"

"The last one I heard of was my awful neighbor, Doyle Nelson," I said. "But that was at least a year ago. Besides, he's still doing time for poaching those maple trees last fall. Maybe you could ask Blackwell's timber manager, Bob Sigurdson. You get along with him."

"So far," Milo muttered. "But Bob will ride the company horse. I heard that after Charlie Pidduck retired last year, Blackwell offered big bucks to lure Sigurdson from the state wildlife department. Jack pays well and he's strict about safety in the mill and in the woods. Your tree-poaching neighbor,

Doyle Nelson, got canned, but he's always had one foot over the line."

"Do you know why any of his former employees were fired?"

Milo shook his head. "I don't remember. Maybe I never knew. Don't get any ideas about digging into Blackwell's operation. When it comes to business, even I don't suspect him of anything crooked."

"I'll take your word it," I said. "I'd rather keep my distance from the jerk."

Thunder rolled and lightning flashed, making me shudder. At least I hoped the late summer storm was the reason. I didn't want to admit I was uneasy.

I operated in a fog during dinner with the Dallas Dodges. Instead of focusing on Clint's account of their road trip in their palace on wheels, augmented by Pootsie's critique of every franchise restaurant meal they'd eaten along the way, I was figuring out how to write up the shooting. If Mitch had arrived sooner, he could have done it, and with less hostility than I felt toward Blackwell. Just after nine, Milo managed to get a word in edgewise to say he had to check with his deputies and that I had to work on the *Advocate*'s online edition. Not only was I gratified, but I was also surprised. I didn't think my husband remembered we had an online edition.

"Dinner's on us tomorrow night," Clint declared as we exited the ski lodge dining room. "That French place on the highway — is it any good? We never got around to trying it on our other trips up here."

I remembered that I had a voice and assured him that it was first rate, at least by our rural mountain standards. Pootsie piped up to say that the place would have to go more miles than a jackrabbit could fly to beat the French Room in Dallas.

I smiled and told them I'd make the reservation for six-thirty. I thought Milo would need time to decompress and fortify himself for an evening with his kinfolk. But Clint wasn't going quietly.

"We figured we'd come by early to check out the work you've done on your house," he said. "Say about five-thirty?"

"Sure," my husband responded. "See you then."

I fumed inwardly as we parted company with the other Dodges. I didn't speak until we were in the Yukon, which he'd parked in the ski lodge loading zone. "Why," I demanded, "were you so damned docile about them showing up tomorrow before we have time to collect ourselves after work?"

Milo looked smug. "Because my big-mouthed brother never gave me a chance to tell him I'm not living in the Icicle Creek Development. That crime scene tape might scare him and Pootsie back to Dallas. Or if Blatt's there with Tanya, he might threaten to shoot them."

"That's terrible!" I declared. But I laughed anyway.

CHAPTER 9

Milo and I left home at the same time Tuesday morning, though we took our own vehicles. The polls opened at eight, so we headed for the Lutheran Church, the site for voters within Alpine's central core. It was no surprise to see that Vida was ahead of us in line.

"Wherever did you two go last night?" she asked in a tone that suggested we'd run away to join the circus. "You missed Darla Puckett setting her culottes on fire."

I was only mildly surprised, Darla being prone to weird accidents and bouts of extreme forgetfulness. "Was she hurt?"

"No," Vida replied on a note of disappointment. "Harvey Adcock tried to stop the sparks from turning into flames, but it was raining so hard by then that they sputtered out almost at once. Of course, Darla accused Harvey of getting fresh with her."

I was about to say that the mild-mannered

hardware store owner was unlikely to make advances to any female, let alone Darla, but just then Vida's niece Marje Blatt came out of the polling booth. Naturally, her aunt waved like a windmill to get her attention. Meanwhile, Milo stood stoically behind me, staring straight ahead in his usual morning antisocial mode.

After marking my ballot, I waited outside for Milo. The rain had stopped during the night, blowing west toward Puget Sound. The air felt brisk, a reminder that fall was only two weeks away. Just as I saw Doc Dewey getting out of his Range Rover, Milo joined me.

"Gerry!" the sheriff called. "How's the shooting vic?"

Doc nodded at me, removed his deer-stalker cap, and smoothed what hair he had left. "I haven't seen Jennings yet, but I checked in with the nurses' station. He's being moved out of the ICU, so he's improving. Who is he? Somebody here just for the picnic?"

I let Milo explain. Patting his arm and smiling at Doc, I headed for my Honda.

Alison was already on the job, giving me a questioning look when I came in the door. "Did you stop at the hospital?" she asked.

"No," I replied, and relayed what Doc had

185

said. "How long did you stay with the patient last night?"

"Oh, I hung out there forever," she said with a disgusted expression. "But L.J. didn't get out of surgery until almost eleven. Then they put him in recovery and told me he'd spend the night in the ICU, so I went home. All those snippy nurses would tell me is that he'd live. I don't know why I went with the ambulance in the first place."

"I'm surprised that Del and Tony let you go along."

Alison lowered her eyes. "I told them he was my cousin."

I smiled. "Was he able to talk before you got to the hospital?"

She shook her head. "He was out of it. Well . . . he was in a lot of pain, so he didn't make sense. And to be honest, I was totally blown away, really, really scared. Do you think I'm an idiot?"

"Of course not," I assured her. "L.J.'s probably glad someone was with him. He may not know anybody in town except . . ." I paused, realizing that Blackwell hadn't shown concern for the injured young man. That seemed crass even for Black Jack, but speculating about what went on in his self-serving mind was useless. "In fact," I went on, "you should visit him when he's feeling better. You can play detective even as you finagle your way into his heart."

Alison looked dubious. "Is that fair when he's in a weakened condition?"

I refrained from rolling my eyes. "Somebody tries to kill the man he apparently works for and L.J. gets shot trying to save him? I thought you wanted to be a detective."

"I do, I really do," Alison asserted, "but I don't want to cause trouble for L.J."

I sighed. "He's already been shot. Get over it, Alison," I said, losing patience. "Are you in or not?"

She gulped once, cleared her throat, and finally nodded. "Yes."

I gave her a thumbs-up gesture as Vida came through the door carrying a lavender Upper Crust pastry box. "Goodness!" she exclaimed. "Everyone is off to an early start today. Almost half the display case was already empty. They were out of raised doughnuts and bear claws. Mitch will be very disappointed." She glanced into the newsroom. "Where is everybody?"

I was about to suggest they might be voting, but Alison spoke first. "Mr. Walsh had a breakfast meeting with Mr. Fleetwood about co-op ads, and Mr. Laskey called to say he was going to interview voters after they left the polling places. He'll check the sheriff's log before he comes here. Oh, and Kip's in the back shop."

Kip was usually the first to arrive, making sure that all things high-tech were in order to start the day. I followed Vida and the bakery goods into the newsroom.

"Really," she said, undoing the box's purple string, "why does everyone think I know something about the poor girl who was strangled and the young man who was shot at the picnic? Neither of them is from Alpine. How could I have any idea of why strangers come here and get themselves into such a mess? Buck feels there must be a connection."

"I don't know how there could be," I said, snatching up a cinnamon-and-sugar-covered doughnut. "The shooter was aiming at Blackwell. Did Buck actually see what happened?"

"No, unfortunately," Vida replied. "He was helping me set out my casserole and cookies. A shame that Buck wasn't a witness. Being retired from the military, he has very keen perception when it comes to firearms."

I wasn't sure what Vida meant, but I respected the retired Air Force colonel. He'd served in Korea and Vietnam, which had given him plenty of experience with weaponry. But Buck didn't have eyes in the back of his head. Vida was another matter. She seemed to know what was going on even when her back was turned.

Leo arrived shortly after I'd moved on to my office cubbyhole. After setting his big advertising case down by his desk, he came to see me. "Spence and I had breakfast at the Heartbreak Hotel Diner," he said, leaning against the door frame. "I drove by the sheriff's office on the way here. Patti Marsh was sitting outside in Jack's Lexus. She must expect him to get sprung."

"Good," I said. "Milo will be glad to see him go. How was your moving experience?"

Leo laughed and shook his head. "Liza told me she'd stored some stuff in the apartment house basement, but I never checked it out. I think she brought everything with her from the house except the walls and windows. I'm not sure where we can put all of it. Sure, the place is two, three times the size of what I'm used to, but still . . ." He stared up at the low ceiling. "What's weirder is we're both used to living alone."

I shrugged. "So were Milo and I."

"That was different," Leo asserted. "You two were . . . close. I mean, in the same town. Small town."

I laughed. "Spare the attempt at tact, Leo. We had a fifteen-year history, going back before you arrived in town. It just took us a long time to figure out the happy ending. We had one false start, as you may recall, and then . . . well, you know the rest."

Leo nodded once. "Tom Cavanaugh. Hell, Emma, when you hired me on his recommendation, I never guessed you'd even met him, let alone that he was Adam's father. After his wife died and you two were going to get married, I thought that was great." He grimaced. "Terrible thing when he got killed. I was afraid you might go over the edge."

"So was I." I gave Leo a weak smile. "The next year was rough. I was a real mess. I didn't realize it at the time, but it was Milo's down-to-earth common sense that helped me get over my maudlin grief. I'd always loved him. I just didn't realize how much."

Leo chuckled. "I resented Dodge from the get-go because I was jealous." He pressed a hand to his forehead. "God, how long does it take so-called adults like us to grow up?"

"We're getting there. You could rent a storage unit at the old Alpine Hotel."

The green flecks in Leo's eyes twinkled. "For all our bad memories?"

"Wouldn't it be better to replace them

with good ones?"

"You're right." He grinned and rapped his knuckles on the doorjamb. "Not everybody gets a second chance. You and I got lucky."

My phone rang. Leo headed for his desk.

"Refresh my memory," Milo said. "What happened with the crazy, mixed-up young woman who turned out to be Kay Burns's daughter after she ended up with a stay at RestHaven?"

"Ren Rawlings left for San Luis Obispo in early August," I replied. "She had to be back there for her teaching job by the fifteenth. Why?"

"Did Kay ever tell Ren that Blackwell was her father?"

"I don't know," I admitted. "Frankly, I was surprised when Ren came to see me before she took off and said Kay had revealed she was her birth mother. I'm not sure if they intended to keep in touch. Ren was very close to her adoptive parents. Why do you ask?"

"Why do you think, goofy?" my husband retorted. "I'm considering possible suspects who might want to waste Blackwell. In case it slipped your mind, wife number one, RestHaven's Jennifer Hood, stabbed him a few months ago, just for old times' sake."

"I never forget a happy memory," I said

— and frowned. "Do you think Jennifer is the one who took a shot at him?"

"Not the one who pulled the trigger," Milo replied. "But she might've gotten someone to do it for her. I'll pay a call on Nurse Hood later. I'm still barricaded in my office until Patti Marsh posts Jack's bail." He paused as I heard a voice in the background. "Doe Jamison just delivered the good news. Blackwell's left the building." The sheriff hung up.

For the next half hour, I dithered over my editorial. During the past few months I'd kept hammering away at the change in government plan. Now that the public was deciding the issue, I had to come up with a fresh topic. Ed's outhouse idea wasn't it. Maybe I should wait until the votes were counted. Then I'd either praise or damn the electorate, depending upon the result.

Still staring at my monitor, I gave a start when Alison came in with the mail. "Double the usual because of the holiday," she said. Seeing there wasn't room on my desk, she dumped all of it on one of the visitor chairs. "Is it okay if I go to the hospital now? Kip told me I could have my calls switched over to him."

"Sure." I grinned at her. "Wild horses couldn't stop you."

She started to turn around, but stopped, looking beyond me to my map of Skykomish County. "I don't think I really loved him."

"Huh? Who? Kip? I hope not. He's married."

"No!" Alison looked shocked. "I meant Justin."

"Well," I said, trying to look serious, "maybe you didn't. It could've been infatuation. What made you change your mind?"

"I saw him at the picnic," she replied. "He was with a girl I didn't recognize. I felt . . . nothing. Nada. Zip."

"That's a good sign," I assured her. "Reactions can't be faked. Your head and your heart are in sync."

She nodded. "So how do you know when you're really in love?"

"You just do," I declared. Except, of course, I hadn't. But I wouldn't admit that out loud.

Mitch arrived at ten-thirty. After grabbing the last two doughnuts, he came into my office. "I stopped at the courthouse to see the county clerk, Eleanor Jessup," he said. "Did you know she was related to Vida?"

I nodded. "At least half of Alpine is. Eleanor's a Runkel. What did she have to say?"

Mitch put one foot on a visitor chair. "Eleanor had heard that voter turnout was heavy, especially for a one-issue election. She thinks that means it'll pass." He paused to devour a bite of doughnut. "Unless they don't like the idea of change."

"Great. How long did Eleanor think it'd take to count the votes?"

"Probably five, six hours, with only eight polling places in the county," Mitch said. "I never realized how many people live west of Alpine Falls by the river. They had to vote at the ranger station on Highway 2."

"We should still be able to have the results before Kip starts the press run. I'll have to come back this evening, though." I hesitated, wondering if Mitch might volunteer to fill in for me. But he said nothing. Brenda didn't like being left alone at night. I broke the silence with a question. "How many voters did you interview?"

"A couple dozen," Mitch answered. "Mixed reactions, including three 'none-of-your-damned-business' replies. Is it a sidebar piece?"

"Sure. I haven't seen your photos from last night. Did you catch any drama?"

"I got shots of Gould hauling Blackwell away, but you and Dodge are in the background." Mitch looked apologetic. "Usable or not?"

I grimaced. "Not, unfortunately."

"You're not gloating. In fact, you both look surprised. How come?"

"Because it *was* a surprise," I said. "Blackwell's arrest was in the log, so we'll run it like any other domestic assault follow-up. Even if he threatened Kay, she has to prove it to make it stick in court."

Mitch still looked dubious. "Will she?"

"She might give it a shot." I changed the subject. "Before the day is done, talk to the sheriff. He may have something new on all of this. As you know, he doesn't always remember our deadline. With a short workweek, he's even more likely to forget."

"If you say so," Mitch said, shaking his head. "Dodge realizes he's married to the *Advocate*'s publisher, doesn't he?"

"Sometimes," I said with a straight face. "By the way, have you met Blackwell's recent managerial hire? It's McKey or something like that."

Mitch nodded. "It's Ken McKean, the new sales manager. I ran into him by accident at Parker's Drugstore. He replaced Jim Tolberg, who retired in June. Seems like a nice guy — told me he came here from a town out on the coast. Didn't Vida put something on her page about the new family in town?"

I nodded vaguely. "She probably did. Between weddings, graduations, and all the other things that go on around here in June, the month is a bit of a blur to me."

"Understandable," Mitch said before taking a bite of doughnut.

After he'd gone to his desk, my thoughts returned to Kay Burns. I realized I hadn't seen her at the picnic. Maybe she didn't know what had gone on with her loathsome ex. I dialed her number at RestHaven.

Kay laughed when I asked how she was. "You sound worried, Emma. I'm fine. I knew Jack would speak, and I didn't want to listen to him. The sound of his voice curdles my blood. I only found out this morning that someone took a shot at him. It'd be crass to say I'm sorry it missed, though I feel for the man who was hit. Will he recover?"

I assured her he would. "Do you know him?"

"No," Kay answered. "Someone — Jennifer Hood, I think — thought he worked for Jack. She was there. Maybe you saw her."

"I didn't. There was quite a crowd — and then a lot of confusion." I hesitated. "I don't suppose you've heard any rumors about who might've fired the shot?"

"Goodness, no!" Kay exclaimed. "If I did, I might thank him. But don't quote me!"

"I won't. Have you heard of anyone he's canned lately?"

"No. How would I?" Kay asked in a reasonable tone. "I have no contact with his timber company. And, as you know, we live in our own little world here at RestHaven."

"True." The facility operated as a virtual fiefdom. Kay was their PR person, but in RestHaven's case the *P* could stand for "privacy" and maybe even "paranoia." Dr. Woo and his staff were beyond tight-lipped. "Let me know when you have your abuse information ready. I'll start focusing on my series later this week."

"I will," Kay said. "Iain Farrell is helping me. He's quite brilliant."

"Good. By the way, does the name Ronnie Davis mean anything to you?"

"Not offhand," Kay replied. "Should it?"

I told her he was supposedly conducting a poll for Blackwell. The name still rang no bells for Kay. "Jack must be doing well with the mill," she remarked. "He may have added more personnel."

"I'll have Mitch check that out," I said. "New hires make news."

After we rang off, I bit the bullet and took

197

on the editorial page. Highway safety was always noncontroversial. Nobody ever campaigned for more vehicular accident victims. In fact, I'd write two short editorials. The opening day for the schools was Wednesday, another safe topic. Readers might be against funding levies and bond issues, but most of them weren't anti-education.

Vida stopped by my office just after eleven. "Where's Alison?" she asked. "I haven't seen her for at least an hour. I heard Lori Cobb was sick over the weekend. Did Alison come down with whatever it was?"

"She's running errands." I wouldn't admit that Alison was sleuthing. Vida was often jealous of other females in my life. There were times when I felt as if I were not her boss but a fourth daughter. She had Amy, Meg, and Beth; maybe I was her Jo. "Do you need her to do something for you? She ought to be back soon."

"No," Vida said, looking owlish. "I was merely curious. Oh! My nephew Billy told me that the big motor home belongs to Milo's brother. I must interview Clint while he's here. I babysat him, you know."

I didn't. Vida claimed to have babysat everyone in Alpine who was twelve or more years her junior. "He'll be easy to find," I said. "I suppose he put that thing in the RV lot off Alpine Way."

"Actually, he didn't," Vida said. "Billy saw it parked by the ski lodge this morning. As you know, Henry Bardeen has a reserved area for RVs on the building's west side. It's mainly for skiers, of course."

"Then you'll know where to find him," I said.

"Indeed I will. Such an outgoing boy, unlike Milo, who kept himself to himself. I thought Clint might go into politics. But he was so very keen on the sciences. He seems to have done very well for himself, though why he had to go to Dallas to do it is beyond me." She shuddered slightly and headed for the back shop.

Mitch entered the newsroom and stopped to pour a mug of coffee before coming into my cubbyhole. "I tried to interview Blackwell," he said, looking irked as he sat down. "He refused to talk and slammed his office door in my face. I went to his second-in-command, Bob Sigurdson. No luck. He insisted he was in the can when the shot was fired."

"Closing ranks," I murmured. "Did the sheriff have anything new on the subject?"

Mitch shook his head. "Just that he was glad to see Blackwell go this morning. The guy's got to have some idea who'd want to

199

shoot him. Is there anybody around here who has a serious grudge against him except the sheriff and those two ex-wives?"

I started to say no, but suddenly remembered what Milo had once told me. "He married another girl here after Kay Burns left him. Her name was Anne Marie Olson. But after their marriage broke up, she moved away. Apparently that was when he took up with Patti Marsh. Her first marriage was a flop, so maybe she doesn't care if Jack has never asked her to be wife number five."

"Staying married isn't easy," Mitch murmured, looking not at me but at my Blue Sky Dairy calendar. He gave a little shrug, picked up his coffee mug, and went out to his desk.

Alison showed up a few minutes later as I zapped Kip my editorial wishes for a successful school year. She sank onto the chair Mitch had vacated and shook her head.

"L.J.'s not good," she declared.

"You mean . . . the wound's more serious than it seemed?"

"Not that," Alison said, frowning. "Dr. Sung told me he'd be fine, though he'll have to stay in the hospital for another day or two. He's a basket case emotionally. I tried to get him to open up, but I flunked."

"Was he making sense?"

"Yes, but he didn't want to talk to me." Alison sighed. "One of the nurses — Julie?" She saw me nod. "Julie said he may be suffering from trauma, like combat soldiers. I didn't argue, but after seeing him so upset at the VI, I think L.J. was on the brink before he got shot. In fact, I wonder if he wanted to be killed, too. Gemma was his twin."

"That's extreme," I said. "He's young, he must have other family . . ." I paused. "You're the only local I know who has some rapport with L.J. Let's go see the sheriff."

A red-nosed, watery-eyed Lori Cobb was at the reception desk. I asked how she was feeling. Improved, she said in a wan voice. Noting that the sheriff's door was closed, I asked if he was in conference. Lori said he was on the phone, but since he hadn't asked not to be disturbed, we should go in.

Milo was hanging up as we entered. "What?" he barked. "Are you two lost?"

I assumed a businesslike air. "Alison has information about the vic's brother," I said after sitting down.

Typically, my husband showed no reaction. "Make it quick. I was about to head out for lunch with Rip Ridley. It's the

201

coach's last free day before school starts tomorrow."

I turned to Alison, who was looking vaguely intimidated. "Go ahead."

"Well," she began, clearing her throat, "I've visited him in the hospital, and he won't talk about his sister's death at all. But . . ." She paused, no doubt taken aback by Milo's intense hazel eyes. "I asked him about funeral arrangements. He wouldn't answer. How weird is that?"

Milo nodded once. "He's not helping us much, either. In fact, he all but stonewalled me. He has to tell his mother, who's been out of the country. She's due back about now, though. Is that it?"

Alison glanced at me. I shrugged.

Milo stood up. "Okay, so beat it. Rip's probably wondering where the hell I am. He's got to be on the football field by one o'clock for the team's practice."

I was on my feet. "Why do the Buckers bother practicing? They'll go two and ten again this season."

"They may not even do that," Milo said, following us out of his office. "They play two new schools. Rip doesn't believe in scouting reports."

Halfway through the open area between the sheriff's office and the front counter, I stopped. "Hey, have you talked to Jennifer Hood yet?"

Milo shook his head. "I called, but she was with a patient. I'll send one of my deputies after lunch."

"What about Anne Marie Olson?" I asked as we went through the double doors.

"What about her? She's been gone for almost thirty years. Are you trying to take over my job — again?" He darted a look at a blue Mustang that had run the arterial at Second and Front. "Damn, I'd better nail that jerk." In two long strides Milo got into the Yukon.

"It's nearly noon," I said to Alison. "Let's go to the Burger Barn."

We found an empty booth at the rear of the restaurant. After we sat down, she gave me a worried look. "Is he always so mean to you?"

The question startled me. "Mean? How was Milo mean?"

"Well . . ." Alison looked uncomfortable. "The way he talked to you. You've only been married a few months. He was insensitive, even rude."

I leaned forward, keeping my voice down. "Milo and I have known each other for sixteen years. We've been friends and lovers off and on ever since we met. From the start, we've had to separate our personal feelings from our work responsibilities. Our jobs often put us at odds. That's always been true of law enforcement and the media. When I walk into the sheriff's office, I'm Ms. Lord, not Mrs. Dodge. I've kept my maiden name for professional purposes. We're used to conflicts in our work."

"It still seems weird," Alison murmured. "I guess it's because you're both older. Love and marriage must be more . . . practical, right?"

I wasn't sure how to answer Alison without violating my own privacy. I resorted to redirection. "Your father and your step-mother were in their early thirties when they got married. How old were you then?"

"Eight," she replied. "Why?"

"Do you remember how they acted with each other?"

"Well . . ." She made a face. "They held hands a lot. Sometimes they'd kiss. But I was just a kid. I think they — especially my dad — didn't want to hurt my feelings about my birth mother. She gave up cus-tody, which was bad enough. I guess they wanted me to still respect her."

"That was considerate," I said. "I admired how they were raising you. It was prudent not to overdo displays of affection. That might've upset you when you were still a little girl."

"I never thought about it," Alison admitted. She seemed wistful. "Maybe I should."

Back at the office, I edited and proofed copy. If there was time and we had space for anything more than the election results, I'd add a brief comment on the op-ed page. Our House & Home editor put out a call for last-minute "Scene" items. She asked if anyone had an election-related sighting.

We were all mute until Mitch finally spoke up. "It's the first time Brenda and I voted here since we moved from Royal Oak."

Vida frowned. "You know we don't include staff members, at least not by name. I could say 'Michigan transplants,' though. Yes, that works." She gave Mitch her cheesiest smile. "It speaks well of Alpine that newcomers become involved in the community."

Just before heading home, I conferred with Kip, telling him I'd zap the election results as soon as I heard from Eleanor Jessup. "It might be as late as eleven," I warned him. "Will that screw up the press run?"

"No," he assured me. "I've had to wait that long when the county commissioners still held their meetings on Tuesday night."

"True," I said. "Leave a two-inch box on the front page, okay?"

Kip nodded and returned to the back shop.

Driving home I wondered if the Dutch Star would be parked in the driveway. There wasn't room on Fir Street's dirt and gravel verge. Sidewalks and curbs didn't exist where I lived, six blocks from the business district. The voters had turned down every local-improvement-district proposal that had been on the ballot for the last ten years.

To my relief, the big motor home wasn't in sight. I pulled into the garage, entering our log cabin via the kitchen. Before I could start for the bedroom to change, I heard a knock on the back door. Warily, I moved closer to ask who was there.

"Just us Dodges," Clint boomed. "We brought our own martoonies."

Taking a deep breath, I unlocked the door. "Hi," I said, forcing a smile. "How'd you get here?"

"We walked from the RV park," Clint replied. "They let us leave our rig there. Say, this is a nice little place you and my kid bro have got here. But what's with the crime scene stuff at his old house?"

"Long story," I replied, leading the way

into the living room. "I'll let Milo fill you in."

"Our niece was just pulling up," Clint replied, commandeering Milo's easy chair while Pootsie sat in my usual place on the sofa. They had plastic glasses for their martinis. Maybe the Dutch Star had its own bar. "So Tanya's living there," he went on. "I thought she was in the 'burbs near Seattle."

"She was," I said, sensing that Milo hadn't revealed his daughter's tragedy with her late fiancé. "Tanya wanted a change."

I'd sat down on the sofa with Pootsie, who gave me a quizzical look. "We heard Tanya was getting married before Bran did. What happened?"

The sound of the garage door spared me an answer. "That must be Milo," I said, getting up and hurrying into the kitchen. "Hi!" I greeted my husband with feigned enthusiasm. "Clint and Pootsie are here."

Luckily, our visitors couldn't see their host's expression. He took a deep breath, squared his broad shoulders, and went into the living room. "You're early," he said. "Why are you drinking out of plastic cups?"

"Part of our traveling party gear," Clint replied. "We bought a top-of-the-line blender just for this trip. Hey, bro, get

207

yourself some happy juice and take a load off."

"I have to change, okay?" Milo managed to sound affable.

Clint waved a hand. "Sure, sure. Wouldn't want the locals thinking you were arresting us. You still got that fire-engine-red Grand Cherokee as your official vehicle?"

Milo paused in the hall doorway. "No. I've got a Yukon Denali."

"Whoo-ey!" Clint shouted, raising his hands. "We can ride with you in that big buggy."

"Right." My husband disappeared into the hall.

I steered the conversation to Clint and Pootsie's twins. Muffy, who I gathered was female, had recently finished her doctorate in environmental sciences at Baylor and was mulling job offers in at least nine different states and a couple of foreign countries. Duffy had attended Texas A & M, Rice, and Hardin-Simmons. I finally figured out that Duffy was a male when Pootsie lamented that it had been hard for him to find his academic niche. Apparently he was now considering an out-of-state school or maybe barber college.

After Milo changed and we both fortified ourselves with a couple of short drinks, he suggested we leave early for Le Gourmand. I excused myself to call Peter, coincidentally half of another set of twins whose parents owned the restaurant. He and his brother, Paul, took turns as the managers. At my humblest, I asked if we could be seated sooner than our original reservation.

"Sure," he said. "I can't refuse the sheriff's wife."

I thanked Peter and rang off.

The evening passed in a relatively peaceful manner, given the vagaries of Milo's relatives. Of course, the in-laws' comments about Le Gourmand suggested they thought our local restaurant lacking when compared to the wonders of Dallas's many fine dining establishments. I drifted a bit while my husband interjected an occasional comment, such as "That right?," "No kidding," and "Huh."

But we had an excuse to escape before Clint got launched on Dallas's undeniable cultural supremacy. Just after eight, Milo managed to catch his relatives stopping for breath and said I had to check election results before the paper went to press.

Pootsie evinced surprise. "Can't you wait for the late TV news?"

"Odd time for an election," Clint muttered, fumbling with a hand-tooled wallet.

"Now where'd I put . . ."

"Emma owns the newspaper," Milo said.

Pootsie's pixie face grew puzzled. "Owns?" She acted as if the word was foreign to her.

Clint leaned across his wife to put a hand on his brother's arm. "I left my damned Amex card in the Star. Can you cover this?" He waved his other hand to take in the restaurant. "I'll make it up to you."

I saw Milo's hazel eyes spark. But he nodded once. "Sure."

The five minutes that followed passed in a haze of my husband presenting his own Visa card to Peter, signing the slip with tip included, and Pootsie nattering away about how she hoped Muffy would take an offer from a Dallas firm, even if it meant less money than the one in Chicago.

The half-mile drive from Le Gourmand into town was mercifully brief. Clint thought they might spend Wednesday looking up old friends in Monroe and Mill Creek. Pootsie reminded him that they should call on his aunt Thelma and uncle Elmer at their farm.

"They gave up the farm five, six years ago," Milo informed them. "They're in the retirement home."

"I'll be danged," Clint said. "Guess I haven't kept up with them like I should.

210

They both still got all their marbles?"

"Aunt Thelma does," my husband replied, crossing the green truss bridge. "Uncle Elmer's another matter. But then he always was."

"He's not a Dodge," Clint stated. "That's good news for the likes of us, bro. Maybe we won't lose it when we get that old."

Milo didn't comment. He was too intent on driving up Alpine Way at least twenty miles over the speed limit. It couldn't have taken us more than a minute to turn off onto Fir and see the RV park up ahead.

"Where to tomorrow night?" Clint asked, leaning close behind Milo.

My mate kept looking straight ahead. "I can't make a commitment yet. I've got a homicide investigation. I'll let you know tomorrow."

"A homicide?" Clint sounded startled. "Hell, bro," he said, clapping Milo on the shoulder, "that's big stuff! You should've told us!"

"It'll be in Emma's paper tomorrow," my husband said. "Have a good night."

Clint and Pootsie got out of the Yukon. I could see the outline of their motor home in the late summer's dying light as Milo reversed out onto Fir, shaking his head.

"Hey," I said, poking him in the arm, "you

211

remembered the paper comes out tomorrow. I'm stunned."

"Lucky guess," he muttered. "I swear Clint gets worse with age. If Pootsie wasn't such a dim bulb, she'd have walked on him years ago."

"She can't be a total dope or she'd never have finished college."

"She didn't," Milo replied, turning into our driveway. "She quit to help Clint finish grad school. Hell, maybe she flunked out. But Pootsie came from money. Her folks were wheat ranchers over in the Palouse, the kind that'd take off for Europe or somewhere in the winter."

We got out of the Yukon and went inside. "I'll bet Clint and Pootsie have a lavish house in Dallas," I said. "Have you seen pictures?"

"Yeah," Milo said, shrugging out of the sport coat I'd given him for his birthday. "They went through a phase of sending Christmas cards with the four of them looking out of different windows. Spanish style, stucco, tile roof, and all that. Swimming pool, fountain, gnomes." He put his arms around me. "You jealous?"

I shook my head. "We've got gophers." I leaned my head against his chest. "And I'd rather have you than your big-mouthed brother."

"Good." He scooped me up, his face close to mine. "Prove it."

I smiled. "With pleasure, Sheriff."

Half an hour later, I rolled over in bed to look at the clock. It was almost eight-thirty. It was too soon for the election results to have been counted, but I still planned to call Eleanor Jessup as soon as I got dressed.

"What's the rush?" Milo asked. "You're suddenly anti-snuggling?"

I started putting my clothes back on. "I'm still working, remember? Say, did you send another deputy to see L. J. Jennings?"

"I sent Mullins." Milo tossed the covers aside and got up. "If Jack shuts up long enough, he can get other people to talk. But he flunked with Jennings. I'll haul him in after he gets out of the hospital. Doc Dewey figures that should be tomorrow."

I pulled on a UW T-shirt. "I don't get it. His sister's been murdered and he's a clam?"

"Not a word. He turned his face to the wall."

"Weird," I murmured. "Unless he's still traumatized."

"Hell, I don't know," he admitted. "I get why she checked into the motel and took

213

the waitress job. But why show up first as herself? You saw her with Jennings at the ski lodge when she was being herself."

"True," I said. "I'm stumped. Oh — what about Jennifer Hood?"

"I handed that one off to Fong," Milo replied, fastening the buckle on his wide leather belt. "He's good at talking to women. Jennifer claims to know zip about the shooting. Fong's inclined to believe her."

"She already got her revenge on Blackwell last winter by trying to scare him to death," I said, starting into the hall. "I'm going to call Eleanor Jessup to see when they'll have the ballots counted."

Eleanor answered on the second ring. She figured it'd be around ten-thirty, ten-forty-five at the latest. I told her I'd call back around then, but in case she should call me, I'd be at the paper by then.

"Why," Milo asked after he'd poured himself a glass of ice water and sat down in his easy chair, "do you have to go out again? Can't Kip handle everything on-site? You usually just call him."

"This is different," I explained. "I have to write the brief story and I can't be sure when Eleanor will know the results. It's my decision whether to hold up the press run. If it gets too late, it messes with our drivers

214

later on. They almost all have other jobs."

"You want me to go with you?"

I smiled at him from my place on the sofa. "That's sweet of you to offer. But no. You have to get up earlier than I do."

"You sure?"

"Yes." The question bothered me. "Why wouldn't I be?"

Milo shrugged. "No reason." He picked up the TV listings. "Not much on tonight. I'll see what the Mariners are doing at Oakland."

That was fine with me. The M's were ahead 7–3 going into the last of the ninth inning. By the end of the game, they'd blown the lead and lost by a run. Neither Milo nor I was surprised. It wasn't a good season for our Seattle Mariners.

I glanced at my husband. It had been a good year for us personally — so far. But September was off to a rocky start. I noticed that Milo was frowning even as he watched *SportsCenter* on ESPN. The arrival of his relatives was distracting, especially when he was investigating a homicide and a shooting. Clint's ties to Alpine seemed tenuous, so the Dallas Dodges probably wouldn't stay long. Still, my other half wasn't one to brood. That bothered me.

But I wouldn't let Milo know it. That would bother him.

CHAPTER 10

I hadn't heard from Eleanor Jessup by ten-thirty, so I left for the office. When I called her from there, they'd just finished the tabulation. The yes vote was ahead by five — which meant an automatic recount. And the absentee ballots hadn't yet been tallied.

Kip looked disgusted. "Why can't we get the votes computerized?"

"Talk to the mayor," I suggested. "Or the county commissioners."

I went into my office to type up the story. It took four minutes to fill two inches on the front page. I zapped the piece to Kip, then joined him in the back shop.

"We're all set, then?" I asked.

Kip nodded. "You can go home. I might get out of here before one."

"I hope so," I said. "Is Chili waiting up —"

I never finished the question. A horrendous boom shook the building and made my teeth rattle. I staggered, breaking my fall against a ream of newsprint. Kip's legs seemed to turn to jelly as he fought to stay upright by the press.

"Holy shit!" he yelled. "What . . . ?" Snatching up his cell, he tapped in what I assumed was 911. My initial reaction had been an earthquake, not uncommon on the West Coast. But Kip's first words confirmed my second guess. "Explosion at the *Advocate*!" he shouted in a quavering voice. "We're evacuating!" He rang off and grabbed my arm. "Let's go!"

I followed blindly, my ears ringing from the explosion. I think I prayed; I know I was terrified. As soon as we were out on the loading dock, I heard the first siren. The emergency crews were coming from behind the courthouse and only had to cover four blocks.

"Oh, Kip!" I cried, choking on the words. "How could . . . was it an accident or . . . ?"

"I don't know." He still held my arm. "Let's move farther away, just in case."

We walked about ten yards beyond the newspaper office — *my* newspaper office — to the rear of the dry cleaners next door. I glanced at the back of the adjacent Venison Inn. There was no one in sight, though I could hear voices.

The sirens had multiplied, sounding as if they were out front. Kip finally let go of me. "I'd better call Chili," he said. "If she hears about this, she'll worry herself sick."

As he turned away, the sirens stopped. I heard shouting and then suddenly I felt what I thought was rain. It wasn't, of course. Feeling stupid, I realized it was water from the firefighters' hoses. The newspaper building was only one story. I moved as far away as I could without getting too close to the railroad tracks. Kip was still talking to Chili when I saw a man hurry onto Railroad Avenue from around the corner.

"Emma!" he shouted. "You okay?"

I recognized one of the EMTs, Del Amundson. "Yes!" I gestured at Kip. "We were the only ones in the building. How bad is it?"

"Not as bad as it could be," Del said. "It's hard to tell, but most of the damage seems to be in the front."

"Was it a bomb?" I asked as Kip joined us.

Del shrugged. "I'll leave that up to the firefighters. But I don't think it came from anything underground. The street looks okay. You two were lucky. Where were you?"

"In the back shop," I replied, my eyes

smarting from the smoke that filled the night air. "If somebody is trying to kill us, they don't know anything about how a newspaper operates on deadline day."

Kip had rung off. "That's crazy," he said. "Who'd want to do something like that?"

I heard another siren. "What's that?" I asked, looking first at Del and then at Kip.

Del chuckled. "Unless my hearing's on the blink, that's the sheriff."

"Oh!" I groaned. "He's going to pitch a five-star fit!"

"Then you better go meet him in case he explodes," Del said.

But before I could react, the Yukon appeared from around the corner of the Sears catalogue store on Third Street. Pulling up about ten feet from where we stood, my husband erupted from the SUV and practically vaulted in my direction.

"Emma!" He gathered me close. "Thank God!"

I could hear his heart beating. What nerve I'd recovered was melting away. Feeling on the verge of tears, I struggled for composure. This was no time to fall apart. "I'm fine. Kip's fine. Really," I finally managed to say while trying to believe it.

"It scared the crap out of me," he declared. "I called 911 to find out what caused the loud boom. Evan Singer told me it was the newspaper."

I could only nod. Milo's hold on me constricted my lungs. "Loosen up," I gasped. "I can't breathe."

I felt him give a start. "What? Oh." He let go, but tilted my chin to study my face. "Are you sure you're okay? You're really pale."

"Del hasn't hauled me off to the ER," I replied. "Kip and I came out here right after the blast. Did you see the damage?"

"No." Milo looked sheepish as he released me. "I was too damned anxious about you. Don't worry about that now. Hell, the building's still standing. I'm taking you home."

"You can't!" I protested. "I have to check everything. Besides, the paper hasn't gone to press. We have to include the explosion."

Del had disappeared, presumably looking for injured bystanders. Kip joined us. "I'm going to talk to one of the firefighters," he said. "Maybe we can still put out the paper."

I finally pulled away from my husband. "We can and we will," I asserted. "Let's find out what's happening in the front of the building. Oh — can you get at a camera?"

Kip thought he could. "Maybe," I said to Milo, "you should go with him to make sure he's safe."

The hazel eyes sparked. "Why not? *You* don't need me." He wheeled around and headed for the rear entrance, where Kip was cautiously opening the door.

I was irked by his reaction, but there was no time to dwell on personal feelings. The prospect of walking around to Front Street was fairly daunting, but I had no choice. Going in the other direction past the VI was about the same distance. My Honda needed a bath. I'd pulled in next to Kip's pickup in front of the dry cleaners. Our usual places had been taken by the patrons of the Whistling Marmot Movie Theatre.

Before I got past the VFW hall, I saw one of the firefighters, Ernie Holt, coming toward me. "Ms. Lord?" he called, sounding surprised. "Are you okay?" He paused, taking in the Yukon. "Where's the sheriff?"

"Inside," I informed him. "Has the fire been contained?"

Ernie nodded. "Any idea how it started?"

"No. It sounded like a bomb." I grimaced. "That's melodramatic, but I can't describe it any other way."

"Then maybe it was," he said in his calm, detached manner. A small-town explosion was a minor incident for the former army chopper pilot and civilian smoke jumper. "We'll figure it out. I'm coming inside to check the interior damage. You want to stay here or . . . ?" He waved a gloved hand at the building.

"I'll go inside, too." I paused, coughing a couple of times. The smoke was settling in behind the buildings. "I have to write up the story. Maybe I can get into my office."

"Let me go first," Ernie said.

The door was open, no doubt to ventilate the back shop. Sure enough, it was smoky inside. I could see my back shop manager, but not the sheriff.

"Where's Milo?" I asked.

Kip was checking the press, but he looked up to nod at Ernie, who kept going. "In the newsroom, I guess. He's investigating. He called in Heppner and Jamison. Everything in here is okay as far as I can tell. The smoke's already clearing a bit."

"Dare I see if my office survived?" I said, as much for myself as for Kip. I did note that the wall that separated my cubbyhole from the back shop was intact.

"Wait for Dodge," Kip advised. He paused to wipe his eyes with a Kleenex. "The fire's out. I mean, it might smolder a bit, but there aren't any flames. Maybe we got lucky. You could write your story in here."

"I will," I said, looking at the clock on the opposite wall. "It'll save time. It's almost eleven-thirty. We can cut some of the Labor Day background story and jump it to page three. Give me two inches, front page, above the fold, okay?"

"Got it," Kip said.

I had to talk to Ernie Holt to get an official quote — or at least an unofficial guess — as to what had caused the explosion. I stiffened my spine, sneezed once, and made my cautious way down the hall to the reception desk. The smoke was still fairly thick. I stumbled over a toppled coffee mug and then again on a half-burned SkyCo phone directory. Voices were coming from the newsroom. One was Milo's, but I didn't recognize the other male speaker. Turning at the entrance from the reception area, I looked out onto the rubble-covered sidewalk. The scene resembled old photos of London during the Blitzkrieg. I swore under my breath.

"Emma!" Milo barked my name.

I stepped carefully in the direction of his voice. The sheriff and the firefighter I didn't recognize were standing by what was left of the coffee urn and the table on which it had stood. The acrid smell was much stronger here, making me feel a bit queasy.

"Look out," the sheriff said while I picked my way through the rubble. As I got closer to him I could see Doe Jamison rummaging around Vida's mangled desk. What was left of her visitor's chair resembled charred kindling. A few feet away, Leo's work space seemed miraculously unharmed, as was Mitch's on the near side of the room.

"Your office survived," Milo said without inflection. He gestured at the firefighter, whose face I couldn't quite make out in the smoky semi-darkness. "Do you know Mark Pittman? He's new to the volunteer fire-fighting ranks."

Mark, who wore grimy gloves, didn't offer his hand, but nodded. "It's not too bad, ma'am, all things considered."

I wondered if he avoided calling me by name because he didn't know what it was. I suspected Milo hadn't acknowledged that I was his wife. From the thunderous look on his face, he apparently wished I weren't.

I nodded. "Once it's cleaned up, it should only take a couple of days to repair the front," I said, forcing a feeble smile. "If it had to happen, better now than in December."

"Yes, ma'am," Mark said. "Excuse me, I have to get back to work."

"Thanks. I want to put your addition to the volunteer firefighters in the paper. But please call me" — I shot a glance at Milo, who was talking to Doe — "Mrs. Dodge."

"Sure," he said with a curious expression. "Good luck."

Milo left Doe to whatever she was doing and followed me as I started for the back shop. I'd gotten as far as the rest room door when he put a big hand on my shoulder. "Why'd you do that?" he asked gruffly, turning me around to face him. "You're always Ms. Lord at work."

I rubbed my irritated left eye. With the sheriff looming over me, it took a moment before I could find my voice. When I did, the explanation tumbled out in a rush. "You're mad at me and I hate that. This mess is bad enough, but it hurts more when you act like . . . It's not *my* fault somebody blew us up! And I'd always rather be Mrs. Dodge than Ms. Lord, and besides, it's after hours." I threw myself against him and burst into tears.

"Jesus!" Milo said under his breath. "You are such a pain in the ass." He held me tight and I felt him take a deep breath, followed by a heavy sigh. "My poor little messed-up kitten. Hey, now you know how I feel when you try to tell me how to do my job."

I sniffled and snuffled before I spoke. "I only want to help you."

"Right," he muttered. I felt, if not heard,

him chuckle. "How long are you going to be here? I'm asking because I have to stick around for a while. I'm not letting you go home alone. We'll go together."

"Half an hour at most?" At least I'd stopped crying. "Is that long enough for you to wind up whatever you're doing?"

Milo had loosened his hold on me but still kept one arm around my waist. "Yeah, it should. Pittman told me their crew will stick around for a couple of hours, maybe longer. There's some damage to the dry cleaners, but they can't get a hold of the new owners."

"The Hermansons," I said vaguely. "I've only met them twice."

He kissed the top of my head. "Okay, do whatever you need to so we can go home. We're both sleeping in tomorrow."

"But I have to be back here by —"

"No, you don't. Public safety is my responsibility. I'll handle that . . . Mrs. Dodge."

I didn't argue.

Shortly before one a.m. we pulled into the garage. Doe would drive my Honda to our log cabin. I was too beat to ask if Milo had any ideas about the explosion. Besides, his usual response was that "it was too early in

227

the course of the investigation." In this case, it was also too late at night. But at least the paper had gone to bed before we did.

When I awoke a little after nine, Milo was already dressed. He was on his cell when I staggered into the kitchen, but hung up almost at once. "How's my sleepy little wife?" he asked, ruffling my tangled hair.

"Sleepy," I replied, leaning against him. "Have you eaten?"

"Yeah, just finished." He tipped up my chin to study my face. "You sure you're okay? I should get to headquarters."

"Yes, go to work. Find out who tried to put me out of business."

Milo started for the garage door. "Oh — Vida called. She's, as she put it, 'agog.' Her recipe file got ruined."

I laughed. "Finally some good news. Most of those recipes dated from her predecessor's World War Two file. Mrs. DeBee had dishes like Meatless Monday Meatballs and Battle of the Bulge diet meals."

Shaking his head, my husband went on his way. I made short work of breakfast with a bowl of Cheerios. By nine-forty I was slowing the Honda to pull into my usual spot on Front, but most of the parking spaces were off-limits by order of the fire department. That was a mere inconvenience compared to the newsroom's devastation. Oddly enough, though the old frosted glass in the front door was cracked, it wasn't broken. The bomb — or whatever it was — must have been thrown inside via the only window, which was above Vida's desk. I wondered if this had been a mean-spirited prank as opposed to a serious hate crime.

I turned left by the Venison Inn, then took another left to park out back on Railroad Avenue. Vida's Buick and Mitch's Taurus were already there. So were four other cars, probably from the adjacent businesses. I almost smiled when I saw the bundles of *Alpine Advocate*s waiting to be picked up by our drivers.

The back shop was empty, but Alison met me in the hall. "Kip left a note," she said. "He didn't finish until going on four, but he'll try to be in by noon. I didn't know anything about this until I got here this morning. I almost passed out."

In daylight, the reception area looked fairly normal except that a new coffeemaker stood on a stool in front of the counter and the usual pastries were laid out on an apple crate. In the newsroom, I saw Vida sitting on one of my visitor chairs at a card table.

"Well now!" she exclaimed. "You're finally here. Leo bought the new coffee urn at Harvey's Hardware. I'll have to replace my computer. Have you contacted Brendan Shaw about the insurance?"

As usual, Vida seemed to have forgotten who was in charge. "No," I replied. "One thing at a time. This is my first look at the place in daylight. Let me grab some coffee and check out my office."

"It's fine," Vida declared, following me through the newsroom as I went in search of my mug. "Except for some ash, of course. What does Milo have to say about all this?"

"Not much," I said, looking around my cubbyhole. "You're right. My hand vac and a damp rag should accomplish the cleanup. Where are Mitch and Leo?"

Vida informed me that Leo had gone to Pines Villa to fetch his laptop for her use and Mitch was checking with the firefighters for any updates to our lead story. "I assume you'll go online presently," she continued. "Do you know how to do that without Kip's help?"

"Yes," I snapped. "I'm not a total computer imbecile. Give me five minutes to check out the premises."

Vida looked affronted. "Really, Emma, I'm only trying to help. How do you think I feel with my recipe files ruined? I'll have to start from scratch. Many of those menu items were classics of their kind."

And, I thought, just about as dated, but I sympathized. "I know. I'm still upset. Have you talked to your nephew Bill yet this morning?"

"Of course," she responded. "Billy's on duty today, despite helping out last night." She grimaced. "I believe he was staying with Tanya when he was called in by Milo. Lila will be wild if she finds out."

"Lila should be glad Bill's involved with a young woman who isn't already saddled with kids or an ex," I said, retrieving my mug. "Did he have any idea when someone will show up to start repairs?"

"Not really," Vida replied while we retraced our route back to the reception area. "But Dick Bourgette called to let you know he'll be by later to determine how he and his sons can rebuild the outer and inner front walls. Perhaps they can start today."

"They'd better. I want the glass in the front door replaced, too. I'll call Brendan right away."

"Yes. That's a priority," Vida murmured.

As if she needed to remind me.

Brendan wasn't as helpful as I'd hoped. He hedged, as insurance agents do, about bringing in an adjuster or an estimator or whatever title was held by whoever would try to get out of a big payoff.

"You know how it goes around here these days," he said in his chummiest salesman's voice. "Everything's inflated in this part of the country because of all the rapid growth in Seattle's greater metro area."

"This is Alpine," I said. "We haven't grown that much."

Brendan chuckled. "But aren't you always writing editorials about how SkyCo's residents have to adjust to change?"

It took me a couple of seconds to overcome my surprise that anyone actually read my editorials. "Look," I said, "just get somebody to assess the damage so that my staff and I aren't going to blow away in the first big fall windstorm, okay?"

Making soothing noises, my agent assured me he'd have someone on-site before five. My next call was to Eleanor Jessup at the courthouse to get the election results.

"We have to do another recount," she said, sounding exasperated. "We always count twice to make sure, but the tallies didn't agree. Then, when we got it right, the absentee vote had to be recounted. We're all cross-eyed by now. We may not have the total verified until tomorrow. I'm not even sure all the mail-in votes are here yet. You

232

know how careless Marlowe Whipp can be with his deliveries."

I knew only too well, so I told Eleanor to keep me posted. I finally had time to go through the paper to make sure there were no serious glitches. Given last night's turmoil, it was a wonder that half the pages weren't upside down. But the only oversight was that I'd forgotten to delete the Mickey O'Neill big-rig incident. All things considered, that was negligible. I'd just put the issue aside when Alison appeared with the mail. I asked her why it had arrived so late.

"Marlowe couldn't come in the front way and he didn't want to vary his route, so he left it at the dry cleaners," she explained. "Mrs. Hermanson just got around to bringing it over now." She leaned closer and lowered her voice. "L.J.'s release this morning is confirmed."

"That's a bit soon," I said. "Will he stay at the ski lodge?"

"Yes," she replied. "At least for a day or so. He's still recovering. Now that he's not loopy, he may recall I said I was his cousin. He'll think I'm a head case. I feel like a total twit."

"Interview him," I urged her. "You work for the paper. Reporters often use ruses to get stories. The public's not interested in how we dig for news." I checked the time. "If L.J.'s being released today, it'll be at eleven. It's now five to. You'd better hustle. Where's your car?"

"By the Sears catalogue office," Alison said.

"Good. So go, girl." I gave her a thumbs-up gesture.

Mitch's expression was quirky when he leaned into my office a few minutes later. "Do you know any World War Two buffs around here?"

I looked up from a Forest Service news release. "You mean collectors or veterans?"

"Either one." My reporter sat down in what was now my only visitor chair. "According to Ron Gustavson of the firefighting crew, the explosion was probably caused by an old-fashioned hand grenade. Maybe two of them. Dodge agrees."

"Gee, I'm glad the sheriff let me know," I muttered. "But," I went on in my normal tone, "I only heard — and felt — one explosion."

"They could've been thrown simultaneously," Mitch pointed out.

"True. I suppose no witnesses have come forward?"

Mitch shook his head. "The Whistling Marmot's second showing didn't get out for another forty minutes. The VI stops serving dinner at ten and the bar's never very busy on a Tuesday night. Everything else on both sides of the block was already closed."

I sighed in frustration. "But what was the point? Anybody who wanted to put us out of business would've aimed for the back shop. I assume Milo doesn't have any new theories since I saw him this morning."

"I didn't talk to Dodge," Mitch said, his face now grim. He and Milo hadn't been on good terms since Troy Laskey's escape from the Monroe Correctional Complex. "He wasn't in when I stopped by earlier. Then, a few minutes ago, he had his door closed."

"Okay," I said, "we'll leave theorizing to the experts. I'll post what we have, but check back with Gustavson and the sheriff this afternoon."

Mitch stood up. "What about the shooting victim?"

"Alison's checking on him," I said.

"Alison?" Mitch, always touchy about turf, scowled. "How come?"

"She met him." It wasn't really a lie. "She accompanied him in the ambulance."

"Oh." Mitch seemed appeased. "I didn't realize . . . Jennings, is it?" He saw me nod. "I didn't realize he'd been here for more than a few days."

I shrugged. "Young women work fast when it comes to good-looking young men. Cut Alison some slack. She's been through a bad breakup." I put on my most sympathetic smile for Mitch — and for Alison.

"I gathered something like that had happened." He grimaced. "I overheard her on the phone last week. She's young, just learning how rough life can be." Shoulders slumping, he turned away and went into what was left of the newsroom.

I'd learned my first major life lesson when my parents were killed on the way back from Ben's ordination as a priest. But Alison had been much younger when her mother was murdered. I didn't really know which of us had felt more bereft.

A few minutes later Eleanor Jessup delivered more annoying news about the election results. "The recount shows the yes vote has fallen behind by five," she said, sounding frazzled. "But we still don't have all the absentee ballots in." She spoke the last sentence as if she were gritting her teeth. "How does Marlowe keep his job? He's the worst mailman we've had in this town since Holy Ole Olafson."

"Before my time. Why was he called Holy Ole? Was he a religious freak?"

"No," Eleanor replied. "It was the holes in his mailbag. He let his dog, Snorri, sleep in it, and that animal was a champion chewer. Ole refused to get a new bag because Snorri loved his so-called bed."

"Snorri was aptly named," I remarked. "Okay, just keep me posted. Thanks, Eleanor."

Kip was as good as his word, showing up before noon to take more photos of the damage. He'd been dog-tired at first light and wasn't sure the photos he'd taken then would reproduce well in our next edition. By chance, Brendan Shaw showed up moments later with an adjuster in tow.

"Coincidence," he told me in my cubbyhole. "Fritz Segal's from Wenatchee and was heading home from a meeting. We've done some seminars together, so he stopped by to see if I was free for lunch. He can check out the dry cleaners and the VI, too. But neither of them look as if they had enough damage to collect."

"Lucky them. Lucky you," I added, seeing Dick Bourgette heading for my cubbyhole. "He's here to make an estimate on the repairs. Why don't all you big business types work it out?" I greeted Dick and exited via the rear door. I was not only tired but hungry.

By the time I walked past the Sears catalogue office and reached Front Street, I spotted Milo heading to the Burger Barn. I yelled at him, but a Snohomish Heating Oil truck cut me off. After I dashed across the street, he'd already gone inside. I found him staring at the specials on the blackboard. I had no idea why. He always ordered the same thing. For that matter, I usually did, too. Over the years, we'd learned it could be risky when the Burger Barn's cook had a sudden yen to get adventurous. The pulled pork sandwiches were still high on my Repulsion Meter.

"Hey," I said, tugging at the sheriff's regulation shirt, "remember me? I'm your wife."

Milo turned. "So you are. How's it going with your open-air newspaper operation?"

"We're surviving," I replied. "Are you sitting down or are you doing takeout?"

"I was thinking about takeout, but you're here, so we might as well sit." He grabbed my arm, dragging me to an empty booth near the back. Obviously he intended to ignore the No Smoking sign.

"Don't sound so thrilled about my intrusion," I said, scooting onto the booth's well-worn padding. "I was hoping you'd have news for me."

"The only news I've got is that Blackwell isn't talking," Milo replied. "He claims Jennings was passing through and volunteered to help hand out Jack's literature. That's bullshit, of course."

"It is," I agreed. "Does Jack still insist there's no reason anybody wants to kill him?"

"You bet. Hell, I almost get that," Milo said, pausing to light a cigarette. "He provides a big chunk of the local payroll. But his bravado doesn't wash. If someone risked taking a shot at the bastard in full view of several hundred people, whoever it was will try again."

Our waitress showed up with coffee. We gave Jinnie or Jennie — I didn't quite catch her name tag — our standard orders. She didn't seem surprised. Maybe we looked as boring as the Burger Barn's menu.

"Have you talked to Patti Marsh?" I finally asked.

Milo shook his head. "We can't get hold of her. I wonder if Jack's told her to go to ground. Sure, she loves the SOB, but Patti doesn't always think before she speaks. He may want to make sure she doesn't say the wrong thing."

"That's possible," I allowed, though I couldn't imagine what Patti might know about someone trying to kill the love of her life. "Any . . . ah . . . ideas about who blew up my poor newspaper office?"

"Not yet." He shot me a sardonic look. "Hell, Emma, these long weekends slow everything down."

I leaned forward and lowered my voice. "Even as we speak, Brendan Shaw and Dick Bourgette are figuring out how to fix the place. Your crew and the firefighters had damned well better finish the so-called explosion investigation so Dick can put up at least a temporary wall. Otherwise I'll demand a deputy to guard the premises after hours."

The sheriff was unmoved. "I've got some sleeping bags at my old house. You want me to dig them out so we can spend the night there?"

"Don't get cute, big guy," I warned him. "I'm not in the mood."

"Hey," Milo retorted, "I can't hustle Snohomish County about the lab work we have to send over there. What I *can* do is have a deputy cruise by every half hour. Now that Vida's recipes are toast, what've you got that's so damned valuable?"

"Well . . . computers. Cameras. Files with sensitive information."

The sheriff remained unimpressed. "What

cameras? Doesn't Laskey keep his with him? Vida has hers in the Buick. You can't take a decent picture. And what the hell kind of 'sensitive' stuff is in your files? An escape plan when Ed Bronsky shows up with his next nutty idea?"

"Vida might have confidential information," I asserted.

"If she did, it would've been with her recipes. Or under her crazy hats. You told me she never takes notes." He stopped talking as our burgers, fries, and salads arrived.

After sixteen years, I knew when to give up arguing when Milo was in full sheriff mode. I changed the subject. "Have you checked into Jennings's background?"

"He sounds legit. Mullins talked to a guy at Micron who said Jennings is on vacation from his marketing job. His last workday was a week ago Friday."

"He came straight here from . . . Boise?"

"Right." Milo sounded suspicious. "How'd you know that?"

Evasion was pointless. Even from the beginning, I'd never liked deceiving the sheriff, and I liked it even less now as his wife. "Alison's obsessed with the guy. She went to pick him up at the hospital and take him to the ski lodge."

"Right. But Henry Bardeen was clueless

241

about a connection between Jennings and Blackwell." Milo frowned. "None of this plays for me. Alison had better watch it. At least she seems savvy."

"She is. You remember what she was like when you were investigating her birth mother's murder."

"I do." His expression was wry. "She ditched evidence to shield her dad. Alison gave it to you and you didn't tell me about it." He reached for his wallet. "You finally turned it over when it was too late to matter. It'd serve you right if I made you pay for your own lunch."

"You're a real jerk," I said. "I can pay. . . . Hey, what about the rifle?"

"The initial ballistics report indicates it was an ordinary hunting rifle," he replied. "Probably a Winchester or a Remington — one of the more common makes. There are hundreds of those in SkyCo. It'd help if there'd been a witness. But nobody's come forward."

"Do you know from where the shot was fired? You said earlier you thought it might have been from the mall."

Milo finished his coffee. "Yes. You've got forest on three sides of Old Mill Park, so unless the shooter climbed a tree, the shot had to be fired from the Alpine Mall. We've got an idea of where the shooter stood in order to see between the trees by the park. There's a steel ladder on the roof that goes up to the top of the second-story section. Alpine Way's a fairly busy street, but that's the problem — drivers are watching traffic, not scenery." He stood up. "I'll buy your lunch, but you can leave the tip."

"Gee, thanks," I muttered, taking out a couple of dollar bills. "I never thought I'd marry a miser."

"I'm not cheap, I'm just careful," Milo said, putting a hand on my rear after I got out of the booth. "Who paid for the re-model?"

"Um . . . well . . ." I stopped when we got outside and looked up at my husband. "I keep forgetting that, too. Are you mad?"

"No." He ruffled my hair. "Figure out a way to avoid Clint and Pootsie, okay? If they call, tell them we've gone into hiding after your office got blown up last night."

"Okay." As I walked back to the *Advocate,* it occurred to me that Milo's excuse was actually a good idea. Maybe I should take him up on it. But we both had our jobs to do. Still, I wondered who had tried to keep me from doing mine.

CHAPTER 11

Dick Bourgette had left a note asking me to call him. I complied, reaching him at home, where his office was in their basement. He told me the insurance information wouldn't be available until the next day, but he could frame up the front before it got dark.

"Don't worry about overtime," he said. "Dodge did right by me when my sons remodeled your log cabin. John and Dan loved doing the job. A log cabin was a first for them. I'll only charge what your insurance will cover. Shaw's one of us, too, but don't let on how we Catholics stick together in a Protestant majority."

"You're too kind," I declared. "Were you at the picnic?"

"We got there late," Dick replied. "Mary Jane and I went to Lynnwood to celebrate our youngest granddaughter's second birthday. We missed the excitement, although we wondered where that giant motor home had

244

come from. It took up half the street."

I grimaced. "It belongs to Milo's brother and his wife. They're visiting from Texas."

Dick laughed. "It's Texas-sized, all right. It sure attracted a lot of attention. I'll see you in an hour or so."

I thanked Dick and rang off. A few minutes later Vida stood in my doorway. "A Ms. Compton is on my line. She asked if we know of a young woman named Gemma Jennings who's visiting here."

"Who is she and why does she need to know?" I asked.

"I gather it's a relative." Vida paused. "Perhaps I should put her through to you. My phone survived, but it makes odd noises. I'll listen in, however. I wouldn't want Ms. Compton to think I'm derelict in my duty."

"Never that," I remarked with a straight face.

I waited for her to transfer the call. It took over a minute, probably because Vida was giving a long-winded explanation. I identified myself as soon as I heard the caller speak.

"I'm Georgiana Compton," she said in a cool, crisp voice. "I hate to trouble you, but I've just returned from a European cruise. I live in Coeur d'Alene, Idaho. I've been trying to track down my daughter, Gemma Jennings. A neighbor told me that Gemma was visiting Alpine. Is there any chance you know how to reach her? She's not picking up her cell."

I wasn't going to be the bearer of bad news. "You should call the sheriff's office," I said. "Let me give you the number." I rattled it off. Ms. Compton thanked me and hung up. Vida practically flew into my office.

"Why," she demanded, "didn't you tell her to call the brother?"

"Maybe she did, but he was still in the hospital, where cells don't work," I said. "Grim news should be delivered officially."

"Well . . . perhaps." Vida sighed. She glanced over her shoulder. "I see Alison is finally back at her post. Wherever did she go this morning?"

"She had some errands," I hedged.

"It's going on two," Vida noted, checking the Bulova watch her late husband had given her over forty years ago. "Does Alison have a nursing degree I don't know about?"

I chose to play dumb, which wasn't difficult, since I had no idea what Alison was doing. "Don't ask me. I'm not her mother."

"True." Vida frowned. "If you were her real mother, you'd be dead."

Given what had happened to the *Advocate,* that was not a cheerful exit line.

I didn't talk to Alison until Vida had gone off on whatever task she had tucked under her blue sailor hat. When I finally went into the front office, our receptionist was glum.

"The nurse appears displeased," I observed, keeping my voice down.

"I'm totally bummed," she murmured through taut lips. "L.J. won't talk to me. Not even after I offered to help him settle in at the ski lodge. I went with him anyway, but he wouldn't let me into his suite."

I leaned against the counter. "Can't talk or won't?"

"Won't. He did tell me to take off." She turned away to stare at the wall.

I considered my words carefully. "He's grieving and he's been shot. You have to make allowances."

Alison finally looked at me again. "You're right. I'm acting like a total drama queen. Maybe I should never have gone on that Alaska cruise earlier this summer."

I was puzzled. "What did that have to do with anything?"

She sighed. "My BFF, Kelly — you don't know her, she lives in Everett — wanted to go because she heard men outnumber women in Alaska. She's been thinking about moving there. The whole time we were gone she kept talking about how we women either get married in our early twenties or not until we're a lot older. She mentioned at least two dozen girls we'd gone to high school with who were already married and that our prime time was running out. I guess her attitude's contagious. I came back here and maybe I pressured Justin a little. That's when he said we should cool it for a while. I knew what *that* meant."

"But you're not sorry now, are you?"

"Not really." She smiled faintly. "At the picnic I saw several girls still in their teens chasing little kids. I'm not ready to do that yet."

"Some of them won't have the dads around for long," I pointed out. "You know the divorce statistics."

She eyed me curiously. "It must be different when you're older. I mean, it can't be as exciting."

I just looked back at her. "Why not? We've had more practice."

Alison's eyes widened. "Oh! I never thought about that."

I merely smiled.

Eleanor Jessup called around three-thirty to

say they'd done the recount twice and — amazingly — Marlowe had found the remaining absentee ballots. He'd tucked them away in "a special place" but forgotten where that was. Luckily, another postal employee had decided to clean out the office refrigerator and found the ballots behind the dill pickles.

"The final tally shows that the yes votes won by eleven," Eleanor announced in a weary voice. Then she paused. "That's the good news. The bad news is that Jack Blackwell is calling for an investigation. Apparently, he wants to hedge his bets. We can't certify the election until we get a court order. That may take a few days. Judge Proxmire took this week off."

"Great," I said on a sort of groan. "I assume it's okay to post the unofficial count? And is Jack's legal maneuver official?"

Eleanor told me the results could be made public, but Blackwell would have to follow procedure with his stalling tactic. That might take until next week. I rang off and went in the back shop to have Kip post the not-so-final results. He still looked worn out.

"Leave early," I said. "You need a nap."

He didn't argue. Fifteen minutes later, he stopped by my cubbyhole to say he was going home. I urged him to stay awake until he got there.

Dick Bourgette was as good as his word. He showed up shortly before five to say he and his sons would start putting up a temporary wall as soon as we cleared out of the office. I thanked him, and with Alison's broken romance lingering in my head, I inquired after his daughter, Rosemary. She, too, had recently suffered through a breakup.

Dick grinned at me. "I take it you haven't talked to her lately?"

"No. When I've been to the courthouse I've been in a hurry or she was plying her trade as prosecuting attorney. What's up with her?"

"Evan Singer," Dick replied, referring to the 911 operator who also owned the Whistling Marmot movie theater. "Brief as her romance was with the movie script writer, Rosie got serious about film as an art form. She asked Evan about those old movies his grandfather had stored in the theater's basement." Dick's blue eyes twinkled. "They seem to be hitting it off."

"That's great," I said. "I knew Evan had been seeing someone in Sultan for quite some time. I assume they broke up?"

Dick shrugged. "I guess so. Not that we're

rushing her. But hitting the big four-oh this year seemed to affect Rosie quite a bit."

"At that age, I was settling in as a small-town newspaper owner," I said. "In some ways, it seems like a lifetime ago. But I can testify that life doesn't end at forty."

Dick grinned. "It doesn't end at sixty, either. Hey, I'd better let you go. John and Dan should be here any minute. I'll check back tomorrow about the insurance."

I thanked Dick and gathered up my belongings. It still felt strange to look out from my cubbyhole and see Front Street instead of the wall, the window, and Vida at her desk. Stranger yet was that I was leaving via the rear door. It could have been worse. I could be wading through rubble.

Milo didn't get home until almost six. Predictably, he was grumpy. "SnoCo's backed up more than usual because of the damned long weekend," he groused after bestowing a halfhearted kiss on me. "Why do so many dumb-asses have to get drowned on a holiday? Why don't they just stay inside and drink themselves stupid?"

"Did anyone from here drown?" I asked at my most ingenuous.

The sheriff glared at me before tossing his hat at the peg by the front door. He missed and swore under his breath. "No. But as usual, we're last in line over in Everett. How soon are we eating?"

"Twenty minutes? Or do you need time to unwind?"

He picked up his hat and set it on a peg before answering. "I'll change first. Save the daffy questions until I'm holding a drink."

By the time he returned to the kitchen to collect his Scotch, I had the potatoes boiling and the broccoli ready to cook. "Where's the meat?" he asked, faintly dismayed.

"It's salmon fillets. You like them. They take ten minutes. Let's sit in the living room. I want to hear all the things you're not going to tell me."

Milo heaved a sigh as he followed me to our usual places. "I can tell you Blatt went up to the ski lodge to talk to Jennings. He didn't have much to say."

"Poor guy," I murmured. "Did you let his mother know?"

"He didn't mention his mother. The guy's not in very good shape."

I was puzzled. "Wait. Didn't Ms. Compton call you?"

Milo scowled at me. "Ms. Who? What are you talking about? Did you hit the sauce before I got home?"

"No!" I took a deep breath. "Georgiana

Compton — Gemma's mother in Coeur d'Alene — called our office this afternoon. I didn't want to give her the bad news, so I told her to contact you."

"Jesus. This is . . ." Milo paused. "I wonder why she never got hold of me. Did somebody call her after she talked to you?"

"How do I know? Who'd do that? Nobody around here knew she existed except L.J."

My husband stroked his chin. "I wonder if it was Blackwell. But how would he know Ms. Compton?"

"When did he give up his mills in Idaho and Oregon?"

Milo considered briefly. "Twenty years, at least. He's so full of himself that he wants a hands-on operation. That was tough with mills in three different states."

"True." It was my turn to think. "There has to be a connection. Two siblings from Idaho don't come to Alpine on a whim. They had a purpose."

"It almost sounds like an undercover job," Milo said wryly. "But if they were hired by someone, say a government agency, why wasn't my office alerted? Unless we're talking hocus-pocus in high places, that's the usual drill."

"The feds haven't always kept you up to speed," I reminded him.

"That's what I mean," he asserted. "Those cases involved undercover work, high finance — state and federal stuff. We can rule out Fred Iverson and the Venison Inn being mobbed up, so that leaves Blackwell. But he owns a logging company, for God's sake."

"What if Jack made a pass at Gemma and things got ugly?"

Milo leaned his head against the back of the easy chair and gazed at the beamed ceiling. "You're off to fantasyland again. Sure, now and then the bastard might try to get laid by somebody other than Patti Marsh, but I doubt he'd pick on a waitress from the VI. Are we going to eat or are you trying to starve me?"

I got off the sofa. "The salmon's almost ready," I fibbed. "Relax. You haven't finished your Scotch."

Milo shook his head. "You haven't turned on the oven. You're lying again, little Emma."

"I hate you." I shot him a dirty look and stomped off to the kitchen.

"Right," my husband muttered as the doorbell rang.

I heard him cuss before he got up to see who was there. Then he cussed again before opening the door. "Hi, Clint," he said. "What's up?"

I almost lost my grip on the oven door. Keeping out of sight, I quietly closed the oven and tried to hear Clint's answer.

". . . pals from Wazzu . . . the Swifts in Sultan . . . Aunt Thelma . . . how she puts up with . . . always was weird . . . a damned Remington 700! How the hell did it get in our . . . stand here all night?"

Curiosity got the best of me, so I ventured into the living room. Clint was already in the house. By the time I reached my husband's side, Pootsie was skittering through the door, looking bug-eyed.

"Hi," I said, but neither of the other Dodges seemed to hear me. Clint was eyeing both the easy chair and Milo's almost-empty glass of Scotch.

"You got any more of that stuff?" he asked.

"Hold it," my husband said, putting out a long arm to stop his brother from moving toward the chair. "I want to see that rifle. Let's go."

The Dodge brothers went, but Pootsie stayed. She made for the sofa, but at least she flopped down at the opposite end from where I usually sat. "Have you got martooni makings?" she asked.

"I think I have gin, but no vermouth," I replied. "Is there anything you'd like instead?"

Pootsie blinked several times. "Vodka tonic?"

I made a face. "I don't have tonic, either."

"Well, shoot!" Pootsie looked as if she'd like to shoot *me*. "Okay, I'll be a sport. Vodka rocks will do."

"Fine." I forced a smile. Pootsie remained in place, which was just as well. I didn't want her to see my dinner preparations. She might get ideas about joining us. After pouring her drink, I topped off my Canadian and 7-Up. I wanted to fortify myself in case Milo and I were in for the long haul.

When I returned to the living room I looked through the picture window but realized I couldn't see the motor home. "Where's the Star?" I asked, handing Pootsie her drink.

"The RV park. Where else?" She stared at me as if I were Alpine's Village Idiot.

"Oh." I sat in my usual place. Since they'd gone on foot, our spouses wouldn't be back right away. Milo would have to get a deputy to take custody of the Remington. I was stuck with Pootsie. "What's this about a rifle?"

Her face contorted slightly. "That was the darnedest thing. It was between the bed and the wall. We didn't see it until I changed the sheets. I thought we'd borrow your washer

256

and dryer. Have you eaten yet?"

I couldn't lie. "No." Then I settled for a fib. "We were thinking of going out." *I* was thinking about it now that the in-laws had arrived.

"We'll go with you. I hope Clint remembers to get the wash. He was so upset about the gun that he forgot to grab it on the way out."

At the start of the tourist season we'd run a story about the RV park and mentioned its laundry facilities. But Pootsie had seen our new washer and dryer when they'd come in the back way on their earlier visit. I was up a stump, as the old-time loggers would say.

"Where will we eat tonight?" Pootsie asked. "The ski lodge has so many heavy Scandinavian dishes. What else have you got around here?"

"The Heartbreak Hotel Diner. You probably saw it after you crossed the truss bridge."

She wrinkled her pug nose. "A *diner*?" She made the word sound obscene. "How about going . . . what's that bigger town where the jail is?"

I bit my tongue to keep from asking if she liked prison food. "Monroe's over an eighty-mile roundtrip," I said. "I doubt Milo wants to leave town when he's working a murder investigation and trying to nail whoever bombed my newspaper office last night."

Pootsie burst out with an ear-rattling howl. "That's funny!" she managed to get out between yuks. "You're quite a kidder. Hey," she went on, staring at the melting ice in her glass, "how about a refill? Where are the boys? How long does it take to get a laundry bag?"

"Not much longer." Another lie. I hadn't veered from the truth so much since Ed Bronsky was my ad manager and I encouraged him to find new advertisers by praising his nonexistent work ethic. Flattery hadn't worked any better than Ed did. "Let's wait for refills. You and Clint must have had a busy day."

The comment evoked a suspicious look from Pootsie. Before she could respond, the phone rang. I picked up the receiver to hear Alison on the other end. "Guess what?" she exclaimed. "L.J. asked me to dinner Friday night to apologize for acting like a total jerk. I am so hyped!"

I tried to ignore Pootsie's curious stare. "He must be feeling better. Do you know where you're going?"

"No," Alison replied. "It could be Mickey D's. I don't care. Do you think I'm insane?"

"Of course not. I'm glad for you. We'll talk more tomorrow, okay?"

"Sure. Oh! Hang on." She turned away from the phone to speak to someone. Lori, probably, since I heard a female voice in the background. "We've got company." She lowered her voice. "It's that pollster doofus, Ronnie Davis. He's asking to be buzzed in. I wonder what he wants. Talk to you later."

I put the handset back in the cradle. "Sorry," I said to Pootsie, who looked as if she'd be frowning if her forehead had any wrinkles. She'd probably had a face-lift. Or two. "That was one of my —"

Just then the Dodge brothers returned. "Mission accomplished," Milo announced. "Let's head on out."

Pootsie leaned forward so far that I thought she might fall off the sofa. "Where's the wash?" she demanded of Clint.

Her husband grimaced. "Hang it, Poots, I plumb forgot! We can pick it up on the way back here, okay?"

Somehow Milo was staying calm, though I knew he must be seething inside. "I'm afraid that won't work. I have to go to headquarters, and Emma's going with me so she can post the latest homicide investigation news on the paper's website. Besides, you both have to come to my office to get

259

fingerprinted so we can rule out your prints from any others that haven't been smudged into oblivion." The last words held a trace of disgust.

Clint looked bewildered. "We were thinking of taking off tomorrow."

"You still can," Milo responded. "You're not suspects. Let's go."

Clint's bewilderment gave way to irritation. "We can't park the Star in those skimpy diagonal spaces on Front Street. That's a pain in the butt, bro."

"So's murder," Milo retorted. "Come on, Emma. We're out of here."

But Clint was shaking his head. "No can do, kid. The least *you* can do is give us a lift down there. Then maybe one of your deputies can cart us up to the RV park."

Milo hesitated but gave in. "Fine." He was first through the front door. Clint grabbed Pootsie's hand to lead her from the house. Bemused, if not relieved, I suddenly realized that my husband had forgotten he'd put the Yukon in the garage. I made my exit through the kitchen, hitting the door opener keypad on my way out. Milo stormed into the garage with his kinfolk trailing behind him.

"Thanks," he said out of the corner of his mouth.

We rode to headquarters in a loud silence.

We also rode fast. I marveled that Milo hadn't turned on the siren. He bailed out first from the Yukon. The rest of us trailed behind like Gypsies driven from their caravan.

Sam Heppner was at the desk, looking grim. If he was curious, it didn't show. Sam wasn't the emotional type. Long ago he'd learned the hard way that emotions can be ruinous. He'd checked his own at the gateway to manhood. His boss and I were the only ones in Alpine who knew why. Young love had made the deputy old before his time.

Milo introduced Pootsie. Apparently Sam had come to the motor home to get the rifle and had already met Clint. "I need their prints," the sheriff told his deputy.

Heppner went off to get the kit. Milo headed for his office and closed the door behind him. Pootsie was studying the Wanted posters. "That one looks like our gardener," she said to her husband. "I told you I didn't trust him."

"Not our guy," Clint muttered. "Ears are too big. Dang, but I'm hungry. I could wrestle down a steer."

I went inside the counter to pick up the phone on Lori's desk. Blanking on Alison's home phone number, I figured her roommate would have it on speed-dial. Lori did. Alison answered on the second ring. I asked her what Ronnie Davis had wanted.

"I don't know," she replied. "He didn't show up, but he sounded out of breath. I guess I should be flattered that he remembered my name. Too bad he's such a total dweeb."

I lowered my voice. "Why do you care? You're going out with L.J."

Alison giggled. "So I am. Mmm-mmm!"

I disconnected, but the phone rang in my hand. Sam literally had his hands full with the fingerprint kit, so I answered in my best imitation of Lori's "Skykomish sheriff's office."

The voice on the other end sounded startled. "This is . . . *Emma?*"

"Leo?" I said. "I'm filling in. Don't ask why. What's wrong?"

"Liza and I have an unexpected guest here at Pines Villa," my ad manager replied just above a whisper. "The pollster, Ronnie Davis. He says somebody tried to run him down. He came inside just ahead of us when we were coming back from getting takeout at the Chinese place in the mall. Alison buzzed him in, but he glommed on to us instead of going upstairs to her unit. He's kind of a wreck."

262

"Damn. I think Doe Jamison's on patrol. I'll pass this on to Milo, okay? Don't let Ronnie eat all your beef chow yuk."

Sam had finished fingerprinting the Dodges. As I got up to alert the sheriff, Pootsie was whining that the procedure had ruined her manicure.

"Hey, Poots," Clint was saying, "you can probably get yourself a mani and a pedi here tomorrow. Maybe we can stay over one more . . ."

I didn't need to hear the rest. When I opened the sheriff's door he looked at me as if I were contagious. "What?" he barked.

"Leo's harboring Blackwell's pollster, who claims he's being menaced. Pick up line one." I slammed the door and backpedaled away.

The other Dodges had disappeared. "Where did they go?" I asked.

"To wash up," Sam said with a rare droll expression. "Who called?"

Before I could answer, Milo erupted out of his office. "You're on, Heppner. Check out a possible stalking vic at Pines Villa, Leo Walsh's apartment. I'll cover for you here."

"Got it." Sam grabbed his regulation hat and made his exit.

"Crap," the sheriff said under his breath as he sank into the chair his deputy had just vacated. "Where'd they go? Somewhere else, I hope."

"They're cleaning off the gunk," I told him as I sat down again at Lori's desk. "Do you have a plan?"

"You mean for —" Milo shut up as Clint and Pootsie returned. "Hey," he said to them, "you might as well go over to the Burger Barn and get something to eat. Or the Venison Inn by Emma's office. I'm stuck here."

Clint scowled; Pootsie looked as if she'd swallowed a furball. "Ick," she said, heightening the illusion. "We want a real meal."

Milo shrugged. "Then call Henry Barden and have him send his courtesy car to pick you up. You can eat there or collect the Star and go . . . wherever."

Pootsie looked at Clint. "We could head on back to the French place. That was okay."

"Oh . . . ," Clint sighed. "Guess we don't have much choice. You coming, Emmy?"

"I can't," I said. "I have to cover the story."

"What story?" Pootsie asked.

But a disgruntled Clint saved me from answering. "Skip it, Poots. I'll call Bardeen. It seems we hit my old hometown in the middle of a crime wave." He reached over to pick up the phone on Lori's desk. After he'd made his request for a ride and hung up, both lines rang almost immediately. Clint grabbed Pootsie's arm. "Let's wait outside," he said with a miffed glance at Milo. "My kid brother and his little woman seem busy."

My call was from a tourist who wanted directions to the ferry dock. I asked him where he was going. To Lake Chelan, he told me. I told him he had to drive there. He swore — and hung up. Milo was dealing with an accident by the fish hatchery. He passed that on to Doe Jamison.

"I feel like a jerk," my husband declared. "I actually wouldn't mind seeing Clint and Pootsie if they'd mellowed over the years. But dammit, they drive me nuts."

"You've got company on that ride," I assured him.

He reached over to touch my hand. "What would I do without you?"

I smiled. "You'll never find out. You're stuck with Emmy." I looked outside. The ski lodge's Town Car had arrived. "There they go."

"It's a good thing Pa never lived long enough to see how Clint turned out. He'd have kicked Clint's ass all the way to Tacoma. Ma wouldn't have stood for it, either."

"I wish I'd known your parents," I said.

"They were dead when I moved here, right?"

Milo nodded. "A couple of years before you showed up. Pa had a massive fatal heart attack. Ma lasted less than a year after he died. She just sort of slipped away. They weren't that old — late sixties. They'd dated for a couple of years, then Pa joined the merchant marine instead of waiting to be drafted. They got married as soon as he got back from the war. Clint was born before their first anniversary."

"She must've missed him terribly. Your sister had already died of cancer, right?"

My husband grimaced. "Emily was so damned young. That really crushed Pa and Ma. They took my divorce hard, too, especially since Mulehide wasn't very good about bringing the kids up here to see them after she ran off to Bellevue with Jake the Snake."

The phone rang once more, and Milo answered it. Whoever it was went on and on. He leaned his head on the hand that wasn't holding the receiver. Finally he spoke.

"If the prowler's gone, Ms. Grundle, there's nothing we can do. Are you sure it was a person and not a possum? . . . Isn't it too warm for anyone to wear a fur coat? . . .

But you reported a possum last . . . I know, they aren't really dead. That's why people say 'playing.' " Milo sighed and put down the receiver. "Grace Grundle again. She hung up on me. At least she didn't get around to reminding me I never raised my hand to answer a question in school. I'm glad she doesn't know Clint's in town. She thought he was brilliant. I figure he was a suck-up."

"You told me he was a good student," I reminded my husband.

"Yeah, he was, but Clint knew how to play the game with —" Milo broke off. "Here's Heppner. Maybe we can get out of here. Well?" he said as his deputy came inside.

Sam yanked off his hat. "This Davis claims a pickup tried to run him down when he was crossing Alpine Way to get to the Lumberjack Motel. The dumb bastard can't describe the vehicle except to say it was blue or black or charcoal. I took him to the motel and told him to look both ways before he crossed the damned street."

Milo had gotten out of Sam's chair. "Did you ask him why he was in town to take a poll for Blackwell?"

The deputy's angular face looked mystified. "No. Who said he was?"

Milo pointed to me. "That one. Davis told

Walsh the same thing. Didn't Leo mention it to you?"

"Walsh was on the phone when I got there and Mrs. Walsh must've been somewhere else. It looks like they just moved in, right?"

"Right," Milo agreed, and sighed. "Never mind. It sounds as if the guy probably wasn't watching where he was going. We're out of here, Sam. You're back in charge. Mrs. Dodge is about to take a bite out of my arm. She gets ornery when she's hungry."

Sam didn't offer any commentary, but merely said good night. Despite knowing that my mate was probably hungrier than I was, I asked him to go out of our way and drive by the *Advocate*. I wanted to see if Dick Bourgette had followed through.

He had. The front of our office was covered in plywood. That was good enough for me. Milo turned up Fifth Street to head home.

"Satisfied?" he inquired.

"Yes. Dick's reliable. I hope the permanent work can get started by the weekend. I wonder if the insurance would pay for overtime."

"That isn't how it works," Milo said. "You should know that."

I made a face at him. "How? Nobody's

ever blown up the place before. And by the way, how's the investigation going?"

"Don't ask me. I haven't heard back from SnoCo's lab wizards."

It was just after seven-thirty when we got home. Somehow, it seemed as if it should be much later. We took the easy way out and ate on the sofa, staring like zombies as the Mariners played an away game at Oakland. Along about the fourth inning, we both nodded off. Later we discovered we'd been watching an afternoon game that was being repeated for evening viewers. We figured that out because even in California the September sun doesn't shine at almost ten o'clock. But we should have slept until the game was over. The A's scored three runs in the bottom of the ninth to win 8–7. It hadn't been a good day for the Mariners, either.

CHAPTER 12

Thursday morning Alison greeted me with a dazzling smile. "I'm going to Francine's Fine Apparel on my lunch hour. I need something totally awesome to wear tomorrow night. What did you wear on your first date with Milo?"

Not yet being completely awake, I had to think about it. "A white blouse and a black skirt. He thought I looked like a nun, so he figured maybe I was some kind of crazy Catholic who'd been kicked out of the convent. Trust me, there was zero action."

"Bummer," Alison said, but her eyes still danced. "What happened to the pollster?"

I related Ronnie Davis's adventure. "In case L.J. turns out to be a dud, Ronnie's staying at the Lumberjack Motel."

Alison made a face. "Ewww. No thanks."

Her phone rang, so I headed into the newsroom, where Vida immediately confronted me. "Well? Who blew us up?"

I explained to her and to Mitch, who was pouring himself some coffee, that Milo was waiting for the lab reports to come from SnoCo.

"Twaddle!" Vida snapped. "They take forever over in Everett. That town has grown too big for its britches. They simply can't handle the extra work we require. I don't care about Blackwell's silly quibbles. The final election results will no doubt stand, which means the county commissioners and Fuzzy Baugh are out."

"We still have to go through the motions," I reminded her.

Mitch was now armed with coffee and a fat cinnamon roll. "I went to the Grocery Basket last night because we ran out of eggs. Jake O'Toole told me there's a rumor that Blackwell is going to name himself county manager before the vote is officially validated. I guess he can do that if the two old guys don't object."

"No!" Vida shrieked, holding on to her beige pillbox as if she thought the peacock feathers on it might take wing. "That can't be legal!"

Mitch looked bemused. "Tell that to Blackwell. Did you think he'd go quietly?"

"No," I said. "But I can't see how he could appoint himself to a new job without input

271

from some kind of citizens' advisory board. I didn't run the statement Jack left here because it was blatant self-promotion."

Vida's gray eyes snapped. "Of course it was! You must write an editorial insisting on citizen involvement. Fuzzy Baugh may be an old fool in many ways, but he's leery of Blackwell. Fuzzy grew up amidst some very shady machinations in Louisiana. Such a history. Huey Long, Jim Crow, and Hurricane Katrina. My, my! How can people live in such places?"

"There are upsides," Mitch said. "When I was in college, one spring break a bunch of us went down to New Orleans to listen to —" His phone rang. "Later," he mumbled, hurrying to his desk.

Vida followed him with a gimlet eye. "Fiddlesticks. I can imagine what a group of college boys would do in a place like that. Utter depravity." She stalked off to her card table.

I went into my office. Despite the temporary plywood facade, a sense of normality was creeping over me. The last week had taken its toll, disrupting my thought processes along with the daily work routine. Letting Alison do a bit of sleuthing might not produce results, but at least it would keep her spirits up.

Meanwhile, it was time for me to assume my investigative reporter role. Mitch would handle most of the actual coverage, but it was my job to do some digging behind a big story. The problem was where to start.

The sheriff's department was on my reporter's beat. If — a big if — Milo revealed anything after hours, that was gravy. The murder victim's brother was a primary contact. Tomorrow Alison was going to dinner with him. Blackwell was an obvious, if touchy, source who might cooperate with Mitch. So far, their history was reasonably noncombative. That left me with peripheral witnesses. While most people's powers of observation are limited, there was always a chance of finding a nugget among the dross. That had happened during previous homicide investigations, and often only in retrospect had a casual comment proved crucial. I began jotting down names of those I'd seen by the podium right after the shot had been fired:

Fuzzy Baugh
L. J. Jennings
Bob Sigurdson
Mickey O'Neill
Ed Bronsky

Ed. Had I sunk so low? Yet he'd be tickled pink to relate what he saw — and even what he didn't see. I hoped I could tell the difference.

I'd met Bob Sigurdson, Blackwell's timber manager, but he'd take the party line. I'd seen Mickey O'Neill around town, but I'd never met him. My most vivid memory was of him as a young man barely out of his teens. He'd given the eulogy for his father, who had been killed in one of Alpine's infamous family feuds.

That left Fuzzy. Despite his age and failing health, he had a certain amount of acumen about people. Best of all from my perspective, he didn't like Blackwell.

I headed off to the courthouse under clouds so low that they covered part of the building's dome. There was no hint of rain. By noon, the sky would begin to clear and we might have sun in the midafternoon. Alpine is at the three-thousand-foot level, and its weather can change from hour to hour, especially with summer on the wane.

Bobbi Olsen, the mayor's secretary, greeted me with a toothy smile. "His Honor is in," she assured me. "He seems improved. I think the excitement at the picnic revitalized him."

"Were you there?" I asked.

274

She shook her head. "Only for about an hour. Jim and I had been invited to dinner at his brother's in Snohomish. We missed all the excitement. Go on in. The mayor's always glad to see you."

Fuzzy did look pleased, but he didn't look well. His pale, wrinkled face was drawn and the dyed auburn hair seemed wilted. Nor did he make the effort to rise from his chair.

"Emma, darlin'," he said with a hint of his Louisiana drawl. "Do sit. I was greatly disturbed by the explosion at your office. We live in perilous times. Has your intrepid mate discovered the perpetrator?"

"Not yet," I admitted, then added in a burst of wifely loyalty, "I'm sure he will. I'm here because of the shooting at the picnic. I believe you were very close to it."

Fuzzy nodded slowly. "Indeed I was. Irene had gone off to fetch me some lemonade. My throat was parched and I'd planned to make a brief speech countering Blackwell's self-promoting county manager propaganda. Of course the shooting prevented any of that from taking place. But the poor young man!" The mayor sadly shook his head. "His sister meets a terrible end and then he gets shot. I understand they were visiting."

"Yes," I agreed. "The brother's now out of the hospital. What puzzles me is why he lunged into the bullet's path. Had he seen the shooter? Was he hired as Jack's body-guard?"

Looking grave, Fuzzy leaned forward. "Oh, no! I was only a few feet away from . . . Jennings, is it?" He saw me nod. "The young man was looking at Jack. He didn't lunge, he stumbled because someone pushed him."

I stared at the mayor. "Who?"

"Alas, I couldn't see who was next to him. Two rather stout women were blocking my view. And then . . ." He held up his liver-spotted hands. "Pandemonium broke loose."

"Whoever pushed him may not have done it deliberately. Nobody knew that a shot was going to be fired. There were also quite a few people who'd downed several beers and weren't steady on their feet."

"Alas, too true," Fuzzy allowed. "The Labor Day picnic has always been an occa-sion for some of our fine citizens to celebrate with excess."

That much was true. The mayor's lemon-ade had probably contained a dose of Southern Comfort. I confessed that Milo and I hadn't had a good view of what was going on. "What's your reaction to Jack's protest of the election results?"

"An exercise in futility," he replied with a wry smile. "I'm surprised he didn't have some of our dearly departed cast their votes from the cemetery." He winked.

I stood up. "Maybe that's why Jack challenged the election. Either way, he could still end up as county manager."

"He won't." Fuzzy's hands tightened on the arms of his chair. "Mark my words, sweet Emma, that will never happen."

I wondered what the mayor meant. But before I could ask, his phone rang. "Ah," he said with a smile, "my dear wife, Irene, the mayor's mayor."

I took my cue and left. Going down the courthouse stairs, I looked over to the sheriff's office, where the Yukon was in its usual place. I crossed the street, passing by the U.S. Forest Service, where Tanya was employed. I smiled, thinking that she couldn't have gotten much closer to Bill Blatt's workplace unless she'd tunneled her way into headquarters.

Lori was on the phone, looking a bit peaked. Jack Mullins glanced up from his monitor. "Don't you see enough of the big guy at home?" he asked with his puckish grin.

"I hardly know he's around," I said. "He spends all his time playing Dungeons and

Dragons on his laptop."

Jack glanced over his shoulder, apparently to make sure the sheriff wasn't in sight. "Does he even know what that is?"

"I doubt it. *I* don't know what it is, but Adam asked me to give it to him for his birthday in June. He told me it'd make the long Alaskan nights not quite so long. Of course, that was during their period of endless daylight. He may be holding it in reserve for later."

A serious expression came over Jack's round face. "Did you hope he'd be a priest or was that your brother's idea?"

"It wasn't mine. In fact, I wasn't happy about it at the time. I've never known if Ben suggested the priesthood to my son, but I doubt it. I think Adam was simply influenced by his uncle's example."

Jack smiled. "We need good priests. How long is Adam stuck up there in Alaska?"

"No clue. It's been five years." I stopped, seeing Milo come out of his office.

"What now?" he asked, sounding grumpy. "Did your plywood fall off?"

"I have some information for you from Fuzzy Baugh," I said. "Get a refill of that sludge you people call coffee and I'll tell you."

Lori had hung up. "We should change

brands. It can't be the coffeemaker. It's new."

Knowing it wouldn't matter even if Starbucks's Howard Schultz came from his Seattle headquarters to make it himself, I reserved comment. Instead, I asked Lori how she was feeling. Improving, she insisted, and she hoped to be recovered by the time Cole Petersen returned to town. Seeing that Milo had refilled his Seahawks mug, I followed him into his office.

"Well?" he said, sitting down.

I cut to the chase. "Fuzzy says L.J. wasn't trying to save Blackwell. He may have been pushed."

Milo took a sip of coffee, his hazel eyes skeptical. "No kidding."

"You don't believe Fuzzy?"

The sheriff set the mug on his cluttered desk. "Even if it's true, what the hell does it mean? As far as I know, Jennings wasn't hired as security."

"Did you talk to his mother, Ms. Compton?"

Milo sighed. "We don't have her number. Lori called Vida, who told her to talk to Alison because, as you damned well know, she'd answered the original call. Alison said it came up as 'out of area, private number.' Hell, shouldn't Jennings have told his mother what happened?"

"She'd been in Europe," I said. "Maybe that's why L.J. was so anxious to get rid of Alison when she took him home from the hospital. He'd make that call from a private line."

"The hospital's lucky to have their own phones," Milo said. "Doc Dewey swears they haven't gotten any new equipment in five years. Blackwell's not beating the drums to pass a hospital bond issue. When it comes to improvements around here, he hasn't done a damned thing since he became a county commissioner."

"That's true," I agreed. "I wonder if I'll get any letters today from people who are unhappy with Jack's lack of performance since he took over from Alfred Cobb."

"Hell, Emma, the locals are too damned apathetic. SkyCo's been strapped for cash for so long that they don't expect anything out of their public officials. Last year it was Engebretsen's turn for reelection and his only opposition was a goat."

Before I could say anything, Lori came to the doorway. "A Ms. Compton in Idaho is on the phone, sir. She's the Jennings girl's mother and wants to know how soon the body will be released."

"Tell her we don't know," Milo replied.

"SnoCo figures the autopsy should be finished later today. We'll call her back then."

Lori nodded and disappeared. I stood up. "Let me know, too," I said. "And by the way, why do you act like you're never glad to see me when I come here?"

Milo shrugged. "Reflex response. For sixteen years you've badgered me for information and half the time I can't go public."

"True," I admitted. "But that was then and this is now. Since I'm your wife, you could cut me some slack and not act as if I'm a pest."

"You are a pest. And on my turf, you're Ms. Lord."

I rolled my eyes. "Logic. I hate it. Goodbye, Sheriff." I made my exit.

The mail hadn't yet arrived by the time I got back to my office. Alison informed me that Dick Bourgette had gotten the new frosted glass for the front door and that Evan Singer — who had some artistic talent — would replicate the original lettering. John and Dan Bourgette might be able to start framing the new front wall in the afternoon, if we didn't mind the noise. I told them we didn't.

The rest of the morning sailed by, though I hadn't yet addressed my next editorial.

Vida's suggestion about calling for a citizens' advisory board to study the county manager proposal had merit. But it'd take time to put such a group together. I considered urging Judge Proxmire to deal quickly with Blackwell's request for an investigation of the vote count, but she would be back soon and might render her decision before our deadline.

When lunchtime rolled around, I realized I wasn't hungry. Vida was in one of her frequent diet moods, bringing carrot and celery sticks from home. Leo was lunching with Gus Swanson, owner of the local Toyota dealership. Kip always ate in the back shop from a sack lunch his wife, Chili, made for him. And Mitch went home to eat with Brenda. When I came back from the rest room right before noon, Alison had already left. Her console was ringing, so I picked up the receiver.

"Emma?" the sheriff said in surprise.

"Yes, I work here," I said, surprised that Milo should be surprised.

"I didn't call your direct line because I figured you'd left for lunch."

"Are you asking me to join you?"

"No, Lori'll pick up my lunch," he said. "I have to stick around. Guess who landed on the Forest Service strip off Highway 2."

"It's too early for Santa Claus. Who?"

"Georgiana Compton. She's on her way to see me. One of the rangers is driving her into town."

"No! You mean, she has her own plane?"

"I guess, unless she hijacked it." My husband hung up.

I considered my options. I couldn't barge in on the sheriff and Ms. Compton. I'd wait for Milo to tell me about their meeting. He might not unload, since the exchange between them would be "part of an ongoing" et cetera. Lurking discreetly outside of headquarters crossed my mind, but the forest ranger who played chauffeur would probably whisk the visitor away to meet with her son, L.J. Maybe my best bet was going to the ski lodge.

Seven minutes later I was turning off Tonga Road and pulling into a parking place. The clouds had lifted, revealing the ski lifts that ran up Tonga Ridge and the face of Mount Sawyer. I got out of the Honda, walking briskly to the ski lodge entrance — and stopped. Alison's Audi was parked in the second slot from the circular drive.

I should have guessed where she'd gone. Shifting from one foot to the other, I nodded vaguely at an older couple who were coming out of the lodge. A valet rushed to get their car keys. I decided to go back to the office. But before I could turn around, I saw the valet open the front door for Alison.

"Emma!" she cried, hurrying down the steps. "What's wrong?"

"Nothing," I replied. "I thought you were going clothes shopping. Dare I ask why you're here?"

She glanced at the older couple who were getting into their car. "I went to see how L.J. was doing, but as soon as I got here, he had a call on his cell. He went into the other room and when he came back, he told me I had to leave. He was expecting a visitor and seemed upset. Should we wait to see who it is?"

"Let's get in my Honda," I murmured, not wanting to be overheard.

"No." Alison had also lowered her voice. "My car's closer. We'll get a better view."

She had a point, so we both settled into the Audi. I felt like we should be wearing slouch hats and rumpled trench coats. "The visitor," I informed Alison, "is L.J.'s mother."

Her jaw dropped. "His mother?" she exclaimed.

"Yes. Even L.J. has a mother."

"I suppose he does," she murmured. "How do you know? What's she doing here?"

"What do you think? Her daughter's been murdered. Her son was shot. Why wouldn't she be here?"

Alison stared through the windshield, frowning. "Because she might be next?"

That idea had never occurred to me.

Ten minutes later, we were still waiting. One of the valets had given us a curious look. Worse yet, I was starting to feel hungry. Just as I was about to say that Ms. Compton might have been delayed, a white U.S. Forest Service SUV pulled into the parking lot.

"Do you think she's rich?" Alison asked. "I mean, did she hire a private pilot or did she fly her own plane here?"

"Milo figures she's well-off," I said. "There she is."

Georgiana Compton had gotten out of the SUV. Before going up the steps, she turned just enough so we could see her patrician profile. She was a tall, slim woman with a dark, silver-streaked pageboy haircut. Her ecru slacks and matching tunic didn't look as if they'd come off the rack.

Alison looked anxious. "What do we do now?"

"Nothing," I responded. "We might as well leave. They need time."

"What if she insists he goes back home with her?"

"She probably will. I assume they'll have a funeral. L.J. will want to help with the arrangements."

"He may never return to Alpine." Alison sounded borderline morose.

"I wouldn't blame him if he didn't," I said, opening the car door. "I wonder why he and his sister came here in the first place."

"He never said." Alison stared through the windshield. "I guess there's no point buying something amazing from Francine. I'm handing in my detective badge."

"Don't be so hard on yourself. The case hasn't been solved." I started to get out of the Audi, but stopped. "Do you still want to try your hand at writing a story for the paper?"

Alison finally looked at me. "Well . . . I guess. Why?"

I explained about Blackwell's recent hiring of Ken McKean. "Vida gave him a brief mention back in June, but otherwise he's slipped under the radar. While Mitch ordinarily would do the story, he and I are starting a series on domestic abuse. He gets

286

touchy about turf, but my reason will be that I don't want to overload him."

"I wrote some articles for the school newspaper at Everett High. I did humor." She made a face. "At least my stuff seemed funny when I was seventeen."

"You wrote for your peers," I said with a smile. "That's all I ask of you now."

"Okay." Alison shook herself. "There's nothing funny about what's going down here."

"That's true. Be careful. I mean that." But I couldn't tell if Alison heard me.

I stopped at the Grocery Basket to pick up a chicken sandwich, a bag of chips, and a Pepsi. Turning off Alpine Way to Front Street, I saw the Yukon in its place. It was just after twelve-thirty. If Milo had eaten at his desk, he might fill me in on Ms. Compton.

Jack Mullins was the only one holding down the fort. He grinned when he saw me come in. "You must've heard the boss man was seeing another woman."

"She's also rich and good-looking," I said, leaning an elbow on the counter.

Jack made an effort to tame his unruly red hair. "It was a closed-door session. I tried listening at the keyhole, but I didn't hear any moans of passion."

"There is no keyhole," I said.

"I guess that's why I couldn't hear any-thing. Go ahead, confront him," Jack said as I went into the area behind the counter.

I knocked and got a gruff "What?" in response.

I opened the door. "Ms. Compton is a dish," I declared. "I, too, have seen her."

Milo frowned. "You did? Where?"

"At the ski lodge." I sat down in one of his visitor chairs. "I didn't talk to her, though. She looks as if she's holding up fairly well."

"I figure she's on a lot of heavy-duty drugs," Milo replied. "Or she's in shock."

I unwrapped my sandwich. "Is she taking her son home with her?"

The sheriff ran a big hand over his face. "No. She told the pilot to take off and go back to Coeur d'Alene. Ms. Compton is out for revenge against Blackwell. She's asking for trouble. Is that a chicken sandwich?"

"Yes. Didn't you eat already?"

"I kept getting interrupted. I'll have some of your chips." He reached for the bag.

"Is there a Mr. Compton?"

"There was," Milo replied. "He's dead. Gemma and L.J. are her only kids."

I swallowed a bite of sandwich. "Where

did the money come from?"

"Silver mining back in the day, on her grandfather's part. Why didn't you get two bags of chips?"

I stared at the empty bag. "You hog! You ate almost all of them!"

"You should eat faster. Or buy more chips." His gaze was steady — and guileless.

I surrendered. "Why is Ms. Compton zeroing in on Blackwell? Not that I'm defending him, but he seems to have been the shooter's target."

"That's what's interesting," Milo said, eyeing the half of the sandwich I hadn't yet eaten. "She didn't say. But she let something slip out before she left."

"And?" I ate the last bite of the first half and snatched up the other half of the sandwich.

"Ms. Compton was vague about that," Milo replied, looking disappointed as I held the sandwich with both hands. "But she referred to him as 'that bastard, Jack Blackwell.' Then she walked out."

"Did she say why her children came here in the first place?"

My husband shook his head. "She dismissed the question as a lark, some kind of vacation adventure. I don't believe it."

"Whatever happened to the serial killer theory?"

"The Jennings girl's murder fits the same MO as the two in SnoCo," Milo said. "Young girl in her early to midtwenties killed in an empty house. But something's off."

"Hey," I said, leaning forward in the chair, "why are you telling me all this? Isn't it part of what you call 'an ongoing —' " I suddenly remembered the postcards Kay Burns and Jennifer Hood had received. I told the sheriff about them. "I'll bet Ms. Compton sent them."

Milo looked thoughtful. "It fits. But what's the Compton-Blackwell connection?'

"Maybe we're about to find out," I said. "Have you got a picture of Gemma?"

"Only a postmortem shot. Strangulation victims don't look too good." The sheriff grimaced. "Another thing — you've got Alison involved. I told you that was a bad idea. If Ms. Compton is going after Blackwell, keep your spy out of the way." His hazel eyes flashed. "You got that, little Emma?"

I did. But I wasn't sure how I could stop Alison. She'd been bitten by the need-to-know bug. Sometimes that bite can be fatal.

A head-on collision in the horseshoe loop

of Highway 2 east of Alpine required the sheriff's presence at the scene. It was almost one o'clock. I called Mitch's cell to see if he'd left for the office yet. He hadn't, so I told him to check out the accident site. There were, according to Milo, possible fatalities. On that somber note, I went back to my office.

Vida immediately confronted me. "The official insurance person was here with Brendan Shaw. He'll have his estimate later today. His name is Kronauer. He looked shifty to me. He's from Seattle. No doubt he thinks we're small-town dupes."

"Maybe we are," I said. "But I trust Brendan."

"This Kronauer probably thinks Brendan is easily hoodwinked, too," Vida asserted. "Evan Singer called. He'll have the new front door glass tomorrow afternoon. By the way, I've having him on my radio program tonight. I'd planned to ask Bobby Lambrecht, but he's still settling in as the new bank president."

"Were Bob and Miriam at the picnic?" I asked.

"Yes, but they came late, so they missed the shooting." She made it sound as if that had been the event's highlight. Maybe it was, all things considered. Vida was still talking. "Evan is presenting another film festival in January at the Whistling Marmot. The previous one was very successful, though I didn't attend. Some of the titles were rather off-putting. *Vertigo* indeed! A movie about an ophthalmologist? Really now!"

"Anything else?" I asked in a faint voice, always taken aback by how much new information my House & Home editor could acquire in a very short time. In fact, I wished I'd taken notes.

Vida tapped her cheek. "Let me think . . . oh! My despicable sister-in-law, Mary Lou Blatt, is back from wherever she went and is positively foaming at the mouth because she missed all the excitement in the Icicle Creek Development. It serves her right for leaving Alpine in the first place."

Naturally, Vida would disapprove of anyone even temporarily abandoning her beloved hometown. "You could fill her in," I said.

"I could, but I won't." Behind her big glasses, Vida's gray eyes seemed to dance with pleasure. "Mary Lou despises not knowing what goes on around here."

That trait seemed to run in the family. I merely nodded.

Mitch returned ten minutes later. "One

dead, three injured," he said from the doorway to my cubbyhole. "Fatality's an older Wenatchee man who may've had a heart attack. His Nissan Stanza crossed the center line and hit a Chevy Tahoe. Husband, wife, and ten-year old boy were taken to Leavenworth for treatment."

"Why not here?" I asked. "It would have been closer."

"They live in Leavenworth," Mitch replied. "They wanted their own doctor. The injuries weren't life-threatening."

"Was the older man alone?"

Mitch nodded. "Driver's license says he lives — lived — in Waterville. Where is that?"

"The other side of the pass, north on Highway 97," I said.

"Nobody local, then," Mitch murmured, tugging at one of his long earlobes. "Not worth a picture?"

"Not unless we get desperate. We could run the photo," I went on, "to show the dangers of Highway 2, even in good weather."

"It's dicey, especially with drivers who go too fast and don't know the highway." He started to turn away, but stopped. "There was a local on the scene. Just before I was about to leave, one of Blackwell's guys drove a tractor out of the Forest Service road. Not

Engebretsen, but . . ." He frowned, trying to recall the name.

"Engelman?" I said. "Fred Engelman works for Blackwell."

"That's it." Mitch grinned a bit sheepishly. "After a year, I should be able to ID more of the locals."

"It's an endless process. I still haven't figured out all the limbs on Vida's family tree."

He chuckled obligingly as I saw Kay Burns coming my way. "I think I've got a visitor."

My reporter bowed out, nodding to Kay, who nodded back. I noted that Vida was nowhere in sight. If she had been, the newcomer would've been accosted by now.

"Good heavens," Kay said as she sat down. "I heard about the explosion, but I hadn't yet seen the result. In fact, I've never been inside your office before. Have you any idea who did the damage?"

"Not yet," I replied. "We're lucky it's not a lot worse."

"I suppose." Kay paused, her blue eyes traveling around my cubbyhole. "Maybe my timing is bad. I intended to goad you about beginning the domestic abuse series in next week's edition."

I hesitated. "I'd rather wait until we're

geared up for fall. Is there a reason to start earlier?"

Kay smiled. "I've been discussing the topic with Iain Farrell. We've become quite close lately. Being a psychiatrist, his input is invaluable. He seems abrupt, but underneath he's a very caring, sensitive man."

Given Kay's history with men, I figured that "underneath" referred to her bedsheets. But that was her private life. My problem with Farrell was that we'd gotten off to a bad start. He'd come off as an arrogant, self-centered jerk. "He approves of you going public?"

Kay nodded. "Very much. He's offered to help. Over the years, Iain has written many articles for professional journals. We're very lucky to have him here in Alpine."

My evil thought was to wonder how such a psychiatry rock star had ended up in our woodsy mountain aerie. But I kept that query to myself. "You mean," I said, probing Kay's intentions, "you'll suggest what I should emphasize in my articles, or do you mean I use direct quotes from you and Dr. Farrell?"

"Well . . ." Kay clasped and unclasped her hands. "Given his vast knowledge, the articles should be published in his own words."

Wanting to keep things amiable, I smiled. "You're talking to an editor, Kay. Unedited copy is anathema to us. That's how we earn our keep. I can be gentle, though."

Kay's face tightened. "Iain has his own writing style. As you know, each profession has an individual way of communicating with the public."

I knew all too well. Specialized practitioners often wrote in obscure language that might as well be Urdu. "Trust me," I said, still affable, "Iain's not the first whose style might need tweaking. And whatever we publish must have a local angle."

Kay seemed puzzled. "You mean naming names of people who've been involved in domestic abuse?"

"Of course not," I asserted. "This is a small town, a small county. While the problem is universal, environmental factors play a role. Alpine isn't Manhattan or even Seattle. I have to think local in terms of a smaller, relatively isolated community."

Kay's eyes focused on my Blue Sky Dairy calendar. "I'll have to discuss this with Iain. As RestHaven's PR person, I always have to consider our image before going public."

"That's fine." I was puzzled about Kay's motives, but I didn't know how to tactfully express my reaction. "I realize that your role

296

in this was triggered by Jack's abuse of you, not only recently, but going back to your marriage. I also recall that earlier this summer, Jack and Iain got into it during a meeting at RestHaven. Blows were exchanged. Is that why Iain has become so involved in what he thinks should go into the *Advocate*?"

Kay looked grim. "He was defending my honor when he hit Jack. Iain's concerned about my welfare."

I figured that wasn't the only thing about Kay that concerned Farrell. He was single. I didn't know if he'd ever been married or had children. My interview with him before RestHaven's official opening had been as brief as it was disagreeable. "That's very considerate of him," I said.

"Jack had the gall to file charges against Iain." Kay couldn't hide her contempt. "The man is reprehensible. I can't imagine Iain ever being disrespectful to a female."

I could, since he'd been downright insulting. "All the more reason to humanize the articles," I said.

"Iain is very human — and humane," Kay declared, standing up. "I'll discuss our conversation with him. He may not like any tampering with his writings. You realize he's outstanding among his peers."

"I've read his credentials," I said woodenly. "Keep me posted."

Kay assured me she would, but my mood had soured during our meeting. It didn't improve a few minutes later when John and Dan Bourgette showed up to start taking down the temporary plywood. Kip stopped me before I could ask the brothers if they could wait until closer to quitting time.

"I told them it was okay," my back shop wizard explained, looking apologetic. "Fleetwood's hour-turn news at three predicted rain by early evening. It's clouding over again."

I sighed. "Needs must. Vida's getting out of the way. She's folding up her card table."

Kip mustered a grin. "Better than folding up her tent. But tomorrow we can park out front and use the main entrance later on."

"Let's hope so," I said as my phone rang.

"The so-called bomb," the sheriff informed me, "was what the firefighters figured — a hand grenade. Two of them, in fact. What are we having for dinner?"

"I don't know yet. Hey — where are the Texas visitors?"

I heard Milo heave a sigh. "I got a half-assed message from Clint earlier. They were visiting his old pals who live somewhere between here and Bothell. Instead of going back to Dallas the way they came, they'll head over Snoqualmie Pass and drive all the way to Sioux Falls before they turn south."

"That sounds like a long haul," I said.

"Do you care? Do I care? Let's hope they take off tomorrow."

"What about the wreck?" I asked.

"Old guy may've had a heart attack. Laskey was there. Didn't he tell you?"

"Yes, but I thought you might have confirmation in case we run more than a couple of inches. Otherwise, the only local angle is Fred Engelman on a tractor."

"You work that out. Wait — what do you mean?"

I recounted Mitch's sighting of Fred coming off the Forest Service road. "I'm guessing the tractor was the kind for hauling out logs."

Milo didn't say anything for a moment. "There's only one of those roads off that loop of Highway 2. That area was logged back in 1986. It'll be another twenty years before those trees can be harvested. Why the hell was Engelman on that timber parcel with a tractor?"

"Don't ask me," I said. "Ask Fred. I didn't live here in 1986."

"I will, goddammit," Milo growled — and

299

hung up on me.

I alerted Mitch that his mention of Blackwell's employee on Forest Service land might be a story.

Mitch was intrigued. "You mean Engelman — or Blackwell — is poaching timber? I thought Jack's business practices were above reproach."

"They have been," I assured him. "For all we know, Fred likes to ride his tractor around the woods. One of the Overholts used to drive his tractor all over around here because he insisted it was easier to handle than any of his horses."

Mitch shrugged. "To each his own."

A little after four, Vida stomped into my office. "I'm leaving early. Kip's installing my new computer, so I might as well go home to prepare for my radio program. I should do some background on the films Evan is showing this summer. I must confess I haven't watched a motion picture since I took Roger to see *Casper,* a very sweet story about a friendly ghost." She grimaced, perhaps envisioning the jerk in his jail cell. "He didn't care for it. I suspect it frightened him."

"How old was he then?" I asked.

"Thirteen," she replied. "He was always such a sensitive child."

300

I imagined the jerk poking his finger in his mouth and making blurping noises. Vida probably felt he was emotionally over-wrought. It had been four months since Roger had gone to prison. I wondered how long his grandmother could go without seeing him. Maybe she was hoping he'd get out early for good behavior. Unfortunately, that would be out of character for her grandson.

"I can't help you with current movies," I admitted. "I'm not much better at keeping up. Evan won't need prompting. He's very knowledgeable on the subject."

"I do hope he talks about wholesome films," Vida murmured. "I've heard that some of the foreign pictures he's shown are quite risqué."

I assured her that Evan's on-air decorum would be fine. He had changed dramatically from the wild and woolly pot-smoking goofball who'd arrived in Alpine fourteen years ago. As the county's prosecuting at-torney, Rosemary Bourgette wouldn't get involved with a flake. She'd already done that and was too smart for a repeat.

By quarter to five, her brothers were making enough noise to set my teeth on edge. I sent Leo and Mitch home, then went into the back shop to deliver the same message to Kip.

He, however, demurred. "I can't really hear it back here," he asserted. "Besides, I'm not done setting up Mrs. Runkel's new computer."

I wished him good luck, then went to tell Alison she could quit for the day. She nodded in a detached manner before she looked me in the eye. "Do you think L.J.'s mother has taken him away by now?"

"I doubt it," I replied. "Milo thinks she's here to raise hell. Don't ask me for details. I don't know any."

Alison frowned. "Now I'll worry about both of them. Who's she going after? Or has the sheriff found out who shot L.J.?"

"Not yet," I said. "Remember, L.J. wasn't the target."

"Does Ms. Compton know that?"

"I imagine Milo told her." I smiled encouragingly at Alison. "Go home, relax, watch a movie with Lori." I felt like adding it had better be "wholesome" in case Vida was taking an evening stroll and looking into windows where residents hadn't yet pulled the drapes. "There's nothing you can do about L.J. or his sister's murder. Oh — don't forget *Vida's Cupboard* tonight."

"Right." Alison wasn't enthused. "Okay,

I'll pretend the last week was a bad dream."
I decided not to remind her that it had
been worse than that. "Nightmare" was the
word that came to my mind.

CHAPTER 13

Five minutes later, Kip and I were the only ones left in the office. I stepped outside to say goodnight to Dan and John, who were framing up what looked like the beginning of a real wall. "Will you quit if it rains?" I asked.

Dan grinned. "That won't stop us unless it's a deluge. We're natives, remember?"

I laughed and wished them good luck before going back inside. My Honda was parked out on Railroad Avenue, so I started for the back shop. A woman's voice called to me before I got past the rest room. I turned to see Fred Engelman's wife, Janie, standing in the open area where the Bourgettes were working.

"Did you want to see me?" I asked, motioning for her to come in.

"Yes. I am. Looking for you," Janie replied in her typical choppy way of speaking. "I need advice."

"You mean to send into Vida's advice column? Just write to her and she'll answer it in the paper."

Janie's eyes darted around, perhaps assessing our damage. "No. About what I saw. At the mall."

"You mean . . . what and when?"

She glanced over her shoulder, presumably to see if Dan and John were eavesdropping. They were both on ladders, so all I could see was their feet. Apparently, Janie felt reassured, though she still kept her voice down. "The shooting. I was there. At the mall."

I realized I hadn't seen either Engelman among the picnickers. It would have been prudent for Blackwell employees to show up for their boss's big speech. Jack was the type who counted heads.

"You saw . . . what?" I asked.

Janie nodded. "A man. Climbing a ladder. On top of the building. Carrying something. In a long case."

She paused for so long that I thought she'd run out of words. "What did you see next?" I finally asked.

"Nothing." She blinked several times. "I wanted to buy socks. The store was closed. I left."

"What did the man look like?"

"Medium. Dark clothes. Baseball cap. Back was turned." She shrugged.

"Did you hear the shot?"

"No."

"What time was it when you saw him?"

"Four? Maybe five. Later, maybe. My watch broke."

I was beginning to think Janie's brain had broken, too. But she wasn't as stupid as her strange speech patterns suggested. "Why didn't you tell the sheriff?"

"I've been gone. My sister got sick. In Mukilteo." She scowled. "Should I?"

I glanced at my own watch. It was one minute to five. "He's probably leaving about now. But you really should talk to him or one of his deputies tomorrow, Janie."

She thought about it for almost a minute. "I'll see. Goodbye."

I watched her wander out through the open area, stop on the sidewalk, look up at the Bourgettes, and stroll leisurely out into traffic. Brakes screeched, horns honked, and somebody cussed in a startled voice. Janie kept walking until she got to the other curb.

Maybe she *was* as stupid as she sounded. Shaking my head, I went into the back shop and out the door.

Milo got home twenty minutes after I did. His kiss was perfunctory. There was no sign of the Dutch Star at the RV park, he informed me. Before I could comment, he went off to change clothes. I resumed peeling potatoes. I was thawing lamb steaks in the microwave when my husband reentered the kitchen.

"I couldn't get hold of Fred Engelman," Milo said, taking glasses out of the cupboard. "Maybe he's still roaming the woods on the tractor."

While my husband made drinks, I recounted my visit from Janie Engelman and what she claimed to have seen at the mall.

Milo ran a hand over his forehead. "I'll be damned if I know how Fred was able to quit drinking after he and Janie got back together last year. I always figured she was what drove him to drink in the first place."

"She's a quirky talker," I allowed, putting the lamb steaks in the oven. "Let's sit. It was a long day."

We settled into our usual places. Milo lighted a cigarette before asking what I thought of Janie's eyewitness account.

"It's a muddle," I admitted. "Translating what she says is always problematical. Her sense of time is vague and her description of the guy is sketchy."

Milo looked thoughtful. "Did she see the rifle?"

"No. She only described the long case he was carrying."

"Right." Milo sipped from his drink. "Hell, it could've been a workman with tools."

"On Labor Day?"

"He was laboring," my husband said with a straight face.

"You don't believe that."

"Hey — I have to consider possibilities, including Janie being nuts."

I decided to give up that argument. "Fine. What I really want to know is if you found out anything new about the explosion."

Milo's expression was disparaging. "If I had, I would've told you."

"Sometimes you do and sometimes you don't. I guess I won't tell you the latest about Kay Burns."

"Is she conspiring to off Blackwell?" Milo sounded hopeful.

"No." I paused. "What if . . . ?" I let the idea dangle.

My husband looked thoughtful. "I know what you're thinking, but I doubt Kay's involved in trying to shoot Black Jack. That'd be too easy on the bastard. She wants to bring him down by humiliating him. Whatever she does, she'll do it publicly, which is why she's using you."

The last words stung. "She *is* using me," I murmured. "I wonder if this is payback for telling her I knew Ren Rawlings was her daughter."

Milo shrugged. "You couldn't blame her for keeping it a secret, especially since Blackwell's her father. Hell, if Kay hadn't left Jack before she had the kid, Ren would've grown up here in Alpine instead of being put up for adoption."

"You're right," I said. "Kay only had one other child by a different husband. The son and his family live over in Leavenworth. I suppose she sees them quite often since she moved back here. Blackwell's rotten temper has screwed up a lot of lives."

"Damned right," Milo agreed. "Which should give us plenty of suspects who might have wanted to off the guy. Except it doesn't. I can't think of anybody around here who qualifies. The only one who seems out to get the SOB is Ms. Compton, and she just got here."

I heard the oven timer go off. "Save the rest of your musings for dinner. We're eating in five minutes."

"That means ten," Milo said. "Maybe I'll have another cigarette."

"You're trying to quit, remember?"

"After the last week, I'm trying to forget,"

he shot back.

"I have quit," I said over my shoulder as I went into the kitchen.

"No, you haven't," Milo called after me. "You're just in one of your non-smoking lulls."

I refused to argue. And, to my dismay, I'd put the lamb steaks in to bake, but forgotten to turn on the oven. After I turned the dial, I gritted my teeth and leaned against the door to the living room.

"Make that fifteen minutes," I said sheepishly.

Milo didn't bother to look up from the *Sports Illustrated* he was reading. "Twenty," he muttered.

I didn't argue about that, either.

We didn't discuss the current investigation again that night. In fact, we didn't talk much at all. I remembered to turn on Vida's program, but for once she was out of her element. The first half of the fifteen-minute "chat," as Spencer Fleetwood liked to call it, went back to Evan Singer's arrival fourteen years earlier. She queried him about how his love of movies had won over his grandfather, Oscar Nyquist, owner of the Whistling Marmot Movie Theatre. After the commercial break, Vida launched into the subject of how fortunate Evan was, having been born into an upper-middle-class family in Seattle but eventually settling in Alpine. He adroitly derailed her by soliciting listeners' suggestions for what SkyCo cinema buffs would like to see in the January film festival.

After we were in bed, I asked Milo if he felt okay. He'd nodded off once during Vida's show and twice later in the evening.

"Yeah," he said, wrapping his arms around me. "It's been busy the last few days. At least the tourists should be gone after this weekend."

"School's started," I remarked vaguely, twisting around to look at him. "Are you sure that's all?"

I felt as well as heard him sigh. "I ran into Doc Dewey today. He and Elvis Sung still need another doctor. I need two deputies. But we're both out of luck because Blackwell and the two daffy old coots won't spend the county's money. It's damned frustrating. Gerry and I haven't had a vacation in almost two years."

"I know. You two didn't get to take your fishing trip. And we never had a honeymoon."

"Are you sorry you married me?"

I laughed. "Since I'd never been married before, the concept eluded me."

"You were going to go on a honeymoon with Cavanaugh."

"Only if we got married in the first place. He was killed instead."

"Hell of a way to avoid getting married."

"That's mean. You told me you never thought Tom would get around to marrying me even though our son was almost thirty by then."

"I was right."

"I hate you."

"That's okay." Milo hugged me tighter. "God, I'm glad I married you. Tricia would've made me sleep in the garage."

"I wouldn't have a garage if it hadn't been for you."

Milo was quiet for a moment or two. "It's that damned Blackwell," he finally said. "I feel as if he's waiting to pounce. I've felt like that since he became county commissioner."

"I know. There's got to be a way. . . ." I stopped.

"A way to what?" Milo finally asked.

"I don't know," I admitted. "But when I figure it out, I'll tell you."

"Maybe you shouldn't," he said in a serious tone. "You can be a cunning little devil when you want to get your way."

"Never with you."

"No. No," he repeated, with a sigh that evoked contentment.

I fell asleep in his arms.

To my great relief, the Bourgettes were already on-site when I arrived at eight o'clock Friday morning. Not only was the new wall finished, but the front door was usable, though the broken glass hadn't yet been replaced. Evan couldn't get around to it until Harvey's Hardware opened at nine-thirty. John and Dan wanted me to choose a paint color. I told them I wanted to stick with brown. It fit well with the other un-imaginative storefronts on Front Street. I cringed at the memory of the yellow paint job Ed Bronsky had let a movie company use on our building when he was still ad manager. The connotation of "yellow" and "journalism" had evaded Ed in the same way that the meaning of the word "work" did.

Mitch was already in the front office, hav-ing been assigned to the bakery run. "No Italian slippers," he complained. "I should've called to tell them they're my ad-diction."

"Remind whoever has Monday's turn to get some," I advised. "The Upper Crust often has Italian slippers to kick off the

313

week." I winced at my unintended pun, but my reporter didn't notice. He was probably still lamenting the lack of his favorite pastry.

Vida and Leo arrived together, though not amicably. They were, in fact, arguing.

"Really, I can't know everything," she declared, one hand adjusting the brim of her straw hat with its magenta band and matching rose. "How would I know what became of Ronnie Davis after someone supposedly tried to run him down?"

Leo shrugged. "Where's your nephew Deputy Bill when you need him?" he asked in an innocent voice.

"Billy is not obligated to tell me everything that —" Vida stopped, noticing that Mitch and I were present. "Well now, we have an outer wall. That will definitely go into next week's 'Scene,' self-serving or not."

Apparently Leo had also dropped the argument. "Lemon-filled bear claws," he noted. "Try not to eat all of them, Laskey. It's unfair that you never gain weight."

Seeing Kip come in from the back shop, I went into my office. I usually waited until my staff had gotten their goodies before I checked out what was left over. Besides, I needed more caffeine to become fully alert. I was still staring at my blank monitor when Mitch appeared with a raspberry bear claw and a mug of coffee.

"What did happen to that Davis guy?" he asked. "The last I heard was after he asked Leo for help."

"That's all I know," I replied. "If he was hired as a pollster, it must've been a temporary gig. Check him out. He's supposed to be working for Blackwell, but you can use the newcomer angle. He's staying at the Lumberjack Motel."

"Speaking of Blackwell," Mitch said after swallowing a chunk of bear claw, "how come we don't have any spies working for him?"

"Because he runs a company that's the local economy's backbone," I replied. "I've never criticized his business acumen. That's why I'm surprised somebody apparently took a shot at him. Trust me — if Milo or I could find out anything detrimental, it'd make news."

Mitch looked thoughtful. "There's always something that's off. There was in Detroit."

"This is Alpine," I said with an ironic little smile.

My reporter didn't look convinced. "Human nature doesn't check population statistics. Are you sure you don't know someone who works for Blackwell who wouldn't rat you out if you asked a few questions?"

"I doubt any of his employees would

complain to us," I said. "Jobs are too hard to find around here. Hold off. Maybe we can back-door this."

Mitch glanced into the newsroom. "Vida?"

"Younger." I gestured at Alison, who'd entered the newsroom with a FedEx delivery for Leo.

"Good luck," Mitch said, looking as if he thought Alison or I would need it. I figured we both would.

Ten minutes later, when my phone rang I didn't recognize the male caller's voice. "I want to see you in my office at eleven o'clock," the man said.

Maybe it was a wrong number. "I'm sorry. Who is this?"

"Iain Farrell," he replied, sounding impatient. "We'll converse when you get here." He hung up. I felt as if I'd been talking to Milo.

I stared at the receiver for so long that I didn't realize Leo was in the doorway staring at me. "You look miffed," he said, sitting down. "Don't tell me it's an irate reader."

"That I can handle," I assured him. "Dr. Farrell is another matter. Have you ever had to deal with him?"

"Just a brief encounter for RestHaven's

316

opening last February," Leo replied. "He was terse, but that was fine with me. I only wanted a heads-up on his photo in the double-truck ad they took out for the special edition. He okayed it despite the fact that he looked like a werewolf. I haven't seen Farrell since."

"That image suits him," I said. "He wants to see me. I suspect it's about him joining forces with Kay Burns for the domestic violence series she agreed to help us put together."

Leo wore his off-center grin. "Is Farrell in favor of domestic violence? It probably gets more patients for RestHaven."

"I don't think they have to solicit patients. Which is interesting, now that I think about it." I gave Leo a quizzical look. "They must rely on referrals. Why would people outside of the greater Seattle metro area come eighty-five miles away from their homes and families to be treated for dependencies or medical rehab?"

Leo lifted a bushy eyebrow. "Because they want to get away from their families? Maybe they drove them to drink in the first place. When I was in my days of Scotch and roses, I drove on autopilot. It's a miracle I didn't kill myself or somebody else when I was at the wheel. Did you tell me Rosalie Reed had her practice on Seattle's Eastside?"

"Yes, that's where Spence met her. They've gone public since Rosalie's husband died."

Leo nodded. "Maybe she recruits patients from the greater Seattle metro area. Some of our advertisers have mentioned that Rosalie and Spence shop together. They bought a new bed for her condo at Parc Pines. Queen-sized."

"She didn't need that for her husband while he was a mental patient at Rest-Haven," I pointed out. "The poor guy had problems even before Rosalie came here."

"In some weird kind of way Spence and Rosalie seem right as a couple," Leo said. "I figured him to go for a flashier type. I always wondered if he put the make on you."

"Never," I declared. "We have no chemistry. And I'm not flashy."

"You've got dash, if not flash."

I laughed. "Save the flattery for advertisers. Speaking of which, how are we doing?"

"Getting there." His green-flecked eyes danced. "Why don't I ask Blackwell if he'd like to buy a bigger ad to show that somebody taking a shot at him only makes him more macho?"

"I like it. Go ahead."

Leo rapped his knuckles on my desk. "I will. I'll go see him now." He stood up. "If I don't come back in a couple of hours, call the sheriff. Or maybe he wouldn't care if Black Jack broke my neck."

"Yes, he would," I asserted. "He knows I need your ad revenue. He got over being jealous of you a long time ago."

"Right. Dodge figured I was harmless." For a fleeting moment, Leo looked wistful. "I guess I was. But now it doesn't matter."

I smiled. "You got Liza back. Maybe you never really lost her."

Leo looked up at my low ceiling. "Maybe. But I lost myself for a long time. Liza's tougher than I am. Thank God."

Later that morning I was still arguing with myself about obeying Iain Farrell's insolent summons. But as a journalist, I couldn't let my emotions dismiss a news source. I decided to take off for RestHaven.

I paused at the reception desk to tell Alison where I was going. She was on the phone, but pointed at the new pebbled glass in the front door. I went outside, where Evan Singer was getting on his bicycle.

"Looks good," I called to him. "Did you give Alison your bill?"

Evan, who had never quite outgrown giving the impression that he was all gangly arms and legs, grinned. "No. I'm not charging you. I want to see you and the sheriff at the opening of my film festival in January. I'm kicking off with *High Noon.* I've never seen Dodge at the Marmot since I took it over. He owes me."

"I'll do what I can," I promised. "It'd be our first movie date."

"That's a deal. I haven't seen you there, either."

I winced. "We don't get out much."

"You two were at the picnic, but I never had a chance to say hello," Evan said, waving a long arm at Ronnie Blatt in his UPS truck. "I got involved helping Rosie round up some of her nieces and nephews. Those Bourgettes are a lively bunch. I haven't been around children that young since *I* was a kid."

I asked Evan my obvious question. "Were you in the crowd when the young man got shot?"

"No," he replied. "Rosie and I figured the kids would be a distraction during the speeches. We herded them down to the river so they could splash around for a while before they ate. Bad idea. Some poor girl was crying her eyes out. Rosie tried to talk to her, but she told us to get lost. So we did."

"Do you know who it was?"

Evan shook his head. "No clue. Rosie thought she'd seen her before, but couldn't remember where. Maybe she lives somewhere else along Highway 2. There were several people at the picnic I didn't recognize."

The cast iron clock tower by the bank showed 10:58. After thanking Evan for his artistry with the window glass, I told him I was off to a meeting. He hopped onto his bike and pedaled away before I could get into my Honda. I pulled into RestHaven's parking lot at 11:05. If Farrell pitched a fit over my tardiness, he could unload on *his* shrink. But the guy was so arrogant that he probably counseled himself.

Remembering where Farrell's office was located off the atrium that had once been the Bronsky family's indoor barbecue pit and bowling alley, I kept going. I was almost there when I heard someone call to me. Turning my head, I saw Sid Almquist coming my way.

"Ms. . . . ?" he began, apparently forgetting my name. "Did you check in at the desk?"

"I didn't know I had to," I said. "I haven't been here for a while. I'm Emma Lord from the newspaper. We met a couple of months ago."

Sid's thin face looked embarrassed. "Sorry, Ms. Lord. I knew you looked familiar, but . . ." He offered me what passed for an apologetic smile. "You came to see . . . ?"

"Dr. Farrell." I gestured to my right. "Isn't his office over there?"

"Yes, but you'll have to sign in," Sid said. "We've tightened up things around here lately. It's for the sake of the patients, of course."

I figured if they got any tighter, visitors would have to receive engraved invitations before they could get into the facility. "Okay, fine. Thanks, Sid."

I went over to the redheaded young man at the desk and signed in. Two minutes later, I entered Iain Farrell's office. He looked up from a sheaf of papers and glared at me. "You're late."

"Security detained me," I said, not waiting for him to offer me a chair, but plopping down across from his sleek mahogany desk. "Sid's memory for faces needs work."

Farrell looked perplexed. "Why should he remember you?"

I hesitated, not wanting to get Sid in trouble. He and his family had been through hard times several years ago after Blackwell had bought out the old Cascade & Pacific Mill and fired Sid along with everybody

322

else. But what had popped into my mind was that a security guard should remember faces. I stared at Farrell. "Why do you care?"

He arched one of his black eyebrows before picking up a pale blue file folder. "Let's move on. We've already lost valuable time. I've put together an essay on domestic abuse. I assume you prefer a hard copy."

It wasn't a question, so I didn't answer. We locked gazes for an instant before he handed over the folder. I thanked him.

"Of course," Farrell said, no longer looking at me but at his desk calendar. Maybe he was hoping his next appointment would be someone whose company he enjoyed. "Do you understand domestic abuse?" he asked, now staring beyond my left shoulder.

"Legally? Or in depth?"

"In any way." Finally he looked directly at me. "Did your father beat your mother? Did your parents beat you?"

I stifled a smile. "My parents were smart enough to devise other forms of punishment. Depriving us of things or activities was their disciplinary method."

"You were fortunate," Farrell said somberly. "Many children of your — of our — generation were not. Savage beatings were common. Often those heinous practices become a cruel legacy."

I had to ask the question. "Do you have children, Dr. Farrell?"

He looked faintly startled. "No. I never married. Why do you ask?"

"I just wondered if you did, how you'd raised them." I shrugged. "But you don't deal with children in the rehab unit, correct?"

"No. We deal only with adults of legal age who have alcohol and drug dependencies." He cleared his throat. "We've gotten off-topic. You realize there are many forms of abuse — physical, emotional, sexual, and economic. You may dismiss economic abuse as less likely to occur in a First World country such as the United States, but I assure you that's not the case. As you might surmise, the male is usually the abuser. Inner cities and isolated communities are prime examples." Farrell paused, presumably for breath.

"Communities such as Alpine?" I said, for lack of anything more cogent. Frankly, I wasn't sure where his diatribe was going.

"Yes, a classic situation." Farrell leaned forward. "Isolated, small population, timber town, lost its economic base in the eighties, struggling to survive ever since. I wasn't aware of all those factors when I accepted the job. But the environment is perfect for my project."

"Which is?" I asked.

Farrell sat back, stroking the chair's upholstered arms as if they were cats. "You wouldn't understand."

"Probably not," I agreed. "That's a pity. Then I can't explain what you're submitting to me. My readers and I would need an interpreter. I'm afraid I've wasted your time — and mine." I clutched my purse, preparing to stand up.

"You can't be serious." His black eyes widened and his skin darkened as he took umbrage to new heights. "How can an ignorant, uneducated readership learn unless you study all of my works so that you can present them in a language they can understand?"

I was on my feet. "They understand English. Save your academic treatises for your erudite peer group. They'll appreciate your expertise. My readers would not."

I stomped out of his office and didn't bother to slam the door behind me. It was only after I reached the exit that I wondered why Farrell hadn't uttered a parting sally. Maybe he was overcome by someone disagreeing with him. At RestHaven, he was surrounded by congenial peers and pliant patients. He didn't seem to socialize much.

If he had, Vida or I would have heard about it. By the time I got to the parking lot, I stopped trying to figure out Iain Farrell and focus on my own motives.

That's when I realized I'd shot myself in the foot.

CHAPTER 14

Alison stared when I came through the door. "You look bummed. What's wrong?"

"I screwed up with RestHaven's Iain Farrell," I said, leaning on the counter. "It's not the first time, but now I've probably pissed off their PR person, Kay Burns. And that means I've lost a source, maybe two. That's never a good thing." I paused, switching gears. "Are you seeing Heather Bavich at the ski lodge on your lunch hour?"

"I thought I would, but won't she be busy playing hostess?"

"Not for lunch. She only has to do that for the dinner crowd. You'll find her in the office or at the front desk. Have you met her?"

"Yes. Justin and I ate there a few times. Heather seemed nice. She's pregnant."

I nodded. "It's their second child. And before you ask, Heather is in her midthirties and has been married less than five years."

Alison's eyes grew wide. "What was wrong with her?"

"Nothing. She was having a good time being single. Give it a shot, Alison."

"You must think I'm a total dweeb," she lamented. "If only there were more eligible men around here." She paused. "Hey — is L.J. still at the ski lodge?"

"As far as I know," I said. "I haven't talked to the sheriff since he got to work."

Alison's face had brightened. "Maybe I will go chat up Heather."

The mention of the sheriff reminded me that I hadn't asked Mitch if he'd noted anything of interest on his visit to headquarters. I managed to catch him just as he was leaving to have lunch at home with Brenda.

"Nothing big," he replied. "A couple of non-local DUIs, possible prowler on River Road, a domestic abuse call that turned out to be one of those 'no harm, no foul' reports."

"Okay, it all sounds pretty tame."

"Right." Mitch put on his sport coat. "The only thing about the abuse call is that Mullins mentioned it was the third or fourth one at that address in the last few weeks. But when a deputy showed up, it was the same old story. Makes you wonder, doesn't it?"

"Yes," I agreed. "Did Mullins say who called?"

Mitch shook his head. "I didn't ask since we never print names unless charges are pressed."

"True. Say hello to Brenda for me."

"I will." He ambled out of the newsroom. I went into my office and called the sheriff's direct line. "What now?" he growled, obviously having seen the *Advocate*'s number come up on his Caller ID.

"Gosh, you sound like you're grouchy," I said. "And just when I was thinking of treating you to lunch."

"You mean at home?" Suddenly he didn't sound so crabby.

"No, Sheriff. I don't do nooners. The Burger Barn is as erotic as it gets when I'm *at work*. Which is why I'm calling. Who was involved in those repeat domestic disturbances?"

"Why do you care?" Milo retorted, back to being grumpy. "You never run names."

"Because — as I told you — I'm planning a series on the subject," I explained, reining in my own temper. "I'm curious about the type of victim who gets beat up and never files a complaint. I call it research."

"Shit. Let me check . . . Okay, it's on Disappointment Avenue," Milo said, sounding almost civil. "Mickey O'Neill and Yvonne Mertz. Mickey has two or ten beers and beats up his girlfriend. When the bleeding stops and he sobers up, she forgives him. Sad, but typical. Hey, I like that idea of a nooner. Want to try it?"

"No, I don't. But I'll meet you at the Burger Barn."

"No, you won't. I'm eating in. I'm busy." He hung up.

I'd forgotten to ask my jerk of a husband if he knew what had happened to the other Dodges. I'd assumed they would've returned last night from visiting Clint's old friends. But with the Dutch Star, they weren't concerned with figuring out where to sleep while they were on the road. Their bed was always with them.

Having been rejected by Milo, I no longer was in the mood for a burger. Maybe Vida would like to have lunch at the Venison Inn. I looked into the newsroom, but she'd already left. Leo was also gone. I decided to drive to Pie-in-the-Sky at the mall.

Being more alert than when I'd arrived at work, I paused to take in the *Advocate*'s new facade. It looked much like the old one, except cleaner.

The first person I saw when I entered Pie-

330

in-the-Sky was Patti Marsh. She didn't look pleased to see me. I returned the feeling.

"Hi, Patti," I said as I got in line behind her. "They're busy today."

She wasn't in a mood for pleasantries. "That ornery SOB you married had a lot of nerve busting Jack at the picnic. He'd just damned near gotten killed! I bet Dodge would have cheered if the bullet had hit my guy."

"Charges had been filed against Jack," I said, keeping my voice down and wondering if Patti was sober. It was only early afternoon, but that made no difference. "It was Dwight Gould who arrested your guy."

"Gould!" Patti spat out the name. "He's still screwing Kay, isn't he? Why? It's been a hundred years since they were married."

I refused comment. "Kay hasn't dropped the charges. If Jack hadn't posted bail, he'd still be locked up."

"That skank Kay can't prove squat," Patti asserted with a toss of her short, gilded hair. "She's still pissy because Jack got tired of her so fast after she dumped Gould. And her with six husbands!"

"Not quite six," I said, moving up in line. "I didn't see you at the picnic. How come?"

Patti turned her heavily made-up face away from me, apparently to study the

331

menu on the blackboard that hung over the serving area. "I had that one-day bug that's going around. It always starts up when the kids go back to school."

"They didn't go back until after Labor Day," I pointed out.

"You know what I mean," Patti retorted. "Labor Day weekend. School starts. What difference does it make?"

I shrugged. "None. You recovered. That's the main thing."

Patti looked suspicious. "Is that sarcasm?"

"No. Hey, it's your turn."

"Oh! Right." Patti, whose attention span was shorter than a gnat's, turned to the dimpled young woman behind the counter. I heard her ask for a blueberry pie and a cherry pie. As the clerk boxed up her order, Patti spoke to me over her shoulder. "I don't bake anymore, but Jack doesn't know that. If you see him, don't let on, okay?"

"Sure, Patti." As she turned away, I shook my head. I was used to her mercurial mood swings. But what planet was she living on where she thought Blackwell and I ever had a civil conversation? I suppose a woman who put up with his physical and verbal abuse could deceive herself about a lot of things.

Patti picked up the pies. "Remember," she

whispered, "mum's the word."

"Got it," I murmured as she headed out of the shop.

I couldn't help feeling sorry for her. Patti was living in her own version of pie-in-the-sky.

I'd just finished my pastrami and Havarti on light rye when Mitch returned from lunching at home with Brenda. I asked how she was getting along with her weaving.

"Good," he said, leaning on the back of one of my visitor chairs. "She feels better when she's busy and her mind — as well as her hands — are occupied. She's getting some local orders lately. Leo's idea for a classified ad in the paper is paying off. Except," he added with a self-deprecating smile, "he wouldn't let me pay for it."

I laughed. "His generosity extends only to fellow staffers. I'm indebted to him. After Ed Bronsky quit when he inherited money, Leo single-handedly saved the paper from going under. What also helped was the community college opening here. The downturn in the logging industry had almost sunk the entire county."

Mitch nodded. "If only something could've saved Detroit when the auto industry tanked. Say . . . do you know where the sheriff went a few minutes ago?"

"No. I know he was eating in. Where was he headed?"

"Toward Alpine Way," Mitch replied. "He didn't have on the flasher or the siren, but he pulled out pretty damned fast."

"Check in with him later." I smiled apologetically. "I'm clueless."

My phone rang. Mitch took his cue and went into the newsroom.

"Emma," Alison said in a breathless voice. "Guess what? I didn't talk to Heather Bavich at the ski lodge because I ran into L.J. right after I got here. I had lunch with him and his mother in the King Olav dining room. Ms. Compton's incredible!"

"You mean," I asked, "how she's holding up regarding her daughter's murder?"

"I'm not sure she's dealt with it on an emotional level. She's internalizing it, I guess, maybe channeling everything to find out who killed Gemma. I told her I worked for the newspaper, so . . . well, I never let on to L.J. that I wasn't a reporter. He and Ms. Compton both think . . . hold on."

I waited for what seemed like more than a minute, but probably wasn't that long.

"The sheriff just came in," Alison said, speaking very fast. "I'm in the lobby. Ms. Compton asked to see him. Is it okay if I don't come back right away?"

"Yes, of course. But be careful."

Alison giggled. "Why? Won't Dodge protect me?"

"Yes, but only while he's at the ski lodge. I mean it. Okay?"

"Sure. Got to fly." She rang off.

I'd barely put down the phone when Vida tromped into my office. "It's one-fifteen. Where's Alison? I saw her leave for lunch a bit early. Is she ill?"

"She's out restocking the reception area. A few things got broken." I hated lying to Vida, but I didn't want her to know that Alison was sleuthing. Up until the last year my House & Home editor had been my partner in nosing around local homicides. However, the more recent victims had been outsiders. Vida lost interest when the deceased had no apparent ties to her beloved Alpine.

"What things?" she demanded, leaning both hands on the desk and pinioning me with her penetrating gray eyes. "You're hedging."

I surrendered. "Sit. You know she's got a huge crush on the good-looking guy whose sister was murdered." I saw Vida nod just once as she settled onto a visitor chair. "Ms. Compton arrived. She appears to have taken a proactive stance in the investigation. Even now, Milo is meeting with them at the ski lodge."

Vida fiddled with the tassel on her royal blue velvet cloche. "Is that wise? Of Alison, I mean. She's very young and woefully inexperienced."

"She's smart," I said. "I think that in some ways she's mature for her age." *Except when it comes to men.* But I didn't say that out loud. "Maybe having her birth mother murdered made her grow up faster."

"Perhaps," Vida allowed. She stood up, shaking out her sky-blue pleated skirt. "I hope Alison knows what she's doing. I'll have to talk to her to make sure. Young people have very little judgment when it comes to so many things. Especially dealing with other people."

"That's how they learn," I said.

"Perhaps." With a swish of pleats, Vida departed.

Alison returned just after one-thirty. "I didn't want Mrs. Runkel to get out the thumbscrews," she confided in a low voice. "I went down the hall and through the back shop to get here."

"She's on the phone now," I said. "Well?"

"Ms. Compton is . . ." Alison paused, searching for the right word. "Indomitable?"

I looked at her curiously.

"Of course she's grieving over her daughter, but she's focused on bringing the killer to justice. The sheriff came to see her."

"How did his meeting go with her?"

"I don't know," Alison replied. "She left King Olav's to meet him in their suite. By the time I got back to our table, she and Dodge were gone. L.J. and I were alone." She smiled. "He told me to call him Larry."

"That's . . . nice. Why not L.J.?"

"He said that's only for professional purposes," Alison explained, now serious. "There are two other Larrys who work at Micron and they've been there longer. But he must've quit if he's working for Blackwell."

Milo had told me about the Jennings twins coming here as a research project for Gemma's travel book, but I was convinced that Ms. Compton had sent those postcards to Kay and Jennifer. The business card L.J. had left at the Venison Inn might mean he was still a Micron employee. I told Alison I didn't know what to believe.

"It *is* confusing," she allowed. "But I can't believe L.J. — that is, Larry — is dishonest."

"Face it, Alison," I said, "you don't really know the guy."

"I'm getting there." Alison looked faintly pugnacious.

"Relax," I urged. "Ms. Compton will take Larry back home with her. You're smart, you're pretty, and whether you believe it or not, you're too young to worry about finding a husband. Enjoy your freedom. When I was your age, I was in no rush to get married."

"You already had a son," Alison said. "Didn't you want to find someone to be a father to Adam?"

"He had a father. He just wasn't around when Adam was growing up. My brother filled the role."

She seemed to sense she should back off. "That was good for all of you."

"It was. As a priest, Ben may be called Father, but he earned the title as his nephew's role model."

Alison nodded. "Adam must've admired Ben a lot."

"He did," I agreed. "Adam seems very satisfied with his vocation."

Alison stood up. Maybe she realized she was treading on foreign territory. "I'd better get back out front."

I smiled. "Go for it." The truth was that I hadn't been happy when my son revealed he was going to study for the priesthood.

Never having had the typical family with a dad and husband in residence while I raised Adam, I'd looked forward to him creating his own family. Instead, he'd chosen the Church and celibacy. The only bright spot was that I might become a step-grandmother to Milo's grandchildren. Assuming his children had any, of course. So far only his son, Brandon, was married. The ceremony had taken place less than a month ago. Tricia and the mother of the bride had been on hand along with two grandmothers. I'd felt like excess baggage. Maybe I was too touchy. I was still getting used to being a wife. The price for unconventionality didn't come cheap.

The rest of the afternoon passed without crises, histrionics, or disasters such as another bomb sailing through the window above where Vida sat at her new, if used, desk. She and Leo had found a suitable replacement at Goodwill during the lunch hour.

"It's maple," Vida said as she gathered up her belongings just before five. "Very solid. The new chair is secondhand as well. The real loss, of course, is the recipe file. I'll start replenishing it over the weekend with some of my own recipes. I still have quite a few of my mother's. She did such clever things with Jell-O."

I refrained from asking what — or how. In fact, *why* might have been the most pertinent question. Instead, I said I hoped she'd have a relaxing weekend. That was probably wishful thinking on my part. The concept of my redoubtable House & Home editor withdrawing from the world to take her ease was unimaginable. Frankly, I couldn't envision her in retirement. Maybe she'd change her mind. Her job provided an excuse for prying into the lives of her fellow Alpiners. Vida was in her midseventies, but I'd seen no signs of her slowing down, nor had she added more than a few wrinkles since I'd met her in 1989. She had no urge to travel and her only hobby was gardening. Buck Bardeen occasionally visited his offspring in other parts of the country, but otherwise he seemed content to keep close to home. As a career Air Force officer, he swore he'd seen it all. Maybe he and Vida would finally get married. And maybe pigs would fly.

Alison was leaving just as I came into the reception area. I asked if she had plans for the weekend.

"Larry called a while ago to ask me to dinner with him and his mother," she said as we exited the office. "I wish he could have stayed with the original invitation for just us."

I pointed out that he could hardly do otherwise under the circumstances.

Alison made a face. "Right, I get it. Ms. Compton's not only overwhelming, but super opinionated."

"Some people are both," I said. "But once you get to know them, they have other, more appealing qualities." But that was before I met Ms. Compton.

Traffic on Front Street was heavy — for Front Street. Several drivers slowed down by our office, probably to check out our new facade. That was an item for Vida's "Scene."

"Hey, Alison," I said as she started to get into the Audi, "check in with me this weekend, okay?"

She shielded her eyes from the sun over Temple Mountain. "You mean if I find out anything amazing?"

"Yes, of course. But," I added, moving closer and lowering my voice as an older couple from St. Mildred's passed by, "I want to make sure you're safe. Let Lori know what you're up to, okay?"

Alison laughed. "You sound like my mother. They're back from the ocean. Maybe I'll drive over Sunday to see them."

"Good idea," I said. "Say hi to them for me."

I got into my Honda and rolled down the window on the driver's side. The day had turned surprisingly warm. Officially, it was still summer. Before global warming, snow had come to Alpine as early as August. According to Vida, old-timers recalled years when there had only been two months without a snowfall. In winter, the accumulation was sometimes eight feet deep. Sepia-toned photos showed the houses perched on uneven ground like mountain goats, with front and back at different levels. There had been no road into Alpine back then. Access was only by train. The town's early residents — some two hundred and fifty of them — had been a hardy, close-knit, and resourceful bunch.

The phone was ringing when I entered our log cabin via the kitchen. I rushed into the living room, but the call had gone to voice mail. I waited for whoever it was to leave a message before picking up the receiver. Father Dennis Kelly's mellow voice informed me that the parish council planned to hold a Thanksgiving dinner for people who were alone for the holiday or unable to afford a traditional turkey meal. He apologized for not calling during office hours, but he'd had a crisis.

The holiday dinner was worthy of mention, but Father Den's "crisis" smacked of news. I called him right back and asked if he'd resolved his problem.

"Another poor girl who needed sanctuary from a man," Den replied wearily. "I just got back from taking her to the shelter at the Alpine Hotel. There must be a dozen women staying there right now, and half of them aren't even from Skykomish County."

"They want to make sure the jerks can't find them," I said. "I'll interview some of the victims at the shelter before I write the domestic abuse series. I know you can't give me names, but was this latest one a local?"

"A recent local," Den replied after a pause. "Cradle Catholic, but currently not practicing her faith. Young, vulnerable, pathetic. She spent the night in one of those shacks out on River Road. No money, either."

"A runaway?" I asked.

"No. She's of age, though barely. Her account's garbled, but I think she's from somewhere along the Highway 2 corridor. I got the impression she was living with a relative before she came to Alpine." He uttered a sigh. "We middle-class Americans, especially around here, like to pretend the

343

lower class merely doesn't have as big an income as we do. We ignore the poor, the ignorant, the uneducated. For a black man, I sometimes lack a social conscience. Damn, Emma," he sighed, "I didn't mean to deliver a homily."

"If you can remember what you just said, work it into this week's sermon," I responded. "You've already got me feeling sorry for her. Maybe I should stop by the shelter tomorrow to start my interviews."

"I just blew the poor girl's cover," Den said in faint dismay. "Can you feign amnesia?"

I heard Milo come into the kitchen. "I'd never use names in such a touchy a series."

"Understood. But if you want to interview me, you can use mine."

"I plan to do that," I assured him. "I'll call you to set up a time next week." We rang off just as my husband came into the living room and flopped into the easy chair.

"A time for what?" Milo asked. "You got a rendezvous with your lover?"

I gave him a dirty look. "I can't even get my lover to kiss me when he comes home."

"You were on the phone. I figured it was business."

I got up from the sofa. "It was. I was talking to Father Den about the battered spouse series. He had, in fact, just come back from hauling another poor female off to the shelter."

"I don't suppose he told you who it was."

"He never does." The query made me curious. "Why do you ask?"

He shrugged. "Just curious. Frankly, I wish the shelter hadn't been moved from the old Doukas house, but the damned thing was falling down. Having it in the hotel is a security problem. We get at least one call every couple of weeks about a husband or a boyfriend who shows up trying to find the woman he's turned into a victim. Most of the volunteers from your church are older and can't fend off those bastards. Then we get called in. It's a damned nuisance."

"Isn't that your job, Sheriff?"

"It wasn't as big a problem with a house," Milo asserted. "Easier to secure. Why can't Kelly hire somebody instead of using volunteers?"

"Because he doesn't have the money," I said, starting for the kitchen. "The county owns the hotel and should come up with funding for it. Maybe they can with the commissioners and Fuzzy going off the dole." I stopped and frowned at my husband. "Why aren't you changing your

345

clothes?"

Milo's face became unreadable, an expression I'd come to know over the years, especially when he was interrogating me about a homicide investigation. "I have to go back to the office."

"I guess there's no point asking why?"

"Right."

"Then I'll start dinner."

"Fine." He picked up the *Sports Illustrated* with its annual NFL preview. "Want to pour me a drink?"

I leaned against the kitchen doorjamb. "Are you serious?"

"Uh . . . I guess not. Never mind. I should be back at headquarters by six-thirty."

I had to make dinner quick and simple. Luckily, Milo liked it that way. A few minutes later, I'd just put the skirt steak in the frying pan when he came into the kitchen and wrapped his arm around my waist.

"Why didn't you run like hell when I asked you to marry me?" he asked as I leaned against him.

"I can't decide what held me back," I said in mock dismay. "Was it your charm or your sensitivity?"

Milo kissed the top of my head. "I still don't know how I finally snagged you."

346

"Stop saying that. I was a real bitch, fooling myself and trying to fool you because I thought Tom Cavanaugh was the only man I could ever really love. If I hadn't been such an idiot, you and I could've gotten married a long time ago."

"You were worth the wait." Milo let go of me. "Maybe I will have a quick shot. You want one?"

"No. Dinner should be ready in ten minutes. Go relax."

I was dishing up when I heard my husband's cell ring. I could only catch a few words at his end of the conversation. As soon as he disconnected, I told him dinner was ready.

"Dare I ask who that was?" I inquired, sitting down at the table.

"Mullins," Milo replied.

"That's all I get?"

"Yep."

"You look worried. Or," I went on, studying his expression, "mad?"

The sheriff sighed wearily. "There's too damned much going on right now. Don't ask."

"Not even about Ms. Compton?"

"Rich women are a pain in the ass, but she's got a right to demand that her daughter's killer is, as she put it, 'brought to

347

justice for his monstrous act.' And she's not exactly pleased about her son getting in the way of a bullet meant for somebody else. Which reminds me, the slug matches the Remington."

"Gosh, that sounds like news," I drawled. Seeing Milo grimace, I switched gears. "I can't blame Ms. Compton. If she sent those postcards, she may feel guilty for Gemma coming here and getting killed."

"She's out of her element in Alpine," Milo replied after devouring a chunk of skirt steak. "This isn't Coeur d'Alene. I get the impression she runs that town. I can see you're still curious. You get one more question."

"Autopsy report?"

"I got it at four-thirty. Manual strangulation causing asphyxia, but didn't break her neck. There were other, minor bruises, indicating she put up a minimal struggle."

"Meaning?"

"It was broad daylight, so she was probably killed at my old house in the downstairs room where Blatt found her," Milo explained, looking as if the words pained him. "I told Tanya to stop kicking herself for leaving the key out for the phony Realtor. She couldn't know it was a trick. Gemma may have gone to the house with her killer or

348

been lured there. It's a damned shame nobody saw them, but there it is."

"It must have been a man, right?"

"Probably," Milo conceded. "The SnoCo ME, Colin Knapp, told me the victim was in good physical shape. He figures she worked out or played sports. She's not as young as you seemed to think. Closer to thirty than twenty is as close as Knapp will say."

"She seemed younger when I saw her at the ski lodge coffee shop," I remarked.

"Looks can fool you," Milo said. "Being rich can't hurt when it comes to wrinkles, but it didn't keep her from getting killed. Gemma was attacked from behind. There were thumbprints on her throat."

I winced. "Ugh. Maybe I shouldn't ask for details. Did you ask why L.J. was handing out Blackwell's circulars?"

"Jennings told me he volunteered because it let him interact with the locals, same as Gemma was doing with her waitress gig. Face it, something's weird about this whole thing. I feel as if I'm being conned."

"You're right," I agreed. "It may be a con, but I can't see you as the target. If Ms. Compton and her kids are from Idaho, who'd be the Alpine pigeon?"

"Beats me," Milo admitted. "My first

choice would be Blackwell, but when somebody tried to shoot him at the picnic, L.J. was not only in plain sight but ended up taking the bullet. Gemma was already dead."

Briefly, we were both silent. "I give up," I said. "At least for now. Any word from your relatives?"

"Oh." Milo grinned. "Not all my news is bad. The Dutch Star's AC stopped working in Bothell. God help Clint and Pootsie if they're not able to travel in total comfort. They're stuck there for at least another couple of days. Clint thought that after they got the thing fixed, they might head into Seattle for a day or so and then drive down I-5 into Oregon and . . . whatever. Maybe we've seen the last of them. You got pie?"

"No. I've got some of those snickerdoodle cookies left, though."

"Aren't they about two weeks old?"

"Approximately," I admitted. "How come you haven't eaten all of them by now?"

The sheriff made a face. "What would my deputies think if they knew I ate something called a snickerdoodle? Besides, they're stale."

"How about some fruit?"

Milo pushed his chair back and stood up. "Are you trying to starve me, woman?"

"No!" I got to my feet. "I'm trying to keep you trim and healthy," I said, coming around the table to put my hand on his arm. "Do you want to get as hefty as your brother?"

The hazel eyes snapped. "Hey — don't start something we can't finish. It's six twenty-five. I'm out of here."

I retreated. "You're a real beast. Do you think I'm trying to —"

His cell went off before I could finish. Milo yanked it out of his pocket and stopped at the door to the garage. "Dodge here," he barked. Then his expression changed to dismay. Or maybe it was disgust. Sometimes I had trouble reading him. "Okay," he said, "I'll handle it. Not that we can do much. It's up to the medics. I'm on my way." He shoved the cell back in his shirt pocket and opened the door.

"Hey!" I yelled. "You can't go off without telling me what happened!"

He started to get into the Yukon. "Shit! Oh, hell . . . some woman tried to off herself at the shelter. She's on her way to the ER." He slammed the SUV's door shut, turned on the engine, and reversed out of the garage at warp speed.

It might have been an emergency call for the sheriff, but it was breaking news for me.

351

I guessed that Milo would head for the Alpine Hotel, but I'd go to the hospital. Ordinarily, I don't chase ambulances. This was different, given the domestic abuse series I was planning. I knew there wasn't much information I could learn from the victim, but I'd get a sense of how the battering cycle could play out into an attempt at self-destruction.

As I turned off Fir to drive down Third, twilight was settling in over Tonga Ridge. At Cascade Street, I passed St. Mildred's, wondering how often Den heard the emergency siren and rushed off to comfort a parishioner. Like Milo, Doc Dewey, and Dr. Sung, my pastor was never off the clock. To a lesser extent, neither was I.

I pulled into the loading zone on Cedar. After having gotten a ticket last February for parking there, I'd taken Milo's advice and obtained a permit. I hadn't heard a siren since leaving home, so I assumed the patient had arrived. I went inside and headed for the ER.

To my surprise, Alison and Lori were in the waiting room. I hurried over to where they were sitting by the aquarium. "Who's sick?" I asked, keeping my voice down.

"I am," Lori said in a feeble voice. "I should never have come back to work so soon. I think I've got pneumonia." She turned away and coughed, as if to prove it.

Alison looked peeved. "I tried to tell her to stay home Tuesday, but she wouldn't listen. I don't nag. Why are you here? Are you sick, too?"

"No, this is business." I glanced at an older couple who were sitting a half dozen chairs away. "I'm following a possible story lead. I'll tell you about it later."

Before I could make my getaway to the ER ambulance entrance, a nurse I didn't recognize summoned Lori. Both young women stood up.

"I'm coming with you, ditz," Alison said to her roommate. "If I don't, you might try to convince me you've had a miracle recovery."

By the time I reached the emergency drop-off area, Del Amundson and Tony Lynch were getting back into their van. I called to the medics, who turned at the sound of their names. Del, as usual, looked amused. The always serious Tony had been on the job for only a year.

"What's up?" Del asked.

"My curiosity," I replied. "Professional, not prurient."

The veteran medic chuckled. "It usually is. How's life with the sheriff? Does he ever loosen up when he's away from the job?"

I shook my head. "I'm still waiting for him to smile. But then we've only known each other for sixteen years. Dare I ask who the patient is?"

Del's smile disappeared. "I'm not sure. Honest, Emma. Even if I were, I couldn't say."

I nodded. "She was from the shelter, right?"

He nodded back. "Pathetic little thing. Tried slashing her wrists. I doubt if she's much out of her teens."

"No ID?"

"There wasn't time to find it," Del said. "We got the impression she'd just arrived."

My heart sank, for both the girl and Den. "Will she make it?"

"She might. Clancy Barton had just arrived to take over the evening shift, so he went to check on the new arrivals. He caught her in the act. Neither Tony or I recognized her."

Tony, who was solemn by nature, looked even grimmer than he usually did. "My guess is she's a runaway. But don't quote me."

"I won't," I assured him. "It's not a story. The sheriff went to the shelter, so he'll find out what he can about her. I'll check back at the hospital later tonight."

"Go for it," Del said as another call came through. "Got a wreck out on the highway by Cass Pond. Take it easy, Emma."

"Right," I murmured, wondering why I'd come in the first place. I could have stayed home and learned as much by making a couple of phone calls. Maybe, I mused as I drove up the hill, I was getting too old to chase stories. On the other hand, not only was my reporter older, but he didn't like leaving his wife alone at night. Mitch attended at least a couple of meetings that were on his beat, but on one recent occasion, he'd taken Brenda with him. Maybe she liked meetings. I don't.

I was still mulling as I slowed down to turn into the driveway of our log cabin. A motorcycle roared by my Honda before coming to an abrupt stop some fifty yards away. The rider removed his helmet, apparently staring at the overgrown road to the neighboring Nelson house. There was something vaguely familiar about the young man, but at the moment it eluded me. I turned off Fir and drove into the empty garage. Obviously, Milo wasn't home yet. I went into the living room to close the picture window's drapes. Again I heard the motorcycle nearby. Then, as I reached for the drapery cord, I saw the biker roar past our house. Something had struck me about his rusty red hair and the pugnacious way he was leaning forward. It was Mickey O'Neill, whose hobby was beating up his girlfriend.

But what bothered me was why he'd stopped to check out the Nelson house. The only occupants were Laverne Nelson, her daughter-in-law, Sofia, and the toddler, Chloe. I couldn't think of any connection between the Nelsons and Mickey. He'd slowed down after seeing my turn signal. Did that mean he recognized me? If he had, so what? I hadn't seen him up close since his father's funeral six years ago. Even in Alpine, there were a half dozen aging tan Hondas.

But there was still something about Mickey that bothered me.

CHAPTER 15

I phoned Father Den to tell him what had happened to the girl he'd brought to the shelter. He was predictably upset.

"I wondered what the siren was for," he said. "I always do, since I'm only a block away from the hospital. I'll call, but there's no point in going over there until tomorrow. The poor girl's probably still being treated and then she'll be out of it."

I asked Den to call me in the morning to let me know how she was doing. He assured me he would.

I'd just finished the dinner cleanup when the phone rang half an hour later.

"Bronchitis," Alison announced. "Not pneumonia. Which is worse?"

"How do I know? Didn't you or Lori ask Doc Dewey?"

"It wasn't Doc," she replied. "It was Dr. Sung. He's really kind of attractive. How old is he? He's not married, right?"

"He's single, but he's got a girlfriend over in Leavenworth," I responded. "He skis, and I think he met her up at the pass a few winters ago when we had real snow. Besides, he's in his midthirties."

"So? Older men are more mature."

"That's . . . generally true," I said. Then, wanting to get off the subject, I asked how Lori was feeling.

"Beat," Alison replied. "But the antibiotics should start kicking in by Sunday. Hey, did you hear about the mystery girl who was rushed to the ER? A nurse told us somebody said she was a runaway hooker from Monroe who sneaked herself into the reformatory to turn tricks and she'd been attacked by an inmate's girlfriend who was visiting him."

"That sounds like a typical wacky Alpine rumor," I declared. "And it's not called the reformatory anymore, it's the Monroe Correctional Complex."

"Whatev'. You know what I mean. You don't believe it?"

"No, I do not," I assured her. "I don't know who she is, but she ran away from an abusive man and then . . . she hurt herself. That nurse should keep her mouth shut."

"Oh, crap! I liked her version better. Now I'll have to tell Lori it's not true. In fact, she's calling me. Now *I'm* a nurse. Later, Emma."

Wearily I put the receiver back in its cradle. No wonder I felt a headache coming on. It might have been a short week, but it had been a long day. After taking two Excedrin, I collapsed on the sofa and watched the Mariners eke out a win over the Orioles. At least the M's were having a better day than I was. That wasn't saying much, since they were at the bottom of the American League West. But I was far from getting to the bottom of our latest murder.

Milo got home a little after eleven. I was sitting up in bed reading David McCullough's *1776*. My husband leaned over to kiss me.

"I got done an hour early," he said.

"Done with what?" I asked innocently.

"My job." His expression was vexingly blank as he headed for the bathroom.

"Clam!" I yelled after him.

He kept going.

I went back to *1776*. A few minutes later my annoying mate got into bed. "Why are you reading my book?" he asked.

I stared at him. "I thought you'd finished it."

"Not quite. Where's *John Adams*?"

I gave Milo a dirty look. "He heard you

come in, so he jumped out the window."

"Not his sort of thing. Kind of a dull guy."
He reached over to retrieve the book.

"That's why I quit reading his biography,"
I confessed. "I like McCullough, but Adams
isn't a very sprightly subject."

"*I* finished it," Milo said. "Find yourself a
book I'm not reading."

"No. I'll just lie here and ask you a lot of
annoying questions."

"Don't. I'm beat."

I studied his face. He did look tired. He'd
put in a fifteen-hour day, which wasn't
unusual. I reached into the nightstand and
pulled out an Agatha Christie mystery I'd
read so long ago that I'd forgotten who-
dunit. "See?" I said. "I'm being quiet."

Milo kept his eyes on his book. "No,
you're not. You're talking."

I knew when to shut up, focusing instead
on Hercule Poirot grooming his elaborate
mustache while exercising his little gray
cells. Ten minutes and a second murder
later, my eyelids felt heavy. Milo turned off
the light. I curled up next to him and fell
asleep in the sanctuary of his arms.

We both slept until almost nine. Milo got
up first, heading to our recently added
bathroom. I burrowed down under the cov-

ers for another twenty minutes. Saturday was my only day to be lazy in the morning.

Unlike work days, when we rarely spoke to each other, our leisurely awakenings made us more talkative. Milo was eating breakfast when I arrived twenty minutes later. "Since when," he asked, "do you dream about Marlon Brando?"

"Brando?" I said in disbelief. "I never had a thing for him. I admired his acting, but why would I dream about him?"

"You ever see him in *The Wild One*?"

"No," I replied, sloshing coffee into a mug. "I think it came out before I was born."

"I saw it years ago on TV," Milo said. "Outlaw biker movie. It was pretty good for what it was. You were talking in your sleep again, saying something about motorcycles and Marlon or Mitchell. Some *M* name, anyway. You got a thing for Laskey?"

"No. His real name is Menachem. I never recall dreams unless they're really weird and wake me up."

"Guess it wasn't that weird," Milo said.

After I sat down, the first jolts of caffeine brought my brain into focus. "Oh! I know why I dreamed about bikers. Mickey O'Neill came by on his motorcycle when I got home last night."

Milo frowned. "He came by *here*?"

"No." I explained how he'd zoomed by before pausing at the Nelson house. "There's something off about the guy, but nothing weird happened."

The intense hazel eyes were unblinking. "So why would you dream about it?"

"Well . . . Mickey beating up his girlfriend. In fact," I went on, "I checked with the medics about the call you got at the shelter. What happened when you showed up?"

"Clancy Barton was taking over from his dad, Frank," Milo said. "The old boy's almost ninety, but he's got all his marbles. He told Clancy to check on the new arrival because, as Frank put it, 'the little gal looks like the calves chewed her.' "

"Colorful old guy," I muttered. "Did his son follow through?"

"He did. Frank had to go off to his supper, so Clancy went to see her. She'd already made a couple of cuts on her wrists." Milo grimaced. "I had Dustin check in with the hospital around nine. She was stable, but wouldn't be moved out of the ICU until morning."

"I take it nobody recognized her or made inquiries?"

"Only us."

That reminded me to call Father Den. But

362

first I had to fortify myself with food. Milo always made his own breakfast during the week because he had to leave for work before I did. But sometimes on weekends, I played the part of the good wife and made it for him. This Saturday wasn't one of those times.

"Can't you put your dirty dishes in the dishwasher?" I asked.

Milo looked up from the *Seattle Times*. "You say I load it wrong."

"You do. At least not as efficiently as . . . Never mind." I sighed and took a cereal bowl out of the cupboard. I'd settle for corn flakes and the *Times* sports section. My husband always read that first.

I'd almost finished eating when Milo put aside the rest of the paper. "Lot of 9/11 commemorative events going on this weekend," he said. "I'm surprised Blackwell didn't have the commissioners do something here so he could play up to the crowd. Is he hedging his bets until the recount's a done deal?"

"Judge Proxmire's back in town Monday," I reminded my husband. "I hope she acts fast to certify the election. Maybe I should talk to Rosemary Bourgette when I see her at Mass tomorrow. She might give Diane a nudge."

"It can't hurt," Milo said, getting up. "I'm going to my den to see if I can fix that yard vac you busted. How'd you do that?"

I shot him a dark look. "If I knew, I wouldn't have broken it in the first place."

"Twit," he said, mussing my hair before heading out of the kitchen.

The digital clock on the stove read 10:22. Father Den should be back in the rectory after saying the nine o'clock Saturday Mass. I went into the living room to make the call. Den answered on the third ring.

"She's out of the ICU," he informed me, "but Dr. Sung says she'll stay in the hospital at least until tomorrow. The cuts were fairly superficial, but she's dehydrated and malnourished. From what she told me, she hasn't eaten much lately."

"You figure she ran away from an abuser or . . . what?"

"Honestly, Emma, I'm not sure. She's holding out on me about who he is and what happened. Obviously, she'd been beaten, and not just in the last twenty-four hours. Elvis told me there were also some older bruises."

"Do you know her name?"

"Yes," Den replied, "but I can't tell you."

"You could tell the sheriff."

Den didn't respond right away. "So he'd

tell you?"

"No! Of course not," I said sharply. "But the jerk's a criminal. Whoever he is, he can't go around beating up women without being held responsible. You know that."

"I do," Den allowed. "The information isn't under the seal of the confessional. It's not the first time I've been in this situation, but it's damned awkward. The abusers need help as much as the abused. They're bullies, but generally they're as low on self-esteem as the women they beat up. Sometimes the roles are reversed."

"I don't want to badger you," I said. "But I should be taking notes."

"Go ahead." Den sounded bemused. "That way I won't have to repeat myself."

On that note we rang off.

Five minutes later Milo reappeared. "Your lawn vac is toast," he said. "What the hell did you do with it? Don't you empty it every time you use the damned thing?"

"No," I replied. "It takes a while for it to fill up. Usually."

"If it'd been any fuller, it would've *blown* up," he growled. "I'm off to Harvey's Hardware to buy a new one." Milo stomped off to the garage.

I finished cleaning up the kitchen and started the dishwasher. My next chores were to vacuum and dust the living room. I'd just finished when Milo returned from Harvey's looking very pleased with himself.

"Want to see the new lawn sweeper?" he asked.

"Sweeper?" I echoed. "I thought you were buying a lawn vac."

"It's better than that thing you had," Milo asserted. "That was a piece of junk. What did you pay for it?"

"I don't remember," I admitted, following him outside. "Under a hundred dollars?"

"That figures," he muttered. "Well? How's this little hummer?"

I gaped at the machinery on the lawn. It was red and black with a handle, wheels, a funnel, and I wasn't sure what in the middle. "It's nothing like my old lawn vac," I said in an uncertain voice. "Is the red and black round thing an engine?"

"You bet," Milo replied. "Briggs & Stratton, one thousand CFM. You can push it instead of stumbling around to drag it behind you. Ball-bearing semi-pneumatic tires, sturdy chute. You won't get all tangled up like you did with the old one."

"Nyuh." I was overwhelmed. "H-h-how m-m-much?"

"End of summer sale. Harvey gave me a

real deal." Milo looked very proud of himself.

I finally collected my wits. "You paid cash?"

"I usually do." He put his arm around me. "Little Emma, how long does it take you to figure out you're not on your own? Besides, I don't throw my money around."

I sighed. "I'm so used to living from paycheck to paycheck." I looked up at my better half. "It's habit. And I forget sometimes that I'm not alone."

"Try to remember," he said solemnly. "Okay?"

I smiled. "Okay."

He smiled back and kissed the top of my head.

Milo had to try out his new toy, though he first showed me how to operate the Troy-Bilt Walk-Behind Jet Sweeper, as it was officially known. With a name like that, I felt it should have a room of its own.

I resumed my domestic duties while Milo tended to yard cleanup. Shortly before noon, the phone rang. I cringed when I heard Kay Burns's voice.

"I'm afraid you've upset Iain," she said, her tone frosty. "He's a very sensitive person."

"I don't like doing that," I said calmly. "But Iain was very difficult."

"He's candid," Kay responded. "Occasionally people misinterpret him. You should apologize to him."

"He's the one with no manners," I said in a reasonable tone. "Farrell owes me an apology. Enjoy the rest of the weekend, Kay." I hung up.

Milo came in through the front door. "What's for lunch?" He stopped to stare at me. "Whoa! You're pissed. What's wrong?"

"Kay Burns," I replied. "She wants me to apologize to Iain Farrell for being a jackass."

My husband looked puzzled. "*You* were being a jackass?"

"No! *He* was. Didn't I tell you he was a jerk when I talked to him?"

"I thought Farrell was always a jerk. Remember when I had to bust him after he slugged Blackwell? I hated doing it, but Jack filed charges."

"Between those two, I wouldn't know who to root for," I muttered, getting up from the sofa. "Are you really hungry? We had a late breakfast."

"I ate before you did," he reminded me. "Should I go pick up burgers?"

"That's a bother," I said. "I'll make you a sandwich."

"Skip it. I'll go to the Burger Barn. I can park in my usual slot and jaywalk to the other corner."

"You should ticket yourself," I called after him. But he was already out the door.

By the time I finished cleaning both bathrooms, Milo still wasn't back with the burgers. It was almost one o'clock. Maybe he'd stopped at headquarters to make sure whoever was on the desk was awake. I stood at the front window, watching for the Yukon to pull into the driveway. Two boys on bicycles, an aging VW, a pickup filled with junk, and a young couple pushing a stroller went by, but I saw no sign of the sheriff. Three more cars and one RV later, I was starting to worry. Maybe I should call his cell. I was heading for the phone when I heard the Yukon pull into the garage. I met Milo at the kitchen door.

"What happened?" I asked.

"That sonuvabitch Blackwell's what happened," Milo said angrily as he dumped the bag with our lunch on the kitchen table. "He saw the Yukon at headquarters and thought I was there. Heppner told him I wasn't, so Jack left. Unfortunately, that's when I came out of the Burger Barn. Blackwell wants to sue me."

"For what?" I asked.

"For being alive, as far as I can tell," Milo replied, then pointed to the bag. "You may want to heat up that stuff. It probably got cold while Jack was shooting off his face."

I put our lunch in the microwave. "What triggered this latest outburst?"

"I haven't found out who tried to kill him."

"I thought he didn't have any enemies."

Milo poured the last of the coffee into a mug. "He says he doesn't, that it has to be a nut job, but I still have to find out who it is. At least he didn't repeat his accusation that one of my deputies tried to shoot him. Gould would be the most likely suspect, but he was right there in the crowd in plain sight. Hell, for all I know it could be some loony just passing through."

"Do you believe that?"

"No." He sat down at the table. "Jack and Farrell had that row at RestHaven a few months ago, but I doubt the nut doctor would take a shot at him. I don't remember what they were fighting over, except that it had something to do with Kay Burns."

"Her honor, as I recall." I paused, thinking back to what had started the fracas that had landed Farrell in jail. "You were on the scene."

"After the fact," Milo reminded me. "It

was crazy. Mullins and I never did figure out who started the rough stuff. Then I had to bust Blackwell for slugging Kay."

I removed the burgers and fries from the microwave and brought them to the table. "A pair of egotistical alpha males," I said. "Even if Kay was married to Jack almost thirty years ago, I doubt that he'd be jealous if she and Farrell might have something going on."

"Who knows with Blackwell?" Milo muttered. "His ego's as big as Alpine Baldy."

"So's Farrell's. Say, have you heard anything more from Ms. Compton?"

My husband shook his head. "She's still here, but so far she hasn't done anything illegal."

We concentrated on eating for a few moments. "Maybe," I finally said, "you should check deeper into Ms. Compton's background. She's rich, but how did she get that way?"

Milo didn't look enthused. "You think she held up banks?"

"Of course not. But the family wealth was founded on silver mining. You know all the tales about sinister doings with the miners in the old days."

"So after a hundred years somebody followed the Jennings twins to Alpine?" The

371

sheriff's expression was beleaguered.

I tried to look ingenuous. "It's not impossible."

"*You're* impossible," Milo muttered after chewing the first big bite from his second burger. "According to Ms. C., Gemma's murder was random. She might buy into the serial killer theory."

"Does she know about the previous murders?"

Milo made a face. "I thought about telling her, but it's conjecture. Besides, you know I have my own doubts. Georgiana Compton is not your typical mama. At first I wondered if she was on some heavy-duty drugs. But her eyes were clear and I couldn't see any other signs that she was doped up. The word that describes her best is 'cold.' "

"Random or not, Gemma's still dead. Unless . . ."

"Unless what?" Milo asked.

"Unless it wasn't Gemma who was killed," I said slowly, "and it was Sarah."

My husband's eyes sparked. "You mean Gemma's played the part of Sarah before?"

"I don't know," I admitted. "It just occurred to me. But Ms. Compton's on a mission."

"You got it," Milo agreed. "If she finds who killed her daughter, I hope she's not armed, because she's definitely dangerous."

We spent the rest of the afternoon doing more yard cleanup. I got to use the fancy new lawn sweeper, which definitely was a vast improvement over the old lawn vac. A little after five we retreated to the chairs in the back yard.

"Let's eat out," Milo said.

I made a face. "I'm dirty and sweaty. I'd have to shower and get dressed. It sounds like too much effort."

He shrugged. "Your call, little Emma."

"Stop calling me 'little.' I'm average. I recently checked. You're the one who's a freak."

"No, I'm not. If I were in the NBA, I'd be a squirty little guard from off the bench."

Trying to picture my husband as "squirty" was beyond me. I was about to say so when I heard a motorcycle nearby. I couldn't see the street from the backyard, but I could tell it was getting closer, as if it had turned off the street — and then stopped.

I nudged Milo, who appeared to be resting his eyes. "I think that motorcycle went into the Nelson driveway," I whispered. "I bet it's Mickey O'Neill."

"So?"

"Oh, never mind. I'm going inside to clean

up. Then we can go to dinner."

I was at the picture window when my husband came into the living room. "God, but you're snoopy," he said, putting a big paw on my shoulder. "Are you already trying to make up for not having Vida around if she actually retires? Why do you care what the Nelsons are up to as long as they aren't bothering us?"

"I'm wondering what the connection is between them and Mickey O'Neill," I replied, keeping my eyes glued on the street.

Milo shrugged. "Mickey's worked at Blackwell Timber for seven, eight years. Maybe he knew the Nelsons before Doyle got fired."

Before I could answer, we heard the motorcycle rev up. A moment later Mickey appeared with Sofia Nelson hanging on to him. They roared off along Fir, heading east.

"There's your answer," Milo said, removing his hand from my shoulder. "Both Nelson men are in the slammer, so Mickey's consoling the younger Mrs. Nelson. Maybe he got bored thumping on his girlfriend."

I grabbed the front of Milo's shirt. "You've got to talk to that poor girl who got beat up so badly. I'll bet she's Mickey's squeeze. If you don't, I will, and I'll do it this evening."

Milo looked impatient. "Jesus, Emma, if

374

this is for your abuse series, you talk to her. I'll bet she won't talk to a man. Can you wait until tomorrow?"

"She might be released tomorrow." I paused. "But it wouldn't be until eleven. I could go to the hospital before Mass."

"Do that. Maybe you can talk her into pressing charges. Let's move. I'm hungry."

I never argue with the sheriff when he needs to eat. Predictably, we went to the ski lodge. By the time we finished dinner around seven, dark clouds were gathering over Alpine Baldy. An end-of-summer thunder-and-lightning storm was in the offing. Although the air felt heavy, all was deceptively calm during the rest of the evening.

It was three in the morning when a rumbling noise awoke me. I rolled over to see if Milo was awake. He wasn't, so I cuddled up next to him. It had been a short yet demanding workweek, but journalists and law enforcement are always on the job. I went back to sleep and didn't wake up until I heard a phone ringing. Milo was fumbling for it on the nightstand. As he listened to whoever was at the other end, I could tell from his expression that it was bad news.

CHAPTER 16

"The storm knocked out the power," my husband informed me as he rang off. "It's nine-seventeen."

I sat up in bed, trying to focus. "Good grief! When will the PUD have it restored?"

"An hour, maybe," Milo replied, getting out of bed. "It's been out since around . . ." He glanced over at the digital clock on my nightstand. "Three-twenty. I'm going to get dressed and head to work. We may have road damage, among other problems."

"Don't you need coffee? Food?"

"I'll get something at the Burger Barn," he said, heading for the bathroom.

I hustled my butt out of bed so I could get ready for church. At least I'd have time to fortify myself with caffeine and some cereal. Except, it dawned on me, the coffee-maker was out of commission. Cheerios would have to suffice. Obviously, my brain wasn't yet in gear.

Milo left the house by nine-thirty. I watched him back down the driveway in a benign late summer rain. Apparently Mother Nature had spent her wrath while we slept.

My plan to go to the hospital before Mass had been dashed by waking up too late. But all was not lost. St. Mildred's was catty-corner from Alpine General. I'd make a discreet exit during the recessional hymn. There was still no power by the time I got to church. The rain stopped before I left home, though the clouds lingered. Six white candles on the altar made a brave show. Not that we needed light to read the liturgical responses — we knew them by rote. I sat in the last row next to Jack and Nina Mullins. Discreetly I asked Jack if he expected to be called to duty. He said he wouldn't be surprised, having heard the big guy was on the prowl.

The lights went on just before the Eucharist was distributed. "Fiat lux!" Father Den exclaimed with a big smile. The younger people who'd never heard the Mass in Latin looked puzzled.

I made my exit as planned. Jack and Nina remained, so apparently Milo had all the help he needed. I hurried over to the hospital and up to the patient floor. The hospital operated its own generator, so it hadn't been affected by the outage. Constance Peterson was the nurse on desk duty. I explained why I had a professional interest in the young woman who had been beaten and asked where I could find her.

"She already has someone with her," Constance replied. "A cousin, I believe. I cannot fathom how women put up with brutal men. She's lucky to be alive. But go ahead. It's the third room on your right."

Constance was of Amazonian proportions. I felt like saying she was lucky that she looked as if she could fend for herself. But that might offend *her* and she'd put *me* in the ER. I headed down the hall and entered Room 3B. I wasn't surprised that the "cousin" was Alison. At least she had the grace to look embarrassed.

"Hi, Emma," she greeted me, regaining her aplomb. "This is Yvonne. She goes by Vonnie. As soon as she gets dressed, I'm taking her home. Why don't we wait in the hall while she finishes getting ready?"

"Why don't we?" I murmured, smiling at the pale, woebegone blond girl in the bed. She looked like a scared rabbit. Alison and I retreated from the room.

"How is she?" I asked when we were far enough away that Vonnie couldn't hear us.

"Physically, she'll mend," Alison replied. "Emotionally, she's a mess. She strikes me as a born victim. But I haven't gotten her to open up very much."

"Where will you put her in your apartment? It's not that big. Or are you evicting your sick roommate?"

Alison paused to allow an orderly with a mop to get by us. "I'd never do that to Lori. I'm taking Vonnie to my parents' house in Everett. I already called to say we were coming. You know they're solid. And I don't think the poor girl ever wants to see Alpine again."

"Did she say who beat her up?"

"No. She's too scared of him." Alison's expression was conspiratorial. "You know who it was?"

Briefly, I explained the Mickey O'Neill connection. "Did she tell you that Father Kelly was the one who took her to the shelter?"

Alison shook her head. "But she admitted she tried to kill herself. How can a girl put up with being treated that way? What kind of family background would let . . ." Words failed her. "It's beyond bad. I'd better check on her. She might try to climb out the window."

I stayed in the hall. I could hear Alison offering words of comfort, but Vonnie's responses were both brief and faint. Realizing this might be my only chance to talk to her, I decided to stick like wallpaper to the two girls until they rode off in the Audi.

Three minutes passed before they joined me. Vonnie's right cheek and chin were bruised; her forearms showed fading yellow patches; the left wrist was bandaged. She walked as if she were afraid that the next step would take her over a cliff.

Alison spoke first. "This is my aunt Emma," she told Vonnie. "She was very upset when she heard what happened to you."

Vonnie's pale blue eyes darted a furtive glance at me, but she didn't speak. I let the girls lead the way to the elevator. Once we got there, I spoke up. "Let's not rush out of here. There's a small waiting room just beyond the nurse's desk. Why don't we sit for a few minutes? Maybe Vonnie would like some water."

Alison took the hint. "I'll go get it. Maybe I can find some juice."

Vonnie timorously eased her frail body into a chair as if she feared the upholstered arms might tackle her. Alison offered a reassuring smile before going in search of juice.

I sat down next to Vonnie. "Did you eat breakfast?" I asked in my kindliest tone.

She grimaced. Maybe it was her reaction to hospital food. I wouldn't blame her. From what I'd seen over the years, most of it looked like sponge or parts of an old saddle. When Milo had had his gallbladder out over a year ago, he swore that the turkey he'd been served was baked newspaper pulp.

"Scrambled eggs and toast," Vonnie finally replied. "Oh — bacon. I couldn't eat all of it."

I didn't blame her. "They have to keep meals bland. Alison will probably fix you something edible."

She stared straight ahead. "I'm not hungry."

"I think you've been through some rough times lately," I said, trying but failing to make eye contact. "Do you have family around here?"

"Family?" The word sounded foreign on her tongue. "No."

"Have you lived very long in Alpine?"

"Not really."

Frustration was setting in. I had no choice but to take off the kid gloves, but I kept my voice gentle. "How did you meet Mickey?"

She jerked her head around to stare at me. "You know Mickey?"

381

"Not all that well, but he grew up here," I replied matter-of-factly. "I've seen him at church." It was true, but it had only been for his father's funeral.

Vonnie looked away. "He doesn't go to church now. At least not since I knew him."

"Is he still living in the O'Neill family home?"

"I guess. I mean," she went on, giving me a jerky sideways look, "it's where his father lived with Mickey's uncles. He told me he fixed it up after they died."

I remembered that the O'Neill house had fallen into disrepair even when Rusty and his brothers were still living there. But the ramshackle dwelling Paddy O'Neill had built for his bride on Disappointment Avenue sixty years ago was shielded from the street by maples, cottonwoods, alder trees, and berry vines. If Mickey had made improvements on the house, he hadn't yet gotten around to the landscaping.

"Is the house nice inside?" I asked, keeping the conversation on neutral ground.

Vonnie shrugged. "It's . . . so-so. Mickey didn't like to clean anything but his guns."

"He collected guns?"

"Not really." She paused, looking at her bandaged wrist. A pensive expression crossed her face; perhaps she was wondering how she'd reached a point where death seemed preferable to life. "Well," she slowly went on, "I guess he sort of liked his guns. He was big on World War Two stuff. He seemed to admire Hitler. He told me the Irish didn't fight in that war. Mickey thought that was smart of them because the English hated the Irish."

No surprise there from Mickey's point of view. "Did he ask you to do housework?"

"No. Just cook." She finally looked me in the eye. "And screw, night and day. That's the only thing Mickey wanted to do. Screw, screw, screw!" She pounded her left fist on the arm of the chair. "I hate him!"

Before I could respond, Alison appeared with a bottle of what looked like orange juice. I had a feeling she'd been listening from just outside the door. "Let's book, Vonnie. Mom'll have lunch ready by the time we get to Everett."

I stood up, but wasn't quite done with Vonnie. "In case I need to get in touch, where's your family?"

She looked blank. "I don't know where my father is. I don't remember him. Mama was in Burlington the last I heard. Or was it Bellingham?" She looked up at the ceiling. "I know it begins with a *B*. Is that the one with all the sailors?"

"Bremerton?" I suggested.

"That sounds right. I've never been there." Vonnie looked as if she didn't care. "I don't know where my two brothers are. I haven't seen them in a long time." She didn't seem to miss them, either.

I lagged behind as Alison took Vonnie's hand to lead her out of the room. It was such a pathetic sight that I felt on the verge of tears. At least the poor waif was in safe hands. That should have cheered me. But I had the feeling that the Vonnies of this world are easily led. They're either too trusting or they've learned the hard way that trust is fragile and often betrayed. Maybe Alison and her parents would help Vonnie feel that life was worth living.

Milo was home when I returned, reading the paper and drinking coffee. The Seahawks were playing the Jaguars in Jacksonville, but he had muted the sound. After hanging up my jacket, I kissed the top of his head for a change. "Any outage problems you couldn't solve, Sheriff?"

"Nope," he replied. "There were only a couple of fender-benders that happened while it was still dark. It's going on noon. Did Kelly keep you after church for bad behavior?"

"As if." I sat down on the sofa and related

my hospital visit. "You remember Alison's parents. They're good people."

Milo nodded halfheartedly. "I doubt they remember me with any warm feelings. The last time I saw them I was trying to finger her dad for killing her birth mother. That must've been over ten years ago."

"That's right," I said. "Alison was only twelve."

He turned off the TV. "The Seahawks are losing this one. Did you see Rosemary at church?"

"No, she must've gone last night." A sudden thought came to me. "I wonder if Vonnie was the girl Rosie and Evan saw crying down by the river at the picnic."

"Could be," Milo allowed. "Your point being . . . ?"

"I'm not sure," I admitted. "Except whoever she was, she had a problem. Maybe an abusive boyfriend?"

"They're out there," Milo said. "Nobody knows that better than my deputies and I do."

"Maybe I should start running names. What do you think?"

"What's your libel liability?" he asked, but didn't wait for an answer. "The calls are a matter of record. The abuser's only recourse would be to sue my department for false ar-

385

rest and sue you if we screwed up. Hell, it might do some good if the baddies had enough sense to be embarrassed. What do other newspapers do?"

"Only small-town dailies and weeklies carry those reports," I replied. "I haven't checked other papers lately, but most do what we do with approximate addresses and let readers figure out who's involved. It's different if the victim files charges, but you know that's rare. Maybe Alison can talk Vonnie into following through."

Milo lighted a cigarette. "You seem to like Alison. How come? Or are you just relieved to have a female on the staff who doesn't try to act like she's the boss instead of you?"

"I'm used to Vida's domineering ways," I said. "Alison's smart. It's a shame that her cosmetology course was cut. Maybe she'll eventually find another community college job. The receptionist's job is a no-brainer for her. My only criticism is that she's hell-bent on getting married. With her smarts and work ethic, she's way too young to care about settling down. Money's no problem because her birth mother left her a trust fund. I thought the travel bug might bite her after the Alaska cruise, but I gather it didn't. I will say that the events of the last ten days have got her attention."

"Murder and attempted murder will do that," Milo said dryly. "But I warned you not to let Alison get in too deep. It's damned dangerous."

"I told you," I reminded him, "she and Vonnie went to her parents' house in Everett."

My husband wore his familiar stern look. "Alison's coming back tonight or tomorrow. She's still a kid. You're not. You know better."

Unfortunately, I did.

After I finished reading the *Seattle Times* without finding any tie-ins for local stories, I called Rosemary Bourgette. Her pleasant recorded voice asked me to leave a message. I chose not to, since my query was work-related. Rosie deserved a day off.

Milo had spent most of the hour in his den, going over his fishing gear. He reappeared a few minutes later while I was watering the three bloomless orchids on the kitchen windowsill. He looked out of sorts. Before I could ask why, he spoke first.

"Have you thought about visiting Adam up in Alaska?" he asked, leaning against the refrigerator.

"Not really," I replied. "In fact, he told me I shouldn't because I'd pitch a fit about the way he lives in St. Mary's Igloo."

"You could meet him in Ketchikan. He gets time off, right?"

I was put off by the suggestion. "You want to get rid of me? What's wrong?"

"You know damned well what's wrong," he growled. "Blackwell. He can't take me on personally because he figures I'd beat the crap out of him, and he seems to have backed off on his investigation threat. So the only way he can mess with me is with you. And don't think he wouldn't do it. I want to keep you safe until all this crap with him and the recount blows over."

I was aghast. "Oh, Milo!" I gasped, and threw myself against him. "I won't leave you!" The words were muffled against his denim shirt.

"I mean it," he said, putting his arms around me. "If not Alaska, what about visiting that old pal of yours in Portland?"

I moved just enough so I could look up at him. "I can't. I won't. I'd worry about you so much that I'd get sick. Please. Drop it. Besides, it's my job. Journalists don't run out on their responsibilities to the public."

He grimaced. "You're a stubborn little twit," he muttered, tightening his grip on me. "I still can't believe you love me so much. Maybe that's why I stopped having the dream."

I moved just enough to look up at him again. "What dream?"

Milo sighed and loosened his hold on me. "I started having it after you dumped me the first time around. We'd be sitting together on the sofa and I'd mention getting married someday. You'd move away from me, saying we needed a break from each other."

"That wasn't a dream," I said in a forlorn voice. "That was real."

"It was both," Milo asserted. "I dreamed it over and over until last winter. I'd leave your house and walk toward my Grand Cherokee . . . and the dream would end. It was as if you could throw me out, but you couldn't make me go away."

Briefly, I closed my eyes. "No, I couldn't. Deep down, I didn't want you to go. I was an idiot. And you're still here. That's why I won't leave you now."

He sighed. "Fair enough." I could swear there was a catch in his voice.

Clint called just before we were about to eat dinner. Like his brother, he hardly needed a phone when he was angry. Milo took the call into the living room, but I could still hear Clint cussing his head off. He must have run out of breath, since I finally heard my husband speaking in a reasonable tone.

"It *is* the weekend. Why can't you rent a car in Bothell and drive to —" Milo winced and held the phone away from his ear. It was probably just as well that I couldn't catch all of what Clint was saying. Suddenly the phone went silent except for the dial tone.

"Holy crap," Milo uttered in a dazed voice as he came back into the kitchen. "My jackass of a brother doesn't like to be inconvenienced. The part he needs for the motor home is out of stock and the place that has it is south of Seattle. They're stuck in Bothell at least until Monday."

"You don't seem very sympathetic," I said.

"I'm not." Milo sat down at the table while I dished up mashed potatoes, peas, and pork chops. "Clint says everything is more efficient in Dallas. To him, Seattle is still a freaking one-horse town. Big D runs like clockwork, twenty-four hours a day, seven days a week. He sure as hell has forgotten his roots in Alpine."

"Did he say if they'll head back this way?"

"If they end up in Fife, they might as well keep going south. It's a good thing I had the Dutch Star processed while they were still in town."

I stared at Milo. "You did? You never told me that."

"You didn't ask," he replied.

"You know I'd . . ." It was an old bone of contention between us, useless to dig up and gnaw on. "What did you find out?"

"The rifle was my main concern," Milo replied. "Except for having been recently fired, it was clean. But there were fibers and hair in the Star that didn't belong to Clint or Pootsie. With those kids checking out the motor home, it's damned near impossible to ID anybody. I can only rule out prints we have on file."

"Can you eliminate anybody from the evidence you did find?"

Milo didn't answer until he swallowed whatever he'd been eating. "There were two light natural hairs. Fibers were dirt mixed with sand and grass. Work all that out."

"In other words," I said glumly, "what you'd expect to find by the river at the park. That's no help."

My husband merely nodded.

Monday morning the clouds hung in close to Alpine's rooftops, especially over our log cabin uphill from the river. Staring at the contents of my closet, I realized it was time to put away any sleeveless apparel. When I finally staggered into the kitchen, I noted that Milo had abandoned his summer uniform.

"What?" he growled, looking over the top of the *Seattle Times* sports section.

"Huh?" I responded, fumbling in the cupboard for a coffee mug.

"Skip it." He disappeared behind a photo of a Jacksonville Jaguar intercepting a pass from Seahawks quarterback Matt Hasselbeck.

It was a typical morning conversation. Neither of us liked starting the day. We probably weren't sure we even liked ourselves, let alone each other.

Milo left just before seven-thirty, and by eight o'clock I was able to drive by rote to the *Advocate* office and pull in next to Kip's pickup. I was sufficiently aware to notice that the clouds had lifted to the four-thousand-foot level of Tonga Ridge.

Alison wasn't yet at the receptionist's desk, but I figured she'd stayed overnight at her parents' house. The drive to Alpine from Everett was taking more time as the city continued to grow. Leo and Mitch were both on hand. I assumed Kip was in the back shop.

"Who's got the bakery run?" I asked.

Leo had been staring at the coffee urn,

apparently willing it to finish perking. "Alison had it," he replied, "but she'll be late and called Vida to ask her to sub."

Mitch's long face looked longer than usual. "The Duchess may be cranky when she gets here."

"Great," I muttered, heading for my office.

I was downloading my email when my phone rang. I grappled with the receiver and heard Alison's voice. "I'm past Startup," she said. "Everett traffic was gruesome!"

"Where's Vonnie?"

"Still in bed. Mom's volunteering at the Food Bank today, but she won't go in until later. I'd better hang up. I've got some kind of big rig ahead of me that's going about ten miles under the speed limit."

"Be careful," I urged, but a click indicated she'd already rung off.

Two minutes later, Vida made her entrance wearing a maroon turban with a gold medallion plastered on the front. She reminded me of a swami. "Healthy offerings to start the week," she announced. "Whole wheat muffins and coconut macaroons. With autumn almost here, we won't get as much exercise."

"In case you haven't noticed, Duchess," Leo said with a wry expression, "I never exercise. I took a vow to avoid physical exertion in my heavy drinking days when I fell off the jungle gym at my kids' grade school during Mothers Against Drunk Driving Night."

Vida gave Leo her gimlet eye. "Now that Liza's here, I'm sure she's doing the cooking. Didn't you tell me she's half Italian? All that pasta! My, my!"

"Liza hates pasta," Leo declared. "Besides, she's always had to watch her own weight. We eat like skittish birds."

Mitch peered at the items Vida was placing on the pastry tray by the coffee urn. "Macaroons with no frosting?" he said in a woeful voice. "I'm the skinny one, Vida."

"It's not merely a matter of weight," she asserted. "Rich foods in general aren't good for any of us. In fact, all of this nonsense about low-carbohydrate diets ignores counting calories and consuming fatty foods."

"It does?" I said, unsure if Vida knew what she was talking about.

"Of course." She actually glared at me. "You may also be slim by nature, but have you taken a good look at your husband since you got married? I swear that Milo has gained at least five, perhaps ten pounds."

"No, he hasn't," I shot back. "In fact, he hasn't regained the weight he lost last year during Tanya's medical crisis."

Vida harrumphed. But before she could say more, a young man entered the newsroom. He stopped suddenly, staring at Leo. "Mr. Walsh?" he said.

My ad manager has an excellent memory for faces. "Ronnie Davis, right?" Leo said, setting down his mug to shake the newcomer's hand. "I didn't know you were still in town."

Ronnie looked puzzled. "You work here?" he asked after a swift glance around the newsroom, which now included Kip.

"Yes," Leo said affably. "If you're here to buy an ad, I'm your man."

"No." He uttered a laugh that was more like a hiccup. "I want to make an inquiry about somebody. Who's in charge?"

Before I could get out even a squeak, Vida spoke up. "I've lived here all my life," she said with her cheesiest smile. "Just who is this person you're asking about?"

Ronnie looked uncertain. "Could we do this in private?"

"Of course," Vida said, leading the way to my office with Ronnie following her like a trained seal. I took up the rear. Naturally, my House & Home editor didn't look pleased. Neither, in fact, did Ronnie.

I scooted around them and sat down at

my desk. "I'm Emma Lord, the *Advocate*'s editor and publisher," I said, smiling. "Have a seat."

Ronnie clumsily plunked himself down in one of the visitor chairs. Vida, obviously annoyed, remained standing. "Well?" she said to Ronnie.

"This may sound kind of weird," Ronnie began, forced to shift his gaze back and forth between Vida and me, "but I work for a nonprofit polling company, Truth or Else. I was hired by Blackwell Timber to take a poll about your recent election." He paused to take out a handkerchief and blow his nose. "I was supposed to get paid after the poll was taken, but Mr. Blackwell is stalling. He says the results of the vote aren't final because there's going to be a recount. Is that true?"

The last swivel of his head was at me so I answered. "Yes, Mr. Blackwell has challenged the election. But I don't see what the ballot count has to do with holding up payment for your polling."

Ronnie's pale blue eyes brightened almost imperceptibly. "I don't either. That's why I wanted to find out if Mr. Blackwell is trustworthy."

As much as it galled me, I was candid. "When it comes to business, he has an excellent record. His employees speak highly of him."

"They do?" Ronnie looked at Vida and then at me. "So how come somebody tried to kill him at the Labor Day picnic?"

"That's a good question," I said, seeing Alison coming our way. She must have just arrived since she was still wearing her linen jacket and carrying her hobo bag. "If you have any ideas, feel free to let us know."

Before Ronnie could respond, our receptionist tapped Vida on the shoulder. "You have two calls on hold and another to call back, Mrs. Runkel. Maud Dodd from the retirement home is anxious to talk to you. One of the residents died last night."

"Another one?" Vida exclaimed in exasperation. "That's three since the last week of August." She stalked off to her desk while Alison shrugged, rolled her eyes, and headed for the coffee urn.

I figured that Ronnie might relax now that our House & Home editor wasn't looming over him, but his jaw muscles seemed to tighten. I asked if he'd stayed in Alpine to make sure he got paid.

"Well, yes," he replied. "I'm usually reimbursed as soon as I turn in the polling results or else my fee is deposited directly into my business checking account. I decided to stay over for the long weekend because I knew there was a bank holiday. Besides, I'd never been in Alpine before and it's in a pretty setting."

"You've had a stressful visit. I heard about a near accident, which is how you ended up at Mr. Walsh's apartment. I'm sure you'll get paid. Mr. Blackwell runs a solid operation."

Ronnie looked at his hands, which he'd folded in his lap. "I'll take your word for it."

"It could be an honest mistake. The shooting incident may've disrupted the usual smooth flow of business at the timber company. Were you at Old Mill Park on Labor Day?"

"No." Ronnie awkwardly pushed the chair back and stood up. "I did some hiking over the weekend. Thanks for listening." He slunk away through the newsroom.

Ronnie's anxiety was contagious. I felt uneasy. But I didn't know why.

CHAPTER 17

After pouring a mug of coffee and grabbing a muffin, I headed back into my office. Leo joined me a couple of minutes later.

"What did you make of that kid?" he asked, leaning on the back of a visitor chair.

"I'm not sure," I confessed. "Something's off. I noticed you were lingering by Mitch's desk. Did you overhear any of what Ronnie told me?"

"Enough," Leo replied. "He didn't offer me a business card after Liza and I gave him shelter. I didn't see him give you one, either."

I shrugged. "He probably knows we aren't going to do any polling. Besides, I think he's had enough of Alpine, especially since he hasn't gotten paid by Blackwell."

Leo finally sat down. "Did you check out the name of the polling company Ronnie works for?"

"No, but I can. I'll do it now." I typed

Truth or Else into the search engine. "I'm getting a bunch of quotes . . . Oh, here it is. A research and public opinion organization out of Omaha. No field offices listed."

"Omaha?" Leo frowned. "I'd expect Blackwell to hire local or at least a West Coast outfit. Fleetwood once told me there were a ton of pollsters in the Seattle-Tacoma area. Hell, maybe Davis was trolling for the home office and got lucky. Is he sticking around?"

"Who knows? Maybe, after a week's wait, he has another polling assignment. The Omaha company may dun Blackwell. Did you hear of anybody who was polled by Davis?"

Leo shook his head. "Liza would have been at the apartment most of the time, but you have to be buzzed to get inside the building. Do you think Ronnie's sketchy?"

"Not really." I paused. "But he seems kind of on edge. Not getting paid can have that effect."

"I should check to see if Fleetwood knows anything about the guy," Leo said, getting up. "It's time to have lunch with Spence so we can toss around joint promotion ideas for the rest of the year. We've got the opening of fall quarter at the college already covered."

"Good work," I said, always thankful for my ad manager's diligence. "Why don't you and Liza come to dinner Saturday night?"

"I'll let her know." Leo glanced out into the newsroom, taking note of Vida, who was on the phone. He moved closer to my desk and lowered his voice. "We ate — I use the term loosely — at the Duchess's house last Saturday. It reminded us of the old TV game show *Twenty Questions,* when the panel members asked if the mystery subject was animal, vegetable, or mineral. We're still not sure what Vida served. My guess was art gum erasers. Liza opted for garters. Buck Bardeen was there and lapped it all up."

"He's a brave man," I said. "Buck served in both Korea and 'Nam. Maybe he was a prisoner of war at some point. That might help him survive Vida's efforts in the kitchen."

"Above and beyond the call of duty," Leo murmured, and went to get another muffin.

Shortly before nine, Alison presented me with a manila envelope that had my name printed in bold black letters with "Private" underneath in smaller ones. "Marlowe Whipp must be off today because the mail came early," she said. "This was under it. Somebody must've dropped it off while I was in the rest room."

I was curious, but wanted to know more about Vonnie. "Sit," I said, and asked about the poor girl.

Alison sighed. "She's like a child. I'm not sure what she'll do when Mom goes off to the Food Bank. I'm guessing she'll stay put because she has no place to go. But I can't be driving back and forth to Everett to check on her. Worse yet, I can't get her to open up. It's like she's in a state of shock."

"She probably is," I said. "Is there any chance your mom can stick around?"

"Maybe. The volunteer schedule's pretty flexible." Alison sighed. "It's so sad. I have to play this by ear."

"Look," I said, keeping my voice down, "Vonnie should have a complete medical exam. If you want to take off and go back to Everett, do it."

Alison stood up. "I might. But I'll wait for Mom's word on Vonnie's status."

"Fine." I smiled. "You may be the only friend she's got. The Vonnie Mertzes of this world don't have friends. They only know abusers who turn them into victims."

"That doesn't speak well for men, does it?"

My smile disappeared. "It doesn't speak well for women, either."

The mail was mostly junk. There were three letters to the editor, one lauding the favorable vote to change county government and the second demanding that the results be overturned. The third letter insisted that I fire "Vita Rinkel" because she hadn't covered the Burl Creek Thimble Club's July and August meetings. That one was unsigned, so I wasn't compelled to run it in the paper. Besides, the club never met during the summer. I opened the manila envelope last. A handwritten note bearing my name was on top of what looked like at least a couple of dozen printed single-spaced pages.

Emma — Here is Dr. Farrell's presentation on domestic abuse disorders. You'll note it's divided into three sections: "Definition of Terms in Popular Culture," "Causes and Types of Abuse," "Treatment and Prevention." There can be no editorial changes since even slight text alterations by a nonprofessional can alter the meaning and hinder the reader's understanding.

It was signed "Kay," but she might as well have added "By Imperial Decree." My initial reaction was to chuck the whole thing in the wastebasket, but I decided to at least flip through Iain Farrell's pedantic musings.

The first page confirmed my worst fears: "From the earliest times of recorded human behavior, violence has besmirched our fragile planet." Not a lead that would grab readers' attention. Not news, either. Farrell's musings went into the recycling bin along with the rest of the junk. If Kay didn't like it, she could write a letter to the editor.

Mitch returned from his rounds just after ten-thirty. "Judge Proxmire ordered the recount," he informed me, leaning against my office doorframe. "They'll do it at two o'clock, with the county commissioners and Mayor Baugh as witnesses. Is it a photo op?"

"Yes," I said. "Are Engebretsen and Hollenberg up to the task?"

"Allegedly." Mitch looked bemused. "I'm not sure Engebretsen sees very well, and Hollenberg can't hear thunder."

"They're both in their nineties," I remarked. "They've served SkyCo well in their time, given how tight funding has been around here. I'd wondered if they'd retire after Alfred Cobb died last December and Blackwell replaced him. I suspect Jack wanted the old boys to stay on for window dressing."

Mitch nodded. "Neither of them seemed with it when I first started covering their meetings. Not much has gotten done, either. Having come from the land of power-hungry union bosses, I'm guessing Blackwell's waiting until they keel over before making his own move. I figure that hasn't happened fast enough for him."

"Exactly," I agreed. "Jack's not stupid. For all I know, he could have some good ideas."

"True," Mitch conceded. "Nobody else around here seems very innovative."

As he went to his desk, I couldn't help but wonder if my reporter was including his boss. He had a way of putting me on the defensive. Before I could brood about it, my phone rang.

"Emma?" a familiar voice from the ski lodge said. "It's me, Heather Bavich. I'm putting through a call from Ms. Georgiana Compton."

"Go ahead," I said, intrigued that I was finally getting a chance to talk to the allegedly indomitable mother of the murder victim.

A moment later a cultured female voice reached my ear. "Ms. Lord," she said as if she were calling roll. "Are you free to meet me in the lodge's Valhalla Suite at eleven?"

My watch showed ten forty-five. "Yes. Is

there something you want to put in the newspaper?"

"Perhaps. I'll see you in fifteen minutes." She rang off.

Having spent over thirty years working on newspapers, especially in Portland's Tri-Met area, I'm fairly immune to dominant personalities. But if not intimidating, there was something off-putting about Ms. Compton. Granted, I'd seen her only once, when she first arrived at the ski lodge. Maybe it was Milo's description of her as an atypical mother on a mission. Not that I blamed her. Losing a child is the ultimate tragedy.

I left my Honda in the care of a young parking attendant who was probably a college student. Glimpsing the big clock over the main desk in the lobby, I saw that I had two minutes to spare. Heather was on the phone, but she waved at me. I went down the hall to the Valhalla Suite, where I pulled the big brass knocker on the door.

It opened almost immediately. "Emma Lord," Georgiana Compton said in a tone that indicated if I'd ever had an identity crisis, she'd just solved it for me. "Come in."

I'd been in the suite before. There were two bedrooms flanking a well-appointed sitting room. Ms. Compton gestured at a pair of charcoal armchairs. "Do sit. Coffee?"

"No thanks," I replied, choosing the nearest of the two armchairs. "I reached my caffeine limit at work." I hesitated just long enough for my hostess to get seated. "I'm so sorry about your daughter. I never got to know her, but I did see Gemma a time or two." I wouldn't mention that she'd waited on me in her Sarah guise at the Venison Inn.

Ms. Compton lifted her head. She had a long neck that was partially concealed by her blouse's silk cowl collar. The item had not come off the rack. "Gemma was lovely. In every way. But," she went on with a wry expression and a chilling look in her opal eyes, "I won't be maudlin. How well do you know Jack Blackwell?"

There was no reason to be coy. "I met him sixteen years ago when I moved here," I replied. "I've never liked him, but he's a good businessman. Jack is Skykomish County's biggest employer."

"That wasn't the question." Ms. Compton didn't hide her disappointment. "I understand you own the newspaper. As a journalist, you should be a keen observer of human beings. What are Blackwell's weaknesses?"

My response didn't require much thought. "His ego. His temper. He lacks self-control under pressure."

"Ah!" She almost smiled. "That's very helpful. And it fits him."

It was time to turn the tables. "How well do *you* know Jack?"

"Not very well on a personal level," an unfazed Ms. Compton replied. "I met him only once many years ago. He killed my husband. Are you sure you don't want a beverage?"

Trying to hide my surprise, I declined her offer. "Do you mean . . . literally?"

Ms. Compton gazed up at the knotty pine ceiling. "My husband, Russell Jennings, was intelligent, but naive, especially about people. He'd graduated from Whitman College the previous year, a month before we were married. Russell was unfocused about a career, with a vague notion of eventually teaching at the college level. Now that he had a wife, he felt he should get a job. Blackwell had an opening at his mill up in Idaho's panhandle. Meanwhile, I was pregnant with twins. There were problems. I required complete bed rest, so I stayed in Coeur d'Alene. In my eighth month, my doctor brought me tragic news. Russell had been killed in a freak accident. A large cedar was being felled and it veered in the wrong direction. My husband was literally crushed and died instantly. Sheer carelessness on the part of Blackwell's men. I went into labor that night with Larry and Gemma."

Georgiana Compton had told the story without emotion. I wondered if she'd related it so often that the recital had become mechanical. I didn't blame her.

"You thought Blackwell was involved?"

"Of course." Her opal eyes held a touch of reproach. "He owned the timber mill, he employed the incompetent men. Ergo, he was responsible. The law didn't agree, though. Bribes were no doubt proffered."

"But you remarried," I said. "That must've given emotional and financial stability to your children."

"No, no, no." Ms. Compton made a slashing gesture with her right hand. "The Compton name means something in Idaho's silver mining history. I was born into wealth. Russell took my name instead of the other way around. However, I gave our children my husband's name as a memorial."

I wondered if Ms. Compton was plugged into reality. Suppressed grief might have unhinged her then, as it seemed to be doing now. "That was generous on your part."

"It was the right thing to do," Ms. Compton asserted. "Russell and I had been married for only a year, but we loved each other most fiercely. That's why Blackwell arranged for Russell to have his fatal accident. The wretched villain wanted to marry *me.*"

I wasn't surprised. "You knew Jack had already been married at least once?"

She uttered a scornful laugh. "No, nor did I care. I despised him. Oddly enough, he shut down his logging operation soon after I told him to go to hell. I figured that's where he'd come from in the first place."

The phone rang on the teak table between us. Ms. Compton frowned, but picked up the receiver on the third ring. I recognized Heather's faint voice at the other end.

"Put him on hold for a moment," Ms. Compton said. "I'm just seeing Ms. Lord out."

She hung up, so I took the hint and rose from the chair. "Thank you for inviting me here. Of course," I went on as she walked me to the door, "I won't go public with any of this."

Her eyes widened. "But you must! That's why I summoned you. Every word of what I've said must be on the front page of your paper."

I forced a smile. "I'll do my best."

But what would be the best for the *Advocate* might not be good for Ms. Compton.

■ ■ ■ ■

The return drive took me by Milo's head-quarters, and I couldn't resist comparing notes on Georgiana Compton. It was almost noon. Maybe we could have lunch together.

Mullins was on the phone, but he grinned and signaled for me to enter the boss's lair. Milo looked up from some paperwork. "Nooner?" he said hopefully.

"I'm working," I retorted. "Can you confer with me over lunch at the Burger Barn?"

"My idea's better, but what the hell." He hauled himself to his feet. "You're mud-dled."

"I am. That's why we must talk."

"I'm not sure I'll like what you're going to say."

I didn't respond. We entered the Burger Barn, where Milo nodded at the GM deal-ership's Nordby brothers as we headed for a booth at the back. "Well?" he said after we'd sat down across from a middle-aged couple I didn't recognize.

"Before I unload, tell me more about your impression of Georgiana Compton other than that she's not a typical mother and is on a mission."

411

Milo scowled. "She's wound way too tight. She'd be better off letting loose and crying her eyes out or going into a rage and howling at the moon."

I withheld comment as Kippy or Kimmy showed up with the coffee carafe and an order pad. We responded like robots. I wound up the account of my meeting with Ms. Compton just as our burgers, fries, and salads arrived.

Milo turned thoughtful. "So," he asked, "how much of that goes in the paper?"

"Not much and none online," I replied. "Except for the factual background on her husband, it's hearsay. What's left is almost more suitable for Vida's page — 'Murder victim's mother claims daughter's body.' That she flew in from Idaho is of minor interest. I'll also mention that her son was struck by a stray bullet."

"I forget," Milo said, looking somewhere beyond me. "What exactly did you say in your article about the shooting?"

I wouldn't answer until he made eye contact. "You never read it."

"Hell, I was busy. Besides, your office blew up."

"So it did." I sighed. "The picnic article was bare bones. Unknown shooter, bullet wounded bystander, under investigation, sheriff baffled."

"How many times have you said 'sheriff baffled' in the paper?"

"Never. But it often comes to mind."

"Twit. You can pay for lunch. In fact, I'll order dessert." Milo grabbed the menu. "What the . . . fudge bar pie? M&M soft serve sundae? No wonder I skip dessert here."

"It's a good thing. Vida thinks you're getting fat. See you at home." I scooted out of the booth.

The couple who had been sitting across from us had made their exit just ahead of me. The woman was getting into a maroon Isuzu Trooper. I heard him tell her to be careful out on the highway. As she backed out into traffic, I noticed a Blackwell Timber parking permit in the right-hand corner of the windshield.

"Mr. McKean?" I said, smiling.

He turned with a slight frown. "Yes?"

I put out my hand. "I'm Emma Lord from the *Advocate*. We'd like to do a newcomer piece on you and Mrs. McKean."

His handshake was unenthusiastic. "We're not very interesting."

I felt like saying most people aren't. "Alpiners are always interested in why people move here. As I recall, you came here from the Grays Harbor area."

He nodded. "We spent almost twenty years there. The logs kept getting smaller." He paused as Milo came out of the Burger Barn and ignored me. That was fine. He knew I was working. I noticed Ken Mc-Kean's earnest blue eyes following my husband across the street. "Is that the sheriff?" he inquired.

"Yes. I gather you two haven't met."

"That's right," McKean said. He had thinning fair hair and a bland face that would be hard to pick out in a crowd. "No reason to." But his gaze continued to follow Milo.

"Were you at the Labor Day picnic?"

"No." He finally looked back at me. "Our son and his wife had their first baby on September first. We drove to Brier to meet the little fellow."

"Congratulations," I said. "I'll call you later this week to arrange a time."

McKean nodded again. "My life won't make a very exciting story."

"A new baby's a good start," I assured him. "Our readers like reading about families."

"Laura — my wife — may insist you run a picture of Jayden," he said with the hint of a smile. "Say, is the sheriff a stand-up guy? We saw you having lunch with him, so as the newspaper editor, you'd know, right?"

The question surprised me. I should have been candid and told McKean that Milo was my husband. But the reporter in me opted for discretion. "Yes, Dodge's integrity is absolute. He's very good at what he does. I've known him for sixteen years."

"Interesting," he murmured. "Always good to know whom you can trust when you're new to a place. Nice to meet you, Ms. Lord."

McKean walked away in the direction of the courthouse in the next block. I crossed Front Street at the corner and barely made it to the sidewalk when a blue pickup hurtled past me. With a screech of brakes, the driver pulled into an empty slot by the sheriff's headquarters. I knew that truck. I paused and watched Laverne Nelson clamber out of the cab and stomp into Milo's domain.

Discretion told me to keep going to my office. Curiosity turned me in the opposite direction. Despite having lived next door to the Nelson brood for sixteen years, I rarely saw them. The trees and bushes between our properties provided a natural barricade.

When I came inside the double doors. Laverne was railing at Jack Mullins. "So what if Sofia's of legal age? She's still missing, you worthless piece of crap!"

"Hey," Jack said in a reasonable tone, "it sounds as if Sofia left your place on her own. Did she mention she was meeting somebody?"

"How do I know?" Laverne shouted. "With Luke locked up, she gets antsy. That was Saturday, this is Monday."

"Right," Jack said dryly. "Does she have a cell phone?"

"She's not picking up," Laverne replied, big bust and heavy thighs straining at her polyester pantsuit. "I've tried calling her a half-dozen times since late Saturday. Sofia wouldn't leave Chloe alone for that long. At least," she added, dropping her voice, "without checking in. I'm alone with the kid. Chloe's a handful now that she's walking."

"Where is she now?" Jack inquired, his voice casual.

"In the truck. Where else? I won't leave her alone."

"She's alone in the truck," the deputy pointed out. "Bring her in here or go home."

Laverne hesitated, then glanced outside. "Chloe's fine. Are you going to put out an alert for Sofia or just sit on your dead ass?"

Jack looked innocent. "It's the only thing I can sit on. You think I'm procrastinating?"

"Don't get cute, Mullins," Laverne snapped. "Fancy words don't cut shit with me. Get your other lazy deputies looking for Sofia or I'll ram my truck through the front door."

"Not smart," Jack said calmly. "Then you'd get busted, and who'd take care of Chloe?"

"I'd keep her with me. Do your damned job and find Sofia!" She wheeled around and stormed out of the building.

Jack shook his head. "How will Chloe survive growing up in the Nelson family?"

"Don't ask me," I said. "I was waiting for Laverne to slug me, but she didn't even notice I was here."

"She's not the noticing kind," Jack responded. "Your other half saw her coming and closed his door."

"I wondered. Dare I knock?"

"Do it gently," Jack advised.

I rapped discreetly. "It's me, your loving wife."

I heard Milo grunt something unintelligible, so I turned the knob and went inside.

"Is the Nelson pain in the ass gone?" he asked. "Or did you miss the show?"

"I caught most of it," I replied. "Did you hear what she wanted?"

"Yeah. Her voice carries like a foghorn.

Why aren't you sitting down?"

"Because I have to get back to my office," I said. "Did Mullins know we'd seen Sofia Nelson ride off with Mickey O'Neill Saturday?"

"No. But even if he did, it doesn't explain why Sofia hasn't come home."

"True." I paused, realizing Mickey would be at work today. It seemed strange for Sofia to hang around an empty house. But that wasn't my problem. "By the way, I met Blackwell's recent hire, Ken McKean. He asked if you were a stand-up type."

Milo scowled. "He's studying me? Why? Did Jack hire him as an assassin?"

"He didn't seem dangerous. In fact," I went on, "he's ordinary-looking, even bland."

"Good guise for a hit man," Milo muttered. "Think Lee Harvey Oswald."

"Right," I agreed. "By the way, could you run a check on Iain Farrell's background?"

"Farrell? Why?"

"Humor me," I replied, and fluttered my eyelashes. "I'll make it up to you."

He glowered at me. "Beat it, you ornery little twerp. You already nixed the nooner."

Milo returned to his paperwork; I returned to the newspaper.

CHAPTER 18

Alison was at her desk when I entered the office. "No need to rescue Vonnie?" I asked.

"Mom already did that," she replied with a crafty grin. "She has a knack for dealing with stressed-out girls. I was one of them after Dad remarried and she had to win me over."

"You were lucky, and so was she. Your father made a good choice," I said, then shut up as Alison's phone rang.

Vida looked up from whatever she'd been reading. "Well now! You've been gone for over two hours. What happened? I was quite worried."

I translated "worried" as "curious." "I was working," I replied. With Leo and Mitch listening in, I related my recent activities.

Vida took umbrage at my abbreviated account of the Compton interview. "Of course," she said, "I sympathize with the loss of her daughter, but that doesn't justify

419

meddling in local affairs. Blackwell's our major employer, even if he's disreputable in his private life."

Leo chuckled. "In other words, Duchess, Jack's a scoundrel, but he's *our* scoundrel."

Vida shot him an arch glance. "I prefer taking the high road with our economy."

"What happens when Blackwell retires or dies?" Mitch asked. "Will his second-in-command take over?"

For once, I beat Vida in responding. "I met the new hire, Ken McKean. He struck me as rather meek, but I could be wrong. Bob Sigurdson has a more commanding presence."

"Bob is also a longtime resident," Vida pointed out with pride.

I was surprised at her endorsement. His daughter was one of the girls her grandson Roger had tried to lure into prostitution. But when it came to her hometown, the fuses blew in Vida's usually rational brain.

Kip had entered the newsroom. "Have I missed a staff meeting?"

"No," Vida said, "but while we're all here, we should start thinking about 'Scene.' Last week's effort was a bit feeble." She moved closer to the front office. "Alison! Do join us."

As usual, my mind went blank, though I

used the pause to assign the McKean feature to Mitch. He was also the next to respond to Vida.

"The power outage fouled up all the clocks and bells at the public schools. The kids who hang around outside and wait for the second bell were all given tardy slips. I heard that last night from Principal Freeman at Cal's Chevron."

Vida nodded approval. "That should teach children to be more aware of time. Kip?"

"Can we mention our new look out front?"

"Well . . ." Vida adjusted her glasses, which had slipped down a bit on her nose. "Yes, that's really not self-serving since we hardly blew ourselves up in the first place."

Leo spoke up. "They removed the spray paint from the Parc Pines residents' directory."

Vida frowned. "We never mentioned it last week. I don't want to turn 'Scene' into a brief article about how the owner dealt with a prank. Have you something else?"

Our ad manager hesitated. "Yes, if you can stand another student sighting. High school kids getting on the bus and griping about being back in the classroom?"

"Well . . ." Vida tapped a pencil against her cheek. "A more positive slant: 'Alpine High youngsters bid farewell to summer as

421

they board the school bus.' Yes, that will do."

I was next, and I'd had time come up with an item: "Janie Engelman stopping traffic on Front Street. Yes, she was jaywalking, but she has to be caught in the act to get fined."

"No, no." Vida shook her head. "That's embarrassing, Emma. Even for a ninny like Janie." She lowered her voice. "Especially now."

"Why?" I asked.

Vida's turban nodded toward my office. She let me go first and closed the door behind her, but remained standing. "I lunched with my niece Marje Blatt," she began. "You know Rocky Sorensen, who works for Blackwell. He injured his back and had to see Doc Dewey. Nothing serious, though. Then," she went on, leaning closer, "he mentioned they were short-handed because someone had been recently fired."

I fell into Vida's trap of wanting me to beg for gossip crumbs. "Did Rocky say who it was?"

She grimaced and straightened up. "It seems that he only overheard bits and pieces. The three names that Rocky caught were Jeff Gunderson, Mickey O'Neill, and Fred Engelman. If it's Fred, I feel sorry for him and Janie. They've had their trials over the years."

Vida was right about the Engelmans, who had divorced at one point. Janie had made an unfortunate — and brief — second marriage, while Fred tried to curb his drinking. He only overdid it on weekends, but his version of a cure had been to check himself into the jail for the weekends. Naturally, the solution irked the sheriff. But early in the new year, Fred finally conquered his boozing and the Engelmans remarried.

"If," I said, "Blackwell's firing someone, it's the first dismissal since Doyle Nelson last year. I'll say this for Jack — his turnover rate's low."

Vida agreed. "He also pays well, working conditions are satisfactory, and on-the-job injuries are infrequent, especially given the dangers in the woods and the mill. He's always had a good head for business."

"I wonder where the seed money —" My phone rang. I picked up the receiver, but Vida didn't budge.

Jack Mullins was on the line. "Just wanted to let you know the allegedly missing Sofia Nelson has been found. In fact, she's talking to your big stud."

"Is Sofia apologizing for her mother-in-law jumping the gun and reporting her as missing?" I asked for Vida's benefit.

"No," Jack replied, sounding bemused. "Sofia's filing assault and battery charges against Mickey O'Neill. She's a mess."

"I never thought I'd say anything good about a Nelson," I said, "but hooray for Sofia! Of course, she's not a blood relative. Has she got bruises to prove it?"

"Sofia looks as if she just came out of a brawl at the Icicle Creek Tavern," Jack responded. "In fact, I had Fong take her to the ER. Later, Emma. Got a call on the other line."

Before I could put down the receiver, Vida demanded to know what she'd missed. I repeated what Jack had told me.

"White trash," she murmured. "The O'Neills and the Nelsons. Why can't people use *sense*?" Vida opened the door and walked away in her splay-footed manner.

She hadn't reached her desk before Mitch poked his head into my cubbyhole. "I'm off to the courthouse for the voter recount tabulation. I hope I can get a decent photo."

"You will," I assured him. "You're creative with a camera. Let's hope Engebretsen or Hollenberg doesn't keel over during the counting. It has to be done three times."

"That would make for a more dramatic shot," Mitch said. Judging from his expression, he was serious. I suppose that was part of the reason he took such good pictures.

I decided to needle my husband. I called his direct line, but Mullins answered. "The big guy took off. Don't expect me to tell you where, because if I do, he might deck me."

"Deck you or dock you?" I asked, irritated as usual by Milo's deputies' tight-lipped attitude, even if I grudgingly understood.

"Both, maybe," Jack replied. "Hey, it may show up in the log, okay?"

"I'll wait," I said, and rang off. But I had an inkling where Milo had gone. If Sofia Nelson had filed charges against Mickey O'Neill, the sheriff would haul him in. I doubted he'd go looking for Mickey at Blackwell Timber. He wouldn't want the aggravation of running into Black Jack. Besides, Mullins had mentioned that Sofia's wounds were fresh. That indicated Mickey wasn't at work. I hurried through the newsroom, pausing to tell Alison I was following a story lead. Mickey's bad behavior would fit into my domestic abuse series.

I turned left on Front, right onto Icicle Creek Road, and then another right onto Disappointment Avenue. The short street had been named years ago by miners who thought there was gold in the vicinity. There

425

wasn't. Only three houses stood on the dead end: one owned by an elderly couple named Trews, the second by Gus Lindquist, and the third, which had originally belonged to Mickey's late grandfather Paddy O'Neill.

I spotted Milo's Yukon but was surprised to see a cruiser pulled up behind it. I parked on the verge some thirty feet from the two vehicles and got out of the Honda. The property was so overgrown that all I could see of the house was the roof, the new chimney, and part of the upper story. I'd been inside once, after Mickey's father and his two uncles had been murdered. If the younger O'Neill wasn't much of a house-keeper, he wasn't a gardener, either.

I heard Milo before I could see him. "Quit stalling or we'll break down the door. Do it!"

Anxiety was creeping over me like an al-lergic reaction. What if Mickey came out shooting? It was one thing to hear about my husband's dangerous duties, but it was very different to be a witness. My feet had a will of their own, forcing me closer to the scene. I was within ten yards of Milo and Dustin when the front door flew open. Mickey ap-peared with his hands in the air. He was unsteady and shouting incoherently. All I could make out was "bitch" and "had it coming." Then he started down the steps and fell flat on his face.

"Shit!" Milo bellowed as Dustin bent down by the fallen Mickey. "Is he conscious?"

"No, sir," he deputy replied. "He passed out."

"Put him in the cruiser," the sheriff said. "Maybe he can sober up in a cell."

"Got it," Dustin responded, typically unflappable.

"I'm going inside," Milo muttered, turning to Dustin. "If I'm not back in half an hour, the rats may've eaten . . . What the hell?"

He'd seen me. I should have made my getaway when Mickey collapsed, but I was spellbound by the drama. "I'm a journalist," I asserted. "I'm covering this story."

"You're a moron!" he bellowed. "You could've gotten shot."

"So could you," I retorted.

Milo took off his regulation hat and brushed back his graying sandy hair. "Emma . . . ," he began, but paused to wave at Dustin, who had put the unconscious Mickey in the cruiser and was now behind the wheel. "Dammit, it's a wonder my hair hasn't turned white. You're reckless and you scare me. What if Mickey had come out shooting?"

"Then I'd have had a bigger story," I replied, trying to look ingenuous.

My husband just shook his head. "Go away now. I have work to do."

"Let me help," I offered. "I've been in the O'Neill house before."

"No, you . . ." He stopped. "Hell, why not? Back then you ignored my official order to keep out. At least you're with me this time."

"Thanks," I said as we went up the porch steps. "What do you expect to find?"

"Why should I tell you?" Milo shot back as we went inside.

"Because I'm . . ." I gasped at the sight of what my tidy mother would have called a pigsty. "Maybe I should've stayed outside after all. This place smells bad, too."

My husband shook his head. "You thought I was lousy at cleaning when I lived alone? Hell, I was right out of *Good Housekeeping* compared to this mess."

I wouldn't argue. We literally had to walk a narrow path into the living room. The floor was covered with discarded clothes, pizza and TV dinner boxes, beer and other liquor containers, CDs, boots, tools, and a couple of porn magazines. The air smelled not just stale but fetid.

"Um . . . what are we looking for?" I asked.

"Weapons," Milo replied. "Let's try the basement. That's where his old man and his uncles kept their heavy-duty hardware."

After we went downstairs, I asked what he expected to find.

"It's what I don't find that matters," he replied, opening the door of a large, battered wooden cabinet. "Mickey's got a real arsenal in here. His dad and his uncles had enough weaponry to man a fort. Collecting firepower must be hereditary with the O'Neills." Milo stepped aside so I could see for myself.

"I suppose it made them feel powerful," I said, staring at the array of rifles, handguns, and even what looked like a machine gun.

The sheriff reached into the top shelf and removed an Adidas shoebox. "I'll be damned," he murmured before letting me see what was inside. "Hand grenades."

I shuddered. "You think Mickey blew up the *Advocate* office?"

Milo gave me a reproachful look. "You know I don't speculate. These are the kind that were used in World War Two."

Vonnie's words came back to me. I told Milo that she'd mentioned Mickey's interest in the conflict. "Could Blackwell have had Mickey try to put me out of business?"

"Maybe," Milo allowed, taking a last look at the guns before closing the cupboard. "That complicates things. There's no Remington in the cupboard. What do you make of that, my cute little investigative reporter?"

I thought back to the events at the picnic. When the shot had been fired we'd just turned away, but I remembered what I'd seen immediately afterward as I turned around and the crowd by the bandstand scattered: the wounded L.J., close to Blackwell; the mayor in his wheelchair; Bob Sigurdson; Ed Bronsky; and, on one side, next to the tall evergreens, Mickey O'Neill.

"I don't get it," I declared. "I saw Mickey standing next to Ed."

"Loggers climb trees," Milo said without expression. "They sometimes have to go very fast. In the pandemonium that broke out after the shot was fired, the only person who might've noticed Mickey's sudden arrival is Ed. Have you talked to him?"

"No," I said glumly. "I had no reason to. And being so self-absorbed, Ed wouldn't have picked up on Paul Bunyan and his blue ox, Babe."

"Right. You could ask him, but all he'd say is that Mickey was there. That wouldn't prove a damned thing. Besides, we've got enough on the guy."

"Why," I demanded as we came upstairs, "would Mickey try to shoot Blackwell? He works for him."

Milo waited until we were outside to answer. In fact, he took out his cell and punched in a number. "Dustman? . . . Have you got the perp settled in? . . . Good. There may be other charges besides battering. Did you ask about the job? . . . I figured as much. Are you back on patrol? . . . Okay, come back to O'Neill's place. It's unlocked. Go to the basement and take everything out of the big cupboard. . . . Right. And be careful. There's live ammo in there."

We started walking to our vehicles. "What job?" I asked. "Blowing up my office?"

Milo shook his head. "We'll get to that. Mickey needs to sober up first. If you mean is he still working for Blackwell, I doubt it. He sure as hell wasn't on the job today."

"Vida had an inkling about that," I said.

"For once, don't tell her," the sheriff responded, opening the Yukon's door. "She'll wheedle it out of Blatt eventually. He's on evening duty. A good thing Tanya likes to stay up for the late-night TV shows. What's for dinner?"

"Soup," I said, starting for the Honda.

"Chicken noodle or tomato."

"Hey!" Milo called after me. "I take you on an afternoon outing and I get soup?"

I kept walking — and thinking. Even if Mickey had tried to shoot Blackwell, who killed Gemma? I sensed there was still a murderer in our midst. Milo's serial killer idea struck me as wrong. Something about Gemma's death seemed more personal. On the other hand, she was a stranger in Alpine. Maybe I was wrong, too.

Mitch still wasn't back from the courthouse. I assumed he was waiting for the final tally. If either of us had half a brain, he should have gone later. Vida and Leo were also off somewhere. I was stalled on my will-of-the-voters editorial. Judging from the previous varying totals, the turnout had been good, a hundred shy of the number of ballots cast in the last presidential election. Naturally, I'd praise SkyCo residents for carrying out their civic duty.

Meanwhile, I had to write a rough draft of the piece about the O'Neill arrest. I was collecting my thoughts — and trying to stay awake — when a bemused Alison came to see me.

"Ms. Compton is here. She says it's urgent."

"I already saw her. Why didn't she come straight in here?" I asked.

Alison rolled her eyes. "She prefers being announced."

"Then tell her I'm receiving."

Moments later, Georgiana Compton glided into my humble office. I offered her one of our thrift store visitor chairs. She eased her designer-clad derriere into it and smiled.

"How quaint all of this is," she murmured. "The town, too. Even your mayor, Mr. Baugh, is quaint."

Not the word I'd have chosen, but I smiled. "You've met Fuzzy?"

"Yes, I've just come from his office," she replied. "I wanted to make arrangements with him for a gathering to commemorate my daughter, Gemma. He agreed, of course. It'll be held tomorrow at six in the ski lodge banquet room. You must post it on your website."

"I will," I assured her.

"Excellent," Ms. Compton declared. "Refreshments will be served. Everyone is welcome. Mr. Bardeen has promised to take care of any crowd overflow."

I wondered how much money had changed hands. Of course Ms. Compton was wealthy. "Have you written down the

433

invitation's wording?"

"No." she replied. "Though I did consider calling it 'a celebration of Gemma's life.' "

"That's appropriate," I said. "I may use that."

Ms. Compton rose from the chair. "I'm sure you'll do a fine job. You seem competent. Thank you." She glided off in the same way as she'd come in.

Mitch returned just after four-thirty, looking frazzled. "The government change won by six votes. Is that good news?"

"It depends on who ends up in charge," I said. "Did you sit through the whole thing?"

"No," he replied sitting down at his desk. "It's a nice day, so I wandered around taking so-called creative photos, even a few in color. The shots of the ballot counting aren't very imaginative. Baugh wasn't there, except toward the end. I heard he had a meeting with someone, but I wondered. He hasn't been well lately."

I allowed that was true, but the mayor had, in fact, met with someone. I explained about Ms. Compton's visit and showed him what I'd had Kip post on our website.

Mitch seemed skeptical. "Why here? Why not in Idaho?" he asked.

"They'll no doubt have a service there," I said. "Ms. Compton is an unusual woman."

Mitch shrugged. "Not to mention bereaved. Do you want me to cover it?"

"You don't like to leave Brenda. Or would she want to come with you?"

He shook his head. "It's hard for her to handle sad things."

"Then I'll stand in for you," I volunteered.

"You sure?"

"Yes." I smiled at Mitch. I didn't add that I wouldn't miss Georgiana Compton's macabre extravaganza for all the designer outfits in Francine's Fine Apparel.

Back at my desk, I called the sheriff's office. Mullins answered. "I won't claim this Mick as any kin of mine. He's a real piece of work. Until fifteen minutes ago, he was still sleeping it off. When he woke up, he couldn't believe he was in jail and thought he was dreaming. Mickey doesn't realize his nightmare's just begun."

"What charges are being brought against him?"

"Other than beating on the Nelson girl, I won't know until the love of your life finishes with him," Jack said. "Dodge may be late getting out of here. He's got to touch base with King County before he takes off."

"King County?" I echoed. "What's Seattle got to do with Mickey?"

"Nothing I know of," he replied. "Use

435

your charms on him when he comes home."

"What charms?" I retorted. "Okay, Jack, I surrender."

"I'm sure you will," Jack said in his cheeky fashion. "Later, Emma." He rang off.

I went into the front office to ask Alison if she'd heard how Vonnie was doing.

"Oh, shoot!" she exclaimed. "I didn't check earlier, but Mom was taking her along to the Food Bank. I'll call later. Hey, what's with Ms. Compton's big whoop tomorrow?"

"Exactly what my post stated," I replied. "And yes, it's a bit off-the-wall."

"So is she," Alison remarked.

I didn't argue.

Naturally, Vida was agog. "Really now!" she exclaimed as we were about to go home. "Who does this woman think she is, taking over our ski lodge in such a high-handed way?"

"Don't knock it," I said. "It puts money into Alpine."

"Perhaps," Vida allowed. "But it still rankles."

Rankling Runkel was a major offense in SkyCo. At least she shut up as we exited the office. After the morning clouds lifted, it had turned into a fine late summer day. The sun was glinting off the tin roofs of older houses, a reminder of when Alpine's snow

436

had often been eight feet deep. Cotton-woods, maples, and mountain ash trees showed their first hints of fall color. I smiled as I turned onto Fir Street and saw our log cabin beyond the cul-de-sac. Home. Once *my* home, now *our* home. I was still smiling when I went inside.

By five-thirty, I wasn't smiling. Milo must still be dealing with Mickey O'Neill. It was a good thing I'd never intended to serve soup. I'd already thawed the ribeye steaks when my husband arrived ten minutes later. He looked weary but greeted me with a heartfelt kiss.

"O'Neill's such a dumb bastard that I almost feel sorry for him," Milo said, heading off to change his clothes. "I'll answer your half-assed questions after I've wrapped my hands around a Scotch."

Five minutes later, he was as good as his word. I'd poured both our drinks and we were sitting in our usual places. I let him speak first.

"Mickey was canned by Blackwell last week," Milo said after taking a sip of Scotch. "Sometimes it's hard to know whom to root for."

"Why did he get fired?"

"For poaching trees in a prohibited area," he replied. "Mickey's account was garbled about where it was, but sometimes he'd disappear from where he was supposed to be working. Blackwell got suspicious and sent Fred Engelman to look for him. After a couple of false starts, Fred spotted Mickey on that loop road off Highway 2. Fred hated being a snitch, but he needs his job."

"When Mitch was at the scene of that accident on 2, he mentioned seeing Fred coming out of the woods on his tractor," I said. "Did Mickey own up to poaching?"

"No," Milo responded. "He insisted he stayed on the right parcel. But if Fred ratted him out to their boss, he's in for it. That's a more serious charge than the one for abuse because those trees are on federal land."

"What would Mickey do with the trees?"

"Sell them to musical instrument makers or commercial builders," Milo said. "There's a big market for wood. We'll check the O'Neill property behind the house. The timber must be somewhere in that jungle. I told Blatt to stop by there while he's on patrol this evening."

I was more concerned about the possible attempt on Blackwell's life. I asked if Mickey had owned up to firing the shot.

"Hell, no," Milo retorted. "Our lab didn't come up with anything, but it's limited. I sent Doe Jamison to Everett Friday to let their high-tech wizards have a go at it. They haven't gotten back to us yet. At this point, it's circumstantial evidence. But he'll break. He's a spineless bastard." He held out his glass. "How about half a refill?"

I was surprised. "Okay," I said, and went into the kitchen. After filling his request, I topped off my own glass.

"Something's bothering you," I declared when I got back. "Would you like to tell your goofy little wife?"

Briefly, he looked conflicted as he sipped from his fresh drink. "Oh, hell, you can keep your mouth shut. Our King County liaison, Bill Conrad, called about a Mrs. Willis who's worried about her daughter, Shannon. She's an investigative reporter for one of the news services and often goes undercover, though she checks in every week with her mother. But no word from Shannon for nine days." Milo paused to light a cigarette.

"Did her mother think she was headed for Alpine?"

"Not necessarily. But Shannon had mentioned she was doing a series involving the timber industry. Mrs. Willis contacted several other logging towns. No luck. I told Conrad my wife owned the newspaper and maybe Shannon had checked in with you.

Has she?"

I shook my head. "Did Conrad describe her?"

"No," Milo replied. "Given the nature of Shannon's job, her mother didn't want an APB put out. She felt it'd screw with her daughter's investigation. When do we eat?"

"Twenty minutes." I didn't admit I hadn't yet started and hustled into the kitchen. My heart went out to Mrs. Willis. I wondered if Shannon was never coming home.

CHAPTER 19

The rest of the evening was mercifully calm in our cozy log cabin. We knew it was the lull before the storm. Ms. Compton wasn't throwing a party *for* Alpine. We suspected there was something devious behind her commemoration of Gemma's life.

Tuesday morning brought rain along with my first visitor, the last person I wanted to see before I was fully awake. At eight-fifteen, Ed Bronsky waddled into my office.

"Hey, hey, hey," he greeted me in an annoyingly chipper voice. "You'll never guess what came to me in a dream last night!"

Fifty pounds of mashed potatoes and gravy plopped into my mind's eye, but I merely said, "What was that, Ed?"

"The big event tonight," he replied, clutching two Danishes he'd purloined from our morning pastries. Ed sat down in a visitor chair that creaked in protest, but he didn't seem to notice. He'd already broken one of its predecessors. "Mrs. Crampton'll need an emcee. Sure, Fleetwood's the obvious choice, but he'll be broadcasting the shindig. So with all the experience from my years keeping the *Advocate* afloat, my autobiography, and my other media experience, I'm a natural for the job."

Job. My sleepy brain evoked not a task but me as the biblical Job, exhibiting patience with Ed. "Talk to her, not me. She's at the ski lodge. By the way, she's *Ms. Compton.*"

Ed, who was chewing a chunk of Danish, scowled. "Iddntdatwahyithed?"

I skipped the translation. "You should probably check first with Henry Bardeen."

Ed swallowed. "No problemo. Hank and I go way back. We've played tennis together."

I'd never heard anyone refer to Henry as "Hank." The ski lodge manager was very self-conscious about his dignity, despite the obvious toupee. Even more disconcerting at this hour of the morning was picturing Ed playing tennis.

"It's best to call on Henry early in the day," I said. *Hint, hint.* "Later on, he gets tied up with guests checking out."

"Good idea," he agreed, hoisting himself out of the chair with all the grace of an elephant executing a pirouette. At least Ed wasn't wearing a tutu. "I'll go up there right now. See you on the main stage tonight."

He bustled away, but paused to snatch up another Danish. I'd never asked Ed what he'd seen while standing by the podium when the shot was fired. Being so self-absorbed, he'd probably forgotten what happened and was envisioning his emcee's role at the memorial.

After finishing a third cup of coffee, I was ready to tackle my editorial. Starting off with kudos for the big voter turnout, I emphasized the closeness of the election and urged the SkyCo residents who had opposed change to give in gracefully. The search for a county manager would be challenging. While a knee-jerk reaction to choose a local might be tempting, it'd be prudent to cast a wider net for an experienced candidate.

"George Engebretsen and Leonard Hollenberg have served long and ably as commissioners," I wrote. *Take that, Black Jack,* I said to myself. "But times have changed with tremendous growth on this side of the Cascades. What SkyCo needs is a full-time executive who will have no distractions beyond the good of the county. We deserve the best because you, the conscientious voters, have said so."

It took me over half an hour to write the editorial, but I was pleased with the result. I'd already told Kip to make room for a front-page box covering Ms. Compton's memorial extravaganza. I was wondering about any other loose ends when Alison brought in the mail.

"I suppose L.J. and his mother will go back to Idaho after the event for Gemma," she said in a doleful voice.

"You can't expect them to stay here forever," I responded. "He does have a job."

"Right." She grimaced. "I guess there's still Ronnie Davis."

"He hasn't left town yet?"

"No," Alison replied. "We were out of milk this morning, so I ran over to Safeway. He was there buying magazines and recognized me. He likes the area and is thinking of moving here. His Seattle rent is sky-high."

"I get that," I said. "Hey, if he does, why don't you give *him* a makeover?"

Alison looked as if she was considering it. "It wouldn't make him taller."

"He's taller than you are."

"Not by a lot." On that note, she went off with the rest of the mail.

Mitch returned from his rounds just before eleven. "Blackwell wanted to post the first-offense five grand bail money for

444

O'Neill. Dodge was furious and added an arson charge for bombing us. That quadrupled the bail amount. Blackwell got mad, so Dodge told him Mickey was also a suspect in the attempt on Jack's life. They almost got into it, but Mullins and Blatt intervened."

I held my head. "Then what happened?"

"Blackwell still insisted it couldn't be Mickey and that the shooter had to be a deputy." Mitch's expression was bemused. "Dodge told him he had a witness who'd seen the shooter and would swear it wasn't anybody who worked for the sheriff's office. Besides, he could account for all of his deputies from the log except Doe Jamison, and the witness had seen a man. Do you know who this witness is? Dodge wouldn't say, of course, in case Blackwell went after the person."

"Yes," I replied. "but Milo told me in what I call conjugal confidence." There was no way short of under oath that I'd identify the scatty Janie Engelman. She probably had seen the shooter, but her account could easily be ripped to shreds in court. "Obviously, Mickey needs a lawyer who'll plea-bargain the charges. The truth will come out. For once, Blackwell's ego has screwed up his judgment. I wonder what's rattled him."

445

Even as I spoke the words, I pictured the indomitable, vengeful Georgiana Compton.

After our reporter went to his desk, I went to the front office where I asked Alison if Vonnie was still staying with her parents.

She laughed, which was a good sign, given her earlier gloom. "I think they want to adopt her. My folks have been suffering from empty nest syndrome since I moved out."

"Are you implying your parents would let her move in?"

Alison nodded. "Mom retired early from her city job. She got tired of all the infighting. Volunteering isn't enough. She needs to go to work or take on a big project. Vonnie *is* one."

I didn't argue.

At five to twelve, the newsroom was empty and I was applying lip gloss. Looking up from my compact's mirror, I saw an agitated Patti Marsh hurrying in my direction. She closed the door behind her and all but collapsed into a visitor chair.

"Am I a fool?" she asked, clutching her snakeskin purse as if I might steal it.

I avoided answering the question. "Why are you asking *me*?"

Her eyes darted all over my office, but she ignored my query. "I just turned down fifty grand. Is that crazy or what?"

"Who offered the money and for what?"

Patti, who seemed sober, finally focused on me. "That Compton woman whose daughter got offed. She's putting on some big deal about battered women. She had the nerve to ask me to get up and unload about Jack not treating me right. Hell, it's just his way when he gets pissed off about stuff. It's not like it's personal."

"It's also not right, Patti," I declared. "Deep down, you know that."

She shrugged. "Jack's got an important job. He needs to let off steam. Don't tell me your big jerk doesn't give you a hard time when he has a bad day."

"Milo gets grumpy," I said, "but he never resorts to violence. Never."

"So? Everybody's different." Patti paused, biting her lip. "You think I should've taken the money?" She didn't wait for an answer. "What then? I'd lose Jack and I couldn't stay in Alpine. I've always lived here. I'm too damned old to start over." Fumbling with her purse, she stood up. "I gotta go for my noon appointment at Stella's Styling Salon. See ya."

Patti scurried off. She'd never explained why she'd chosen me as a confidante. There was no need. She had no women friends and her daughter, Dani, lived in L. A. Her whole world was Jack Blackwell. Over the years, I'd shown her kindness, which she'd taken for friendship. I suppose that really wasn't such a bad thing.

It was ten after twelve when I entered Milo's headquarters. Mullins grinned at me.

"Can't resist him, huh?" Jack said. "I suppose it's his boyish charm."

"I've never seen a picture of Milo as a child," I admitted. "Only of him as the groom in the *Advocate* story about his first wedding."

"I missed that. I was probably about eight and not into romantic stuff. Unfortunately, I changed later on and got married."

"Jack," I said, "you should stop making cracks about —"

The sentence was cut off as Milo came out of his office. He looked surprised to see me. "Why aren't you at lunch?"

"Why aren't you?" I retorted. "I got held up by Patti Marsh."

Milo scowled. "Literally? Did Blackwell cut off her allowance?"

"No. Are you going to eat?"

"Not here," he replied. "You can join me. Lori's still barking like a seal, so I told her to stay home." He pulled out his wallet, handed Jack a twenty-dollar bill, and told him what we wanted. The deputy probably knew our orders by heart, since he'd been making the Burger Barn run for almost as long as I'd known him. "If there's any left over, buy yourself some ice cream."

Jack had stood up. "You're confusing me with Bill Blatt," he said, heading for the door. "That's how his aunt Vida rewards him for telling her what's going on with our investigatons. How come she hasn't been pestering Bill about the current one?"

"Victim's not a local," I responded. "Newcomers don't count."

Jack shrugged and went on his way.

Milo sat down at his deputy's desk. "You're here because . . . ?"

I first commiserated about the Blackwell dust-up, which evoked a look of disgust and a couple of grunts. Then I moved on to Patti's visit.

The sheriff expressed surprise. "She's dumber than I thought. Oh, hell, she and Blackwell have been together for over twenty years. In some weird way, I get it. Maybe he doesn't beat her up as often these days."

"I suppose that's possible," I allowed. "Have you any other news for me?"

Milo scooted Jack's chair away from the desk and stretched out his long legs. "I do,

449

which is why I'm eating in. I got a call from the SnoCo sheriff half an hour ago. A fisherman was coming off the Sky at Reiter Ponds by Gold Bar this morning. It was starting to really come down, so he ducked into an abandoned shack." My husband's hazel eyes fixed on my face. "You got it. Another dead girl. The killer's still out there."

I had a flock of questions, but he put up a hand. "Let me finish. This one was younger, maybe late teens. No ID. The ME's preliminary autopsy report says she was strangled and could've been killed at least a week ago. Of course they're checking missing persons reports, but — this is speculation on their part — she could be a hooker. As you know, their disappearances don't always get reported."

"Does this mean the killer's changed his MO?"

Milo rubbed at his forehead. "No. The girl wasn't on a street corner in Gold Bar selling herself. The guess is that the killer picked her up in town and lured her to the river."

I considered the new information. "The time of death might be over the Labor Day weekend, right?" I saw Milo nod. "Wouldn't there be a risk of the killer encountering other fishermen at Reiter?"

"Maybe," he replied. "But Gemma was lured to her death here in town."

"True." Something niggled at the back of my mind, but it was as elusive as the flash of a rainbow trout in the Skykomish River.

Just then Jack returned with our lunches. Before we could retreat to the sheriff's office, though, Heppner called in a four-vehicle collision by Baring with probable fatalities. Sam needed some help.

"Goddamned rain," Milo muttered, grabbing his jacket and hat. "Don't eat my burger, Mullins, or you're on suspension." The sheriff rushed out to the Yukon.

Jack looked puckish. "I never even got ice cream."

I removed my share of the order. "I'd stay to keep you company, but I doubt your boss will be very cheerful when he gets back."

The deputy's eyes twinkled. "For Dodge, that *was* cheerful."

The rest of the workday played out in its usual routine. Milo's disposition wasn't much improved when he got home a little after five-thirty. He did remember to kiss me, but his first words were gloomy. "Two killed outright, eight injured, nobody local. Gerry and Elvis will need medical treatment of their own before the night's over. What's for dinner?"

"Ask Ms. Compton," I responded. "Her event starts at six and there's food."

"Shit!" Milo bellowed. "I forgot. I'd better go with you. I should've assigned a deputy, in case there's trouble. I won't bother to change. I wonder if Blackwell will show up."

"Good question," I said. "If not, he'll send a spy. Are you going to make a drink?"

Milo looked uncertain, but then shook his head before he sat down in the easy chair. "I'll wait until we get to the shindig. By the way, I heard from Marje Blatt about Iain Farrell's background. Marje is good at that sort of thing. No wonder Vida relies on her."

I'd flopped onto the sofa. "And?" I prodded as he paused to light a cigarette.

"You know the official bio," Milo replied. "Chicago native, Milwaukee practice, taught at Marquette until seven years ago, when he resigned and moved to Butte, Montana, where he worked with prisoners at the Silver Bow County jail. Three years later, he moved to Redmond. Since that's near Bellevue, I figure he met up with Rosalie Reed and she recommended him for the job here."

"The change from Marquette University to the Butte jail sounds odd," I said.

"Yeah, it does," Milo agreed. "That's why

I followed up with a call to Marquette's security office. I got zip. I'm waiting now to hear from the Milwaukee cops."

"Good," I said, and suggested that we leave for the ski lodge. "I suspect there'll be a crowd. I heard Fleetwood's five o'clock newscast while I was driving home. He's broadcasting it live, of course."

"Nothing you can do about that," he said, kissing the top of my head.

"I'm used to it." After hitting fifty, there were lots of irksome things I'd had to get used to. Except murder. I never got used to that.

The banquet hall had been added on shortly after I'd arrived in Alpine. It could accomodate two hundred people for a sit-down dinner, but the only off-limits spaces on this cloudy evening were a curtained stage at the far end, two bars on each side, and a coatrack. A smaller conference room was in the basement.

When we arrived at five to six, there were at least a hundred Alpiners on hand. Or foot, since most of them were anxiously waiting for the bartenders to start serving. I didn't recognize any of the servers, including a platinum-haired young woman who was signaling that she was ready to take orders. Apparently, Ms. Compton had hired from outside. That wouldn't please the locals, but maybe they'd forget to bitch after the third free hit.

Milo had already been engaged in conversation by Coach Rip Ridley. I glimpsed Spencer Fleetwood chatting with Leo, while Rosalie Reed and Liza Walsh regarded their menfolk with indulgent smiles. Behind me, I heard the voice of Janet Driggers, wife of the funeral director, Al.

"We almost didn't come. Ms. Compton stored the stiff with us, but we won't get a burial fee. I insisted we boycott this bash and stay home to try out our new sex swing, but Al thinks it might make him airsick."

I gave the ever-bawdy Janet a dubious look. "Does he get queasy on the free flights you get for working at the travel agency?"

"No, but I do." Janet's green eyes grew serious. "What's with Ms. Compton? I only met her once at the funeral parlor. I've seen all kinds of grief, but she's utterly glacial. Can you imagine her having sex?"

"I haven't tried," I admitted, "but she did bear two children."

"I figure she bought them," Janet declared. "Let's get drinks."

We moved to the platinum blonde's line, which Milo and Rip had just left with glasses in hand. Uniform or not, Milo was officially off duty. Janet and I moved up a couple of places as the lights dimmed. A moment later the curtain parted to reveal a female figure in a simple green dress. The crowd immediately quieted.

"My name is Jennifer Hood Blackwell. I married Jack Blackwell when I was very young and naive. He abused me in every possible way. I left him as soon as I summoned up the strength. I have never been with any other man since. I don't hate men. But I lost my trust in the male sex. I hope and pray that someday, somehow, I can trust a man. At least I still have hope." Jennifer turned away and disappeared into the dark part of the stage.

The crowd was stunned into silence. Finally, tentative applause broke out. There were some negative murmurings, too, probably from Blackwell workers. Whatever the onlookers were expecting, it wasn't Jennifer Hood denouncing the local timber baron.

"Holy crap!" Janet exclaimed in a stage whisper. "Did you know Jack was her ex?"

"I did," I confessed. "But it was never for publication."

Janet craned her neck. "Is he here?"

"I haven't seen him. I doubt he'd come to a service for someone he doesn't know."

"I heard the brother worked for —" But we were next in line and Janet shut up.

I asked for bourbon and 7-Up; Janet ordered a screwdriver. She emphasized the cocktail's first syllable, but the platinum-haired bartender was blasé. She'd heard it all.

Drinks in hand, we moved away from the bar. The lights blinked three times. Kay Burns was on the stage. She introduced herself as Kay Barton Burns.

"Many of you know me," she went on, "as an Alpine native. I left my first husband — a good man — for Jack Blackwell. It was the worst mistake I ever made. Jack was a beast, both physically and emotionally. My only escape was to leave him — and Alpine. It took me almost thirty years to come back to my hometown, but I'm glad I did because now I can tell you why Jack forced me to go away." Like Jennifer, she walked off into the darkened part of the stage.

I turned to Janet. "If Vida's here, she must be eating this up."

"Is she?" Janet craned her neck. "I'm too short to see one of her crazy hats."

What we saw next was a big screen with a map of Idaho. "This is the Gem State," intoned a resonant male voice-over. "The nickname is worthy, but Idaho has produced more silver than any other part of the country. Timber has also played a big role in . . ."

"What is this crap?" Janet said into my ear as the screen now showed scenic vistas of the state. "A tourist promotion?"

"No clue," I whispered. "Gemma's background, maybe." I refocused on the narrator.

". . . and evil has a name. It is Jack Blackwell."

Shouts erupted from the crowd. There were boos, too, but I didn't know whether they were for or against Black Jack. Then a couple of fights broke out, one in the far corner to the left of the stage and another about twenty feet from where Janet and I were standing. Unnerved, I looked for Milo. Fortunately, he and his regulation hat were tall enough that I could see him shoving his way to the stage. He stopped briefly, apparently speaking to someone. The screen was showing what looked like a mineshaft. I couldn't hear the sound over the onlookers' voices. Then the curtains closed and the crowd quieted.

I think I was holding my breath. Even Janet was speechless. Finally Ms. Compton appeared in front of the closed curtain wearing a long silver sheath that gleamed like armor. "I apologize for any technical difficulties," she announced. "We'll move on to the most compelling part of the evening. My daughter, Gemma, should be remembered not just for all the things she was, but for all the things she could be."

Ms. Compton paused as the curtain opened again. A plain casket sat on the bare stage. Several people gasped and some groaned.

Janet grabbed my arm. "Did they swipe that from us? Where's Al?"

Ms. Compton was still speaking. "For those who never met Gemma, you can now."

Puzzled murmurs filtered through the banquet hall. I caught Henry Bardeen's eye. The ski lodge manager was in obvious distress. His face was pale and the toupee was askew. Whatever hefty price Ms. Compton had paid him evidently didn't seem worth it now.

I looked again at the stage — and blinked. The coffin's lid was being raised, but there was no one onstage except Ms. Compton. She stood calmly, a silver sihouette, gazing at the fully opened coffin.

Gemma Jennings sat up and climbed out onto the stage.

There were gasps and murmurs. Despite my shock, I realized that many, maybe most,

Alpiners had never seen Gemma during her brief stay. Despite Janet's jabbering, I focused on the stage. Mother and daughter were embracing. When they finally let go of each other, Ms. Compton moved to the front of the stage.

"My daughter lives! I have avenged her father's death. Enjoy the rest of the evening celebrating not her death, but her life!"

The two women stepped backward and the curtain fell. Janet was outraged. "You mean we've been storing the wrong stiff? What the hell is going on?" She rushed off, apparently in search of Al.

I wanted to find my own husband, who seemed to have disappeared. Maybe he'd gone to speak to Ms. Compton. Not only had her son, L.J., lied about the identity of the murdered woman, but his mother had publicly accused Blackwell of murder. It was no wonder that the banquet hall sounded like the Tower of Babel.

To my surprise, Henry Bardeen was wiping his brow with a handkerchief and talking to Sam Heppner. Doe Jamison had also appeared, making her way through the crowd. Milo had obviously sent for his deputies. For all I knew, he might've called in the State Patrol. I wouldn't have blamed him.

Sanity — or at least some semblance of order — seemed to have come over the gathering. I wondered if I should try to interview Ms. Compton, but she and Gemma were nowhere in sight. Finally I spotted Milo elbowing his way in my direction. He barked my name, so I hurried to meet him.

"Jesus," he growled under his breath, glaring at Ed, who was trying to get his attention. "Let's blow this place. I've put Heppner and Jamison in charge, but Gould and Fong are standing by. Let's get out of here."

"But I want to talk to Ms. Compton," I protested as he put his arm around me.

"Forget it," Milo said, steering me to the entrance. "She and her kids are on their way out of town. They've got a plane waiting at the landing strip."

"Damn!" I exclaimed as we exited the building. "I should've had somebody take pictures! Why didn't I think of that?"

"Somebody brought a camera," he said. "Look over there."

I looked. Vida was walking to her Buick, but having eyes in the back of her head, she turned around. "Well now!" she cried. "Wasn't that a monkey-and-parrot time! Kay was the star of the show. But I'm certainly glad I didn't have to interview that

Compton woman for my page. I think she's quite mad. Blackwell will certainly sue for slander."

Milo and I didn't argue.

We didn't talk on the way home. My husband was grim-faced for the entire ride and I felt depleted. When we got inside, he poured us drinks. After we'd sat down in our usual places, I was the first to speak.

"Vida's right," I declared. "Ms. Compton is crazy."

Milo nodded. "It's too bad. Either she's infected her kids or they inherited some bad genes. I suppose the county will have to press charges for the son IDing the wrong corpse. Blackwell will sure as hell go after her. For once, I don't blame him, even if he brought some of it on himself. Have you written a story about her?"

This wasn't the time to berate the sheriff for not reading the *Advocate*. "No. She struck me as very strange. But I understand her reaction to her husband's death. Even if she's unhinged, I can see why."

"Weird," Milo murmured, still looking grim. "So who's lying in a coffin at Driggers Funeral Home?"

I hesitated. "How about the missing investigative reporter, Shannon Willis?"

461

The sheriff had to think about it, but after a few moments, the grimness faded from his face. "It could be. She was older than the usual vic, but not by a lot. It was an indoor job. That one really bothers me, because it was *my* house." He got out his cell. "Blatt's on duty and he was the one who found her. I'll tell him to call Mrs. Willis with what I'm afraid is bad news. Maybe Tanya's with him to lend moral support."

Realizing that I was hungry and that Milo undoubtedly was, too, I went into the kitchen to forage for dinner. The digital clock on the stove registered 7:04. So much had happened in the past hour that it seemed as if it should be much later. Kip would have started putting the paper together. I'd told him to keep six inches open on the front page and make room for one of Vida's photos.

All of this was racing through my mind as I put potatoes on to boil, thawed lamb steaks, and cut up a head of cauliflower. Then I set my brain on overdrive to write the story. I took my laptop out to the living room, where Milo had finished his phone call.

"Blatt's sorry he missed it," he said. "Tanya's not there. She went to the gym. When do we eat?"

"Not until I write up this whole mess," I declared. "It's not going to be easy."

Somehow I danced around Ms. Compton's explicit accusations about Blackwell. They were probably all over the county by now. I mentioned that she seemed to hold a grudge against Black Jack, dating back to when he owned a mill in Idaho. But there was no way I could get around the resurrection of Gemma: "L. J. Jennings had identified the murder victim as his sister. The sheriff's department will investigate how or why he made the mistake. Meanwhile, law enforcement is seeking the victim's real identity."

I read what I'd written to Milo, who shrugged. "Too bad you didn't include some of the stuff Ms. Compton said about Jack."

"I don't want him suing me," I retorted. "This was one tricky article."

"Maybe you should add one thing," Milo said.

"What?"

His hazel eyes snapped. "We've still got a serial killer out there. I hope you've yanked your junior sleuth off the case."

I stiffened in my place on the sofa. "I didn't see her in the banquet hall. Did you?"

"No," Milo replied. "But after it started, I

was focusing on Ms. Compton. Maybe Alison decided to skip it. Lori wasn't there, either."

"Damn!" I said under my breath as I grabbed the phone. "I'll call her right now."

Lori answered in a hoarse voice. "Alison decided to call on that Mr. McKean. She told me you wanted her to write a story about him. She left about five minues ago."

"Oh." I was relieved. "I met him, but I forgot to ask where he and his wife are living."

"They're renting a cottage out on the Burl Creek Road while they fix up the house they bought next door. It needed a lot of work." Lori paused to muffle a cough. "I'll have her call you when she gets back."

I thanked Lori and hung up.

And suddenly I panicked. Staggering off the sofa, I rushed over to Milo. "Can you find out where the McKeans are living?"

Milo was staring at me as if I'd lost my mind. I didn't blame him. "What the . . ." But he knew me well enough to take my distress seriously. He got out his cell and asked for the McKeans' number. I prayed they'd be home. I was sitting on the easy chair's arm. I could hear a woman answer. Milo identified himself and asked if Ken was available. Laura McKean said he'd just gone outside.

"He heard an odd noise," she said as I hung over Milo's arm. "An animal, maybe. We've never lived so close to nature before. When we —" She gasped. "Excuse me, I must —" The line went dead.

CHAPTER 20

Milo jumped up so fast that he almost knocked me off the easy chair's arm. "I don't know what the hell's going on at McKean's, but I'm checking it out. The deputies may still be at the ski lodge."

For once, the sheriff didn't seem to object to me going with him. Once we got into the Yukon, he waited until we were on Alpine Way before he turned on the siren. "Okay," he said, "tell me what we're doing. This time I'll admit I *am* baffled."

I was so terrified by what I thought might have happened that I could hardly talk. "Alison. Lori said she was going to interview Ken McKean. They live in a cottage next to the house they're buying. An empty house. I have a terrible feeling that she may have been attacked by the serial killer."

We were already on the Burl Creek Road. "You think McKean's the perp?" Milo asked in disbelief.

"No. He has nothing to do with the murders." I had to stop, still fighting panic.

But Milo knew where he was going. After another mile, he braked to turn into the paved driveway leading to a dark mid-century modern house and a small stone cottage with its own dirt track. Alison's Audi was parked behind the Izuzu Trooper I'd seen by the Burger Barn. The scene was deceptively quiet.

We hurried to the rough-hewn pine door. Milo rapped twice. "Sheriff Dodge here. Open up."

Ken McKean opened the door. The first thing I saw was a disheveled Alison on a leather sofa being comforted by Laura Mc-Kean.

"Sheriff!" Ken cried. "I knew I should've gone to see you about this maniac!"

"Skip that now," Milo said. "Are you okay, Alison?"

I'd already rushed over to stand by the sofa, though I wasn't sure who was trembling the most — Alison or me.

But the girl had spunk. "I'm not dead," she replied in a shaky voice. "That's a plus."

There was room on the sofa for three. "Sit," Laura said to me, patting the vacant leather cushion. "Are you a deputy?"

I sat. "No. I'm a wife." I nodded at the

sheriff. "Alison works for me at the news-paper."

Milo and Ken had both sat down in the room's only other chairs. My husband was the first to speak. "What happened, Alison?"

She took a deep breath, then turned to Laura. "Could I bother you for some water?"

"Of course! Bottled or tap?"

Alison chose the bottled variety. Laura McKean, a small, lean woman with a plain face and short dark hair, hustled off to what was probably the kitchen.

The sheriff tried to hide his impatience, but when he spoke, he kept his voice conversational. "You were coming to see the McKeans, right?" He saw her nod. "What happened after you pulled in?"

"I got out of my car and walked up the paved drive to get a look at the house Mr. and Mrs. McKean are fixing up. I thought I'd ask about their plans." Alison glanced at me. I nodded approval. "I was checking out the garden, too, because it was kind of overgrown." She paused to accept a bottled water from Laura. "Thanks. I don't mean to sound snarky, Mrs. McKean, but those big shrubs were where the guy was hiding."

"Oh, no!" Laura cried as she practically collapsed on the sofa next to Alison. "I knew

468

we should've pruned them back!"

"Now, Laura," Ken said, "you know they told us at Mountain View Gardens that . . ."

Milo cleared his throat. Ken shut up.

"You're saying that your assailant came out of those shrubs?" the sheriff asked, his voice still calm.

"From between them," Alison replied after a swig of water. "He asked — politely — if I lived in the house. I told him I was visiting and that the owners lived in the cottage. He knew the house was vacant, but he was thinking of moving here. We could get in through a window to look inside." She paused to drink more water. "That sounded . . . wonky to me, but we'd walked almost to a side window. He was getting insistent, even . . . agitated. I got scared. I turned around, but he grabbed me and I screamed and screamed. I don't remember hearing Mr. McKean coming out of the cottage, but I heard him yell. That's when the creep let go and took off." She put a hand to her throat. "I was sure he was going to strangle me."

"He probably was," Milo said quietly. "Did you recognize him?"

"Yes!" Alison's pale face flushed. "It was that pollster doofus, Ronnie Davis!"

The McKeans looked blank. I stared at

Milo, who was studying Alison. "You're certain?" he asked in his usual laid-back interrogative style.

"Definitely," Alison responded. "I ran into him once over a week ago, then he came into the *Advocate* office, and I saw him this morning at Safeway." She shuddered. "Ronnie seemed like such a total dweeb. How could he be so . . . bloodthirsty?"

Milo stood up. "Being what you call a 'dweeb' can be part of the reason, Alison," he said. "But mostly it's what goes on up here." He tapped his temple. "Our local serial killers were both very different in physical appearance. Ted Bundy was good-looking. Gary Ridgway — the Green River Killer — wasn't. But they were both wired to kill. Excuse me, folks, I've got an APB to put out." The sheriff made his exit — without me.

"Hey," I shouted, running after him, "what about your wife?"

He turned around. "Huh? Oh. You ride with Alison. In fact, you drive. Bring her to our house and I'll take her to her place when I get back. She needs to unwind."

That made sense, even if Milo had only thought of it when I yelled at him. I went back into the cottage with a question for

470

Ken McKean. Laura was still consoling Alison.

"What did you mean," I asked Ken, "about not talking to Dodge?"

He looked chagrined. "I'd seen that guy looking at the house a few nights ago when I took out the garbage. His back was turned when I asked what he was doing. He jumped, turned around, and wanted to know if the house was vacant. I told him we'd bought it, but planned to remodel. He nodded and sort of slunk away. When I happened to run into you on the street, I was thinking about calling on the sheriff, but then I decided I'd sound like an alarmist."

I posed a question. "You didn't know Ronnie Davis was taking a poll for Blackwell?"

Ken looked puzzled. "I don't know anything about a poll."

I sighed, mentally kicking myself. We should have verified Ronnie's statement with the timber company. I'd flunked one of the first rules of journalism. "No wonder the polling company he claimed to work for was in Omaha," I muttered.

Alison finished her bottled water, and I asked if she was ready to leave. She was, but first gave profuse thanks to the McKeans for saving her life. "When I write my story, I'll include how heroic you've been."

I agreed.

While I coped with the differences in driving the Audi rather than the Honda, Alison mused not on her near-death experience but on Ms. Compton. "So she's gone and taken Gemma and L.J. with her. Why did L.J. say the waitress was his sister?"

"His mother had a plan from the get-go," I replied, and then explained about the postcards to Kay and Jennifer. "The murder had nothing to do with Ms. Compton and her kids, but I suppose it jump-started the campaign against Blackwell. You missed her savage attack on him at the ski lodge. She's one weird woman. Her husband's death festered all these years until she decided to act. I don't know if his death was Blackwell's fault, but he became her target and infected her twins. When L.J. got shot, that was the last straw. She blamed Blackwell, even though he was the apparent target. I think Ms. Compton blamed Black Jack for everything that had ever gone wrong in her life, including hangnails."

I parked the Audi on the verge in front of our log cabin. Neither of us spoke until we got inside. We both collapsed onto the sofa.

"So who was the poor waitress?" Alison asked.

"An innocent victim." I related Mrs. Willis's call to Milo. "He'll have to verify it."

Alison grimaced. "That's awful. About her, I mean. How old was she?"

"Around thirty, I think."

"Was she married?"

I stared at Alison. "I don't think so. Are you still stuck in that rut?"

"Well . . ." She gazed up at the ceiling. "L.J. was kind of a dud when I got to know him. Maybe he *is* as weird as his mother. I suppose I could stay single for another year or two."

"Try at least ten," I said. "I waited half a century and I'm damned glad of it."

I wrote the story about the attack on Alison, which took almost half an hour. I called it in to Kip around nine-thirty. Naturally, he was horrifed. I thought of phoning Vida, but I was too tired. She'd be mad at not being informed, but I'd deal with that in the morning. Milo finally got back home a little before ten. While he was at his office, he'd sent over to the Burger Barn for sustenance. I'd stifled my own hunger pangs with pancetta, Brie, and sesame crackers. We both decided we could use a stiff drink. I posed no questions until he was settled into the easy chair.

473

"Any sightings of Davis?" I asked.

He shook his head. "He had a car, a ninety-eight Kia Sephia. He didn't clean out his motel unit at the Lumberjack, but he's on the run. I sent out an APB. Oh — Blatt heard from Mrs. Willis. She's making it official that her daughter is missing."

I took in everything my huband was saying, but zeroed in on the motel. "I told Alison that Sarah — or Shannon Willis — was an innocent bystander. But she wasn't. She and Davis were both staying at the Lumberjack. Shannon must have had some suspicions about him, so she had to go. That's why she doesn't fit the vicitm profile."

Milo swallowed a big swig of Scotch and lighted a cigarette. "Okay, why not speculate? It's been that kind of month so far."

"I bet I'm right," I asserted, glaring at my mate.

"Hell, Mrs. Willis should hack into her daughter's computer," Milo said. "Maybe Shannon was researching small-town murders or some damned thing."

"What about Mickey O'Neill? Have you interrogated him yet?"

Milo shook his head. "I want him to be sober and I need the lab results from Everett. But he's screwed now that the Nelson girl is pressing charges. If he got a decent lawyer — which he probably won't — he might argue the shooting down to reckless endangerment. But he'll still do time. Hell, I almost feel sorry for him. He came from a violent family and got some bad genes." Milo's cell rang. With a big sigh, he pulled it out of his pocket. "Dodge here."

Whoever was at the other end had a lot to say. I sipped my Canadian Club and tried to be patient.

"Okay," he finally said. "That part's out of our jurisdiction. We'll deal with what's left over tomorrow." He clicked off.

"Well?"

"Down around Sultan, Davis apparently tried to pass somebody on a curve and smashed into a big camper. The creep was obviously going too fast and was killed outright. Maybe that's just as well for everybody concerned."

"What about the other people involved?"

"No other injuries," Milo replied. "He didn't clip the car he was passing and though the camper was damaged on the front and the side, it was still drivable. The two passengers were shaken up but declined medical assistance. SnoCo's stuck with the accident details."

"Do you think they'll agree that Davis committed their murders?"

475

"They would've saved the victims' clothes, so a match can be made with DNA samples. If the killings stop, that's the end of the story. Oh — I heard back from Milwaukee. Believe it or not, the woman who called me has a sister in Monroe. Anyway, she checked back and found out that though the charges were eventually dropped, Iain Farrell beat the crap out of his then girlfriend. The university put him on probation, but he decided to cut his losses and move on. You better not tell Kay. Maybe he's changed his ways."

"Maybe," I allowed. "But he's still a jerk."

"Kay runs to type," Milo said, "though I doubt Gould ever hit her. Maybe she got bored. Some people like danger." He finished his drink. "Let's make an early night of it."

"I'm worn out, too," I said, getting off the sofa. "Those other people were lucky they didn't get creamed."

"Right." Milo was also on his feet. He put his arm around me and kissed the top of my head. "Maybe I can revive a little once we're in —"

The doorbell rang.

"What the hell . . . ?" My husband let go of me. "Maybe it's one of my deputies," he muttered as he went to open the door.

I stood in the hallway and heard Clint Dodge before I saw him — and Pootsie.

"Bro!" Clint shouted as he all but shoved his brother aside to enter the house. "You won't believe what happened to us tonight! We damned near got killed out on that damned highway! Haul out the strong stuff and we'll tell you all about it."

Milo looked at me. I looked at Milo. We made the drinks. We listened. We both nodded off. When we woke up around eleven, the Dallas Dodges were gone.

"For good?" I asked in a sleepy voice.

"Who knows?" Milo responded, stretching his arms beside me on the sofa. "Next time I'll look through the peephole. If they show up again, *we'll* be gone."

Wednesdays were always times of semi-kicking back after meeting our deadline. For the first time since I could remember, I deliberately allowed myself to be late getting to work. Naturally, Vida was agog when I entered the newsroom a little before nine. In fact, my entire staff eyed me with curiosity, including Alison. I'd told her she should sleep in or even take the day off, but apparently she had recovered from her near-death experience. I commended her for her courage and recuperative powers.

But it was Vida who followed me into my cubbyhole and closed the door. I expected her to interrogate me on the details of the previous night, but I was wrong. "I visited my addled sister-in-law Ella last night at Parc Pines," she said after she'd settled onto a visitor chair and adjusted the netting on her felt cloche. "I happened to run into Leo and Liza, who'd gone out to dinner at the ski lodge. We chatted for a bit." She paused, giving me her gimlet eye. "Do you know how the Walshes met?"

I said I didn't, or if I had, I'd forgotten.

Vida looked like a cat in cream. "Leo was just starting his career as an ad man. Liza was working on one of his papers in Orange County as the women's page editor. Naturally, I didn't mention my plans to retire, but I got the impression that Liza is a bit . . ." She paused, grimacing at what she was about to say. "A bit restless here in a smaller town. Ordinarily, I'd advise her to become involved in our many organizations and charities, but . . ." The gray eyes locked with my brown-eyed stare. "When the time comes, of course."

"Of course." I smiled back.

ABOUT THE AUTHOR

Mary Richardson Daheim started spinning stories before she could spell. Daheim has been a journalist, an editor, a public relations consultant, and a freelance writer, but fiction was always her medium of choice. In 1982, she launched a career that is now distinguished by more than sixty novels. In 2000, she won the Literary Achievement Award from the Pacific Northwest Writers Association. In October 2008, she was inducted into the University of Washington's Communication Alumni Hall of Fame. Daheim lives in her hometown of Seattle and is a direct descendant of former residents of the real Alpine, which existed as a logging town from 1910 to 1929, when it was abandoned after the mill was closed. The Alpine/Emma Lord series has created interest in the site, which was named a Washington State ghost town in July 2011. An organization called the Alpine Advocates has been formed to preserve what remains of the town as a historic site.

marydaheimauthor.com

The employees of Thorndike Press hope you have enjoyed this Large Print book. All our Thorndike, Wheeler, and Kennebec Large Print titles are designed for easy reading, and all our books are made to last. Other Thorndike Press Large Print books are available at your library, through selected bookstores, or directly from us.

For information about titles, please call:
(800) 223-1244

or visit our website at:
gale.cengage.com/thorndike

To share your comments, please write:
Publisher
Thorndike Press
10 Water St., Suite 310
Waterville, ME 04901